I0662404

Severed Head Publications
ELEPHANT VINDALOO

Nicola Frost was born in London in 1960. After an infancy in Nigeria she returned to England where she was educated in a convent in Kent. As an art student she moved to central London where she lived for a decade, mostly working in night clubs. She immigrated to the USA in 1990.

Nicola lives in Orange County, New York, where she works as a painter, writer, and furniture designer.

Elephant Vindaloo is her first published novel.

For more information visit:
nicolafrostartist.com

ELEPHANT VINDALOO

A Novel by
NICOLA FROST

Severed Head Publications

Severed Head Publications
5 Water Street, Port Jervis, New York 12771

Copyright @ Nicola Frost 2013
All rights reserved

ISBN 978-0-9891850-3-5

Photography by Martin J. Goldsmith

Photography copyright owned by
Martin J. Goldsmith

Elephant Vindaloo is set in South London's notorious and dilapidated district of the Elephant and Castle. It is staged in the 1980's against the political backdrop of Margaret Thatcher's Britain.
The story revolves around the occupants of eight flats, off one stairwell, of a small crumbling Victorian council estate, over the course of one weekend.

At the top of the stairwell to the right live squatters, Fat Sid and Vince. They make up the rhythm section of a local rock band The Neanderthals. Most of their spare is taken up looking after their fellow squatter's, teenage heroin addict Dolores, baby Jason. To add to their troubles Dolores brings home Little Wing, a beautiful but disturbed runaway.

Next to the squat lives Nick, a reformed drug addict, given over to health foods and exercise. Nick carries a torch for our leading lady, Kate. Sophisticated, brilliant and glamorous, a chance meeting brings her an unexpected date with our equally gorgeous and sexy Jake, a would-be actor/model, and The Neanderthals front man.

Below the squat, filthy disgusting Robert masturbates the weekend away. He is a window cleaner by trade, an electronic wizard by his own design, and has a sinister second career producing home videos.

Next to vile Robert lives Leo, a card-carrying union carpenter. Leo is a kindhearted, cheerful lad; as thick as two short planks, and prone to an ill-fated love life.

Beneath Robert yuppies, Dick and Selene, carry on their routine bondage and humiliation sex marathons, unaware that they are the centre of Robert's latest obsession.

Next to Dick and Selene lives Ruby Rutt, a ferocious gout-ridden octogenarian. Ruby and her best friend Edith hold Saturday afternoon rituals of wrestling, Scotch, and cigarettes. The television blasts at decibels usually associated with adolescent boys, obscenities are yelled, fists are shaken; it is not a sight for small children.

On the ground floor, beneath Dick and Selene, lives Alec Evans. Alec, a depressive pacifist artist, and Greenham Commom* widower, battles with his own growing political unrest as he suffers the continual absences of his self-righteous wife, Monica.

Next door to Alec, Ugandan immigrant Seema Patel rules her husband with silent contempt, instilling terror on a daily basis. She crushes him with the subtlest of eye movements and a deportment of grace and aloofness.

Elephant Vindaloo entertains a host of other characters: Fen, the rag and bone man and his dog, Scud. Gorky, a Polish refugee and his militant mother. Georgie, the gay world's answer to Stephen Hawking. Amorous grandfather Leonard, local villain Mean fuckin' Mike and Margaret, the reincarnation of the first Queen Elizabeth, to name but a few.

* U.S. missile base picketed by woman and their children 24hrs a day for several years.

*"All the world's a stage,
and all the men and women merely players:
they have their entrances;
and one man in his time plays many parts,"*

William Shakespeare

For Brenda

One bleak, chill Sunday night, and the east wind blows. It blows strong and constant. Its damp, icy fingers penetrate your skin, flesh and joints, to the very marrow of your bones. Rain crashes to earth directed by a relentless gale, pounding the tarmac, pummeling the tinny swarms of traffic. A saturated canvas, loose on a trailer, flaps sadly as a torn sail on a ship destined without hope. Wheels endlessly orbit wheels, these two great adjacent circles, this giant junction of South London; The Elephant and Castle. Like some dark, primitive, Boschian machine, its two main cogs turning eternally in this tempest straight from the shores of hell. It spits as it spews; cars, buses, taxis, motorbikes, lorries and cyclists; dark waifish figures surface from its flooding, subterranean, piss-stinking subways. A thousand puddles reflect a thousand lights. Long splinters of water form on the road's tired surface sparkling the red neon words 'take-away'. Opposite, from the foot of the railway bridge, the steamy windows of 'Elephant Vindaloo Indian take-away food' looks homey and inviting.

Traffic out, out into the gray, dank, chaotic, concrete sprawl of South London, through highly condensed, overpopulated suburban S.E. England and then the coast and the European mainland.

And traffic in and around, heading north. Eight bridges, eight means of escape. From Vauxhall Bridge in the west, to Tower Bridge in the east, they radiate like spokes of a wagon wheel across a loop of The Thames, the Elephant and Castle serving as an ugly but well-oiled gudgeon.

East of the north of Vauxhall Bridge is the Tate Gallery of Modem Art. Riverside, sealed archways secure passages to the gallery's vaults that once served as dungeons, incarcerating slaves and petty criminals destined for The Colonies. By the south entrance to dignified discrete Lambeth Bridge is the medieval fortified London residence of the Arch-Bishop of Canterbury. In the summer ancient rose bushes scale these tall walls, sharing their blossoms and perfumes with the outside World. Further east is the grandeur of Westminster Bridge. On its south bank the windows of County Hall and the abandoned offices of the late Greater London Council stare blankly as a dead man's eyes across bridge and water, resting on the archaic Houses of Parliament, its corridors jam-packed with the long-term makeshift offices of the modem day politician of these islands. Waterloo Bridge crosses to where the West-End ends with the elegant, gentle curvature of The Strand, taking one west to Trafalgar Square and Charring Cross Station and two minutes away by foot lays Covent Garden's Bohemian Plaza and Royal Opera House. Blackfriars Bridge, Southwark Bridge, London Bridge, all serve The City of London. One square mile crammed to the brim with a hysterical chaos of working stiffs and traffic, bicycle couriers and runners. Typical of most financial districts of most large famous cities, but maybe in the 1980's, in this country, with this government, one of the most hated. Finally picture-postcard Tower Bridge. On the north bank to its west the ancient prison of the rich, famous, and soon to be headless, The Tower of London. Beefeaters guard, and the giant ravens have clipped wings, for legend says that if the ravens ever leave The Tower, England's sovereign line will fail. Many would wish good riddance and some would wish worse. To the bridge's east a magical mystery tour through some architectural megalomania. The Docklands Light Railway glides on air down a single rail raised high through the St. Catherine's Docks and Canary Wharf development it was built to serve. Child of Thatcherism, costing billions while millions wait homeless, jobless and on hospital waiting lists. Now the cranes of bankruptcy form the skyline as it sits in its unfinished magnificence, only 10 percent leased. So much for the future financial centre of the world.

Once a very wealthy man, also prone to unusual vision, came from over the ocean. He wanted to take London's famous drawbridge with its two towers to the harsh east Californian desert and reassemble it brick by brick. So he asked to purchase the famous London bridge and brought home London's old London Bridge, which, in spite of the popular children's nursery rhyme, is a simple but fine sturdy piece of masonry. Life is full of surprises.

As the Chinese say, whenever you cross over water you cross into another World.

FRIDAY

Over-heated, under aired, a fresher stench of sweat arose over the constant rank odor of filthy laundry, rotting junk food and rodent excrement. In mugs scattered throughout the room molds thrive. Layer upon layer fester on the round surfaces of old milky tea, the most recent white, then any array of colours; light yellow, green, yellow-ochre, brown and even navy. Pornography litters the floor, the table tops, the filthy bathroom, the sticky encrusted counter-tops of the kitchen, living room, bedroom, the revolting unmade bed. Donned in a yellowed string vest and Y-fronts, crotch stained like French mustard, Robert lies in his disgusting nest. Rigid as his ugly penis, his face matching its puce hue, the sounds of heavy boots, whip-lashes and screams fill the room.

In sharp contrast the wall facing him is meticulous. A place for everything and everything in its place. The room's one and only window, Victorian and therefore large, spills daylight onto a spotless work bench. Streamlined and exquisitely made, Robert has personalized it for his specific tastes and traits. At the back of the bench top two soldering irons stand like trophies, nibs clean as a whistle, a best and a spare. To the left front three drawers had been neatly partitioned and well stocked with electronic parts; integrated circuits, resistors, switches, capacitors, circuit boards and the like. In the small cabinet to the right he keeps an oscilloscope, spectrum analyzer and other test equipment he uses for his inventions as well as some more conventional tools in a small tool box.

Above the work bench, on the right side of the window sill, a spindle holds reels of brightly coloured electronic wire, silver solder and a pair of tiny, perfectly sprung wire cutters are attached to the window frame with a strong fine chain. On the left, on a piece of thick green felt, lay a number of small precision tools. Across the window, at about eye level for Robert's small stature, runs a thin shelf with various slots and holes for screw drivers, pliers and wire cutters. Left of his bench is an old museum display case holding an impressive collection of telescopes, binoculars, cameras, telescopic lenses, cameras for film and video, his first ever Polaroid, as well as a whole host of recording and listening devices.

To the right is an old industrial Singer sewing machine that Robert is impressively skillful with. Over the years he has tailored several pairs of overalls for his window cleaning business, all fitted with any number of cleverly concealed slots and pockets. His latest pair are international orange, cut loose with French seaming stitched down on the outside like jeans. This seam runs all the way from the cuffs, under his arms, down to the hemline of the legs, which he always makes too long so they need to be folded over twice and therefore can be loaded with electronic parts and what-have-you. The back is seamed with a low waist. Just before it hit the side seam, Velcro tears open to allow a small pair of antique brass opera glasses to drop into a pocket that is large enough to hang loosely, but is steadied by being stitched into the side seam and therefore difficult to detect. Just below his right hip, held together with two hooks, is a small opening in the side seam into which slots an equally beautiful piece of brass and glass, a one inch diameter, fourteen inch expanding telescope. Inside either side of the front bodice are stitched strips of strong canvas ribbon looped in various sizes from which he hangs any number of small tools. The top of the back bodice is seamed with side panels, a larger central section and a yoke. Into the centre panel he has sewn two layers of denim so that the yoke actually opens by means of an invisible zip and coils of wire can be tied to the inside of the giant pocket by one, two or three loops of wide ribbon. At present he also has a pair of overalls in army camouflage, similar but with more esoteric features for photography and special pockets for lenses and the like.

Greasy smelly Robert does well at his chosen profession. He is good, moderately reasonable and flexible; willing to do the job when one was at work or away for the weekend and collect his money later. Being so creepy very few of his customers wish him to clean on the inside but his professional reputation has earnt him a few small public buildings recently, with all sorts of possibilities. Even from the outside he has become an expert of concealment. His first visit to any new job is purely research. He looks for loose bricks, rotting wood, or simply just frames in need of a good coat of paint. He then makes a good bid to repair the likes, offering his usual flexibility and a very convenient payment scheme. But not all of his prey are his customers, oh no, that would make it far too easy. Robert needs to run the risk of complete exposure, though he fears it even to the extent of entertaining horrifically paranoid nightmares. Such are the perversities of his sickness. Many a time he has successfully managed to remove old telephone wires that entered a dwelling through an ancient hole drilled in the crumbling cement between wall and window frame and insert a battery operated subminiature camera. This in turn is attached to a wireless transmitter smaller than a pack of cigarettes, which he either hides or disguises, and then replaces the old cable. These transmitters are aligned to an antenna on his rooftop and the radio waves are picked up by a receiver in his front room that is wired to his video recorder and finally put down on tape.

Some shelves to the right of his bench are home for his automatic cameras, including a couple of Polaroids and a Kodak Instamatic. Also the only non-pornographic literature on the premises (other than the rent book and a battered old cook book belonging to his paternal grandmother) are kept here. These books and magazines are about electronics, film, video and audio; but while we're on the subject the only reason he still possesses Granny's cook book is neither for sentimental reasons or creative joy. He keeps it in order to bake her chocolate cake which he will eat in one sitting, like an addict, and over the years his teeth have rotted to the extent that his breath stinks nearly as badly as his feet. Anyway, there are also a number of videos tapes, some blank some in production, and others full and labeled with such titles as, 'Slit Sisters' and 'Anal Alley', plus a small light box he uses for editing his creations. Finally, on the top shelf, is an amplifier. A cable coming up through the floor boards runs up the wall to the amplifier, which in turn is connected to two speakers mounted in cabinets high up in adjacent corners of the room.

"Beg for it sow!"

"Hit me, hit me!" Dick and Selene are having their Friday evening sadomasochistic, bondage and humiliation sex marathon.

"No!" bellows Dick. Robert can hear the sound of the spurs and chains on Dick's high heeled, black lizard-skin cowboy boots as he paces around the room.

"Please, please!"

3

"Don't question me sow! You'll earn what I say you deserve; if I say you're not worth the leather, then you're not worth the leather! Lick scum sow, lick! "

A sharp slap then silence follows as Dick presents Selene with some unsavory body part or accessory, then three loud lashes, two landing in the air and one not. Selene whimpers, Dick laughs sadistically, struts to the door, it opens, slams, bolts are drawn, and he changes into his jeans and a T-shirt and goes down the pub. In the meantime Robert goes limp. The session has not been long enough for him. The chronic masturbation of decades had desensitized him and he is desperately dependent on his voyeurism vices as relief to his obsessions. It would be a while before Dick's return, when he would give Selene a good lashing, untie her, and they would bonk like rabbits, maybe for hours. Meanwhile Robert has his rounds to do.

~

Kate sits chin in hand, elbow on table, fingers drumming, listening to Pebble and Scribble squabble. Phoebus in his descent rests momentarily on the apex of an adjacent rooftop, sending the last of the day's brilliant sun rays to pierce the old glass of the majestic library windows, refracting them into fine spotlights that illuminate dust, that moves as if suspended for all eternity by its very lightness of being. Across the floor the windows bear elongated quadrangles of light. One journeys to the table where she sits, shoots up and over the walnut and green leather table top, severing her hand and falls to the floor once again to eventually climb the cedar bookcases and shine on gilt and aged leather.

A week's mounting fury boils within her. The much loved head of restoration had dropped dead at Sotheby's auction last month, moments after losing a Rembrandt to a phone bidder described as a "rap artist" from Brooklyn, New York. Dr. Pebble, his emergency replacement, is already throwing his weight around considerably. Pebble has a low opinion of women, based on utter ignorance and the bitter taste of forced celibacy, so he choose to ignore them unless he has something he can be a shit about. Kate has made it as sure as hell that he has not had reason to fault her.

She has just finished an intense restoration of some small, water damaged sketch books of van Gogh's a week before the preliminary deadline. They are exquisite. She has spent a pleasant hour cleaning and putting away her tools. She's washed her hands, hung up her apron, and with her coat and bag over one arm and the books in hand she descended one flight of stairs to the research library. She passed the offices of the department's two main employees, the bastard Pebble and Professor Scribble. She found the Professor already in the library, he immediately broke forth into an ear splitting grin when he saw her. The Professor loved art, loved van Gogh, and loves Kate. She had set out the books next to each other on the table top and went to report to Dr. Pebble.

"Would you like me to fetch him?" asked the Professor. He is an understanding man.

"Thank-you but no thank-you Professor, I don't need any help with the Doctor," she replied in a tone of voice than ran shivers of delight up and down Scribble's spine.

Kate had knocked on Dr. Pebble's door. Nothing. She then counted to ten and knocked again.

"Just a minute," a curt call had come from inside. He was on the phone, the minutes passed and she heard laughter and joking. Screw this! She had turned to walk away, and of course it was just then that the door had flown open.

"Now! What is it that's so important.....? Oh Miss Lanseer," looking her up and down; it was annoying, he really could not find anything to fault her on.

"The van Gogh's are finished Doctor and in the library with Professor Scribble."

"Already?" he barked.

"Yes, already sir," she said, not without a certain amount of ice in her larynx.

"Well very good, I'll be right along." And with that he shut the door in her face.

Meanwhile the Professor had worked up a lot of enthusiasm, his nose twitched as wildly as a copulating rabbit's and he bounced like an ominous blancmange, rubbing his hands in delight; the fat man's version of jumping up and down. Van Gogh was his favourite painter and he was about to burst forth in

5

unbridled delight when Pebble walked up, took a quick look and said:

"Very good Miss Lanseer. Return the books to security," turned and walked away.

"Dr. Pebble?"

"Yes!" he snapped impatiently over his shoulder.

"Before I go home I was going to ask you if you would be so kind as to lock them in the safe down here so the size could go off over the weekend." He looked at her blankly.

"So the glue can set?" God, was the man a total idiot? There is a prolonged silence before Pebble answers.

"Before you go where?"

"Go home."

"And what is the time now?"

"It's four-twenty."

"And what time are you employed to stay until?"

"With all due respect Doctor, I'm on salary and have just finished an extremely focused project ahead of time. I'm tired and there's nothing worth starting in the very little time we have left today.

"And with all due respect Miss," and he spat the 'miss' both literately and with venom, "I think it's for myself and my peers to designate your timetable. You'll leave at five just like everybody else. Bring the books to my office at four fifty-five," and with that he had marched out of the library only to reappear almost immediately and start this tedious, pseudo-intellectual debate with the Professor.

She becomes aware that her fingers have taken on a life of their own, what she had consciously started in motion was now running on full steam, dangerously fast and at risk of losing all control. Pebble's neck turns red, he spins around and starts to bellow. She springs to her feet, fury blasting a torment like powerful jets of steam. Pebble and Scribble both take a step back in awe of the distraught dragoness, hell bent on deep frying her petrified victim before ripping him to shreds with her bare teeth.

"Shut up you horrible, stupid, little man!"

The men take another step back. Pebble, if he had half a brain, should be scared, very scared. As it was he is stunned into disbelief, the truth can be a difficult thing to face after all, and Professor Scribble shimmers with admiration and wicked delight.

"What I would like to know, you misogynist bastard, is how an idiot such as yourself came by a Ph.D.? How the hell did you get this job? Did you lie on your application or did some sort of old boys' network wangle it for you? I bet you used one of the conventional methods didn't you? Daddy made a hefty donation to your university, or bending over for the right person? Oh don't be ashamed Doc, they say prostitution is the oldest profession you know! "

And with that she picks up her coat and handbag and marches towards the door, her anger echoing throughout the room as her high heels hit the parquet flooring between the bookcases. Scribble was in heaven. What a luscious sound! What a glorious woman!

"You're fired Miss Lanseer, you're fired!" Pebble screams after her, his face beetroot and sweating profusely.

"Go and stick the rough end of a pineapple up your arse, you fucking moron! " and the door swings silently shut behind her bringing the retreating footsteps to a premature halt and Pebble, still staring after her, uttering completely inarticulate splatterings of spittle. The Professor, taking advantage of the Doctors mute state, grabs his coat from the back of his chair, snatches up his battered brief case and runs after her, swifter and lighter on his feet than he has been for years. He takes the stairs and catches up with her coming out of the lift he had just missed, leaning on the wall red faced and out of breath.

"Kate!" Kate is taken aback for a second but continues her rapid exit. Scribble is forced to run alongside of her puffing and panting.

"Professor, I know you mean well but I'm in no mood for it."

"But Kate, you were magnificent!"

"Magnificent and unemployed, along with millions of others."

"Hawkins isn't going to let you go this easily Kate, you're top of your trade, how many bookbinders get to work on projects like van Gogh and the likes, besides ..., " the Professor halts his monologue to step aside & hold open the gallery door for an elderly lady. He has to run once more to catch up with Kate.

"I'm telling you Kate, they'll not let you go over this, you're too valuable and Pebble's a fool."

Miraculously a black cab pulls up outside the gallery and a Japanese couple disembark. Even as a suited gentleman steps up to converse with the cabby Kate, in perfect momentum of stride, gets in and slams the door.

"Elephant and Castle please."

Both men look at her, slightly stupefied. Scribble's round face splats on the window like a large insect, she reaches over and pulls it down.

"Get in Christopher, I'll drop you off at the Oval. But please, I want to be quiet O.K.? I really, really need to be very quiet and very peaceful."

Scribble opens the door and bustles in breathing heavily. He slips, dropping his ancient brief case which splits and spills its entire contents onto the floor.

~

Scud sniffs at the corner of "The Rhinoceros" public house with unabashed enthusiasm. Along with a few of the other neighbourhood mutts, he circles first one way and then the next, nose alternating from sphincter to the streaked polished granite skirting of the pub, where recently evaporated urine still leaves a small puddle on the pavement. He is cocking his leg, adding his own personal touch to the pungent aroma when the noise of a diesel engine pulling up curb side sends his companions off at a trot. He takes a step forward in anticipation, tongue drooping out of the side of his mouth. His face has a snout, similar to a bull terrier, but his ears are pure Alsatian and are vastly disproportionate to his medium-small build. His short, smooth brown fur ends abruptly at his jaw-line and a wiry graying coat sticks out as if he has been electrified and gives him the appearance of someone who has dressed up in a guerrilla suit and forgotten the head piece. Protruding from this mangled mass of matted hair are four matchstick legs which could make it possible to mistake Scud for a small sheep if it was not for a long, filthy, foxy tail that he trails on the ground behind him most of the time.

The door of the taxi cab swings open and female legs with high magenta heals step out onto the flagstones.

"Keep the change driver."

"Why thank-you, Miss."

The door slams and the legs move towards Scud until he is eye-level with the hemline of a very stylish gray skirt.

"Hey Scuddy, how are you boysie, how are you!"

As the figure bends over him a tress of red falls into view and a lily white hand with long pearlized magenta fingernails strokes his head softly and pats him.

Then the legs move away and approach one of the shiny green doors of The Rhinoceros. Its sandblasted frosted glass would have read 'Public Bar' if Scud could have read. There is the loud click of an old brass latch, the door swings open and shut, and the legs disappear, leaving the whiff of beer and Chanel in the air. Scud stares after the legs for several seconds panting and drooling happily. Then he entertains one further thorough nasal escapade at the corner of the pub and, after leaving a final contribution, sets off after his furry friends.

As one steps inside the pub a pay-phone, jukebox, dart-board and the Ladies and Gents are to the left. All along the back wall runs one long brown vinyl upholstered seat and four dark heavy oblong tables. The seat turns ninety degrees at the far corner to accommodate two sides of a table, next to which stand a fruit and a pinball machine. To the right is the bar with its high stools, and between it and the pinball machine is one more table. Here sits Gorky, a tall man in his forties of eastern bloc origins, stroking the pub's nasty alcoholic cat, Slasher. The feline sleeps peacefully on his lap as Gorky argues politics with two younger men, Kevin, a Northerner and would be militant, and whiny Alec, a middle-class pacifist from Purley.

Otherwise there are a couple more tables and a pool table more or less in the centre of the room. There are a few elderly regulars, all men, with the exception of two spindly little old ladies in colour coordinated macs, hats and bags. Every pub in London seems to harbor such a couple. Seated strategically at the corner table giving themselves an optimum view of the comings and goings of the bar, jukebox, both latrines, pool table, dart board and the machines of many coloured lights that whiz, wail, crash, scream, explode and sometimes make der-da, der-da, der-da noises in menacing tones. The little old ladies have legs that look as if they can be snapped like dry twigs between thumb and finger; however they put down, at a moderate speed, bottled beers with the potency of pints, Malts and barley-wines; how they do it seems to be one of the many mysteries of the Universe.

At the bar rat-faced Robert is giving Jake the low down; how to catch people in the shower, performing various sex acts, and so on and so forth.

"Jake, I'm tellin' yer mate, if yer knew what was goin' on, you'd be out there yerself!"

Jake, extra tall, extraordinarily handsome, charismatic and much sought after. You could usually peel women off him by the dozen. Clad in jeans, T-shirt, leather jacket, leather boots and leather cap, he processes a wild spirit and is usually charming. Women go crazy over Jake and he loves it and he hates it too. He can get all the sex and attention he can possibly want but for some reason he never feels fulfilled. Men either idolize him or want to beat him senseless. His few close male friends, in spite of their brotherly love for the man, cannot always reach his wild lost soul.

Jake leans on the bar with both palms and shakes his head slowly left to right in disbelief, smiling to himself.

Kate feels two red hot holes bore into her back.

"Why Kate, what a pleasant surprise!"

Jake and Robert look up. Kate looks around. At a table tucked away by the door Dick Hodgins, yuppie, reads the Financial Times and drinks his pint of lager.

"Good evening Dick how are you?"

"Rare health, Kate, couldn't be better. Yourself?" His good manners have a cutting edge.

"Good, fine thank-you, and Selene?"

"Oh fine, just fine." An unpleasant smile crosses his bland good-looking face as he places a cigarette in his mouth and feels around in his pocket for a light.

"Just thinking of the Sportsman's Diamond lighter of mine some bastard ripped off. Remember?"

How Kate and everyone else wished they could forget! Dick has been ranting and raging about that bloody yuppie lighter non-stop for the last three months.

"Talking of Selene I really should be getting back." He looks at his watch, empties his glass and slides out from behind the table.

"Anyway we're looking forward to seeing you on Sunday. Give us a call some time Kate, pop round. Sel would love to see you" he says insincerely.

10

Good, she had known he would not be able to flog off her Grandmother Martha.

"I may just do that." Kate answers, truthfully enough. So Selene has not told him about tomorrow. That weird brief phone yesterday had unnerved Kate:

"Noon this Saturday, invite Georgie for me please. Don't say anything to Dick. I need to talk," Selene had whispered and hung up. Curiouser and curiouser.

Robert's eyes follow Dick out of the pub and he starts to fidget. He is getting more flustered by the second and is coming out in a hot flush. So close to her, her perfectly formed breasts, her smell, that laugh. He would bet good money that she's a screamer. He just had to get one of his devices into that one's bedroom, he just had to...

"Are you feeling O.K. Robert?" Jake inquires, knowing full well what ails him. Cowardly Robert scurries off to sit at the table Dick has abandoned.

Suddenly Jake and Kate are alone for the first time in a year or so of brushing shoulders. Jake, so seldom without entourage, stands leaning on his left forearm, his right boot crossed over his left. He stares straight into her eyes and starts to grin. And Kate, beautiful inapproachable Kate, sits on a bar stool leaning on her right elbow, head resting in her palm, and slowly returns his grin.

" 'Shall I compare thee to a summer's day? Thou art more lovely and more temperate. Rough winds do blow the darling buds of May and summers lease has all too short a date'."

"Why thank you Mr. Shakespeare."

"May I get you a drink?"

"I'll have a Pils and lime thank you."

Tom serves them and offering his cigarettes around, he looks under the bar and then feels both trouser pockets for his lighter. At six-foot and with sixty-one years he is one of a dying breed, a true working-class gentlemen publican. He had once had the magnificent body of an amateur boxer of 260 lbs in his heyday, and now is still a strong man, but has taken on the outside appearance of tubbiness.

Tom's wife makes a rare appearance in the Public Bar. Cone-bosomed, firm and tightly strapped at the waist, Nancy sweeps in on the high stiletto heels she has never been seen without. She has been complaining for years about her lot as a publican's wife, and so has banished herself to the Salon bar. That way, she says, she will not have to deal with so much 'riffraff'. However, she likes to say hello to Kate when she makes an odd appearance; she thinks Kate is a very nice young lady.

"'Ave yer seen the lighter luv?" asks Tom.

"If it ain't down by the sink, where it's supposed to be, then your guess is as good as mine. I'm beginnin' to think someone eats the bloody things!"

Nancy and Pookie, her pedigree orange poodle, have been to the hairdressers. Nancy had a perm and a tint to match Pookie and Pookie had a trim. They have matching powder-blue ribbons.

"Very nice," lies Kate stroking Pookie's nose, who Nancy often carries tucked under her plump arm. Jake tries to pat Pookie and Pookie tries to bite Jake and continues snapping at his retreating hand.

"She doesn't like men." Nancy says with pride and contempt, and returns to her domain in the Saloon.

"Cheers Tom," Jake raises his glass.

"So what's Sunday?" asks Jake

"My Grandmother's eightieth."

"And Mr. Dick-Head's invited?"

"Grandma's known Selene since she was six."

"So you get The Stiff as well."

"Selene happens to be my best-friend and 'The Stiff' her lawfully wedded husband!" Kate answers severely.

Jake apologizes. Kate bursts out laughing.

"You had me going there, feel my heart." Jake takes her hand and holds it to his chest.

"I'm telling the truth! He is my best friend's husband, I can't stick him and neither can my Grandmother."

"Why's that?"

"She thinks he's creepy and dull. Strange mixture if you think about it. She calls him 'that little shit'."

Jake throws back his head and laughs heartily.

"I like the sound of your Grandmother already! May I buy you another drink?"

They look at each other, suddenly very aware that he has not released her hand nor has she made any effort to withdraw it. A galvanic pull of mutual desires take a leap onto another plateau.

Jake reaches out and with the lightest touch imaginable, brings his index finger to her cheek and slides it down to her jaw, up behind her ear, down the side of her neck and up again. Kate blinks slowly, shutting her eyes a moment longer that she means to, taken by surprise by her own sharp intake of breath.

Meanwhile Robert downs his pint and scurries off, happy about the piece of information he has just overheard.

~

"The Donna Kebab," announces Vince, "part of the new British heritage. What do you think people used to soak up a belly full of beer and throw it up with before the Donna?"

"Just one of life's many mysteries Vince." Fat Sid sits on a red plastic seat which is attached to the table. He is squeezed into a space which for most people was far too wide. His flabby buttocks overhang all three edges of the seat like an oversized cushion. Little Jason, snuggled up like a bug in a rug, sleeps the sleep of the innocent wrapped up in an old Cashmere sweater under Vince's leather jacket.

The Turkish server opens the pieces of pita bread he has warming on the grill with two sweeping movements of a large, wide knife, the tip of the blade was both round and pointed. He starts stuffing them full of raw onion and shredded white cabbage, looking over his shoulder to check on the spicy lump of processed meat roasting before red-hot electrical coils. He rotates the giant vertical skewer to reveal the cooked portion and picking up a long, thin, carving knife he proceeds to slice shreds of the toasted lamb, fat pouring into the tray below. By the time he had finished loading the already heavily laden pocket bread, the kebabs are almost the shape of small rugby balls. The man wraps up the food in several layers of newsprint and Vince pays while Fat Sid lifts his mass to its feet.

Turning left onto the street they soon passed Carter Street police station and continue north along the Walworth Road towards The Elephant.

"Not bad for February," says Sid with his layers of blubber.

Vince shivers. For February maybe, otherwise it was still freezing. He wraps his arms around his chest holding the warm package next to Jason.

"Supposed to be sunny over the weekend," Sid continues.

"I'll believe it when I see it!"

"Well I 'ope they're right. The sun brings people out and I want a full house, I'm sick of playin' for the landlord and 'is dog. And it would be nice to at least break even on beer and petrol."

"Wonder if Jake's back in town yet."

"This evenin' apparently. I might stick me head round the door of The Rhino later, see if he's around."

"Hey, talk of the devil."

"What?"

"Up ahead, looking in the chemist's window."

"Well I'll be damned! I'd recognize that long, lanky, bastard anywhere, but who's that with 'im? If I didn't know better I'd say it's that posh redhead who works up the Tate, what's 'er name?"

"Kate."

"That's it."

In the distance the couple turn their backs and start walking away towards The Elephant and Castle roundabouts. The woman looks sophisticated even from a distance and then a pub door opens changing the couple from monotone to Technicolor for a few seconds; long enough to establish without a doubt the identity of Jake's lady friend.

~

"I told you not to set foot inside this house you little whore! If you had a shred of decency in you, you'd give him up for adoption; and you will not be considered a member of this family until then, be it a christening, a wedding, or even a bloody funeral and that includes mine!"

So, this was going well! Little Wing's mother and her sister Dolores, shrieking on the front lawn, guests watching at every window, neighbours switching off lights so they could peer through the net curtains without being seen.

"So you're saying if I give my son away that makes me O.K., but if I love and care for him I'm a whore?" screams Dolores.

14

It had not been difficult to track down Dolores, much easier than she had thought it would be. A phone number of a Y.M.C.A. given to her by an old school friend of her sister's had led to an acquaintance who had taken over a bed-sit from her in South Norwood. They had given her another number, a neighbour apparently. Someone called Leo. She wondered if this was the father of her nephew.

" 'Ello."

"Hi, my names Little Wing, Bobby gave me your number, I'm looking for an old friend of mine, Dolores?

"Jason's mum?"

"Yes." So that was his name.

"Just a mo."

Little Wing heard receding footsteps, a door opening and a hollow echoing holler.

"Oy! Dolores. Phone call."

Soon came the sound of a door opening and a familiar yap, yap, yap, yap. Little Wing grinned, she would have recognized that voice anywhere.

"Hello?"

"Dolores."

"Yes?"

"It's me, your sister..."

"Trudy...!"

"Yes, yes I'm back in Sevenoaks. I've been here a week. When are you coming to see me? It's Mum and Dads' silver wedding anniversary, they're having a party tonight."

"Are you joking? You must have heard Mum going on? She'd kill me! "

"You're coming to see me, O.K.? I'm inviting you. I'm back, let's get this sorted out once and for all. We can't be scared of her for the rest of our lives."

"Well I hope you know what you're doing, that's all. Don't forget I have some forgiving to do too. That bitch threw me out when I was five and a half months gone, with no money, nowhere to go, and dad just stood there like a stupid wimpy git and let her do it."

"I know."

"I'm not sure about this."

"Dolores she is your mother."

"O.K. but it's you I'm coming to see, O.K.?"

"O.K."

"I've missed you."

"I've missed you too."

"You know they never told me what happened to you. I just came back from Austria and you weren't there. They told me you were sick. They told me you were so sick they had sent you to Switzerland for the air and that no one was allowed to see you."

"We've got a lot of catching up to do."

"I'll see you at seven-thirty."

"Seven-thirty it is Dolores, bye. Hey, by the way, my name's Little Wing now, no one's called me anything else for years."

"Good-bye Little Wing. Hey, this is going to take some getting used to, why Little Wing?"

"That's another story."

"I'll look forward to hearing it."

"Be careful what you wish Dolores, bye-bye."

"Bye."

Now the three women stand under the stars, Dolores and her mother bawling with unbelievable bile and hatred. Her father stands awkwardly, every bit the hen-pecked, pathetic specimen of a man that he has aspired to over the years. It is just at that moment a Land Rover pulls up the driveway, parks and a man and woman get out. Little Wing stares transfixed, paralyzed, she must be dreaming, this could not be happening. The man stares back at Little Wing, the corner of his mouth twitches and then he smirks.

"Now don't you start! We don't want any trouble out of you."

Little Wing now stares at her mother in disbelief.

"You knew? Oh my god! You knew. You bitch! You knew!"

"Now calm down, don't go making an exhibition of yourself, things like this are better kept in the family. You don't want to go upsetting your father do you? You know he has a weak heart."

"Oh my god you fucking knew! That's why you packed me off, that's why you kept me and Dolores apart."

The woman in the Land Rover, her Aunt, calls out her name.

"Shut up! Shut the fuck up! How could you stay with that man, I thought you loved me? Oh, my God Dolores wait for me. Don't try to stop me Mother, I'll blow the lid on the lot of you."

And with that she bolts upstairs, stuffs her few possessions into a small cloth rucksack, sweeps her father's antique silver snuffbox collection in after (the first and last time she will ever steal) and runs down the stairs leaping the last eight and out of the front door. She continues running until she catches her sister up.

"Fucking bitch. I knew she'd be like this, I just knew it! I should have known not to come down. By the way what was all that about?"

"I'll tell you later, can we just get the hell out of here?"

"God you're shaking all over!"

"Yes." Little Wing swallows hard.

"Come on; if we run we'll catch the eight-thirty."

~

Nancy hovers in the alley behind The Rhino watching little Pookie plop neat little turds onto the concrete. Suddenly an eerie feeling sends the hairs on the back of her neck a tingle. A dark shadow steps from behind a shrubbery at the end of the alley and starts moving towards them. The figure stops, still and silent, violin case clutched in his left hand.

"Why Andy! Why didn't yet call out luv, yet scared the livin' daylights outta me! "

Andy stands before her intently, alternating his scrutiny from her to Pookie and back again. Pookie starts to growl.

"That's disgusting!" he says, gesturing at the faeces on the ground with the violin case.

"Nancy! Nancy! Penelope's on the phone." Tom sticks his head around the corner.

"There yer are! It's yer sister luv, come on." And he hurries on back to the pub.

Nancy looks back down the alley. Andy is nowhere to be seen.

~

It was a quiet Friday night for the three occupied Victorian tenement buildings and their workshop yards that made up the small community. A few other locals had stuck their faces around the door of The Rhino for a beer or two, but all in all if there were two dozen people left come chuck out time, that was the sum of it. Shivering under the stars on this cold clear winter's night, they turned up the collars of their jackets and put their hands deep in their pockets as they dispersed in small groups, which in turn broke up as individuals turned into different stairwells wishing each other a good night. Soon they had all vanished and one lone drunk staggered down the road. He shouted I.R.A. a couple of times before urinating up against a wall. He leaned there resting on his right forearm as he relieved himself, soiling a trouser leg and drinking out of a bottle of methylated spirits which he dropped and broke. Then the poor homeless Irishman started to cry. Not for his bleeding hands sliced on the splinters of glass, but for the industrial alcohol he was hopelessly trying to scavenge. Even Scud does not feel like investigating and crosses the road and rounds the corner for home.

SATURDAY

Nick stands in the entrance to his stairwell, up bright and breezy for his daily run. It is still cold but remarkably warmer than the day before and not a cloud is in the sky. It is the first time this year he feels a touch of spring in the air and the birds feel it too. They are giving a hundred percent to a full oratorio; puffing out their plumage and bouncing around on the pavement and in the trees. A pair of squirrels chase each other through the trees for the pure joy of it.

"Oy!" Nick can just make out two skinhead girls down the other end of the road.

"OY!" Nick's left ear drum nearly blows. He looks up the road and sees their male counterpart about hundred feet away.

"Oy!" The ritual continues.

"COME 'ERE YER SLAG and SUCK ME COCK!"

"No! Yer come down 'ere yer cunt."

Nick looks up and shutting his eyes he warms his face with the rising sun and takes a deep breath of pollution. Ahh! Spring and romance in the Elephant and Castle.

~

She wore suede, black suede, tight fitting over the knee boots and mini-dress. In between the hemline of her dress and the top of the boots was a silky thigh. She looked gorgeous. She entered through a rotating door, like a cat intent on its prey, and made her way through the jungle of faces. Taking the goblet from him she emptied it, pouring it in one swift movement down her throat, leaving one drop in the comer of her mouth to trickle down her chin and her throat. Sliding his fingers through her long, lush hair he held back her head and followed the burgundy trail with the tip of his tongue until he reached her mouth which he kissed deeply and passionately. He slid his hand between the warmth of her thighs and gently stroked her there, his hand gliding upwards with each caress until he felt the stocking tops give way to satin soft flesh. Embracing him with both arms she brought her mouth close

19

to his ear. Giving the lobe a sharp little bite, she licked it and whispered:

"Guess what?"

"What?"

She put out her hand and rapped her knuckles three times on the bar. Tom appeared riding on Slasher's back.

"Jake!" shouted Slasher. Kate and Tom rapped three times on the bar. Jake's focus had become fuzzy around the edges and he felt he was being sucked backwards.

"Jake!" Everybody was looking at him as they pounded on the bar or table top three times. Then they melted into pools of mercury out of which grew rabbits, who hopped away through the buttercups and poppies and took flight.....................knock, knock, knock.

Jake rolled over. His clock reads 9.07am. Shit. He had wanted to sleep late today so he could be in good form for tonight. He throws off the covers and slumps his way to the door. Bang, bang, bang Laughter.

"Shut up, I'm coming, I'm coming!" He wished he was.

Fighting with the bolts, the door flies asunder just as Edith the sprightly septuagenarian from upstairs is passing.

"Now there's a sight for sore eyes," she chuckles. Jake immediately covers his privates with both hands.

"Excuse me Edith!"

"No apology necessary dearie, 'aven't 'ad such a rare treat in years," and as she continues her descent she starts to sing 'I've gotta Lovely Bunch of Coconuts'.

Jake steps back allowing the front door to open into the narrow corridor and Vince staggers in quite helpless. He would have collapsed all together if not for the wall to prop himself upon. His arms are folded tightly over his lower chest and he is doubled up uttering shrieks of mirth. And Leo comes swaggering after. If he grins any harder his head will crack and his cranium drop to the ground; not that it would make a notable difference. Jake goes back to his bedroom and dresses. He returns to find Leo seated at the kitchen table and Vince, having filled the kettle and placed it on the ring, is allowing the gas to run before he strikes a match and holds it out at arms' length. Flames flare up around the kettle like a magician's fireball.

"Yee-ha!" exclaims Vince enthusiastically, pulling a perfectly rolled spliff out of the pocket of his leather jacket and waving it under Jake's nose.

"Wake and bake Jake, wake and bake!"

He lights the joint and tilting his head slightly back, he inhales deeply, stopping before the end of each drag to take in a little extra air for maximum affect. Exhaling he blows a whole array of smoke-rings, from the typical Parisian 'O la la' row of little smoke rings to large singular rings which move slowly forwards like phantom jelly fish. From these two extremes he has perfected numerous variations and combinations. For instance, using a soft breath he can send three or four slow moving small rings, then overtake them by passing one or two larger around them. One of his favourites is to blow a large ring and pierce it with a fast small ring, then by changing the direction of his head he can repeat the performance several times until he has five or six of these blossoms in the air around him. He passes the joint to Jake who by this time was complaining loudly. Leo raises a cheek and farts.

"What the hell are you two bastards doing up at this time on a Saturday with nothing better to do than to come bashing on my door?" He inhales deeply himself. Vince sits down and crosses his legs.

"What ails you Mr. Semi-Erectus; sweet dreams? Let's see, Samantha Fox? Cleo Rocos? Marilyn Monroe? Or Edith perhaps?" Leo produces a wet flaccid laugh. "or could it be ...?" and they both said in unison:

"Kate Lanseer!" and then roll around in their seats, giggling like a couple of school boys.

Jake takes a good couple of tots out of the joint and passes it to Leo. Getting up from the table he runs the hot tap and fills the teapot to warm. Leo passes the joint over the table to Vince and Jake resumes his seat.

"Oooh, the silent treatment! If I didn't know you better I'd think you had a little crush going here."

"Cor blimey! Kate Lanseer! I could give 'er one, she's dead tasty," puts in Leo.

"I thought you could give her quite a few," says Jake. Leo colours up.

"Now see 'ere. That's over six months ago now and ..."

"I wonder why crabs?" says Vince. "Why not prawns?"

21

"Or shrimp?"

"Or lobsters?"

"Aw! Come on." Leo is getting whiney.

"Or winkles? But there again we've already had enough winkles for one day, even if Edith only had her fancy tickled. So tell me Jake; Kate Lanseer?"

Jake looks from left to right, his friends grin back. Filling up his lungs he holds the smoke in for a good while and then slowly exhales. He passes the joint to Leo.

"She came into the Rhino yesterday, early evening. She had had a shitty day at work. We talked, we had a couple of drinks, decided we were hungry, so we went to the Pizzeria, ate together and I walked her home ..."

"Oooo! " sing the over-imaginative duo.

"... as I was going that way anyway. She's actually really nice, funny and intelligent and not stuck-up at all."

He finishes abruptly. He is not going to mention that kiss, that one incredible erotic good night kiss. He did not want to talk about it, it was ...., Jake searched for the right word. It was private. Leo looks disappointed.

"So yer didn't give 'er one then?"

"Leo, it is possible to spend some time with a woman without knobbing her." Jake replies.

Leo does not look convinced. Not because of his personal success rate, if it can be called that, but because this was Jake he was talking to, Jake is his hero. Jake always gets laid.

"So, you two getting together later?"

Darn Vince. Vince takes the joint from Leo. Jake takes three mugs from the cabinet to the left of the sink and takes milk from the fridge, smells it and puts it back, opens a new carton and places it on the table with the sugar bowl and three teaspoons. He sits back down.

"Maybe."

There was a general hooting and cheering. Leo stands up and struts in a circle and cock-a-doodle-does like a rooster. Jake and Vince look at each other then, look at Leo, then look at each other again.

"What?" says Leo. Jake and Vince continued to laugh.

"What?"

The kettle begins to whistle. Jake stands and emptied the hot water from the teapot into the sink. He puts in two tea-bags and fills it until just below the spout, placing back the lid and covering it with the tea-cozy to brew. Vince passes the joint to him and looks at his watch. 9.20 am.

"What time's your Grandad's train?"

"Ten-twenty." answers Leo.

"What's this?" asks Jake.

"Me Grandad's coming up from 'Astin's for the weekend and we've gotta go and meet 'im at Waterloo."

Jake hands Leo the roach, who takes a large tote. Coughing roughly he splutters:

"It's all cardboard yet bastard!"

~

"It's gotta be fresh," explains Jerry. Freddy agrees. The children watch from around the corner as Scud squats and strains, elevating his massive tail to deliver the ammo. Normally the other children would never have let six year-olds in their gang, but Jerry and Freddy have shown such talent and imagination that this morning's escapade was more of a symbolic rite of passage than a test. Scud finishes his endeavor and takes a good whiff. All seeming well he trots off and Jerry and Freddy go into action. After a quick look up and down the street they make a dash from around the corner. Freddy opens up the newspaper and holds it down, while Jerry scoops up the faeces with a piece of cardboard purposely brought for the job. Placing the turd down in the middle of the paper they examine the spoils. It's perfect, not too hard, not too soft; good old Scud. Jerry then squirts a little lighter fluid onto the steamy concoction and Freddy carefully crumples the newspaper around it and picks it up. Standing up he proceeds to the stairwell and up to the second floor. Maybe because of the special relationship that exists between twins the coordination of the mission is perfect. No sooner has Scud's mini-missile taken light, than a stone from a well-aimed catapult shoots through the upper left window pane. Robert drops his magazine, zips up and runs to the front door, determined to catch the little bastards this time. But when he throws open the door the burning newspaper takes him by surprise and instinctively he starts to stump out the flames. One stump, two stumps, three stumps, something feels strange underfoot, four stumps, he definitely was not imagining it, slippery and sludgy, soft and sticky, five stumps and then it hits him, a second before the smell confirms his fears.

~

It is bright and cold outside. Jake, Vince and Leo jump up and down, stamping their feet, slapping their hands which they rub fiercely together. 10:10am, they have been waiting over twenty minutes at the breezy Elephant and Castle roundabouts. Here are three separate bus-stops for a zillion buses and to either side of them ramps descend into the maze of subways linking the primary points around the junction, including the silver cube-thing in the middle, where winos drink cheap sherry and curse the whole world. The subways take one to both entrances of the Elephant and Castle Underground Station and the deep antiquated Bakerloo line and the Northern line pass below them. The two tube stations are linked in their turn by a long claustrophobic tunnel with steps and blind bends where Skinheads sniff glue out of plastic bags that move like a third chronically diseased lung.

Behind them are some wide steps leading up to an uninteresting neoclassical church of impressive size and stature that looks more like a Town Hall and is easily forgettable. And in front of them, that which they wish they could forget, horrors of horrors, the olive green Elephant and Castle Shopping Centre. A giant abscess on the arse of The Elephant; its core the Department of Health and Social Security office block, shooting out of its roof.

"I'm telling you, it's a hydrant for the shopping centre," insists Vince. They are discussing the silver cube-thing.

"It's a fallout shelter," says Leo happily.

"It's not big enough," Jake addresses Vince. "I heard it has all the main fuse boxes and the electrics for the shopping centre, roundabouts, and all the buildings around them, which makes a lot more sense to me."

Jake has just decided to disagree with everything Vince says for the pure hell of it.

"Fallout shelter!"

24

"Fallout shelter my arse," says Vince, "it's a hydrant, looks can be deceptive, especially with fluids. Besides that thing could go way down underground."

"I think it's a Sculpture."

"Fallout shelter!" says Leo, all smiles.

"Fallout shelter, fallout shelter, you sound like a bloody parrot Leo!"

"Maybe they built it for the winos." suggests Jake.

"Maybe it's a UFO. Ah, what's this?"

Everyone cranes their necks as not one, not two, but three number twelve buses pass under the railway bridge coming from the Walworth Road. The first bus terminates there and a full capacity of passengers disembark grumbling and moaning. The second, near empty bus, shoots pass like lightning in spite of many a loud angry yell and the third, half full, stops in front of the first and everyone who had been running back to catch it has to turn around and run in the opposite direction. It is a general stampede, every man, woman and child for themselves, Jake and his friends only just manage to leap on board before the conductor shouts full and rings the bell twice. Somebody kicks the side of the bus and it pulls out, cars screeching, horns blowing, and it continues on its endless journey, turning off towards St. George's Circus and Waterloo Road to Waterloo Station, they are now almost certainly going to be late for the old man.

They arrive at ten-thirty only to be told that the train is running forty-five minutes late. So they play hide and seek all the way to the bar, where they spent some time over a quick pint and teasing Leo, which is not really very fair of them considering his limitations. Suddenly it is eleven o'clock and they hurriedly empty their glasses and run to the platform, getting there just as the last of the passengers are clearing the gate. Jake spots a little, white haired, old man. He is standing aside raising his hat as he ushers a very attractive woman and her pretty teenaged daughter before him.

"Madame," he says.

"Thank-you."

"No; the pleasure's all mine!"

"Grandad!" says Leo.

"Hello Sparky!" Grandad is dressed in beige trousers with a brown leather belt, with matching shoes polished like mirrors. He wears a green V-necked sleeveless pullover with a small design in the knit, over a white shirt with a wine coloured bow tie, a Harris Tweed jacket with a matching hat, a green silk cravat finishes the outfit and he carries a medium weight, beige mackintosh over his arm. Leo blushes.

"Leo, Grandad, Leo," he speaks softly into his ear as he takes his carpet bag from him.

"And who do we have here?"

"Me mates Jake and Vince."

"Good to meet you gentlemen. Ahh! Saturday in the city, or more importantly Saturday night. Music! Dancing! Ladies!"

"Well it's good to meet you too Grandad " says Vince grinning, he has already taken to the old boy.

"Leonard, Vince, please call me Leonard. Who ever heard of a Lady who was attracted to a man called Grandad. Not an aphrodisiac in any shape or form."

They walk out into the chill clear brilliance of an early spring day at its finest and cross the busy forecourt to the taxi rank.

"What a splendid invigorating day boys. This reminds me so much of Dorothy. It was a day just like this at the taxi rank outside of Charring Cross Station. What a woman, legs up to here," he holds his hand up to chest level and lowers his head with a slow nod and a knowing look "and blue eyes, like the sky, and dark chestnut hair. She was crying, poor darling, some imitation man who hadn't turned up to meet her. I said, 'weep not for boys who call themselves men!'. That was some night."

By the time they reached the front of the queue and a cab had pulled up, old Leonard was on to Kitty.

"Not her true name you understand. Just a little pet name I had for her because of the way she had of rolling your nipples between her teeth, making this delightful purring sound as she did so. A tiny little brunette doll of a woman, I think you boys have a name for it these days;" he ponders for a brief second, "a sex kitten."

~

It takes Edith twenty minutes walking at a nice relaxed pace to get to her daughter's house. Silvia would have come and picked her up or paid for a cab but Edith would have none of it.

"I ain't ready for the grave yet. If a little bit of what yer fancy does yer good then so does a little bit of exercise. I can still touch me toes yer know."

And of course everybody did know, though it never seemed to stop her from showing off.

"So what time is our lovely girl and those little bastards getting 'ere?"

"I don't know Ma. They should 'ave been 'ere by now. Shall I give 'er a ring and see what's 'appenin'?"

"Let's 'ave a cuppa tea, and if she still ain't 'ere after that, I'll give 'er a tinkle."

Half hour goes by to no avail.

"Yer don't think those little sods got nicked stealin' from Woolies again do yer?"

"Oh for goodness sake Ma, 'ow should I know! Please try to be nice when they show up, it is 'er weddin' anniversary after all!"

"Like it's us who should be bein' nice to 'er. It's that shit of a 'usband's the one who should be bein' nice. A grown man knockin' up a fifteen year-old and 'e soon showed 'is true colours once 'e got that weddin' ring on 'er finger. Poor little thing, 'avin' to work like a black, day and night, to support 'is sorry backside and those little bastards of 'is. And 'ow many times 'as 'e been in and outta prison in the last five years? Next thing yer know 'e'll be getting' caught nicking from Woolworths!"

" 'E was remember?"

"Yes yer right! Pathetic really."

" 'Is family nearly disowned 'im over that one. It was just before 'is old man got sent down for doing over that armoured truck. I never forget the old boy. 'E was sitting right there were you are, 'oldin' 'is 'ead in 'is 'ands and shakin' it with disbelief. 'And to think 'is brother went to Dartmoor[1]' 'e kept repeatin', over and over again."

The doorbell chimes 'London Bridge is falling down'. Edith could quite happily rip that thing off the wall and stuck it up...

"Well 'ello luv, come and give yer old grandma a kiss, how's me lovely girl?"

---

[1] *A notorious prison for hardened criminals.*

" 'Ello Nan." Edith's grandaughter gives her a big hug. Silvia is holding baby Ruth and after the women exchange the customary oows, coos and ahhs over her, Edith turns her attentions to the twins.

"And 'ow's me sweet little great-grand sons?" Jerry and Freddy stand shyly looking from their great-grandmother to their shoes. Freddy wriggles and holds onto his willy.

"Oh there now, yer not scared of yer great-granny are yer?" says Edith with a sugary sweet voice and a big sweet little old lady smile. But they are and Edith knows they are, and they know that she knows they are, and she knows that they know that she knows they are. So all in all they understand each other perfectly.

"Well come on and take yer coats off, breakfast will be right out. I've just gotta do the eggs and pop the toast in."

Beverly takes off the twin's coats and leaves the room with her mother and Ruth.

"Sorry I'm so late Ma but Mike wanted to talk to me before 'e went to meet Dave."

"That's all right luv, it is yer wedding anniversary after all. What I don't understand is why 'e 'ad to invite that cousin of 'is up? Today of all days!"

"It's O.K. Ma, Dave just needed somewhere to stay in case 'is date with 'is old girlfriend didn't work out. 'E probably won't even be there tonight."

Like hell. Silvia wonders how Beverly keeps believing her husband's perpetual lying. She removes the wire tie from a red and white plastic bag with the words 'Mother's Pride' written on it and proceeds to slot square pieces of white bread into the toaster. Silvia then places a bowl of lambs' kidneys and some fried potatoes in the centre of the table, returns to the cooker and pours the raw eggs into a frying pan.

Meanwhile Edith looks at Jerry and Freddy and grins. Jerry and Freddy take a look at Edith and take a step closer together.

"Staying with yer Nan tonight, won't that be fun?" Neither of them answer they just take a step closer and hold hands. They do not look like they are having any fun.

"And yer going to go to bed and go to sleep when yer told, ain't you?" Jerry nods rapidly for both of them, his brother looks at his feet and wriggles again.

"And tell me Freddy, what 'appens if yer don't?"

"The sandman comes." Freddy whispers taking hold of his willy again and looking like he is going to cry.

"And then what?"

" 'E 'olds yer down by yer 'air and rubs grit in yer eyes 'til 'e skins 'em and they're all red and bloody!"

"That's right!"

"And if 'e's in a very bad mood 'e brings the tooth fairy with 'im and she pulls out yer teeth with red 'ot irons! " adds Jerry.

"Yes. And do yer want to know what grown-ups used to do to bad children when I was a little girl when they were in a very, very, bad mood?"

"No!" shouts Freddy. Edith carries on regardless.

"They'd rip off one of yer arms and beat yer round the 'ead with the soggy end."

"Breakfast's ready." Silvia's voice calls from the kitchen. Jerry and Freddy turn heel and run.

Silvia is serving up the eggs and Bev is putting a heavily stacked rack of buttered toast on the table as the boys scuffle into their seats.

"They're always so well be'aved for grand-nanny, bless 'em!" Beverly exclaims. She pours the twins some juice and then sits down. She helps the boys and herself to the kidneys and potatoes before turning her attention to baby Ruth.

Silvia did not answer her daughter but contemplates the boys; she thinks Freddy looks particularly disturbed. She is more than just a little suspicious. When the twins had been three she had caught Edith singing the Ballad of the Ghost of Ann Boleyn to them as a lullaby, stumping and doing actions along with the words, which go something like this:

'With her head tucked underneath her arm,
She walks the Bloody Tower,
At the midnight hour,
She walks the Bloody Tower'!

Freddy has nightmares about lullabies and nursery rhymes. Jack and Jill sing sweetly as they pushed him down the deep well at the top of the hill, Little Bow Peep and her attack lamb leaping for his throat, and Little Jack Horner, psychotic, lurching out of his corner, and at the very mention of Little Miss Muffet's tuffet he would cover his ears and scream.

Jerry has managed to get a handful of marmalade while his grandmother's back is turned and his mother attends to his baby sister. Acting fast he stuffs his hand down the back of Freddy's collar, withdraws it and slaps Freddy's back to splatter the marmalade as much as possible. Freddy then scoops out what he can reach and wipes his hand in Jerry's hair.

"We was just sayin' 'ow well be'aved the boys always are for yer Nan." Beverly looks up as Edith appears.

"That's very nice of yer dearie, maybe I'll sit next to me little Jerry 'ere, make sure they keep up the good work."

Jerry looks horrified and slides to his right and closer to Freddy, who was waiting with a big boogie which he wipes on his brothers leg. Edith reaches behind Jerry and catches hold of the hair on Freddy's temple and gives it a quick twist.

~

"Wondrous Carolyn! My God she taught me a thing or two..."
"We're here Leonard!" interrupts Vince.

The taxi pulls up and drops them off in the Walworth Road across the street from the better of the two greasy-spoon cafes. They risk near death crossing the busy road and it is a stiff door that Vince shoulders open revealing the distinctive gloomy interior of Ali's Cafe. There is no guessing when the small, high ceiling room last had a coat of paint and even on a bright clear day, such as today, condensation runs down its dingy walls and the two opaque windows glazed with thick frosted security glass. The counter, that runs almost the complete right hand length of the cafe, has once had a blue lino surface which has worn almost completely white. Yellowed glass display cabinets sit on top of both ends of the counter, half full of rather unappetizing bread rolls, Cornish pasties, and steak and kidney pies. Battered wooden tables with plastic table cloths are crammed in for quantity not elegance willy-nilly across the floor, with as many rickety wooden school chairs as possible shoved under them, all of which are taken. A disgruntled queue stands in line, blocking off the counter behind which Ali shrieks.

"Eggs up, bacon, beans, bubble[2]!"

A large dull man gets up and reaches for his plate over the heads of those waiting, his eggs nearly sliding off. Leonard ponders.

"Just a moment lads." And with that he walks to the front of the queue and removing his hat he engages Ali, who is rude and bad tempered at the best of times, in conversation. After a minute both men's heads turn towards them and Leonard points at Leo, who waves.

"What's the old bugger up to?" says Jake.

Meanwhile Ali disappears into the back and produces Mrs. Ali from the kitchen; whereabouts Leonard takes her out-reached hand and kisses it, holding it between his own as he speaks briefly to her. Mrs. Ali, known to her regulars as 'that old bat', becomes quite coy and girlish and afterward smiles for a good hour over her hot stove and frying pan. Ali comes from around the counter and hurries out a table of four who are dillydallying over their tea and fags and seats Leonard and the lads, taking their order himself, much to the annoyance of those standing in line. What's more he sends his daughter over with the food cooked especially in fresh lard by Mrs. Ali herself.

"Eggs over, sausage, bacon, beans, tomatoes and chips?" Leo holds up a hand.

"Eggs up, mushrooms and bubble?"

"That's me" says Vince, who is trying to be a vegetarian again. Rita gives him a lurid grin.

"Eggs over, bacon, beans and chips. That must be yours." She places the plate in front of Jake, looking lewdly at him and pushing out her already very ample bosom.

"And just for you Sir... "

"Leonard my dear, call me Leonard!"

"Leonard." And she places down two beautifully poached eggs with bubble and squeak done to perfection.

"Thank-you my dear."

"Mum says the pleasures all 'er's," says Rita, not a trace of Turkish to be found in her broad Cockney accent.

---

[2]*Short for Bubble and Squeak; fried cabbage and potato*

Jake is impressed. It would seem the old boy is not all talk. Ali's cafe usually offers two tantalizing versions of eggs, fried up or over, like it or lump it. It was a pity Leo could not take a page out of his grandfather's book, he usually disintegrated into a blithering idiot when faced with a woman, and of course the little incident last summer had not helped.

"Poached eggs!" exclaims Vince. "How did you pull that off?"

"Vince my dear boy. You'll find in this life that the Ladies are usually only too willing to please, you just have to learn how to ask. My advice to you is love each and every one of them as unquestionable sex Goddess and learn a few complimentary words in as many languages as possible!"

~

Dick opens the door in khaki's and polo-shirt, holding a pewter mug.

"Kate. Hi," he says, with a hint of uncertainty.

What the hell is she doing here she asks herself. Paying the price of friendship she supposes. A friend in need is a friend indeed, indeed! More like a friend in need is a bloody nuisance.

It is practically the same crowd as at the flat-warming party, she could have picked up just were she left off six months ago if she wished. The guests are mostly work colleagues, with a few exceptions. There is Dick's geek genius/idiot brother, her cousin Georgie and herself, Dick and Selene's hairdresser and his friend, a muscular blonde masseur. The geek genius/idiot brother has attached himself to Georgie and sways sole to heel and back again, staring into his glass and grunting in monosyllables as Georgie talks. His rhythm breaks off as he pauses on the balls of his feet, throwing his head and glass back, emptying the contents down his throat and then back on his heels and so on. He replies in superior, shrill, bitchy outbursts. Georgie is across the room, his eyes bulging with horror and disbelief, dry Martini clutched rather than held in his crooked hand. His look implores Kate rather than greets her. She bends to kiss him and squats, resting her elbow on the arm of his wheelchair.

"Kate, what the hell are we doing here! What if there is a God and he's punishing us?"

"Whatever for?"

32

"Oh I think he may have a long list on both of us don't you? Sex and drugs and rock and roll for instance. Having too much fun! General debauchery on my part, and as for you, for not stopping your friend from marrying this idiot."

"Now Georgie, you know the way I feel about letting people make their own mistakes."

"But if you had known?"

"Oh, I'd have shot him after their first date of course!" Georgie lets out a high pitched shrieking laugh. Heads turn.

"Oh dear! Aren't I behaving myself?"

"You know, she did nearly talk herself into getting on a flight the night before."

"What happened?"

"She sobered up."

"So who said drink is a demon?"

"I don't know."

"Maybe it's a friendly demon."

"Maybe sometimes."

"Well here's to sometimes Kate," he raises his glass. "May we drink to thirst and thirst to drink."

Selene, wearing a navy-blue pin striped designer apron, enters with a tray of hors-oeuvres. She waves at them from across the room then starts to scuffle amongst Dick's friends, more like hired help than the hostess. Finally she reaches them and almost jumps as Kate takes the tray from her hand and puts it on Georgie's lap. Kate gives her a big hug, Selene stiffens, nervously glancing to the corner of the room where Dick was keeping a watchful eye. Kate releases her, keeping hold of her hand.

"What's up, you're shaking, and you're as white as a sheet."

Kate smooths Selene's short layered hair back into place. Selene glances around the room, looking at Kate and Georgie occasionally. She reminds Kate of the afternoon the three of them had waited for her parents to return from their summer holidays. Selene had to tell them she had taken out their brand new uninsured Mercedes, which had been delivered whilst they were away, and ridden it off. It had ended up upside-down in the village duck pond after being rolled several times. They had been lucky to survive that one. Kate and Georgie exchange a quick look. Selene seems to pull herself together and focuses her attention more on her two friends.

33

"Thank you for coming. I hope the stairs weren't too much trouble for you Georgie."

"Trouble? Twaggle!" says Georgie. "Ask your husband, he's the one who helped me, he and that glorious black Adonis over there. No my dear, I have no objection in traveling Cleopatra style and I can assure you there's nothing wrong with having a couple of men sweating and panting over you, but if I remember rightly you already know that!"

A grin and a flash of the old Selene sweeps across her face.

"But come on Selene, it's us, Georgie and Kate, your friends. It's you we've come to see and a long time no see. What's up?"

At that moment Dick, wearing the twin apron of Selene's, walks up behind her and says something brisk into her ear, then swooping up the by now empty tray from Georgie's lap he smiles stiffly at him and nods, then does the same to Kate, and strides away to the kitchen. Selene follows meekly behind, then suddenly looking over her shoulder she mouths a loud silent.

"LATER."

"I didn't imagine that, did I?" asks Georgie.

"No" says Kate.

~

Sallow Alec walks along hardly noticing the bright blue day and the brilliant sunlight. As usual he is not where he's at and, as always, his projections are pessimistic and reminiscences depressing.

As he looks up he realizes he is approaching a small group of women and young children, who stand in a circle contemplating something on the pavement. Coming closer he hears a stout woman remark:

"Oh dear, look at the poor thing, it's in pain, you can tell, someone should do something about it."

Looking down he sees a mouse on its back, waving its tiny front paws in the air, the back half of its body is mangled and crushed. It would seem the unfortunate creature has escaped the claws of a cat, only to be stepped upon or run over. Without hesitation Alec walks through the centre of the group, stamps on the mouse, then carries on walking. Behind him little cries and wails begin and someone calls out after him:

34

"Yer bastard! Yer could 'ave waited 'til we got the kids outta the way! "

~

In the Rhinoceros, Leonard savours himself over a good pint of bitter. The lads are onto their second and are beginning to get a little boisterous.

"Pace yourselves gentlemen, pace yourselves. Remember alcohol is no friend to old John Thomas[3]! May I recommend a restful afternoon, a good bath and clean sheets? The Ladies appreciate things like that, don't they Leo?"

"Grandad," he whines "that was last summer."

"Last summer is not so long ago Leo, and let's face it, there were a lot of innocent victims. It's like post traumatic syndrome, not easily forgotten."

When the general laughter and tittering had calmed down Jake managed to question Leonard.

"And what about yourself Leonard, hoping to get lucky?"

"Oh well Jake, I wouldn't rule out the possibility. Many a fine tune played on an old fiddle. Yourself? Anyone particular in mind?"

Leo sniggers, Jake gives him a dirty look.

"I wouldn't have thought you to be the shy type Jake. Someone special eh? You're in love with this one a little already aren't you, and you haven't even seduced her yet, I can tell! Be careful, sometimes the time for something comes and goes and if you don't catch it you may never get the chance again. How I envy you young men, you have it all in front of you. I bet she's very beautiful this one, eh?"

"Yes actually Leonard," he is smiling in spite of himself, "very beautiful."

"Blonde? Brunette? A Negress perhaps? These dark skinned ladies are so exotic, not to mention passionate!"

"A red head Leonard, with blue eyes."

"A red head! Oh, Jake how I love red heads!"

"Surprise, surprise," mutters Vince.

---

[3] *Male member*

"Oh Bernadette, sweet Bernadette. A tiny little thing but as fierce as a tigress, and nearly as noisy as one too! Ahh! Yes Jake, I think we always know the ones we are going to fall in love with and if we had any sense we'd run like hell. But as they say, better to have loved and lost than never to have loved at all," and he held his glass aloft.

"To Ladies great and small!"

"Cheers!" They echo one another, happily clinking glasses.

"How about love at first sight? Do you believe in such a thing Leonard?"

"Absolutely and without a doubt Vince, and if you ever have the good fortune, my advice to you is never, ever let it slip between your fingers, but close your hand tightly around it and hold it close to your heart." Here Leonard seemed to drift off, his eyes suddenly sad and focused on memories almost lost in time.

"And now Leo my lad, I think I am going to take a little siesta. Even if you boys can take the pace, I'm afraid this old boy has to gather all the energy he can muster."

Leo and his Grandad finish their drinks. Taking up his mac and hat Leonard wishes Jake and Vince au revoir, but not before wishing his best to Nancy and acquainting himself with little Pookie, who unaccustomedly takes a liking to him. Edith arrives just as they are leaving.

"Madame" Leonard raises his hat and steps aside to allow her through the door. Edith smiles and gives him a nod.

"What a sweet old man" says Nancy. Tom rolls his eyes muttering under his breath:

"Dirty old sod."

Leonard looks regretfully after Edith.

"Are yer comin' Grandad?" Leo says, holding open the door, carpet bag in hand. Leonard replaces his hat and steps outside.

"Ah Sparky my lad, so many Ladies, such little time!"

Edith waves at Jake.

"'Ello Big Boy!"

"Good afternoon Edith." It was going to take a while to live this one down.

Edith proceeds to the bar to sit with the lunch time locals. Kev, the young ruddy, ginger haired Yorkshireman was busy describing his latest theory for assassinating the Prime Minister.

"All you need is a bike and a hand grenade," this seems logical, everybody knows London traffic stands at a stand-still most of the time, "it would be all timing after that. She would have to be coming out of Downing Street just as a double-decker bus was passing and you'd cycle down the far side of the bus and lob the hand grenade over the top of the bus and ride away like a bat out of hell."

"And you don't think traffic would be stopped to allow the good lady to be chauffeured away in maximum security?"

Thus speaks Gorky, a local enigma, a tall and handsome man. He sits on a low comfortable chair pulled up by the bar and on his lap, as usual, the vile Slasher.

"Alec is something the matter?" Gorky suddenly realizes that his friend had not said a word the entire conversation, which was most unusual.

"I just killed a mouse," says Alec, who then relates the story from beginning to end.

"You did the right thing mate." Kev reassures him.

"I read once of a certain type of Buddhism, I can't remember which one, that says you should never interfere with the fate of another being, and that we're all meant to suffer the fate we're destined however ghastly, and that the pain and suffering elevates our souls for our next incarnation."

"So you saying because you squelched the mouse it's going to have to come back and live the same life over? Ow come on Alec! A bloody mouse!"

"Have you considered the fact that your part in the mouse's death was part of its fate? You mentioned yourself how instinctive the act was."

This seems to comfort Alec somewhat and Gorky was right, the whole execution had been most alien to his character.

"Excuse me Edith, would you like to sit down?"

Gorky stands to weak protest from Edith, placing Slasher down gently. Slasher stretches then hisses twice at Jake, who is coming up to buy a round plus a double shot of tequila for himself. The tomcat then runs behind the bar and stands on his hind legs, helping himself to a bellyful of slops. Kev stands a round for Edith and the three of them. Alec passes around cigarettes and searches for his lighter. Gorky produces a box of matches. Kev will not take third light, waving away the match. Tom produces a lighter from behind the bar.

"First they saw, then they aimed and then they fired," says Tom.

Nobody mocks him, for they had all heard the stories of their grandfathers and their widows.

"Me old boy fought in WWI;" Edith says proudly, "poor love, used to 'ave the most awful nightmares, wake up screamin' in the night. Never would talk about it. 'E would just shake 'is 'ead slowly and say: Edith, war is the most terrible, terrible thing."

They are all quiet, isolated from one another, momentarily lost in thought. Edith looks from one to the other.

"Now there, there, don't let's start getting all depressed now. The past is the past and there ain't nothing we can do by getting miserable."

"The trouble is the imminent threat of war today, there isn't going to be any hand on hand fighting, no great warriors, no heroes. You can flush strategy down the toilet," says Kev. "All there's going to be is some stupid wanker in a uniform, prick in one hand and the other on a button marked Zyclone C, following protocol."

"Have any of you seen the government flyer yet?" asks Alec, "about what to do in the three minute warning? You remove a door, lay it in a corridor sealing yourself in with six bags of sand, with three weeks supplies of food and water and a bucket to crap in, and after surviving nuclear attack and the all clear is sounded one can come out and 'resume normal activities'! "

"Your lady wife still down at Greenham Common[4]?" Gorky addresses Alec. "Yes? Very admirable, but it will do no good you know. So useful a media distraction, to make you think, oh look, they're on television again; maybe it is possible for a mere insignificant little proletarian like myself to make a difference after all! And meanwhile they laugh and spit on you, get on with what they really do not wish you to see. We must recognize all the evils of our enemies and be willing to experience and practice those

---

[4]*U.S. military base armed with cruise missiles .It was picketed 24hrs for some years by the Greenham Common Women, who camped outside the base with their children.*

evils. You must use their low, vile methods. Being nice, being civilized, will not beat them. They do not care what people think or how they suffer. These people are filth, deal with them as filth! Do not try to be heroes. Do what has to be done and be willing to be remembered as scum, if indeed you are remembered at all."

"That's not always so. What about Gandhi, and John Lennon, and Martin Luther King and people like that. They made a difference," says Alec.

"And why not include Jesus while you're at it?" replies Gorky. "Jesus who gave this world a new religious hierarchy, Christianity. Your beloved Richard the Lion Heart, Britain's great Christian crusader for example. After one practically successful battle he was feasting and drinking with his men when a messenger arrived on the scene. Apparently there was an old Muslim woman in a nearby village who, on her death bed, wished to be converted to Christianity. He went immediately to the village where his troops entered the old woman's house, carried her out, bed and all, and burnt her alive. They then returned to their camp and carried on the festivities. As for the great people you mention, they or their predecessors have all been assassinated. That's something to think about, martyrdom is not a recipe for success you must understand."

"Now Gorky luv, I don't think yer being all that fair to Jesus, 'If there's one commandment I give unto you, it's that yer love one another as I 'ave loved yer.'

"As yer youngsters say, that's were 'e was comin' from. Now don't take me wrong, I ain't no Bible basher, but I like to go church on occasion, 'specially if I've got me concerns to worry about, and all I know is 'e can't be 'eld responsible for what people did after 'e died, none of us can. Now I ain't no educated woman, I know that, but no one can tell me that Jesus did nobody no 'arm."

"Dearest Edith. If all the world could think like you it would be a beautiful place. I sometimes wonder if only women could vote what sort of world it would be."

"We could get rid of 'em trouble-makers!"

"And of course complete power of veto, see already dear lady, power corrupts." Gorky smiles sadly.

"But Kevin you are wrong about strategy, strategy is everything, strategy and intelligence, you need infiltrators, spies.

"'Know thy enemy and know thyself and you shall always win.'

"In 645 AD the Chinese T'ang dynasty took an army of a million men into Koguryo, part of what we now called Korea. They failed on their first campaign to capture even one fortress and then they sent a third of their forces off on another conquest who consequently were caught through an ingenious maneuver by a relatively small army. Some accounts say that out of the original million, only 2,700 returned. The button has to be pressed before any bomb can be launched. That button and the launch site may be their most powerful weapons but that also makes them their biggest vulnerabilities."

"I'm for total anarchy. Living by the natural order of chaos and liberation for everyone! " Kev says passionately.

"Oh, anarchy, anarchy, so many of you British talk of anarchy." Gorky replies impatiently waving his hand as if to flip something irritating away.

"How can you know if you want anarchy, chaos is not to be understood otherwise it is not chaos, and you are telling me you want something you don't understand to govern your life?"

"But that's the whole point Gorky, nothing governs your life," Kev says insistency, " 'Imagine no religion, it's easy if you try. No hell below us, above us only sky.' "

"You two certainly seem to like your John Lennon. Admit it, you're just a couple of old hippies at heart! Walking around stoned much of the time, spending your meager Giros[5] you receive from the government you're supposed to oppose so strongly and yet you make yourselves so reliant on, for dope and corporation beer and then complaining. Then when you are challenged by confrontation you go down to the pub, like generations before you ..."

"So how are we supposed to live with no Social Security when there's no jobs and 60,000 homeless in London alone?" asks Kevin.

"You get organized, you don't brew until you explode, face yet another humiliating defeat, only to return to apathy. And wives and girlfriends cook meals and wait for yet another empty evening ending with tolerating a drunken fool who may even beat her."

---

[5]*Social Security check.*

40

" 'Ere, 'ere." says Edith, thinking of her grandaughter's husband.

"Thank you Edith. We had the sexual revolution in the sixties, the rise of so called anarchy in South London and inner cities in the eighties, and what has changed? Ask any woman and they will tell you. Nothing. Absolutely nothing at all. Why do you think history is recorded around war and battles? It is because this is how we nearly always obtain change, it always has been and as long as the world turns it always will. We are fiercely territorial animals. You have to kill and be willing to be killed...."

"Gorky, you can't ..." interrupts Alec.

"No! No don't blame the messenger that brings the bad news. The sooner you can accept that, the better it will be for you. Don't riot; fight battles ..."

"UNDER A BEIRUT MOON, SORRY SON, THERE'S NOTHING WE CAN DO. UNDER A BEIRUT MOON...."

Jake has somehow managed to turn up the volume on the jukebox and is dancing with one of the old stick ladies to Stiff Little Fingers.

"Good God! 'E'll give 'er a 'eart attack!" Nancy has rushed in flustered, torn away from her high society pew in the saloon bar with Pookie tucked under her arm, who immediately starts yapping with all the sudden noise and commotion Jake is causing.

"Do somethin' Thomas, do somethin'!"

Tom starts grinning in spite of himself, that Jake is a comedian, that is for sure. Robert comes in wearing his dirty old donkey jacket and camouflage overalls with a Tesco's carrier bag under his arm. Stopping short he looks solemnly on the proceedings; he is often disgruntled. Then choosing to ignore the free entertainment he walks up to the bar and orders half a bitter; Nancy serves him with the expression of one being forced to smell over-ripe cheese. Tom walks around the other side of the bar and unplugs the jukebox to a general chorus of arrs and boos.

"Now Jake we're going to 'ave enough noise tonight with the bands and what 'ave yer, so I think we'd like a bit of peace 'til then lad."

Jake takes hold of Tom and starts to waltz. Vince realizes he is going to have to help Tom out, Jake could get pretty

41

uncontrollable when he is like this. Walking up behind Tom he taps him on the shoulder.

"May I cut in?"

"By all means Vincent, by all means" replies the landlord.

Taking Jake firmly Vince tangos him straight out of the door.

Vince decides he better get some food into Jake, besides he is due back at the squat to load the truck for tonight's gig. They stop by the corner shop.

"Cold today," says Mr. Patel to Vince, rubbing his crossed arms.

"But bright and beautiful all the same Mr. Patel."

"Oh cold, very, very cold."

Mr. Patel inevitably complains about the weather. His wife looks him up and down. She is by far the more intelligent of the two and does not mind letting her husband know it, not exactly by words but by her silent scorn. His mother's arrival on the scene has not helped matters either. His wife, Seema, had been born into the upper middle-class of the Ugandan Asians and finds her husband's family rather bush to say the least. Her family has lost everything fleeing Idi Amin's regime and having six older sisters and no money to speak of she had not had much of a dowry.

Jake shoots off behind some shelves that divide the shop in two. At the back of the shop Mr. Patel's mother sits in a doorway crossed legged and bare-foot, on a collapsed cardboard box. Grabbing an almost square can off a shelf Jake bends down and holds it prominently.

"Spam," he says softly and slowly, pointing at the can, "there's a lot of ham in a can of Spam."

He has been trying to teach Mrs. Patel a few choice catch phases since her arrival a couple of months ago, it is the first time she has ever been out of Bombay.

"A lot of ham in cam in spam," she replies.

Jake stands up straight and flaps his hands around; he is pleased and frustrated at the same time. Almost, almost. He bends over again. Pronouncing each syllable and placing particular empathizes on certain words he slowly repeats.

"There is a lot of ham .... m, in A can....n, OF Spam....m."

"What the hell are you doing?"

Jake jumps and stands up briskly. Nearly dropping the tin he juggles it with a clatter back onto the shelf. He musters one of his naughty little boy grins and looks sideways at his friend. Vince knows it is pointless questioning him when he is like this, he would only burst into song or something and then he would never get him to shut up, so he sets himself to the task at hand and they are soon giggling amongst the bake beans. Seema sweeps passed every so often to see if they are stealing anything, her Sari flowing gracefully behind her.

Greasy haired Robert has appeared and hovers outside smoking a fag, his old battered Tesco bag in hand, and peers into the store every so often. Mr. Patel looks tentatively over his shoulder and shoos him away. Robert points at his watch.

"Bloody Wop!" he mutters under his breath. There is an aerobics class at the leisure centre starting in an hour, and through a clever system of lenses and mirrors plus an American water repellant developed for wind-screens, he thinks he has made it possible to video the inside of the women's changing room, showers and all. Understandably he is itching to launch his new project.

Jake pulls faces at Mr. Patel as he rings up and Mr. Patel offers short smiles and nods to Jake, he is not really taking any of it in. Seema is in the far comer standing on an upturned crate pretending to tidy the pet food. She looks over her shoulder every so often simultaneously to her husband's side looks as if she is telepathic, her constant look of suspicion versus his constant aura of guilt.

Jake and Vince leave the shop with a roar of laughter and Seema, steps to her left and over her mother-in-law, walks down the short corridor and through a swing door to the lavatory. Mr. Patel follows in silent haste. Stepping over his mother in his turn he listens, ear to the toilet door, to the general unspecific rustle of layers of cloth. As soon as he hears the strong flow of urine he dashes on tip-toe, almost leaping over his mother, to the shop front. Opening the door he can no longer see Robert.

"Psssst, Mr. Smith, Mr. Smith."

"About bloody time." Robert appears from around the corner, where he has been kicking his heels against the wall. Mr. Patel ushers him into his shop, producing a small brass key, as if by magic, and proceeds to unlock the cabinet door under the counter top. He pulls out an assortment of boxes and grabbing a letter opener from beside the till he levers up a loose floorboard. With too much speed and not enough haste he tries to stuff Robert's bag into the cavity, panicking when he cannot get it to fit. He is still flustering around when he hears the lavatory door open. He shoves the floorboard down as best he can and pushes the boxes back in willy-nilly, only just locking the cabinet door in time.

Seema sweeps around the comer to be greeted by both men grinning idiotically at her. She looks from one to the other of them. She dislikes Robert intently and does nothing to quell the look of distaste on her face as she observes the ferrety little man. As she turns to continue pretending to tidy the pet food Mr. Patel quickly hands Robert an envelope which he just as quickly pockets. Seema looks over her shoulder, the men stand in the exact same positions, looking at her with exactly the same stupid smiles on their faces. Mr. Patel gives Robert a look of insistence, motioning his eyes to the newspapers. The latter pulls out a copy of The Sun and asks for ten Woodbines and a box of matches. Seema returns to the pet food and Mr. Patel, limp with relief, rings up the total. Robert pays and leaves. Mr. Patel's heart is beating fast, that had been too close for comfort. Mrs. Patel Sr. reaches out and picks up a can of Whiskas. Canned cat! She shudders & quickly replaces the tin on the self. What a strange culture this was turning out to be.

~

Fat Sid arrives back to the squat[6] huffing and puffing from his assent to the third floor. He kicks the door open and shut with a loud resounding slam which seems to shake the whole building. With his hands full of carrier bags he f's and b's[7] his way sideways down a narrow corridor to the kitchen. He puts the bags down noisily and listens. Not a sound. Everyone is out or not up yet,

---

[6]*In Britain a homeless person may legally occupy or 'squat' an empty premises.*

[7]*Swore.*

44

everyone except that poor little bugger, who sits in his high chair with a whimper on his lips.

"Don't yer start, I'll feed yer in a minute." Sid says to the baby.

He notices a large saucepan on the cooker with a note beside it. He reads it and taking off the lid he grunts approvingly before turning on the gas. He unpacks the shopping and shoves everything in its place, opening and shutting various cupboard doors, tearing a beer from its plastic ring before placing the other three into the refrigerator, along with the milk, eggs and other groceries he has purchased. Everything that belongs elsewhere he puts neatly on the table that someone had cleaned and tidied, along with the can of beer, a jar of baby food, a tiny spoon and a small crackling portable black and white T.V.

He sits down heavily on a kitchen chair and, pulling the high chair towards him, he switches on the football, opens the baby food, and starts stuffing the baby's mouth. This arrangement is going well until the baby pukes all over himself and starts howling. Sid puts down the jar and spoon and opens his beer. Taking a large swig he burps loudly and getting up he farts and scratches his arse. He opens the fridge and takes out a bottle then runs water into a saucepan, which he places on the gas with the bottle to warm. Throwing a soiled T-towel over one shoulder he proceeds to wind the baby. Resuming his seat he takes another sip of beer and shakes his head as he contemplates baby Jason. Poor little sod. He and Vince had decided a couple of months ago that it was less trouble to look after him themselves than to try to get Dolores to, whoever Dolores is and wherever the hell she came from. Now she has brought home this Little Wing who looks even younger than herself. He hopes to hell she isn't under age.

"She says she doesn't mind cooking and cleaning and she could sing with Jake in the band, she's got a great voice."

Sid wipes Jason's face and starts to shovel food into his mouth again. The front door opens and shuts. Heavy boots tread the corridor and the door opens into the kitchen.

"Millwall, ba-ba-ba, Millwall!" Jake chants at the T.V.

"Sssssh!" says Sid and Vince in unison. Too late, Jason starts to howl. Sid gets up and hands the baby to Vince then goes to check the bottle. Vince sits down and bounces him on his knee until he pukes.

45

"I've just fed 'im yer moron."

"God, it's like handling a giant zit," observes Vince.

Jake has found a teddy bear which he shakes at Jason while he pulls faces and dances around playing the fool. Jason looks at him dumfounded for a moment, then brakes forth in fresh redoubled howls.

"For god's sake sit down and stop upsettin' the baby!" Sid snaps. Jake stands still, teddy bear at his side, he looks most put out.

"He doesn't like me!"

"How would yer feel if some great, enormous, noisy git came stampin' inta the room an' started yellin' and jumpin' up and bloody down?" says Sid.

"He's gone right off me! What have you two been telling him?"

"It's a baby Jake! If he's taken any dislike to you that can't be credited to wind, then it's definitely personal, O.K.? Nothing Sid or I can do about it."

Jake sits down on a small stool and leans against the wall, he stares at Vince and the baby.

"Jason, it's Uncle Jake, you've always loved your Uncle Jake." He looks pathetic, seat too small for his long spidery legs, teddy bear in hand.

"Bloody hell Jake, here, don't drop him." Vince passes Jason across the table and fetches a tin from the corner of the top shelf of one of the cupboards. He reaches inside his jacket pocket and produces a pack of cigarettes. Sitting down he opens the tin and pulls out three cigarette papers and starts skinning up a joint. Sid hands Jake the bottle and sits down himself, he already feels half dead, what with facing Tesco's on a Saturday and coming home to this; where the hell is Dolores? It is only an hour or so before they have to begin loading up the van for the gig.

"Where's Dolores?"

"I'll be fucked if I know" replies Sid, as he farts. Jake hiccups.

"Bleedin' Nora. Is that you Sid? I thought it smelt rank when I walked in here! Phew!"

Vince waves his hand in front of his face. Jake hiccups. Sid farts again, Jake starts to giggle. Vince strikes a match flourishing it around to burn off the methane before heating up and flaking off a piece of the cannabis resin into the tobacco.

"What are you cooking Sid, I would say it smelt good if I could."
He lights another match, Sid is famous for his flatulence.

"I brought some spaghetti and a can of tomatoes and some bread, I didn't realize you were making lunch."

Hiccup.

"I spent the last couple of 'ours down the Walworth Road, so we're well stocked up. But I only got 'ome fifteen minutes ago. Yer can thank Little Wing for the stew, I tasted it; it's very good."

"Great, let's smoke this little number and then do it justice." Vince waves a beautifully rolled joint in the air, true to his perfectionist nature.

Hiccup.

"That's not all, take a look in the fridge, 'cook for thirty-five minutes good hot or cold!"

Jake belches and hiccups. Vince stands up and walks over to the fridge. True enough there are two pies covered with cling-film all ready to be popped into the oven.

"The one with leaves is apple, circles cherry." Sid nods towards the cooker.

Hiccup.

"I'm impressed. So far so good, she seems to be keeping her side of the deal admirably."

Hiccup.

"So far. Mark me words there's goin' to be some trouble with this one. She's a sweet 'eart, that's for sure, great cook it would seem, great voice..."

Hiccup. Vince was busy taking one of the pies out of the fridge and placing it in the oven, he nods his head in agreement.

"Very pretty too, shame about the scar, but I'm tellin' yer somethin' ain't right. I can just feel it in me bones. It's almost as if she wraps 'erself it a shroud of pleasantness and uses it as a fence between 'erself and the rest of the world. Know what I mean?"

"We only met her yesterday, she's probably just shy."

Sid looks at his friend. Had he imagined a touch of defensiveness? God this is all he needs.

"Yer probably right. But she is a friend of Dolores, don't forget that."

"Good point O Wise One, now ..."

A colossal snore reverberates throughout the room.

"That bastard's gone to sleep with the baby!" Sid bellows.

~

"You two would shit yourselves!" Gorky laughs; there are noisy objections from Kev and Alec. "You'd crap your pants."

Edith, who has moved on up the bar to say good-bye to Nancy, looks on affectionately.

"Dear lads! Carrying on with their politics as if they'd all the weight of the world on their shoulders."

"Maybe a bit of national service might even the load" says Nancy, as tight lipped as ever as she feeds Pookie cheese and onion potato crisps.

"Thatcher said somethin' 'bout bringin' it back, for the girls as well."

"Might not be such a bad thing" muses Nancy, pulsating her lips forwards, uncomfortable with the thought of empathizing too closely with any Tory policy. Tom and herself are of good Labor Party stock, her father had been a shop steward at Rotherhithe Docks. She reaches for her cigarettes and offers one to Edith who declines.

"Where's the lighter Thomas?"

"Next to the sink where it usually is luv."

"I looked and I can't find it."

"No? Well it was there just a minute ago."

"Yes Mr. would-be Revolutionist and Mr. would-be Anarchist, I put it to you that you haven't got it in you to carry out one lone act of terrorism, however justifiable, without peeing down your leg" says Gorky.

Kev starts defending himself by boasting of former glory and Alec is whining about hypothesis and pacification.

"No Kevin, I'm not talking about street fighting the police with a crowd of other patchouli boot boys, and I'm certainly not arguing hypothesis," he rolls his eyes to rest on Alec. Kev and Alec exchange a look and shift uncomfortably in the seats.

"Perhaps you'd like to spell it out for us Gorky," says Kev.

"Perhaps I would. You two think, if you had to, you could carry out a terrorist attack?"

"Yes." said Kev.

48

"Well if it was for the right causes and ...,"

"Yes, yes Alec, we've examined the deeper recesses of your conscience, and talking all being unwell?"

"Well yes, of course," he says pushing out his pigeon chest, "it would be my duty to mankind. And womankind of course." He adds quickly glancing nervously around him, as if he is expecting a group of man flaying bull dykes to come running out of the wallpaper.

"And you think you could handle a solo mission, regardless of the personal consequences, if it was for the greater cause of mankind?"

"Yes," says Kev, sounding surer of himself by the second.

"Of course," snaps Alec, sounding rather sulky. It occurs to Gorky that there are times Alec reminds him of Pookie, but not wishing to get side tracked he puts the thought to one side. He drops his voice.

"Well, how about testing out your theories?"

"Well, how about it?" says Kev. Gorky glances up at the clock; there is time.

"Meet me in The Windsor Castle at seven. Until then ... "

Gorky stands and toasts them emptying his glass and retrieves his coat from the back of the chair. Slasher, jumping down from his lap, spits at Alec who swallows hard and holds his breath until the cat walks away.

"And Alec."

"Yes Gorky."

"You're a vegetarian aren't you?"

"Well I don't eat land meat or any corporation dairy produce or ..."

"Excellent, excellent. You can bring say, half a dozen good sized baking potatoes, they don't have to be organic."

"O.K." Alec replies meekly. He is beginning to feel rather sick to the stomach. Potatoes, The Windsor Castle. What the hell did he want to meet them there for? The Windsor Castle is a skinhead pub.

~

Jake is in no condition to haul equipment, so Vince, having fed and stuffed him amply, addresses him with a commanding note:

"Get some sleep and get a bath. You've got a date with a sex goddess tonight, remember?"

But Jake does not feel like going home. He crosses the road and enters a cobbled courtyard that runs down the centre of the adjacent block. He is looking for fun and he finds it. Fen is in, he can hear his tinny mono record player halfway down the yard and Scud barking at the gates, trying to get his master's attention. Jake yells a couple of times.

"Fen! Fen!"

Scud lifts his enormous shaggy tail off the ground and starts to wag it. He looks up hopefully at Jake but nothing happens and his tail drops in disappointment. Jake stands back and throws pebbles at the upstairs window. The window screeches up and a pair of large hands appear, one holding the window open and one holding a piece of two by four, which gets wedged between window and window sill so a head and shoulders can protrude. The head is tawny skinned with scruffy black hair, on which sits a shapeless brown felt hat decorated with an array of dried flowers and feathers, a couple of badges and books of matches around it's brim attached with paper clips. His dark brown eyes search the horizon.

"Fen."

Fen looks down, laughs and the hands appear again. They remove the two by four; Jake hears the piece of wood drop onto the floor, followed by heavy footsteps on the bare creaking boards of the old staircase. A door bursts open causing Fen's horse, Queenie, to look around from her manger and whinny. Fen is already talking rapidly in an excited manner as he jostles with the rusty bolt that holds the two gates together. There is a loud click and one of the gates squeaks, swirls and swings open. Scud scurries by, jumping up and down in circles around Fen, as the latter dances a little jig and sings; Queenie whinnies again. Jake slides in and thinks he may as well dance a few steps also.

"Come up, don't worry 'bout those books there."

Which books Fen means is a mystery as a good dozen or so large piles obstruct the staircase on either side.

"Just step over this," he says, pointing to a plastic container of clothes pegs as he pauses to lift a pile of crisp yellow newspapers and throw them on top of an aquarium full of broken alarm clocks. Finally they reach the top of the steep wobbly staircase and step into the infamous Fen's Den.

The walls are covered with pictures, newspaper and magazine clippings, curling photographs, numerous thermometers, some barometers, at least fifteen clocks all saying different times and one running backwards. Mirrors with worn silver hang and stand upright against the wall, there are Frisbees, a couple of amputee action men and other dolls and toys. Old clothing is displayed on mangled wire hangers, as well as goggles, glasses, a kite, the list is endless. From the beams in the ceiling hang a score or more oil burning lanterns, which Fen thankfully never uses. There are also rusted dented pots and pans, chipped cups, old hand tools, extension cords with flaking insulation, a faded Union Jack, broken car parts, some cracked chamber pots and basically a whole array of objects from A to Z. On one wall is the front grill of an old MG, its headlights intact. Around it the wall is covered with hubcaps and license plates. At night Fen attaches crocodile clips from the headlights to an archaic, if not plain dangerous car battery, juiced by an equally archaic and dangerous battery charger. On the other walls he has various neon advertising signs and sometimes for lamps and special effects he uses orange flashing, rotating roadwork lights.

His living area is practically walled in by bookcases, cupboards, tables and chairs, sewing machines, cookers, refrigerators and all sorts of other furniture, which in turn are stacked and submerged under mattresses, piles of books and periodicals, suitcases bursting with moth eaten clothes, broken kitchen appliances, boxes of china and crockery, old boots and shoes and numerous never ending collections including Jake's personal favourite, a small box marked 'Pieces of string too short to save'.

A potbellied stove occupies the centre of the clutter upon which a large army kettle is kept constantly on the boil. Fen picks up a pint glass of milky tea and takes a gulp. Scud drops down in front of the stove to take a nap. Fen has company, a small, flat chested lady friend who introduces herself in a very well educated accent as Margaret.

51

"I'm really Queen Elizabeth the 1st," she explains, "I've been reincarnated to reclaim my throne and bring power into the hands of the common people."

"Long live the Queen!" Fen stands to attention in all seriousness and then giggles.

"Over there," he points, "I think there's a seat under those coats." And leaping with amazing agility over his record player, making it jump just enough to dislodge it from where it is stuck on the doe-dee-do of a T-Rex single, he starts throwing the pile of coats over the top of a bookcase. Sure enough a burgundy velvet armchair with a missing cushion appears eventually and Jake sits down, sinking low into a seat that has originally been expertly sprung and stuffed with horse hair.

Fen reaches up and takes a cracked Wedgewood mug from a hook in a beam and pours milk from a dented tarnished silver jug with a twisted hinge. Picking up a fur hat, he reveals his old green and gilt teapot with a chip out of the red roses that adorns its sides. He pours for Jake after placing in front of him an upturned milk crate that he decorates with a frail, disintegrating, smelly net curtain and plastic roses in a milk bottle. He places a plastic imitation crystal fruit bowl on top that held an impressive collection of sugars. The bottom of the bowl is filled with marbles and coloured sugar crystals and on top are sugars ranging from pink packets of saccharin, sachets from McDonald's and Whimpy, right up the scale to pairs of brown cubes artfully wrapped in rice paper and marked ' The Ritz' or likewise in gold icing. The whole affect is rather Christmasy.

"Well Margaret, how are you going to start out on your conquest to regain the throne?" asks Jake.

Fen looked at Jake in all seriousness.

"We're gonna rescue Terry Waits[8]," he says most solumnly, Margaret nods.

Fen opens an oven door and takes out a dark green Harrods box which has been ripped and stuck back together with gaffers' tape. Inside is a garment which is made from a fabric that looks

---

[8]*Chief envoy to the Arch Bishop of Canterbury. He was sent to Lebanon to negotiate hostage release only to be kidnapped himself and held hostage for over 4 years.*

Moroccan or Afghani or something, but in all other ways resembles a traditional British men's dressing gown. Fen puts it on.

"Plenty of room underneath for cameras," says Margaret.

"And tape recorders," puts in Fen, pulling out a box from under a table and pushing it towards Jake. It is full of filthy cassette recorders and a reel to reel; they all look like they came out of The Ark.

"We'll hire a camel and I'll dress in the latest safari-style outfit."

"I'm the servant," Fen says, removing his usual hat and placing a turban styled ladies hat on his head, it looks like something Nancy might wear, "and I lead the camel over the border at a quiet spot, and then we start our investigation."

And they are just about mad enough to get away with it thinks Jake.

~

Leo is dead on time, good old reliable Leo; there again so usually is Andy, and he is half an hour late; this has never happened before. Luckily Nick their next door neighbour is in, and Alec from the bottom of the stairwell and his mate Kev said they will give them a hand. Alec and Kev come up just as Vince is loading their pre-loading joint.

"Mr. Evans and Mr. Fitzgerald, welcome to the land of illusion, your timing is perfect! Here's a J with your names on it." Vince gets it burning good and evenly and, after taking a good couple of hits himself, hands it to Kev.

"No Serial Killer?" asks Kev.

Serial Killer is the band's behind his back nick-name for Andy their violinist. The band, The Neanderthals, has an electric violin instead of the usual pain-in-the-arse lead guitarist and the arrangement has gone without a hitch until today. Andy is of average height, average build and has short, but not that short, mid-brown hair. He wears clean, comfortable clothing and shoes, always has immaculately clean, manicured hands; basically you can find no fault with the man. He is perfect. Never late, always phones when he says he will, always does at least his share of the work, never moans. He has one beer before he goes on, then he will help load and unload the van, has one more beer, after which he will always politely turn down any offers of hospitality and disappear into the night, only to turn up on the dot for the next gig or rehearsal. And for this he has earned himself the name Serial Killer.

"Not yet. And Jake got as pissed as a newt at lunchtime so Vince 'ad to send him 'ome to sleep it off and 'e's supposed ta be meetin' yer friend Kate later."

Sid's last remark addresses Nick. It stings him like a wet cloth in a gale force wind.

"Anyway thanks a lot for givin' us a 'and, we really appreciate it."

Sid is in his Metallica T-shirt all ready to go, Jason sleeping peacefully, cradles in the crook of his big fat hairy arm.

They are all so preoccupied with the unexceptional blabbing that is going on, that nobody notices Nick as he stands and looks out of the window, eyes full with tears and pain.

Sid puts Jason in the next room for his afternoon nap. More coffee plus another joint and The Neanderthal's late as usual keyboardist Barocco makes a boisterous entrance draped in a blue velvet cloak.

"I am therefore I am!" announces Barocco with a theatrical grandeur.

"Don't you mean 'I think therefore I am'? " asks Vince.

"No!"

"Barocco, I 'ope yer remember what I said 'bout the 'Ammond. If yer must use it tonight then it ain't comin' back up 'ere. It took six of us to get it up last time and even then we nearly dropped the bloody thing, it could crush a bloody cart 'orse," says Sid.

"Oh keep what's left of your hair on fat-so. My brother-in-law's relented to groveling and blackmail, and he's letting me use his lock up under the railway arches opposite here. There's lifting equipment, trolleys and what-have-you, happy?"

"Good, I'm sick of stubbing me fuckin' toe on it."

"Why do the people who own all the equipment always live on the top floor? Couldn't you have found a ground floor flat to squat?" Barocco asks.

"For yer information Mr. my-dad's-stinking-rich-with-a million shares-in-Exxon, the few available ground floor flats are either derelict, burnt out, or stink of infected urine."

"And then there's those mammoth speaker cabinets of yours," retorts Barocco.

"Bass yer idiot! If yer think I'm giving up any of me bass because a lota bloody pansies can't carry 'em, then yer got another thought comin'. "

More steps are heard in the corridor and a familiar yap-yap-yap. Dolores.

"About bloody time!" Now Sid is really pissed off with her.

"Hello everybody. Hello Sid, what's up? You're got a face like a back of a bus!"

Dressed in black, hair dyed raven, pasty faced with her eyes heavily outlined, skinny Dolores, teenage mother of Jason, tactless as a drunk.

"And where do yer get off just leaving Jason alone in the flat like that?"

Another figure slips in silently and stands by the door. She makes such a good job of fitting into the wallpaper that she could have made herself invisible if it was not for the aura of youth, health and beauty that radiates from her, in spite of the nasty scar on her left cheek. Vince swallows hard. He has always credited himself in being brutally honest with himself but nothing could have prepared him for last night. It had been instant and dramatic like in film or a novel but, as they say, truth is stranger than fiction. One minute he had been walking up the stairwell laughing and joking with Sid and all had been well. The next thing had known he had stepped into the kitchen only to be confronted by the back of a barefoot, dainty little figure with long chestnut hair and beautiful delicate hands arranging a vase of daffodils. An overwhelming sensation, truly profound and awe inspiring, hit him square in the guts & melted softly as the fluttering of a butterfly's wings, leaving him weak kneed and mesmerized. It could only be described as love.

"I didn't leave him alone, I left him with Little Wing."

Sid passes his question mark eyes onto the young woman by the door.

"And I left him here because I had to go and look for a job. Dolores told me you were getting up to look after him, and you had said I could leave as soon as I heard your alarm clock go off because you liked to be by yourself first thing."

"I 'aven't gotta alarm clock."

"But that's impossible I heard it go off!"

"And I'm telling yer, I 'ain't got no alarm clock!"

Great, thought Sid, another liar. Vince, who has stormed out of the room only seconds before, returns and places a wind-up alarm clock on the table.

"Look what I found in the pocket of one of Dolores's jackets hanging on the coat-rail outside of your room Sid."

Sid looks at Little Wing. She meets his look easily and strongly enough but looks troubled, as well she might. Sid is much more inclined to believe her than Dolores even though they only met last night. They both look at Dolores.

"Oh, come on!"

"Yer bloody well knew I was out. I always do the food shoppin' on Saturday mornin'."

"What about last month, when your uncle had a heart attack, you didn't do it then."

"Last month, when me uncle 'ad a 'eart attack? For fucks sake, no, that's right. That particular weekend I did not do the shopping and neither am I likely to in any similar emergency, yer silly little cow! What the 'ell 'as that got to do with anythin'? "

"Anyway he's all right isn't he? Where is he anyway, just stuffed in the next room all alone? That's not exactly looking after him is it?"

"I put 'im down ten minutes ago, fed, bathed and changed, yer ungrateful little bitch!"

"If you two keep shouting like this he's going to wake-up," says Vince.

Vince does not like shouting, violence or any type of unpleasantness if it can be avoided. For all his boots, leather and chains he is a peace loving individual, intelligent, well-educated and very entertaining. His blond hair comes halfway down his back and his face is handsome and alive with character. His light-brown eyes are warm and penetrating and hold no malice, his twice broken nose adds to rather than deters from his looks, but by far his most striking feature is his mouth. It is from his mouth one can most accurately read his mind; his vibrant joy and private sorrows, his cautious anticipation and his quiet anger, his gentleness, patience and kindness. This mouth also gives vent to his famous laughter, and no receptive woman has ever walked away unhappy from his bed. Lacking the immediate hit-you-between-the-eye-balls charisma of Jake, he is happy to play second fiddle to his best friend. He has a similar adoration of women as Leonard but not so much in the addictive sense of the latter.

"I'll go and check on him," Little Wing says quietly as she turns to leave the room.

"Oh no you fucking won't! I'll check on him. I'm his mother, me, O.K? Jason's mine," and she pushes past her.

Little Wing looks after her sister not quite knowing what to do with herself; embarrassed by Dolores behaviour and awkward being alone in a room full of men whom she does not know.

"Come and sit down luv and 'ave a cuppa tea." Sid stands up and offers her his seat. He addresses the rest of the room.

"We'll do the speaker cabinets first, then we 'ave to get the 'Ammond down." This last announcement is met by various moans and groans as the men tunnel out into the corridor.

"What have you been up to today then?" Vince sits down in the seat next to her. She enchants him more and more by the moment.

"Dolores went out early to meet someone, so I went up to the West End to check out the bill boards outside of clubs, see what kind of stuff they're showing. I'd only been walking around for half-an-hour when I stumbled on some would-be Blues club. They were holding auditions and I listened for a while and was just turning to go when this man came running out with a clipboard and asked if I was Fiona Tully. So I said yes, and he said you're late hurry up."

"What happened?" Vince grins.

"First off everybody was forty up and they ignored me, they were really stuck up. So after sitting there for a couple of centuries with nobody talking to me I decided to leave and just as I stood up to go they called me, well Fiona Tully, up. So I got up on the stage and people started to laugh and the band leader went to the bar and started talking to someone so loudly that people were turning round and looking."

"So what did you sing for them?"

"My Time After a While!" they both smile, Vince notices she had dimples when she giggles. What the hell is wrong with him? If he goes on like this he is going to make himself puke.

"Then all of a sudden they started being nice to me."

"So you got the job?"

"No."

"No?"

"There was this little hitch."

"What was that?"

"I heard them play." She pulls a face.

"That bad?"

"Oh Vince, they were terrible! I didn't know what to do with myself, I had to keep biting the insides of my cheeks to stop myself from laughing! And then the real Fiona turned up and in the end I made a run for it!"

Vince laughs out loud, she is funny, this is all very encouraging.

"What have you got there?" He points to an old paperback sticking out of the breast pocket of her jacket. She pulls it out and hands it to him, it is a copy of Homer's Iliad. Vince leafs through it for a couple of seconds before he realizes something.

"You speak Greek?"

"VINCE!" screams Sid, "Quickly before Barocco and Alec drop this bloody cabinet!"

~

Selene's 19 year-old brother and girlfriend arrive dressed in trench coats, Doc Martins, and shapeless handmade garments of hemp and naturally coloured wools. They arrive a lot more than fashionably late and once relieved of their heavy overcoats flop down on the settee, sucking face and sticking tongues down each other's throats, her black and his fuchsia hair co-mingling on the upholstery. The other guests mill around them as if they were part of the background music. After about an hour of snogging, three beers apiece and a belly full of food, they steal a bottle of Vodka, up and leave. Someone has the right idea, thinks Kate.

Cousin Georgie is stuck again with the skinny, geeky, genius/idiot cousin or whatever. Dull must be a family trait Georgie noted. He is trying to engage Dick in conversation at every possible opportunity but to no avail. Likewise Kate is trying to get a discrete minute or two with Selene but it is impossible.

"This is impossible," says Georgie. "This is our friend, she needs our help. We're going to have to take the intuitive and I'm going to have to get out of here. So here's what we're going to do. Tomorrow, at Martha's party, she will be opening her presents in the cocktail hour before luncheon. You and I will leave the room and ten minutes later Selene is to excuse herself and leave by the same exit. There will be someone who will assist her. Don't worry about Dick-head, Grandma will be in her element and that should be quite a spectacle in itself. Then finally we may get to TALK, god dam it; is there something fucked up in this picture or isn't there?"

"It's pretty fucked up."

"I'm out of here. Kate my darling, kindly ask the ebony Adonis and that blonde hunk with the tight white jeans and T-shirt if they would be so kind as to assist me."

"Would you like to come over and burn one?"

"Tomorrow my lovely, tomorrow. Right now I have a previous engagement!" His eyebrows rise and lashes flutter, he follows with a cunning smile that says it all.

"Enjoy yourself Georgie." They kiss on both cheeks and hug.

"I know they say ninety-nine percent of sex is in the head but I don't see why one should neglect nor underestimate that one percent."

"Me neither," agrees Kate. And without any further ado, Georgie is whisked away like a true queen.

Outside Georgie and his gorgeous duo behold 'The Neanderthals' and friends.

"All these huffing and puffing, sweating young men in leather! What's a girl to do!" exclaims Georgie, doing his best imitation of a swoon.

"Oh look at Ginger, what a backside, isn't he cute!"

The three of them generally oow and aah their appreciation as they look Kev up and down.

"Give me blondie any day!" Georgie draws their attention to Vince. "Now he's a peach."

"Oooh! I wonder if he's a shower or a grower! That's quite a lunch-box he's got harnessed in those jeans," the masseur notes enthusiastically.

"That little one's so funny! Strutting around like a rooster, bless him!"

"And what about that great fat thing! You know who would like him don't you? Skid-mark Harry!"

The couple hold their midriffs and squeal. Sid bends over showing off his nylon tartan underpants and the crack of his arse.

"Charming!" Georgie says haughtily.

"That's one big nose! It makes Barry Manilow look like a pug." The blonde has progressed on to Barocco.

"He looks Jewish, what do you think?" muses the masseur.

"I think it's still a very big nose."

"He'll be circumcised if he's Jewish."

"Circumcised men always have premature ejaculation!"

"The old round-heads and cavaliers raise their ugly heads again! Cleanliness and scentless virus lashings of hot meat injections for hours on end, now which would I choose I wonder?" Georgie is already beginning to find the couple's rather limited intellect tedious. He takes a deep breath and makes himself relax and focus on the upcoming sin and debauchery. That dreadful party has made him terribly uptight.

"If you had a mouth proportionately as big as his nose you'd be able to swallow your own head."

"If I had a mouth like that I'd have better things to do with it than swallow my head silly! Oh! Now he's cute! Cuddly and handsome, and strong and muscular like a lion!"

"The very namesake, that's Leo" says Georgie.

"Ooow!" The ebony Adonis holds his hands together in delight.

"Though Cancer may have made a more appropriate birth sign for him."

"No! Not the one who had that party last summer?" The blonde holds his hand to his mouth aghast with horror.

"The very one."

"Oh how disgusting and he looks such a dish too!"

Georgie's white 1950's Pullman Mercedes comes cruising around the comer and parks behind Sid's van and now, much to the gay men's delight, it is the band's turn to express admiration and share their lower octave oows and arrs.

Morris, Georgie's driver, helps him embark, his two-toned twosome jump in either side of him, and waving good-bye to the boys in the rock band, they pull away. Georgie gets quite carried away and blows Vince a kiss. They turn right at the end of the street, left onto Kennington Park Lane, right at the Oval and head north of the river for Chelsea.

~

"Little Wing?"

"Yes Delores?"

"I don't know quite how to tell you this."

"What?"

"I lost my wallet."

"Oh! I'm sorry. Can you remember where you had it last?"

"I got it pick-pocketed on the Walworth Road but what I'm trying to say is, you know that snuffbox you gave me on the train last night?"

"Yes?"

"I'd already been to the pawnbrokers."

"Shit!"

"I'm sorry Little Wing."

"Don't be silly Dolores, it's wasn't your fault, it's only money after all. It's just that we don't have much of it, that's all." And she gives her sister a sad little smile.

"Don't worry we'll be O.K."

"Yes?"

"Yes. All three of us. You, me and him." They are both kneeing overlooking little Jason who is sleeping blissfully in the little rocking cradle Sid has made for him.

"Who says you can't choose your family. Screw Mum and Dad."

"You're right, screw 'em. I love you Little Wing!"

"I love you too Dolores."

After hugging her sister Dolores holds on to her by the elbows and studies her face.

"How did you get that scar?"

"A kitten got its claw embedded there and tore a hunk out."

"Err yuk!" she places her hands over her mouth.

Little Wing lets out a single snort of laughter, slowly shaking her head. She has forgotten how tactless her sister can be. She pulls a nail file out of her pocket and walks across the room on her knees towards the iron fireplace. Lowering herself on her elbows she levers a knot out of the skirting board and by inserting her fore finger she removes about a foot long section behind which is a small white cloth bag. Pulling open the drawstring she reaches inside and then hands Dolores a perfectly square silver box. It looks delicate but exquisite, plain and highly polished; its only decor is a fine double line that runs around the edge of a slightly bulbous lid. Its corners are rounded and from each splay a tiny solid leg. Little Wing remembers this one from when she was a child, it has always been one of her favourites, it reminds her of a mustard pot. She replaces the skirting and hammers home the knot with one firm strike from her closed fist.

~

Hot room in a haze. The smell of French cigarettes and Scotch, the sound of obscenities being yelled, fists are shaking, it is not a sight for small children.

"Get him, get him. The bastard!" The bellowing war cry of Ruby, unaffected by her advancing years.

"The filthy swine, the filthy stinking swine!" Edith's shriek is no less savage.

"Foul! Foul! He did it again. The referee must be bloody blind or something!"

"Darn stupid!" Edith chuckles and tips her head backwards emptying the contents of her crystal tumbler.

"He punched our lovely boy right in the kidneys again."

"Get 'im Mincer, get 'im!" Edith manages to shout but still sound menacing, "Kick 'im in the balls!"

Edith and Ruby, eyes glued to the telly, as it blasts at decibels usually associated with rock music and adolescent boys. The neighbours hammer on the ceiling, floor and walls in vain attempts for quiet.

They both boo and hiss and generally continue to pour out their contempt at Mincer's opponent and the ongoing proceedings. The ref delivers a foul to Ape-Eater and the bell rings.

"About time, filthy creature, drink Edith?"

"Don't mind if I do; yerself?"

"Silly question dear." Ruby turns to reach the ashtray and firmly stubs out her cigarette.

Edith gets the decanter from the sideboard and pours. Because of Ruby's bad feet it has become customary for her guests to help themselves, and her of course. Noticing the volume for the first time Edith lowers it. The desperate hammerings stop but not quite simultaneously.

"Whatever are you doing Edith?"

"Turning the telly down yer silly old bitch!"

"I can see that. It's that knocking, it's stopped now."

"Maybe it's 'em next-door havin' a bit of that 'ere 'ere." Edith crosses the room and hands Ruby her drink.

"Whatever are you talking about Edith?"

"Don't be daft, you've been married, yer know what I mean. A bit of nookie, getting yer leg over."

Edith returns to her seat, placing her Scotch on the side table, and lowers herself slowly into the armchair, free falling the last eight or so inches. Her backside sinks into the cushion and she rolls backwards, her feet rising off the floor showing off her nether regions. She continues.

"Our Bev cleans for 'em every Monday and Friday, and their second room, yer know, the one off the corridor, they keep locked ..."

"Whatever for?"

"I'm gettin' to that, anyway, the door it was always locked, two big bolts which look like they came out a church or somethin' and a dead lock. Well, one day when they were away on one of their fancy trips abroad she gets 'er cousin, you know, our Tracy, the one who works up at the 'ospital taking the molds for the 'earin' aids ..."

"That's disgraceful Edith you can get arrested for things like that!"

"... and takes it to the locksmiths, the one in Brixton by The Cock and Dog. Well she takes a quick peek and yer ain't never seen nothin' like it! First off it's entirely black, the walls, the ceilin', the furniture, everythin'. They 'ave wall to wall rubber carpet, leather on the walls with mirrors, well me and Bev reckoned it was leather, Silv said somethin' about P.V.C."

"You've been there?"

"Well Bev wanted to know what we thought."

"Wanted to be three nosey cows more likely."

"I'll pretend I didn't 'ear that. So there's this big black four poster bed with a black sheet, definitely leather this time and the contraptions! All different bits of rope, nylon and silk scarves, straps with studs and buckles, chains, 'andcuffs. And then there was the bed itself, the top and bottom opened like stocks."

"Stocks?"

"Yes, yer know, like they used to 'ave on village greens, and yer'd throw rotten tomatoes at 'em."

"I know what they are. What on earth do they want stocks for?"

"Kinky stuff of course! There were 'oles for arms, feet, 'ead, everythin', all shut up with padlocks. And all around the bed, 'ung on the posts, chains and whips and thin's! Then there's this long post from floor to ceilin' like a fireman's, in one corner a wood chair and a metal chair with 'inges and things and locks to go round yer arms and legs and waist even yer neck. A suede arm chair and all over the walls, like yer never seen, all sorts of chains and devices with locks and leather straps; a regular torture chamber."

The bell rings for the next round. Edith finds the control box for the TV next to her drink and turns the volume up.

"There 'e is, our luvly boy Mincer. Go on, get the bastard! Oh, the filthy swine, the filthy stinking swine!"

Ruby, glass in hand, sits staring straight in front of her, totally confused and bewildered.

~

Seema has to get the shop to herself for a while. It is not going to be difficult, she knows her husband's habits well. He has been glancing at the clock for forty-five minutes now, he will not be able to keep it up much longer. Addiction calling! Addiction calling! Sure enough, less than two minutes later he makes his lame excuses and leaves the shop, she has just under an hour. He has gone to the dogs. If not the horses will do, but the dogs are his drug of choice. He fiddles about fifty pounds a week out of the till and on Saturday afternoons, in less than an hour, he blows it at the Bookies.

With her face pressed to the window she watches his shrinking figure until it reaches matchstick size, turns left and disappears only to reappear a few seconds later and tip-toe back in the opposite direction. Picking up the letter opener she finds by the till she pops the lock of the cabinet open and tuts at what she finds there. All these boxes and bags just pushed in this way and that, maybe it is only this he is keeping from her, this mess. Pulling everything out she spots the obvious, and seconds later she is looking into Robert's Tesco bag examining its contents. It has taken her all of two minutes to discover her husband's dirty little secret.

~

With the help of a big hubbly-bubbly full of gold seal Pakki black and the three beers Jake has stolen from the fridge at the squat, Fen's Den is really hitting party mode.

"We're off to see the Wizard, the wonderful Wizard of Oz!"

Jake leaps around in what limited space there is, arms spread eagle, saucepan on his head, the tin man bellowing like a baboon. Fen the scarecrow who, for some God only knows why reason, marches on the spot with an exaggerate swing of the arms, plastered with an ear splitting grin and only joining in on the 'because, because, because, because, because..'. And Queen Elizabeth, alias Margaret, naturally takes the part of Dorothy, a shrill, tone deaf Prima Donna, bounces around in a pair of red Wellington boots Fen has found for her and wrapped in some Christmas tinsel. Suddenly Jake stops.

"It's no good, it's useless," he cries. "We have to have a lion."

And with that he dashes down the stairs, out of the door, through the gate and out into the main yard pursued by Scud who is really getting into the spirit of things. Standing by the back entrance to the workshops, saucepan still on head, he surveys the street; nothing. Scud drops his wagging mammoth tail and decides to take to his travels. As he rounds the comer he is met by Gorky. The tail elevates itself again and begins its heavy sway, Scud receives the customary pat and kind words. He really is not the sort of dog that anyone would want to give a good hug and stroking to.

"Gorky! You have to come and sing with us! We need you Gorky! "

"An interesting proposition Jake. One at another time I may well have answered to, but today is not the day. I have things to do and plans to be made, and only a few hours in which to do so."

"But Gorky. The Lion, ' We're off to see the Wizard, the wonderful Wizard of Oz, because, because, because, because, because ...' "

Gorky is walking away his hand rises, waving Jake good-bye. Jake stops singing and looks after him and flaps his hands about, what is he going to do now? Then, as if by magic, a figure appears from around the far corner and proceeds towards him, passing Gorky as it draws closer. Angela! And she is wearing a gold trim, leopard-skin, polyester bomber jacket. Perfect! And how many times in one life will Jake be able to say that about a gold trim, leopard-skin, polyester bomber jacket?

Angela that afternoon, as for several years now, has got drunk to go out for a drink, and Angela is going out to drink. It is late Saturday afternoon as her high heels finally totter down the road. She can barely keep it together up there at elevation 4". She wears imitation leather stretch trousers, many sizes too small, with prominent large-tooth stainless steel zips that run down the outside of both legs from waist to ankle. Above the waist she resembles sausage meat oozing out of a too tight skin, she is also large breasted but somehow or other she manages to squeeze it all into a red boob-tube. This part of her she does manage to cover with a certain amount of decorum with the gold trim, leopard-skin, polyester bomber jacket, which could have done with being a size bigger if one really splits hairs. Gold also are her stiletto shoes, the straps of which are already too tight for her poor swollen ankles. Red varnish has been reapplied to both finger and toe nails over many layers of chipped red vanish, and lost are the symmetry of her lips, who's smile had given her her name. Painted red to match her nails, they seem to have a fuzzy pink outline because over the passage of time the surrounding skin has become stained with the acidic clash of sweat, booze, and cheap lipstick.

Jake runs up to meet her, leaping around her like a March hare.

" 'Angie baby, special lady'!"

" 'Ello luv."

"You've just got to, got to, got to, come and be a lioness!"

"What yer talkin' about yer silly bugger. Yet gotta saucepan stuck on yet 'ead."

"Come with me!"

66

And with that Jake lowers his stance to Angela's shoulder level, raises his finger to his lips as he takes her other hand and preforms a crouched, long legged creep while Angie totters alongside. In this manner they proceed down the road, into the yard, to Fen's Den.

After quite a performance, Jake manages to get Angela up the rickety old congested staircase. She fits right in and takes to her role vigorously and with enthusiasm; growling and conducting with a chopstick. This is all very well in the live and let live spirit that suits Fen and Jake, however Margaret suddenly decides as she is Dorothy, it shall be she, if anyone, that conducts.

"I'm King of the Beasts!" says Angie with pride, holding the chopstick behind her back.

"Well I'm Queen Elizabeth the first," replies Margaret.

Fen bursts forth into his high maniac's laughter. Jake flops down into red velvet arm chair and takes the saucepan off his head. He has worked up quite a thirst.

"Hey, Angie baby. How about me and you go hit a few pubs down East Street?"

~

At the other end of the street from The Rhinoceros is the dismal King's Arms. Its harsh lighting makes the red lino floor, red plastic upholstered seats and lack of customers even more distinctive. It is Mean Mike's wedding anniversary and he sits celebrating it with his best friend Rick and his cousin Dave, who is up from St. Mary's Cray for the weekend.

"So I said, look 'ere yer fuckin' cunt, if yer don't fuckin' watch it, I'll knock yer fuckin' teeth so far down yer fuckin' throat yer 'ave to stick yet fuckin' toothbrush up yer fuckin' arse to clean 'em"

"And what did the cunt say to that?" asks Rick.

The door swings open and a pretty petite blonde comes in. She wears a calf length black leather coat, over a powder pink dress with matching high heels, lipstick and nail varnish.

" 'Ere Mike, the Mrs," says Dave. She sees Mean Mike and waves.

" 'Ang about, this won't take a minute."

He gets up and goes over to her. Dave sniggers. There follows a hurried earnest exchange of which only a few snippets drift over.

"... but it's our anniversary Mike .... yer promised.... "

Then Mean Mike begins to get annoyed. If she was a man he would of probably have hit her by now.

"Don't tell me what to fuckin' do woman, no one fuckin' tells me what to fuckin' do!"

"But Michael!" she starts to cry. Rick starts to feel uncomfortable.

"Don't fuck with me woman, not if yer know what's fuckin' good for yer. I'll come along when I'm good and fuckin' ready, now sit the fuck down and have a fuckin' drink, or fuck off!"

She turns and runs out of the pub. Mean Mike struts back over and sits down.

"Fuckin' woman."

"Oh come on Mike, it's yer fuckin' wedding anniversary," says Rick.

"Fuck me, I don't fuckin' believe this! Yer as bad as that stupid fuckin' cow. Yer wanna tell me what to fuckin' do, do yer?"

Mean Mike springs to his feet, nervous heads are turning.

"We can take this outside if yer fuckin' want, nobody tells me what to fuckin' do, no one!"

"No mate, no. Come on Mike. Fuckin' hell. It's me, yer mate, Rick. Sit down, 'ave a beer. It's me round. Fuck me!"

Mean Mike sits down adjusting the lapels of his leather coat, shifting awkwardly from buttock to buttock.

"Well what the fuck are you lot looking at?" he yells, addressing the rest of the pub. Heads turn rapidly away and equally rapidly the hum of conversation starts.

"Fuckin' woman," says Mean Mike. Dave sniggers.

~

Meanwhile tempers are fraying and tensions are drawing tight in the back room.

"Number 83 Hampton Street. Held up at his grandmother's with food poisoning."

"You've got it," confirms Vince.

Barocco struts off. Vince is relieved to get rid of at least one of the high level egos from the general low key hysteria in the room. Vince is worried about the gig. Andy has to show, he is so reliable. Something must have genuinely held him up, Vince was sure of that and he is right. But Jake-who the hell knows what that unpredictable maniac is going to do next. And then there is Barocco with a belly full of Scotch under his belt already, conveniently never seeming to realize that there is more to setting up a gig than his blasted keyboards and now he has brought a baby grand piano too. They probably would have thrown him out of the band a long time ago if he was not so talented, but a wanker never-the-less.

Vince strolls over to where a heated discussion has been brewing for several minutes now between Fat Sid, the lead guitarist of the support band and his girlfriend (the tambourinist), and Patrick the organizer. He stands on the outside of things, his ears listening and taking in everything being said, but his mind elsewhere.

"Maybe we should go on first because A) we've been playin', since you lot where in nappies. B) Because we're much better than yer. C) Everybody's comin' to see us anyway, and D) if yer don't shut the fuck up and stop annoyin' me, I'm going to take yer outside and beat the crap outta yer."

Fat Sid is in no mood to deal with a nineteen year old product of blue collar socialism arguing some supposedly Marxist theory of equality, all because he wants to get his own way. Sid has been brought up on such stuff; he comes from a strong union and Labor party background. He can remember his mother and aunt organizing soup kitchens for picket-lines. Nancy's and his father are friends, they had worked the picket lines together.

"Are you an only child?" Vince seems to suddenly snap out of a trance and surprises himself with his reflex utterance

The guitarist says nothing and looks Vince up and down. Patrick steps in quickly.

"The Neanderthals is the main act, that was the understanding when everyone was booked. So let's finish setting up and get those fucking sound checks over and done with so everybody gets a chance to relax for a while."

Sid takes a good slurp from the can he holds in his hand, his Adam's-apple raises and falls several times before he empties it. Standing up he belches loudly, crushes it in his hand and throws it across the room into a dust bin.

"Suits me." he says simply, dropping a silent fart as he turns round and walks away. The guitarist still keeps his tight lipped vigilance on Vince.

"What?" says Vince. Silence. " What?" he repeats, raising both palms and shoulders.

"KI-HOP!"

Something moves very quickly and the next thing anybody knows the guitarist is laying on the ground groaning. Nick still holds his hand and with a small twist a knife flies out of his grasp and slides across the floor. The guitarist screams and the girlfriend starts to yell blue murder. Nick has got a little carried away and broken his wrist. A lot of people seem not to be themselves today. Then a sticky entity which has been crawling slowly and silently towards them strikes and all priorities change

"Fuck me!" exclaims Patrick when everyone has escaped outside. "Did a rat crawl up that man's arse and die or what? "

~

Leonard returns to the Rhinoceros early this evening, giving Leo a good excuse to take a break from his commitment with The Neanderthals and Fat Sid's flatulence. He has hardly managed to drag his grandfather away from flirting with Nancy, which is pissing Tom off no end, when Edith makes an entrance. Leonard, noting Nancy has returned to the sanctuary of her saloon bar, stuffs a couple of quid into Leo's hand.

"Quick Sparky."

Leo knows exactly what is expected of him. Racing Edith to the bar he slips Tom the money and whispers in his ear. Tom, knowing Edith's poison, rings up and gives Leo the change. Leo strolls back over to Leonard, giant grin all over his face. He has just sat down when Fat Sid comes through the door. He holds his hand like a shot gun and points at him.

"I've gotta go 'elp with the band now Grandad, I'll be out the back room if yer need me."

"You run along and enjoy yourself Sparky, don't you worry about me."

"Leo Grandad."

"Leonard Leo."

Edith orders a drink and rummages through her handbag in search of her purse. Tom speaks into her ear and points to Leonard who waves. Edith turns and snaps her bag shut. She recognizes him from their brief encounter at lunch time, such good manners; she likes good manners in a man. She has not been pursued romantically for ... well, for some time. She stands with her back towards Leonard while she engages Tom briefly in conversation before he has to resume serving other customers. There is really nobody there for her to talk to. Her boys, as she likes to think of Gorky, Kev and Alec, are not there tonight and Nancy is busy in the saloon bar. The only other option is the stick ladies. She is beginning to feel more self-conscience by the second, which she finds ridicules at her age, so she decides to act quickly before she can give it any more thought, and turns and crosses the room to the table were Leonard is seated. Leonard stands to greet her.

"Leonard Humbolt at your service Madame."

"Edith Reese. I trust I'm not intruding?"

"Impossible dear lady, impossible."

~

Gorky and Kev are laughing at poor Alec as they hold the door of the Gents open a crack.

"This punishes him for being late, I knew he'd be late," says Gorky.

"Oh Gorky, don't know about shitting myself! More like pissing myself. Just look at him!"

"He doesn't know what to do with himself does he? Where to look, what to do with his hands."

"No and ....!"

They both roar with laughter. Gorky shuts the door quickly and, being unable to articulate, signals to Kev to hush down.

"Did you see what I saw?" says Kev, relieving himself into a urinal.

"Yes," replies Gorky, "he greeted that skinhead with a Nazi/Peace sign salute."

Kev starts laughing again, Gorky, still chuckling, raises his finger to his lips and opens the door again.

"What's he doing now?" Kev asks.

71

"He's sitting on his hands and staring straight ahead of him."

"Come on, let's put him out of his misery and into the frying-pan."

Gorky's last remark set a chill in Kevin's spine.

Poor little Alec! All 5' 4 1/2" of him sits in his usual oversized thrift shop jacket. This is not to say that he only has one jacket but they all look more or less the same. His thin brown hair hangs around his pale face almost to his shoulders and always looks slightly oily. He certainly has not dressed for the occasion but Kev, much to Gorky's surprise and admiration, has gone the full hog. He has cut off the long straggly pieces that hang around the edges of his cropped ginger hair and dresses in drainpipe jeans, white T-shirt, red braces and a bomber jacket. He also has exchanged his green laces for white and given his Doc Martins a good polishing. They walk up in front of the table where Alec sits shaking and click their heels as they salute him.

"Hail!" they say in unison.

"Hail" Alec replies, as weakly as his salute. They sit down on either side of him.

"Building a little Dutch courage?" Gorky nods towards the Scotch and soda in front of Alec.

"Same again thanks Gorky." Alec answers flatly and quietly, mistaking the question for an offer. Kev hides his amusement behind a cough. Gorky is well known for being tight with cash and pulling stunts such as leaving as it is coming up to his round, like this lunchtime.

"I'll have the usual" says Kev. Gorky goes up to the bar.

"Any idea what this is all about Kev?"

"So far not a whisper."

"Someone just asked me if I was here for the speech."

"What did you say?"

"Yes."

"You should have asked what speech."

"I didn't want them to suspect anything."

"But there's nothing for them to suspect yet."

"I know but I felt kind of strange, paranoid, I even thought I heard people laughing at me."

"Paranoia, my friend, sharpens the senses. A little can be healthy, too much shatters the spirit." Gorky catches his last

72

remark as he brings the drinks over and places them down on the table.

"You must breathe deeply as our Buddhist friends; calm yourself for the task at hand." Lowering his voice he adds. "Did you remember the potatoes?"

"Yes" Alec replies.

"Good, I knew I could rely on you Alec."

"Now Gorky, would you care to enlighten us to what exactly the task in hand is?" asks Kev.

"The mission? Yes we have reached that time I believe. Gather closely and listen. Tonight is no ordinary Saturday night for the ladies and gentlemen of The Windsor Palace. Tonight at 9.00 o'clock their most popular living mentor, Lord Mosley is coming here to address them in person. Are you familiar with the achievements of this particular member of your fine British aristocracy?"

"Yes," says Alec.

"Is that the geezer who uses his manor house to train these wankers for combat?"

"Amongst other things Kevin, yes. Alec, would you care to brief us further?"

"Absolutely Gorky. Fascist connections amongst the royal family, gentry, and extended peerage aren't exactly rare. However, what differentiates Lord Oswald Mosley is, whereas these revelations for the most are embarrassing secrets they wish desperately to hide, he is actively and proudly involved in the promotion of racial hatred in every aspect. As Kevin rightly stated, the grounds of his stately home in Stevenage have been converted into a combat training ground for such groups as The British Movement and The National Front, but his involvement runs deeper and is even more sinister than that. He is known to meet regularly with underground Neo-Nazi groups overseas, specifically in Austria and Germany, and there is evidence connecting him with the illegal import of arms into this country from these outlawed groups."

"God! So what's the plan Gorky?" asks Kev.

"First assassination," he nods at Alec, "and then, just for you Kevin, some anarchy to put the cherry on the icing on the cake."

"You want me to kill ..."

"Shush!" says Kevin.

73

"Quiet." Gorky hushes him simultaneously.

"You want me to kill him!" Alec says in an urgent whisper, "Just like that! In broad daylight, well publight. I'll get myself slaughtered! They'll beat me to a pulp. Sorry I'm not getting myself booted to death for that bastard," he knocks back his Scotch, "you're fucking crazy Gorky, I'm out of here."

"Oh calm yourself Alec, this is no suicide mission. Would I send you on a mission with no hope of return? Believe me I don't want to see you get killed for the fascist bastard either. Strategy, remember Alec? I'm the great believer of strategy, which was my part of the deal. Get another drink down you, then we leave. We've explored the enemy territory, now it's time for terrain."

~

Tonight Kate wears a strapless, black lace bra, matching knickers and suspender belt with fine, black seamed stockings and high black suede shoes. She adorns herself in a stunning black lace evening dress of her own creation. Its neckline runs at an angle under one arm and over the other and a four inches of scalloped lace hangs down from it. The hemline runs at an angle parallel to the neckline and stitched to this is quantities of the same lace of about fourteen inches in length. Blooming beneath her knees, the side that is higher is gathered up further by two satin ribbons stitched to the inside and the outside, tied and held in place by a diamante broach which complements a fine strap that holds the bodice over her bare shoulder allowing the back to drop dramatically. Its one sleeve is not lined and ends in the scalloped lace and, like the main body of the dress, fits tightly.

The flesh of her alabaster face is highlighted and shaded supplely, but together with her vivid red lips and nails the effect is striking and fully emphasizes her magnificent bone structure. Her necklace and earrings are Austrian crystal and on her right hand she wears a simple solitaire diamond ring, a Nepalese snake thumb ring, and on her left hand a large garnet and a bracelet of marcasite.

She carries a black satin evening bag this evening. The bag holds a small silver cigarette case, which in its turn holds a dozen small pure grass joints. Tucked away also is a silver cigarette lighter, perfume, a mirror, necessary makeup for touch up, a comb,

74

toothbrush, an enameled Austrian locket, money, a credit card, false I.D. and a knife that she knows how to use. She makes it her business to always buy top quality drugs and likes to have at least two contacts in each specialty. The grass, a rare treat for the white man in the 80's, she has on regular order from a friend of a friend down the Latimer Road in Brixton. However, the contents of the locket are by far the most intriguing; some tiny cylindrical, cobalt blue micro-dots of mescaline.

There is a quiet knock on her door. When she opens it Barocco stands gawping before pulling himself together.
"Kate Lanseer?"
"Who wants to know?"
"My name's Barocco Isaac, I'm a friend of Jake's. He asked me to give you a message and bring you this bottle of fine Chianti."
Barocco has chosen Chianti because he had taken note of the Pizzeria date the previous evening and thought it would be more convincing. He is pulling the stunt in the first place to get his foot in the door.
"Oh." she says, smelling the whiff of a rat but more intent on the half joint she has in the ash tray. "You better come in for a moment, I was about to leave in a couple of minutes anyway, you can talk to me while I finish getting ready."
And so Barocco finds himself in the holy of holies of erotica, Kate's boudoir, slurping very good red wine and intoxicated by the exotic room almost as much as the hostess.
The room is a room within a room. The door now opens into the corridor but before one faces a finely made sliding screen covered with a textural ivory handmade rice paper. On the wall opposite there are two other sliding screens, both opening up either side of the chimney. Behind these, on steel bars strongly attached across the recesses of the outer room, hangs her theatrical wardrobe. These sliding screens are also doorways to the window and the mantel piece where she keeps her hats. Further screens encase and form the walls of the inner room. In the inner room, and before the mantel piece of the outer, she has placed the smaller of a pair of matching chests, the other larger chest sits at the end of her bed, a luxury, king size mattress, raised on a wooden platform with two draws either side, all treated to the same satin peat brown finish as the floorboards. The bed's cover

is thin and heavy, made from silk and interfaced with lamb's wool. It is edged with a frame of turquoise green within which is an elaborate oriental floral design in black on a gold background, and it is lined in a deep ruby red. In front of the chest, by the bed, is a Persian rug patterned in black and red on a golden background. A large terra-cotta Grecian urn sits in one corner out of which grows silver-white pampas grass and many vines hang from the ceiling. On the floor between the rooms lies clear Christmas tree lights which she has fixed to a dimmer switch and under the central light hangs an upside down Chinese paper umbrella, its handle shortened to give the desired effect, this is also set on a dimmer.

Sitting at her dressing table she lets down her hair and combs it out with her fingers. It hangs in a shining mass of burgundy curls which fall well below her shoulders. She lights the remaining half a joint in the ashtray, smokes for a while then hands it to Barocco and finishes her glass of wine. It is definitely time to go out into the night, out into the big bad city.

"So did he say how long he was going to be?" She speaks to him in the mirror.

"He said he'll do his best, we're due on at nine-thirty, so I hope he gets here before that." Barocco speaks from a low, well-sprung chair of amazing comfort, upholstered in crimson and gold brocade.

Kate ponders. He had not said anything last night about visiting his grandmother, in fact he had given her the impression he was going to be around today helping to set up the gig. Well something could have come up, or maybe he had simply forgotten. She decides to give him the benefit of the doubt, for now.

"Goodness, I hope it wasn't from The Pizzeria last night."

"How do you feel?"

"Fine. Anyway isn't it supposed to take thirty-six to forty-eight hours for food poisoning to come on?"

"Yes. I don't think you have anything to worry about."

"I hope not, it's not exactly a recipe for a romantic evening!"

Here is this beautiful woman, talking diarrhea and to his ears each syllable is so sexy, anything and everything she says sounds sexy; Barocco is a dog. Sod Jake, he should have been on time. His arrogance projects all the way down the evening to a

76

successful, XXX climax. He does not have a chance in hell, even before he throws up.

"Here" she says, putting down an empty bucket beside him. It is all that he can do to take the flannel from her and wipe it round his forehead and temples and the back of his neck.

Barocco has collapsed into a chair at the kitchen table after throwing up violently and noisily in Kate's bathroom. After ten or fifteen minutes of uncontrolled heaving, Kate had walked in with a heavy bucket.

"Lean over the bath," she had commanded. He had been too weak to argue. Crawling on his knees, he did the best he could to obey.

The sensation of a whole ice cold bucket of water suddenly poured over the back of his neck was astonishing. He had sat bolt upright on his heels, eyes popping out of his head sober and nauseous no more. He is exhausted though. Kate opens the window to give him a blast of oxygen completing her rough and ready cure. Now he is just wet and cold, he begins to shiver and as if by magic a towel hits him in the back of the head.

"Would you like to borrow one of these?"

She holds up two shirts. One flowing and made in a kind of satin which changes colour between purple and magenta as it moves, and the other cotton with a paisley design on a black background cut in the style of the early seventies. He prefers the paisley but after his recent bout of vomiting decides to go for comfort.

"Thank-you, you're very kind and I'm very embarrassed."

"Hey, it happens to us all." Kate thinks of many a drunken night. "Just as well you were here in relative comfort, do you think it's some bug you've caught from Jake?" she asks knowing full well it is not.

"I hadn't thought of that!" replies Barocco, grateful for an out. What the hell had been in that joint? He was ridiculously stoned. She pours him a glass of mineral water.

"Here, sip this slowly, are you feeling any better?"

"Yes thank-you." The water is like nectar. "I think a couple more minutes should do it, I can't thank you enough for being so understanding."

"Shout when you're ready, there's clean tooth brushes in the bathroom cabinet over the sink." And with that she disappears back into her bedroom.

Whilst Barocco changes and freshens up Kate stands and stares at herself in a long ebony framed carved mirror. She puts on an antique cloak styled coat of black velvet lined with a coarse mint silk with a gold floral design over which flew silver herons, and fastens it with a silver Phoenix set with an egg-shaped opal.

~

Several pubs, a couple of hours, and many drinks later Jake and Angela can barely walk. They hang onto each other staggering as the pavement swells, ebbs and undulates under them. It is as if they are on deck in a turbulent ocean. People are crossing the road to avoid them, mothers drag their children aside. In many other neighbourhoods they would have been arrested for drunk and disorderly conduct by now, but this is not any neighbourhood; this is East Street off the Walworth Road after dark on a Saturday night, and drunks are a common enough sight. Even so they make an odd couple. Poor Angela, such a sad stereotype, mascara smudged in circles under her blood shot eyes, and Jake all in leathers, looking like he has stepped out of the pages of Rolling Stone magazine, handsome in spite of his disgusting state. Stopping short he gestures to Angela to stay put. She does not get it and stands swaying on her high heels.

"Jake!" she calls out into the infinite abyss of intoxication that surrounds her.

There are many should-be wake-up calls on the slippery, twisted descent of alcoholism. Having to have a drink to go out for a drink is one of them, and Angela had started out drunk that afternoon like so many others. Sometimes one can still see that she had been a beautiful woman. Her once penetrating blue eyes were now almost permanently blood shot. A bone structure as delicate and fine as the most exquisite porcelain is only just beginning to lose itself to bloating, however the satin velvet peach skin that once donned it has been ruined. Caked with badly applied cheap makeup relentlessly for decades, her complexion has become gray and patched with both oily and encrusted dry skin cells. Her hair that had been a heavy wavy mane of dark champagne is now short, stiff and brittle from peroxide. Sitting at her white and gold trim dressing table, sagging under the ruffles of her pink, flowery, nylon negligee, she sips at the remains of last night's bourbon or this morning's Bloody Mary, swallowing aspirin as she tries to focus on the job at hand. Years of men, booze and abuse have rotted away her looks, her body, and finally taken hold of her soul. Her sanity has been questionable for a long time.

Jake has staggered off a short distance to lean against a wall and throw up over some dust bins. He returns to his companion just in time for her to fall into his arms as her legs give way, nearly toppling him flat on his back. Clutching each other as if for dear life, they continue their voyage in the pursuit of folly.

The next pub they reach has its windows boarded up and painted black. Men cheer over the sound of distorted raunchy disco music. A brassiere greets Jake slap-bang in the face like a blindfold. He screams frantically trying to pull it away and when he finally holds it in his hands he stares at it mystified for a few seconds before registering. Letting out one of his manic laughs he removes his jacket and drops it on the floor. Swaying where he stands he attempts to put the bra on over his T-shirt. Angela cackles like an old crow and tries to help. Even between the two of them they are unable to negotiate the hooks and Jake, losing patience, somehow manages to retrieve his jacket without falling over and puts it back on.

From the other side of the catwalk Robert is watching, looking, seeing, spying, eyeing. Jake with that old slag, well, well, well. He has to get to the bottom of this one. He makes his way slowly around the catwalk intent on his prey. His victims stagger off towards the bar, which is four men deep with punters trying to get in their orders before the next act, 'Suzy Sizzle'. Jake, because of his height, loud obnoxious mouth and the wall of men to lean on, gets served remarkably fast all things considered. By the time Robert has made his way over to them they are already slurping and swaying.

" 'Ello Jake, 'ow yer doin'."

Jake squints in an effort to focus, hanging on to Angela for support, his arm around her shoulder. He can hardly hold his head up as he fights to articulate.

"Wobwert, howie Wobwert."

Angela cackles, one leg gives way and she catches hold of Jake's lapel to pull herself up, he wraps his other arm around her and starts to sing.

"Werr uff ta see the wizart, der wonderfa wizat off was!"

Behind the bar the bartender is whispering in the landlord's ear and nodding in their direction.

The Stones blast 'Miss You' from the crackling overhead speakers and Suzy Sizzle makes her entrance to loud cheers and wolf whistles. Jake gives a noisy reception to the music, lets go of Angela, empties his glass of tequila and starts dancing, all legs and elbows, jostling and knocking into those around him. Beer gets spilt, teeth are knocked against glasses, heads are turning, anger is stirring. He is about one second from getting a punch in the mouth when he leaps onto the catwalk. Now the whole pub is booing and cursing him as he performs a cross between a Michael Jackson video and a belly dance.

The landlord signals across the room to two well groomed bearded men, both built like shit-house doors. They are dressed in expensive leather jackets and well cut trousers, and despite the gloom they wear very dark sunglasses. The men barge their way through the audience, clamber up on to the catwalk and taking hold of Jake with their enormous fat hands they throw him to the ground. He falls flat on his face on the rotting floor boards, ingrained with years of spilt beer, the dirt of city shoes, and cigarette stubs. Half stepping, half jumping, they bring their substantial bulks down either side of him and administer a couple of good kicks and punches each before taking Jake by the arms and running him out of the pub, throwing him into the gutter. A last blast of music and cheering meet his ears as the heavy swing door opens and closes behind the bouncers.

He rolls around hopelessly for a few seconds, then gives up and stares up at the spinning stars for a while. When he finally gets some idea as to what is up and what is down, he manages to get up on one knee, where he rests. Eventually, and with great difficulty, he gets onto his feet and starts staggering in the general direction of home.

Angela is confused. It is hot, her eyes are streaming from the cigarette smoke and the mascara that has run into them. She does not understand the commotion going on around her. She starts to cry.

"Jake? Where are yer Jake?"

Some of the men start to laugh at her. Robert catches hold of her as she sways, giving her a good feel up as he does. This is going to be more fun than he had thought. She clings onto him.

"I don't feel well Jake. I wanna go 'ome. Please take me 'ome Jake."

Robert puts down his glass, standing up just in time to catch her again. Better get the bitch home before she is good for nothing. Finally he gets her outside onto the corner of the street and starts looking this way and that for a cab. She has wrapped her arms around his neck and is barely conscious.

"I luv yer Jake," she says.

Robert hopes she doesn't puke over him, that would really piss him off.

~

The Neanderthals are on in half an hour, and still no sign of Jake or Andy, and now Barocco had done a vanishing trick. Vince and Fat Sid sit around a table near the bar with Leo, Little Wing, Dolores and Baby Jason, silent and tense. Dolores as usual is not making life any easier.

"I thought you said he was so reliable? Where do you think he is? Maybe someone should check the Tube, see if there's been a bomb?"

" 'E gets the bus," she is getting on Sid's nerves, just for a change.

"On a Saturday night? With all this traffic? The Tube's quicker. I thought you said that he was clever?"

"This is ridiculous," says Vince, and takes an old worn leather bound address book that is held together with an elastic band from the inside pocket of his leather jacket and with a pocket full of change he crosses the room to the pay phone.

"What do you think he's doing? It's no good phoning him at home. If he was at home he would have called by now wouldn't he? Oh look Barocco's back with Kate, all dressed up like a dogs dinner, silly bitch."

"Wow!" says Leo. Vince nearly drops the receiver and the coin he is putting in the slot.

She walks across the room to the bar with Barocco who is trying desperately to impress. Nancy and Pookie come round from the other bar to wish Kate a good evening. Barocco is busy trying to attract Tom's attention, flashing a fifty pound note around in the air. Nancy and Kate engage in polite conversation for a couple of minutes before Edith approaches.

" 'Cuse me for interruptin' but can I 'ave a quick word with yer dearie?"

"Of course Edith." Edith gestures with a nod towards the Ladies.

"Thank-you Barocco I'll catch up with you later, it's nice to see you again Nancy" she says, giving Pookie the customary stay-on-the-right-side-of-Nancy pat and follows Edith, who tunnels her way like a little mole towards the toilets.

" 'Aven't yer got anythin' smaller? For Pete's sake Barocco 'ow many times do I 'ave to tell yer."

Barocco fishes out his wallet and Tom serves him his usual large Scotch.

"And whatever's Kate's favourite poison is."

"Double Cognac."

"O.K. one large cognac if you please, and whatever you're having Tom."

"Thank-you Barocco."

Leonard was gesticulating frantically across the crowded room. A sour faced Dolores kicks Leo who still, along with Sid, cannot help gawping open mouthed at Kate as she follows Edith.

"Grandad" she hisses and points. Leo grins and waves. Leonard for once gets a little impatient with him, with a gesture of haste he mouths.

"Come here." Leo picks up his beer and crosses the room to his table.

"First things first my lad, first things first, spare key. Myself and the lovely Edith will be forsaking you shortly for a little venture out into the West-End. A film, a short saunter under the stars up to Shaftesbury Avenue, and around Chinatown, with a little something to nibble on if we're peckish, and later, who knows!"

Leo has retrieved the key which he keeps safety-pinned inside the lining of his jacket and hands it to Leonard.

"Secondly, who is that magical sex Goddess who just graced us with her presence? The red head? Oh no, don't say that's Jake's lady. Where is he? Never be late for a lady, especially a lady like that. It's a crime and if it isn't it should be! It's a sin against humanity! It's like not sharing the heart of an artichoke with your lover, pouring vintage champagne down the drain, eating oysters alone, ordering fillet mignon well done. There are some things you just don't do!"

Meanwhile Edith is confiding in Kate.

" 'E's asked me out for a night on the town, the pictures and then a Chinese."

"Well, do you want to go?"

"Yes but yer know these damn men dear. Next thing yer know they want to jump all over yer."

"And you don't want that." Kate looks sympathetic.

"No, not exactly dear. It's just that it's been a long time since I've, yer know, 'ad a bit of that 'ere-'ere, and let's face it, could well be me last. And if I did decide, yer know, to 'ave a bit of nookie, well I read this piece in the 'News of the World' that said that calibus stuff you youngsters smoke can make yer feel randy, an athrodeeseeack or something they called it."

"It's cannabis Edith, and yes, it can indeed make you feel randy!"

"And safe-sex. Who knows, 'e could be some dirty old sod who's been shovin' it everywhere."

"Edith Reese. Are you asking me if I can supply you with drugs and condoms?" Kate tight lipped, fixes a look of intense seriousness on her face.

"Yes!" Edith throws back her head and stands posed with her hand on her hip defiantly.

"Then look no further!"

Vince walks back to the table looking like a man of purpose. Screams of laughter are coming from the Ladies lavatories.

"Keys to the van Sid." Sid fishes them out of the back pocket of his jeans and hands them over with a nod.

"Twenty minutes God willing, twenty minutes."

~

83

She walks as quickly as she can manage on high heels, running a little and keeping well to the curb side as she passes the derelict block and then the wasteland.

In spite of enormous waiting lists Southwark Council has evicted the tenants some years before and sold the land off to private contractors, who in turn went bankrupt after demolishing the first block having not accounted for the extra teams of welders that had to be brought in to cut through the heavy steel girders that construct a lot of early Victorian architecture. As for the remaining block, all but one corner, about two-thirds of the way down a one-way street that divides the derelicts and the wasteland, has been left to rot. On this corner, which had been the side entrance to the workshops' yard, is The Windsor Castle public house. Otherwise vermin run rampant, sewage rats the size of cats, the stairwell's muggers' and rapists' paradise. Not even the most desolate of the homeless are interested in that which had once, only a few years earlier, been a thriving community .Graffitied high up between the shattered windows in very large, green letters, is a single word: S H A M E.

She can hear bad rock music coming from The Rhinoceros, where the lively sound of conversation and healthy laughter greets her from both bars. She makes her way to the public bar hoping to run into her grandmother. Scud hovers near the doorway and as she stops to stroke him the door opens and Leo, not paying attention as usual, walks straight into her, his big clumping boot crushing her tiny Cinderella foot.

"I'm sorry," he says.

"It's O.K." she says and bursts into tears.

Leo at the best of times is near hopeless with women, but tears, what to do about tears? He has no idea. Looking down he notices the geranium in the beer barrel matches her shoes, but when he goes to pick it he pulls up the whole plant by the roots. He hastily snaps off the flower and looking nervously over both shoulders, as if he was expecting Nancy to leap out of the shadows, he shoves the roots back into the barrel, brushing earth over them, half burying the plant in his efforts.

"Don't cry," he says, "yer too pretty to cry." And he stands absentmindedly holding the flower that he then remembers to give

84

to her. She manages a half smile and reaching in her pocket she finds a tissue and starts to dab her eyes.

"Thank you," she says and takes her first proper look at Leo.

Handsome Leo, with his short spiked blonde hair and dark roots, stands like a dense solid rock, his hands in the pockets of his coat. He is not tall but not short either and a little overweight but pleasantly so, plump, cuddly. Somehow a little of his grandfather manages to force its way to the surface.

"Would yer like to go to a party?" She thinks for a moment.

"Yes." She feels herself cheering up considerably. "Yes, I'd like that."

Just a mo then." Leo opens the door. "Leonard!" A pause, "Hey, Leonard, I'll see yer later."

Meanwhile, through the open door Pookie looks at Scud, Scud looks at Pookie. He opens his mouth allowing his tongue to drop out to one side and pants happily, wagging his enormous foxy tail. Pookie looks over her shoulder. Nancy is busy in the other bar. At the last moment she nips through. The door closes, narrowly missing her lollypop tail.

~

"Now tell me about Windsor Place?"

"It's on a one-way street."

"Good Alec! And why is that of the utmost importance to us?"

"Because when the car pulls up he'll be sitting on this side."

"And his chauffeur will be walking around to open the door for his Lordship, so you can be conscience-free about that one. Of course, there will be bodyguards and maybe a welcoming party but you will have to be the judge of that Alec. Collateral is an unfortunate by-product of assassination sometimes."

"I'm not going to let convenience and cowardice fly in the face of principles, it's not one rule for me and ten for everybody else, notice how all the rules change when it comes to saving the skin off one's back ? I'm only doing this if I get a clear shot at him. No collateral! Even in Crime and Punishment everyone lets that one slip by. No one seems to want to remember how one of his justifications for knocking off the old bitch was the way she treated her sister. And what was the first thing he did after killing her? He cleaves the sister's head in two with an axe!"

Gorky, Kev and Alec have joined the silhouettes of the chimney pots against a star rich sky. As Gorky speaks he has pulled open the drawstring of the black cloth bag he carries and taken out what seems to be various plumbing parts. Sitting with his back to a wall, over which Kev surveys the target below, he starts to assemble them. The result looks like a plastic cannon you use like a rocket launcher, which is exactly what it is. On top of the barrel the flint part of a table lighter has been adapted to spark inside the tube by a trigger that twists between finger and thumb. The barrel can be opened at the near-end where a disc the same circumference of the tube unscrews.

Against the stellar backdrop and a large crescent moon Gorky finishes assembling the weapon. He looks in all seriousness at Alec. Alec is pacing up and down smoking a cigarette, his hands are shaking. Gorky has an aerosol can and the potatoes sitting-next to him.

"It goes like this Alec. Unscrew, hair spray, screw up, potato, aim, twist."

"How much hair spray?"

"Not much, don't worry I'll help you. Unfortunately we have not been able to test it, so we don't know about curvature, so be prepared to take a second shot. My money is on it being 90% accurate."

"So what do we do now?"

"Now Alec? Now we wait."

~

Mean Mike, Rick and Dave have taken their Saturday night down to The Rhinoceros. The loud music from the back room vibrates the walls, and through the floor boards and tables the rhythmic thumping of the bass guitar can be felt. Every time the door swings open there comes a blast of the amplified music.

Mean Mike slams down the phone and walks back to where Rick and Dave are standing near the bar, plowing his way through the crowd who jump aside like the Red Sea parting for Moses.

Dave is showing off his prison I.D. number which he has tattooed somewhere on his left shoulder amongst the numerous bad tattoos that cover his entire body.

"There yer go, there it is, 'If lost please return to H.M.P. Brixton No.0684736'."

Mean Mike hovers, glass in hand, dark gypsy eyes darting back and forth, looking for trouble-but finding none.

"Mrs. not 'ome yet Mike?" asks Dave, shit stirring and loving every minute of it.

"Fuck no and if she ain't fuckin' 'ere with me and she ain't fuckin' at 'ome were she should fuckin' be and she ain't fuckin' somewhere inbetfuckintween, then she's got some fuckin' accountin' to do!"

Nose flaring like a wort-hog, eagle-eyed, his hair, which he has managed to grow just below his jaw line since his last incarceration, is of such dark brown it may as well be described as black. A scar from a scalpel runs down the left side of his face. He has a way of shifting from foot to foot or, if sitting, from buttock to buttock, as if his trousers are pinching him in the groin, perhaps they were. And it was trousers he wore, not jeans, and yes, tight around the arse, in black wool. He also wears a black cashmere polo-necked sweater, a black leather jacket, which is pin tucked down the back centre section to the waist. His black leather shoes are highly polished, and around his neck he wears a gold chain with a diamond studded M. The ring he wears on his pinky is vulgar and expensive. To finish the effect he wears a Gucci belt that his niece (who so far is having a much more successful criminal career than her uncle) has lifted for him in Oxford Street.

"Gotta fuckin' piss," he announces to no one in particular and plows his way as before towards the Gents.

If there is one thing better than finding trouble then it is making it. A plot starts forming in his scheming mind as he relieves himself with vengeance into the urinal. Opening a small window of heavily frosted glass just above eye level, he stands on tip-toe, being careful not to piss on his fucking shoes, and watches the proceedings and general comings and goings of the event in the back room. A mini-cab pulls up and he sees his wife's grandmother and some old cunt get into it.

Mean Mike gets back to his friends about ten minutes later. They would, have thought he had been cracking the porcelain if it was not for his gloves, and an increase in the swaying behaviour.

"Where the fuck 'ave yer been?" asks Rick.

Mean Mike motions with his chin to be quiet and move closer; it was the beginning of a conspiracy.

~

They were waiting to catch the No.12 bus from outside the Town Hall on the Walworth Road. Almost opposite is the Labor Party's headquarters which has been purchased for them by the Trade Unions Council. A banner hangs on the building displaying the party's new logo.

"I kinda like it. It's like one of 'em Mills and Booms romance books."

She's right there, thinks Leo grimly. The New Labor Party. What a load of bollocks. A fucking red rose.

It is a five minute bus ride to Camberwell Green but Leo has forgotten that it is far too early for the party so they wander around for a while. As Camberwell Green is not much of a place to wander and they soon get bored and wonder what to do next. They decide they are hungry and look around for somewhere to eat. They find a Turkish restaurant in a rather dilapidated building.

"What do yer think?" she asks. Leo-peering into the dark candle lit interior.

"Looks kinda serious."

By which he means that there seems to be a lot of low budget bohemian types having quiet low key conversations. The interior is low budget too, cracks in walls including missing bricks go unrepaired. The terra-rosa decor is charming all the same and with the candlelight, a few plants scattered around and a plastic rose on every table, it did give off a rather romantic atmosphere.

"And it's cheap, look 'ere. Special set meals for two 7.99, 9.99 and 12.99. And it says yer can bring yer own booze."

So off to the Off-License they go. Leo, facing a whole wall of wine to choose from, feels quite over-whelmed. She picks out a bottle of Blue Nun, he is having none of that, his sister and her snotty husband drunk that, it tastes like gnat's piss. He makes a decision. He is one of the lucky few to have a job and he got a bonus that week, so what the hell.

"Do you like champagne?"

~

88

"Why does it 'ave to be me that grabs the cash box?" Dave whines.

" 'Cause it's you that's from outta town, that's fuckin' why. They're gonna fuckin' recognize me and fuckin' Rick ain't they?"

"But they've seen us fuckin' 'ob-knobbing together."

"So fuckin' what! Yer just some fucker we got talkin' to. Fuck me, everyone knows what a friendly fuck I am! "

Mean Mike hovers from foot to foot, turns up the lapels on his jacket and pulls it down at the hem. Rick looks doubtful.

"Don't worry," says Mean Mike, misreading him, "I won't 'it yer 'ard. Just fuckin' think. There's about two 'undred, to two 'undred and fifty of those fuckin' freaks in there. Five quid each. That's one fuckin' thousand, two 'undred and fifty fuckin' quid minimum. Split three ways that's over four 'undred fuckin' quid each for a few fuckin' minutes work."

And work it is indeed for Mike, coming from a family who usually has at least three members in jail at any one given time. Their crimes range from bank robbery, embezzlement and grand larceny, right down the scale to the more petty crimes that only Mean Mike and Dave seem capable of pulling off and getting caught for at such an alarming rate. They have become quite an embarrassment to Mike's old man, who at present is doing, fifteen years in Dartmoor prison for armed robbery. So the plan is set. Mean Mike and Rick would proceed into the back room where an argument would break out which would develop into fisticuffs. While everybody's attention is consumed by the fight Dave would snatch up the cash box and do a runner. And that was all the planning and thinking that went into that.

~

It is unusual to see a policeman on foot these days not to mention darn risky. Constable Wright had fought for this beat along with nearly every other officer at Carter Street Police Station. Dope smoking hippies and a half-a-dozen or so serious crimes a year was a walk in the park compared with the surrounding neighbourhoods. On an adjacent estate gangs of kids, often numbering a score or more, roam searching for prey, and if not finding any happily fetch some gasoline and set fire to a wino instead. Under the railway bridges and across the Walworth Road live some of the most frightening looking mothers in the world. Dressed in leather and studs they stride the pavements and alleyways, their children tucked behind them. Before them they brandish a brace of Rottweiler or Dobermans, held back with strained chain leashes and a strong arm; nobody blames them.

There have been a couple of complaints about the noise coming from The Rhinoceros. He decides, he better take a look and radios in for back up; you never can be too careful. He remembers the Brixton riots had all started from a controlled burn and suddenly flared up and spread like wild fire. He has heard two versions of the ignition of the '85 incident. The official version is that the family home of a Michael Groce had been raided at 7am in connection with an illegal possession of a firearm. However the story on the street is that Groce had already been tried and convicted, and that the warrant out for his arrest was merely for nonpayment of fine and, to top it all, Mr. Groce had apparently been home in his own flat at the time of the raid. Either way Groce's mother had been shot through the spine and paralyzed. The constable had also been shipped out to the Broadwater Farm Estate riot in Tottenham. There a fellow officer had been macheted to death. A member of the Labor Party who had taken this inopportune moment to try to make a speech found himself caught between advancing lines and being jeered down by the mob.

"Bigger cages-longer chains, bigger cages-longer chains."

And then the petrol bombs had started flying and the officer next to him went up in flames. He had never been so shit scared in the whole of his life.

~

Nancy is checking the Ladies lavatories, yet another unglamourous moment in the life of a landlady she resents thoroughly. Someone has definitely been smoking drugs in there, what would people think! Heavens forbid she should lose any of her regulars like Edith, or someone like that nice young lady Kate Lanseer. Opening the small window in the heavily frosted glass above the wash basins she takes a look out at the comings and goings of the backroom. Suddenly her eyes are diverted by some scuffling on the pavement.

"POOKIE!" she screams hysterically.

Constable Wright has just walked around the side of The Rhino when he hears the sound of shouting and commotion over the noise of the music coming from the back room. Dave, who is looking over his shoulder while running with the cash box tucked under his arm, would have collided with the policeman if it was not for Scud and Pookie. Scud, in his efforts to free himself from the genitalia tug of war has defecated the sidewalk and Dave finds himself skidding in excrement as the copulating dogs move across his path. He falls arse over tit, landing at the constable's feet. The cash box opens and three pounds sixty-seven in change, made up mostly of copper, rolls out into the gutter. The constable stands looking down at Dave as two police cars come screeching to a halt behind him and the door of the saloon bar swings open. The full contents of a filthy cold bucket of water flies through the air, missing the dogs but hitting Constable Wright full force, and soaking Dave where he lays.
"Leave me Pookie alone, yer 'orrible creature!"

~

"This ain't 'alf luvly Leo." Leo, who has forgotten about speaking with his mouth full, grunts and points enthusiastically with his fork at the lamb kebabs.
"Oh, I don't mean just the food, everythin', 'specially the champers. Thanks ever so much Leo, I can't remember the last time anybody ..., " she feels like she is going to cry, "well it's luvly Leo, just beautiful."

~

Alec lights another cigarette. He is usually a light smoker but tonight is different. Everything is different. The touch of the wind feels different; the texture of his clothes feels different. More more, more real, more extreme, more ethereal, more like a dream. They are enveloped from the sounds of the streets by the silence that surrounds them. Two trains pass in the night. He looks at his watch 9.25pm, Gorky had said he'd be late. He cannot remember the sky ever looking as beautiful as it did tonight since he was a little boy, when in his innocence all was new and wondrous. He wonders what Kev is thinking. He wonders if others in his position have felt this way. He thinks of his wife Monica, whom he has seen so little of this year, with bitterness, as someone he had once loved and then changed into a stranger, a sanctimonious selfish bitch as far as he could see. And then he thinks of what he is most desperately trying not to think of. That near at hand, a man, another human being, is looking at the same sky, another human being who will never see the sunlight again because of him and the premeditated act of slaughter he is about to perform. Gorky has indeed chosen a good target there is no denying that. If one was to assassinate Thatcher there are too many ready and apt to jump right into her shoes, like that Tory bastard that preaches the merits of compulsory sterilization for mentally ill and working class women. The Queen would just be replaced by Charles and he by his son, and there would still be the Dukes and Duchesses and all the other inbred relations with their Nazi skeletons in their Saville Row couture closets. This man is different, nobody had just turned up on his doorway with guns and ammo. He had financed a campaign of Fascism and made it his business to purchase and import arms for his own personalized army. It is he who masterminds the advertising, the training and the propaganda on that which his movement is built. Yes, it is very difficult to argue against the value of terminating this particular individual's life. This man is not just exercising his right to freedom of speech, he is organizing hatred and training it to kill.

"Gorky." Alec hears Kev's voice speak with a softness and clarity often used by lovers.

Gorky silently jumps up; Alec notices for the first time how nimble he is. He looks over the wall with Kev for a brief second before both men turn to look at Alec. Their warm breath clouds around them, he cannot see their features. Gorky nods.

"Time."

Suddenly everything seems to speed up. For some reason Alec thinks of Fen's old mono record player playing Starry Starry Night at 78 rpm. Before he knows it he is between his two friends. Gorky is placing the potato cannon on his shoulder and Kev stands as motionless as a statue, potato in his hand, the moonlight shining off his National Health glasses, obviating the windows of his mind and giving him an androgynous appearance.

An old white Rolls-Royce, he had known it would be a Rolls-Royce, is coasting slowly down the far side of the wasteland like a phantom. Two large skinheads appear from The Windsor Palace. One seems to be talking into a cell phone, the other stamps his feet and rubs his hands, looking up and down the road. A police car hovers at one end of the road and from their view point they can see a second parked around the corner. Alec unscrews and removes the disc from the barrel and Gorky sprays a small blast of hair lacquer. He screws the chamber back up again and Kev loads the potato. Alec brakes out in a horrid combination of a hot and cold sweat around the back of his head and forehead, the beat of his heart grows louder and stronger in his ears; he is shaking. The car stops in front of pub.

"Now!" says Gorky.

Alec freezes, the two skinheads step out in front of the car and salute. The chauffeur gets out and starts walking around the car.

"Now Alec, now!"

Taking a gulp of lead ridden London air he shut off his mind, shuts his eyes, and reaching up on top of the weapon takes the trigger firmly and surely and twists it.

If Alec felt everything turning at 78 rpm before, now it spins like a top. There is an enormous shattering of glass as one of the pub's two large windows is struck. They can hear the angry shouts and the screams of the maimed from inside. Within seconds skinheads start to pour out of the two doors, blocking Lord Mosley's means of escape and retreat, you would have thought he had poured boiling water on an ants nest. Alec switches to automatic pilot. He watches his hands swiftly unscrew the barrel once more for a repeat procedure. He keeps his eyes wide and focuses this time, breathing deeply, as his old self, the self he is so suddenly and rapidly destroying, reaches out to grasp him. But before those hypothetical fingers can touch him he has already twisted the trigger for the second time, and this time he is a dead shot.

Suddenly he is sober and everything seems to switch back to normal, except things are not normal. He stares transfixed; all hell has broken loose below. Is this how easy it is to become a killer?

Alec hardly notices himself take the weapon and hand it to Kev. Sirens sound, lights are flashing, the two police cars screech to a halt outside the pub. A small gang brakes off from the main mob and starts across the wasteland towards them. Gorky is pointing and talking about the vulnerability of the positioning of the petrol tanks on the cars. He sees Kev nod his head, Gorky sticks something into the potato before he loads it and Kev aims and fires and a split second later there is an explosion as the back half of one of the police cars goes up. Gorky says there is time for one more shot.

"Are you two fucking nuts? They're onto us, let's get the hell out of here." Alec starts glancing from side to side, judging a safe passage through the roof tops.

The fourth shot goes off taking out the other window of the pub. The skinheads have now almost reached the bottom of the building and are going for the stairwell next to theirs. Gorky walks to the back of the roof and rapidly, but with no signs of panic, unscrews the potato cannon and throws the pieces in an arbitrary manner from the roof top into the dilapidated overgrown empty workshop space below. Alec is starting to climb onto the next roof, more skinheads are heading towards them, police cars and riot squads tear down the road stopping directly below.

"Come back Alec! There's no escape that way. You'll get caught."

"Fuck off Gorky!"

Alec continues his scramble over the ledge. A brick comes loose from under his foot and he nearly falls, he clutches on the inside of the wall for dear life. Kev grabs his arms as Gorky leans over and catching hold of his belt they drag him back on board. By now the skinheads are climbing the neighboring flight of stairs.

"You're mad, you're both fucking crazy, you're fucking ....."

Gorky lands him a heavy slap on the face.

"Now you can do what you want, but if you want to get out of this alive you'll follow me!"

And with that Gorky runs into the stairwell with Kev hot on his heels. Alec stands motionless for a moment, the moment before the skinheads start kicking in the door at the top of the neighbouring stairwell. He follows his friends who slip into a flat on the first landing and a well oiled reinforced door shuts silently behind him and heavy bolts slide into place. Gorky ushers them into the front room where they are greeted by a stout old woman dressed in a black dress, slippers and a white apron, gray hair swept into a lose bun at the nape of her neck.

"Gentlemen, I'd like to present to you my mother. Eva Zaidorf."

~

Jake has finally zigzagged onto home territory. A fifteen minute walk in just under an hour. He finds himself staggering diagonally over the wasteland, away from The Windsor Palace and the ghostly derelicts and towards the occupied part of the estate. Things are going well. After this crossing he has only to round the comer and in two blocks he will be home and dry. Kate Lanseer, here I come! He can now focus with one eye shut and walk relatively straight. As long as he does not speak too much he thinks he can pull it off, which just goes to show what he has his head stuck up.

He is about halfway over the wasteland when he is caught in the head lights of a white Rolls-Royce gliding by like a sled. It passes the derelicts and stops and then there is the explosive noise of shattering glass bursting from its frame. He looks around, swaying on the spot; it would seem someone has thrown a brick through the window of the pub. Skinheads are surfacing from the two doors. Over the screams and crying, of the injured and maimed, there is another loud sound similar but different from the first. From what he can tell a missile of some kind has struck the car, entering through the passenger side window and passing right through and out of the driver's side. The pub's massive broken and unbroken windows shine enough light on the car for Jake to make out a red substance splattered on some of the windows.

He falls to his knees and throws his guts up. A group brakes off from the emerging swarm of skins and starts heading off across the lot in his direction, he can hear their angry guttural cries. He is still doubled up when two police cars come screeching to a halt. The sound of sirens near and far echo around his head. The skins are getting closer. They are out for blood and vengeance and if they cannot find vengeance, Jake has blood that would keep them happy for a while. What is he going to do? He starts to pray. He has not prayed for a long time and certainly not in this manner. There is a word for it-groveling.

"Please God-anything God. I'll stop drinking God. I'll get a nice girl friend and stop screwing around. Anything but this God, anything...."

POW! There is a real explosion this time. The back of one of the police cars bursts into flames. Jake sits up on his heels; it is a truly sobering moment. His vision seems to have cleared and it is almost as if he has forgotten that he is vomiting. The skinheads change their course slightly to the right, just enough to miss Jake, however now the majority of the skins are heading out over the wasteland. A couple more police cars arrive on the scene and there is another crash of glass as the second window of The Windsor implodes.

Fights are breaking out giving birth to bedlam. Jake thinks he will use his new found and probably temporary sobriety to get the hell out of here. Praise be to God! He has just reached the far corner and gets off the block when the riot squad starts to show up in their armoured vans, grills lowered on all of the windows. Jake runs swiftly as an arrow from a tightly drawn bow; he has no intention of being stuck between the devil and the deep blue sea.

~

The room is dominated by a large table set for four on white linen. It has all the appearances of a disturbed meal. The plates are half empty, the odd piece of duck fat pushed to the side. It seems that one of the diners does not care for the sweet and sour cabbage or carrots and has mashed up their potato pancakes in their gravy. Another plate is meatless. There is a silver platter and bread board on the sideboard with the remains of a simmered duck in horseradish, and a braided loaf of challah bread, knives lie at their sides. In the centre of the table almost empty canteens hold the remnants of the cabbage, buttered carrots with parsley, and the potato pancakes. There is also a small gravy boat of the horseradish gravy that the duck has cooked in that needs filling, salt and pepper, and a bottle of red wine which needs replacing. In fact there is one open and breathing on the sideboard. Serviettes lie abandoned on the table top, chairs and floor. Chairs are pushed back from the table and a long low gramophone, dressed in a round crocheted doily and a geranium, plays polkas. Gorky is busy giving swift orders.

"Take off your shoes, Kevin give me that jacket." He bends to sweep up Alec's shoes.

"Alec you look fine. Get your fingers greasy and handle the dishes, cutlery and glasses and everything. There's yours without the meat. Kev I noticed how you play with your vegetables."

He disappears with the shoes, boots and jacket and returns in slippers. He throws a baggy pullover to Kev. The sound of sirens are picking up outside, there are hurried footsteps up and down the stairs, curses and urgent voices.

"When the police knock, and they will, so prepare yourselves, you two go to the window and look out. Just remember my mother invited you, my friends, via me, in the pub last Wednesday night to dinner tonight. You had been here for about an hour, we were eating, we heard an explosion etc.etc. Got it?"

They both nod a quick consent.

"And what about your mother, Gorky? What have you told her? What if she gets scared and cracks?"

"My mother Kevin? Why this was her idea. Who do you think masterminded all this?" he gestures to the room around them and to the window and the scene beyond.

"Don't you worry about mother Kevin, mother survived the Warsaw Ghetto."

Alec has already taken up his position by the window. Outside more skinheads are setting out over the wasteland to meet advancing lines of police. Police cars are arriving every second, distant sirens get louder. What he is witnessing could indeed be described as a scene of anarchy. Arriving police take the burning car to be the work of the fascists. The majority of the skinheads, when seeing the police set against them, think they are backing their assailants. Only a minority of the two factions have any notion of what has really happened, and of these the police are trying to stop the skinheads from taking the law into their own hands; so all in all both parties hinder each other in their mutual aim. The riot police have managed to contain the main part of the pandemonium to the wasteland, while clearing the way for fire engines and ambulances. Pieces of flying glass have cut and maimed a few score of the skinheads, the worse of which lay bleeding on the ground. Also there are the headless remains of Lord Mosley to be removed from his car. Police vans pull up at each end of the block to conduct a search of the roof and rid them of rioters. They proceed to seal the stairwells, top and bottom, in order to carry out their own investigation.

There are three heavy raps on the door. Alec jumps and nearly shrieks.

"Get a hold on yourself Alec!" whispers Gorky. "Breath, breath."

Gorky's mother walks to the front door and starts wailing.

"Go away! I'll call the police!"

"This is the police Madame, Detective 'Ealy and Detective Shaw, if you'd like to look through yer letter box I can show yer me I.D."

"No, no it's a trick, a trick!" she continues to wail.

"Detective forgive my mother. Here," Gorky pulls open the letter box to which Detective Shaw dutifully holds up his I.D.

"See mother, it's all right. It's just the police." Gorky proceeds to unbolt the door and take off the chain. Opening the door he invites both of the policemen into the front room.

"I'm sorry to be disturbing yer," says the detective, gesturing at the abandoned meal.

"No need to apologize detective, we were already disturbed. What on earth is going on?" Gorky helps his weeping mother into a chair while he listens intently to Detective Shaw. Detective Healy walks slowly across the room and stands between Alec and Kev and takes a good look at the battlefield.

"What a bloody mess," he says.

"What the hell's happening?" says Kev.

"Well, we were 'oping yer might be able to 'elp us with that one," he stares pointedly at Kev who returns his look without a problem.

Alec takes his cigarettes out of his breast pocket and then starts looking through his pockets for his Zippo. The detective pulls out a flashy gold lighter, flicks open the lid with his thumb, touches a button on the side and a perfect flame appears. Giving Alec the same attention he has given Kev, he watches him light his cigarette.

"Thank you," says Alec, his voice and hand shake. The detective stares at him a moment longer before snapping the lighter closed.

"So you 'ave to take yer shoes off but yer can smoke. There's feminine logic for yer."

Alec stares at him blankly for a tense two seconds, it is like they are communicating through a satellite.

"Oh, yes, yes, typical, typical." The detective looks at him for another couple of seconds before turning his attention back to Kev.

"We are conducting an 'ouse to 'ouse search, 'oping to find eye witnesses to an attack on The Windsor Palace which, as yer may already know, entertains a radical right-wing clientele. There are some routine questions I need to ask yer, then we can be on our way and yer can get back to yer dinner. First when did yer become aware that something was amiss?"

"Well it's as you see Detective. We were in the middle of dinner, there was an enormous crash and seconds later another. We jumped up and went to the window and looked outside and a police car exploded and people rushing out of the pub and then the other window went."

"And that's the first yer 'eard of it? A crash?"

"Yes."

"And you sir?" he looks over his shoulder at Alec." Ditto?"

"Yes, yes of course, yes."

"Of course, very good sir. Now, do you two gentlemen reside 'ere?"

"No."

"No but just round the corner." Alec hoped his voice did not sound as weird as it seemed to. Detective Healy glances at him for an awkward second.

"Then all I'll be needin' are names and addresses and some proof of identity and Detective Shaw and I can be gettin' on our way. And if you lads remember anythin' later which yer forgot to tell us, don't 'esitate to call me or Detective Shaw at Carter Street."

So names and addresses are taken and all goes routine except Alec has no I.D. on him. Detective Healy quietly says something into Detective Shaw's ear and they look at Alec and nod, Detective Shaw addresses him.

"As we 'ave three witnesses to confirm yer identity we're not going to bring yer in Mr. Evans, 'owever yer must come to the station tomorra with the suitable papers for us to be able to dismiss yer from our lists of suspects. Purely routine but failure to do so may and probably will result in yer arrest, do yer understand sir?"

"Yes," answers Alec quite meekly, he is beginning to feel sick; he throws his empty cigarette packet across the room into the fireplace.

~

Sid sits and scratches his chin. Dolores's yapping goes in one ear and out the next.

"Can I have some money Dolores?" asks Little Wing.

"You'll never guess what. I forgot the pawn brokers closed half-an-hour early on a Saturday."

"They do?"

"Yes.'

"Shit, I've got less than a fiver."

"Her," Dolores hands her a ten pound note, "that should see you through the evening shouldn't it ?"

"Sure, thanks Dolores."

"Where the fu .....'ell is Vince! " Sid may be a big fat slob but he is a well brought up big fat slob and he tries to remember not to curse in front of woman and children. But what is this one anyway? A woman or a child? He has some weird feeling Vince has fallen for her. He knows there is no solid reasoning behind this assumption. Vince certainly has not given anything away, but he is almost certain he is right. He gets up on his feet and gives in to pacing when Patrick comes into the bar. He stands in the doorway, elbows bent, palms up, he shrugs his shoulders, and Sid returns the gesture rolling his eyes to heaven. Patrick fights his way over. He is starting to freak out.

"First you bring your own personal Bruce Lee who breaks Leer's lead-guitarist's wrist, then you try to gas us all, and now Andy and Jake have done a no show. What the hell's going on Sid, Sid where's Vince?" he catches the expression in Sid's eye.

"No no no. Tell me he's taking a leak, fuck it, tell me he's just in the Gents taking a leak!"

"He took the keys to the van and left. He said he would be twenty minutes, that was half an hour ago." Dolores puts in her piece, helping things along nicely as usual.

"Oh no, oh God! What am I going to do? The other band would be terrible even with their guitarist. I got them muddled up with a

100

band called Lure. For fucks sake help me! Think of something Sid!"

Sid sits down heavily, glum and depressed. He smooths his stubble and looks down at the ash tray.

"I could sing."

"What was that?" Sid's eyes raise and look over the table and ashtray, Patrick also looks at Little Wing, their hearts are in their throats.

"I could sing, just until Vince gets back, tide things over for a while." Sid smiles, Patrick looks worried.

"Don't worry Pat, she's gotta great voice."

"I do hope so, please God let it be true, I'll give up beer for a month if something comes off tonight." Patrick turns his back and leaves, boo's are heard, switched on and off by the opening and closing of the door.

"You are an angel!" Sid puts emphasis on each word. "Come on."

She is halfway through her fifth song and the audience, who has been talking over her since the first, is becoming rowdy. Near the stage a small group of around twenty are silent. She sees Vince before anybody else and signals to Sid that she is coming round to a suitable place to end. Vince and a taller man of about six foot come through the first set of swing doors, down the short wide corridor, enter through the frame of the open second doors and proceed down the side of the room to the stage. The other man has his long hennaed hair tied back with a black velvet ribbon. He wears a flowing purple velvet shirt, black patch leather jeans and carries two guitar cases. A wide spread buzz joins the assortment of human braying and cackling, it would seem Vince has returned with a local celebrity. The guitarist jumps on stage and without a word of greeting to Sid or Barocco, unplugs Little Wing about ten seconds before the end of Ghetto Woman. He introduces himself as:

"I've a real gig to get to after this, let's go."

Her miniature audience looks at each other, shake their heads and walk away. Someone says:

"I can't believe 'e did that! What a cunt!"

And finally; after all the moaning and a groaning, and a huffing and a puffing, heaving, grieving, dragging, loading, arguing and mental berating; one final short sound check, over the increasing number of sirens that seem to be passing by, they let out a final sigh and hand their performance over to destiny-just as an hysterical screaming comes from the back of the room. It is a deranged Jake:

"There's a riot going on, The Windsor's been bombed and a police car exploded!"

A large crusty[9] stands forward and places himself in the door frame. He raises his fist and bellows:

"ANARCHY!"

There is a loud barnyard cheer followed by a rapid exodus as most of their audience bottle-neck out of the two sets of doors, turning a sharp left round the corner of the pub. Jake, still donning a very twisted brassiere and much weakened by the adrenaline rush staggers once more. He makes it as far as the centre of the floor where he drops on his knees, then onto his face and passes out.

And the band plays on. It plays to a practically empty house. A dozen or so seriously stoned and tripped out individuals shiver in their coats. Cold hands with white knuckles gripping beer cans. Warm dragon-breath, rising from mouths and nostrils, are infiltrated by the dim yellow beams of spot-lights. It is one of the greatest bands ever, if only together for that one night, it is a gig that is worth its place in the history of British rock. The players are made of such stuff that has made the music companies multi-millions and now, as Punk Rock had predicted, they have been betrayed. Puny songs, sung by puny adolescents fill the airways. Bands without instruments put together in the corporation boardrooms. The CEO's nephew composing three minute formula pop songs, designer labels dress the anorexic youths, their pretty faces and their young dreams are sold and placed under contract.

Therefore it had come to pass that a great web was spun through the bazaar labyrinth of London; crisscrossing over the

---

[9]   *A white, dred-locked sect that favoured facial piercing, trench coats and shapeless clothes coloured with vegetable dyes. Their origins lie with the Stonehenge travelers and they usually lived out of eccentric vehicles or squats.*

entire metropolis and stretching out into the suburbs. It was woven by old cars and vans continuously on the verge of breakdown. Overloaded with amplifiers, speakers, cables, stands, instruments and all the other tools of a musician's trade, they endured; joining together rough pubs with bleak clubs.

And the band plays on. Vince and Sid, the rhythm section, are as solid as a rock. They have forgotten how many bands they have played in together over the last decade, and even more so in the latter half as Sid managed to evolve from Heavy Metal to good old fashioned rock and R'n'B. Tonight they are in top form. Barocco, despite his weak condition is as brilliant as always. A background in classical music gives him a discipline and palette more expansive than most of the best keyboardists around.

Little Wing takes Jake's place. Cramming the lyrics or making them up if she forgets, she takes her directions from Vince. She easily stands her ground as the band's first lady. She has applied makeup as pale as a Japanese geisha to her face and lips, on her cheekbones she has drawn bold crimson Vs with a soft fine lip pencil and carefully smudged the insides of these lines inwards. Her eyes are painted in bold metallic Egyptian style. She dresses in a great many scarves, put together to form which can best be described as a punk belly-dancer's dress and head dress. Her jewellery is a mass of bangles on her ankles and wrists, as well as rings and necklaces. Held above her hips is a fine gold chain on which an antique tear-drop amethyst hangs.

"Sod the age difference," Vince decides, "she's so lovely and fascinating, and talented, I'm going to go for it. If I don't some other bastard will; someone who doesn't give a fuck about her."

As of the great guest guitarist? Living proof that one can be talented, rich, and good looking, but still be a wanker.

And as they say, it's all timing, and Jake is known to have the luck of the devil. It is no sooner than Patrick and one of the bouncers have carried off Jake's limp, lifeless looking body backstage and thrown it on a pile of coats, that Kate and Nick make an entrance.

"He phoned just before we went on," Vince lies, "apparently he's on his way, he said not to wait for him but to go on to the party and he'd see you there. He also apologized profusely."

"God! Where's he coming from, Timbuktu?"

"Essex."

~

Little Wing gets up, leaves the room and treads tentatively around the rest of the house; She feels shaky and holds Jason close to her, lightly touching the wall with her free hand. She had not wanted to come here in the first place but Dolores had kind of bullied her in her brisk fashion. Before she had known it she had somehow agreed to do something without being aware of what it was, and was mean not to drop everything and do it right away.

"They don't need you to load the van," Dolores whines, "sod it."

"Well I better just ask them if it's O.K."

"Of course it's O.K. Oy! Pencil-Dick," she shoves a rather pathetic young man with a wooly hat and goatee, sending him staggering a whole foot or so nearer to the stage, where he continues to stand and stare like a moron.

"Tell Vince and Sid Little Wing's with me," and with that she caught Little Wing by the wrist and swiftly led her outside.

She has rushed her away from the aftermath of the gig, to go to the Elston Street squat and abandons her almost immediately. She hands her Jason and crosses the room, where she sits down and snuggles up to the man of the house, speaking sweet nothings and nibbling on his ear. After ten or so minutes of this, just as Little Wing is getting really, really pissed off, they get up and Dolores follows him out of the room. She holds up her hand as she leaves.

"Five minutes," she mouths.

Twenty minutes pass and she does not return. Little Wing sits on a foam mattress on the floor. Across the room four very drunk young men sit at a table shouting over the music on the stereo, smoking and drinking beer, and ignoring the rest of the room. Various mattresses and cushions and one easy chair are placed around the room, none too clean. Five people, that is one on the easy chair, four leaning against the walls on the floor like Little Wing, sit around and stare straight ahead, eyes half-mast. In a corner a couple roll around entwined with each other. The floor looks like it has not been swept, cleaned, or anything for at least

104

three months and on it lay five dogs, a pair of Dobermans and various smelly mutts.

The ground floor of the squat is uninhabitable, making the main living quarters the first floor. This consists of three large rooms and a rather unpleasant bathroom. In the next room through the open doorway she sees someone draw a large circle on the wall. He walks away and takes his place along with a dozen or so other people, rolls up the sleeve of his velvet green jacket and pulls out a syringe and shouts:

"Go!"

And each with their own syringe start drawing blood and using the circle as a target. As soon as the going gets fast and furious, the majority of them stop while continuing to cheer on the remaining couple, who are going at it with such earnest they fail to notice everyone laughing at them.

She crosses the landing to the other room. Its high ceiling is lost to gloom, out of which spider's webs hang like Spanish moss. The bay window is boarded up from the outside and pieces of broken glass hang loosely in the frames. The dusty bare boards are carpeted with numerous sleeping bags and blankets; some are already occupied with comatose sleepers. But no Dolores. The only place that is left is the two small rooms at the top of the next landing. She treads softly up to the top of the staircase. Looking through the right door she catches site of her sister's reflection in a large cracked mirror.

"Come on Danny, come on! You said you'd shoot me up."

Danny steps forward, his back obscures Little Wings view. He steps back; the rubber tubing is still around Dolores's arm. She sways ever so slightly and smiles ever so slightly too, with her pinhead eyes and leaden lids.

"Oh Danny, oh Danny!" Danny takes her by the shoulders and lies her down gently on his single bed, and then he takes off the rubber tubing and looks after his own needs.

Afterward he lies down beside her, and taking her in his arms, they drifted around together embraced in opium fairyland. He has a small fridge in his room filled with beer and water and there were clean buckets for puking. You have to give it to him, the guy has style. It seems like Dolores has found herself a really good catch.

~

Detective Healy takes in the view from the roof tops. The tow truck is taking Lord Mosley's car away. There are only six ordinary police cars and a fire engine left, and the latter is almost packed up and ready to go. He still has to make some kind of statement for the press and write his report. He turns his back on the site and rubs his eyes. Where the hell did that other lot come from, rounding the comer all of a sudden, like a stampede of infantry from Planet of the Apes? Shit. He lights up and walks to the back of the roof and looks at the crumbling red bricks on top of the wall. Some are missing, recently, judging by the amount red dust that still lay on the ground; red dust with a clear footprint in it, a footprint that seemed to carry on in the direction of the stairs getting fainter and fainter before it disappeared altogether before the old Polish lady's front door. Interesting. He radios down for the photographer. He goes back over to the cigarette stubs, all ground under heel, all except one, which looks like it has survived a hasty footstep. Opening his coat he fishes out a long pair of tweezers from of his breast pocket and gently eases It up and, holding it up to the moonlight, he examines it at close quarters and then with his lighter. A Winston, interesting, very interesting. He drops it in a plastic bag together with the empty cigarette packet that had bounced back out of the fire place and he had surreptitiously managed to pick up and put in his pocket.

~

Little Wing sits up at the kitchen table with Sid. Still wrapped in her coat she sits with both hands in her pockets and shivers. Steam rises from two mugs of creamy hot chocolate on the table. Sid brushes back his greasy brown hair as he leans over Jason holding a bottle. There is a rap on the door far too loud for the time of night. Sid mutters. He could guess who it was. He stands up and hands the baby to Little Wing who takes him into the bedroom. Sid opens the door and Jake takes his balding head in both hands and gives him a big kiss on the forehead.

"Get off yer poofta!"

Jake, Vince and Barocco follow Sid down the corridor into the kitchen. Sid sits back down at the table and takes a sip of his hot chocolate. Jake excuses himself.

" 'Ow did yer do that?" Sid asks Vince moving his eyes briefly towards the bathroom door.

"First we stuck him under a cold shower."

"Hmmm." Sid, nods his head slowly in approval.

"And then we made him shower" put in Barocco.

"Yes." says Sid, nods faster and pulls a face.

"And then we gave him amphetamines!" Sid sits still and thinks for a second.

"Yes I suppose that was all yer could do really. Any idea where 'e'd been?"

"No."

"Not a dickie bird" says Barocco shaking his head.

"And what about the 'Date'?"

"All taken care of. One well thought-out excuse,"

"Food poisoning."

"Exactly. And some well thought-out humility "adds Vince.

"Yer groveled for the bastard."

"Yes. And luckily she was with Nick Perry, a good friend of hers so it would seem, and he whisked her away before she got a chance to see him. We're catching them up at the party. Are you coming?"

"No, I think I'll stay 'ere with the little one."

"No Dolores ah?" Sid looks up at Vince.

"Little Wing brought 'im 'ome from Elston Street where it seems Dolores is spending a lot of time lately." They both know what that means." Seems she 'as got a thing going with Danny Day."

"He's the worse!"

"He's the man! The man with a lot of H in his hand." Barocco looks at them both.

"Of course." says Vince sadly.

In the bathroom Jake combs through his hair with his fingers and puts his leather cap back on. He studies his face for a moment in an old oblong mirror (which is engraved with a BR in the centre) and then produces a package from the fifth pocket of his jeans. Holding it up to the light he can clearly see through the plastic bag that he still has all four of the tiny, little squares of blotting paper. Each square is marked exquisitely with a gold spine black dragon; he has been saving these all week. He takes one out and places it on his tongue and scooping up a handful of London tap water he swallows the unholy wafer.

In the centre of the kitchen Little Wing stands rocking a sleeping Jason.

"He's so good," she says. Vince and Sid nod like proud parents, smiling affectionately. Jake enters the room and finds himself quite taken by her. Not surprisingly neither of them recognize each other from earlier.

"Little Wing Jake, Jake Little Wing" says Vince simply.

"Little Wing, hey that's some name you've got there Little Wing. Where did you get that from?"

"That's my secret," she replies with a smile on her face.

"I love secrets. Coming to the party?" Jake asks her.

"I don't know. I'm tired."

"Oh, come on," he starts massaging her shoulders. "You'll get a second wind."

"Oh well, maybe."

Vince and Sid look on solemnly. They are not going to put up with this, not with Little Wing. Jake is turning on his male charm big time, they have seen it all a thousand times before.

"Jake, can I have a word with you mate?" Jake follows Vince into the front room but not before pulling a face at Little Wing and making her giggle. When they reach the front room Vince turns abruptly on Jake.

"Lay off!"

"What?" Jake sounds hurt.

"You know what. Little Wing. Pick on someone your own size. I've scraped, lied and groveled to keep your date for you with Kate. You know you're meeting up with her later, now don't blow it!"

"You interested in her?"

"Who?"

"Little Wing?"

"Actually she does rather intrigue me."

"Want to give her a good fucking do you?"

Vince met Jake eye to eye, Jake's aggressive, arrogant smirk met a sad look.

"You know, sometimes Jake you can be a real arse-hole."

They return to the kitchen where Sid is nursing the baby again and Little Wing Is yawning after her long day.

"Come on." Jake picks up Little Wings jacket from the back of her chair and starts helping her into it.

"Will you be O.K. here with Jason, Sid?" she asks, as Jake hurries her out of the room.

"Don't yer worry about me princess, I'm just fine."

Vince, Barocco and Sid exchange looks that could cut ice.

~

Leo and his lady friend have been standing in the corner now for nearly half an hour observing the scene. She yawns. She does not look particularly interested in the drinking and drugging going on around her and Leo is bored also. It strikes him that although this may be fun enough with the lads, having a few bevies and a joint or two, it isn't much of a place to bring someone on your first date. Even though the rock band is in the next room it is still near impossible to hear each other without shouting and she had said over dinner that she likes disco and soul music. Besides where were the others? He has been somewhat anticipating their company to keep the evening entertaining.

~

Nick and Kate have not gone straight to the party, oh no; Kate insists on taking a couple of detours.

"Don't worry, I'll pay."

It is not the money Nick resents but the pursuits. He has fought his own battles with drugs some years before and certainly does not need any reminders of that life style. In spite of the passionate love he feels for Kate he is pissed off. At the first stop, after waiting outside listening to the driver moan for more than ten minutes, Kate has come out with a no-no. She jumps in the cab and gives the name of a road in Battersea. Battersea! Nick cannot hide his look of annoyance from her.

"Last port of call," she says, "I checked first."

After another ten minute wait and ten minutes of the driver's negativity, Kate finally emerges and tells the driver to stop the clock and pays him with a generous tip. Nick gets out and slams the door. He wonders what is going to happen when she has spent all her last month's salary on coke. The chickens were certainly going to come home to roost then.

~

"At a time when we need a strong socialist Labor Party more than any time since the thirties," Vince gestures with disgust at the red rose banner on the Labor party headquarters over the road, "and that's what they spent half their time debating at Blackpool. Logo's, image, advertising."

"And have you noticed how they never question Tory policy, they just argue how they could do it better," puts in Barocco.

"And selling off the nationalized companies. How can you sell something that belongs to the country? At risk of sounding simplistic, it's stealing, plain simple stealing. Those shares are going very cheap and to whom is the interesting question. Hello, what's Jake up too?"

Jake is holding Little Wing's hand and crossing over to the other side of the street.

"Hey Jake! Jake! What's up man?"

Jake points to the window display of the chemist.

"Shout if you see the bus coming," he yells.

Barocco rolls his eyes. God knows what he wants to show her, he has the weirdest sense of humor sometimes. Vince frowns observing them at the window. Jake, pointing, says something and they both giggle. A bus pulls up obscuring his view.

"They've started to find T.B. in some of the dead tramps they're bringing in, first cases for decades." Barocco's father is a famous surgeon, a lung specialist.

"Shit." Vince looks grim, the government's deliberate sabotage of the National Health Service infuriates him.

"Yoo-hoo!" There are two high pitched rings on the bell from the bus opposite and it pulls off. Jake is waving like a blithering idiot and calling out of one of the small sliding windows before disappearing to the upper deck with Little Wing. Barocco, looking after the bus, misses seeing Vince's jaw lock and his face go white with fury.

~

"This was ever such a nice idea of yours Leo. Oh look! Don't it look luvly! "

They are halfway over London Bridge on their way back to The Elephant when they pause to take a look at Tower Bridge against a spectacular stellar backdrop. Leo notices her remove a shoe as she leans on her elbows and rubs her instep against her shin before replacing it. He contemplates her high heels, he has forgotten all about them, her feet must be killing her.

After giving the party another ten minutes to no avail, he had struggled desperately, grabbing at straws for ways to keep her entertained. His first thought was a walk around the deserted financial district to take a look at some of the buildings he was working on. He reproached himself immediately. What a stupid suggestion, women were not interested in stuff like that. Much to his surprise she seemed delighted with the idea, so they had walked back up to Camberwell Green and jumped on a night bus going up north of the river to Algate.

They zig-zag through cobbled Huguenot streets of the East End to Spitalfield's market, where the early birds are already hanging fresh carcasses. The market is all under one roof and dimly lit, its corrugated sides are up leaving it open to the elements. A few pubs holding special licenses in order to cater for the butchers' nocturnal existence help spread light on the scene and the surrounding streets.

They carry on east for a small distance until they hit Brick Lane, once a Jewish area lying just north of Cable Street, where an English Lord and his fascist Black shirts had provoked the famous riot of 1936. It now houses Pakistani residences and both sides of the narrow street are lined with restaurants, many still open.

"We never did 'ave any dessert. What do yer say we 'ave some of that pistachio ice cream?"

"You mean that 'ard green stuff?"

"Yeh."

"Oh, I don't know, I never 'ad that before, looks kinda funny. What's it like?"

"It's delicious!"

"Yeh?" She does not look convinced.

"Yer know what, they do mango too. Why don't yer 'ave that and if yer like the pistachio we can swap."

Which is exactly what happens.

"Oh Leo it's delicious!"

"I told yer so! 'Ere," he pushes the green ice cream towards her and takes the mango.

"Oh Leo, that's not fair, yer wanted the pistachio."

"It's O.K. I like 'em both," he sticks his spoon into the orange mango ice cream and takes a big mouthful as if to prove his point.

Afterward they head off in the general direction of home through the empty business district of The City of London.

"Yer see they're not pullin' 'em down anymore. They gut 'em, or sometimes they do pull 'em down but leave the front up so it looks the same like, from the outside. Then they rebuild 'em and we come in and fit 'em out. See what I mean?"

He points to a prime example. She takes his arm and snuggles up. She finds him ever so interesting. He has shown her new buildings of glass, their lobbies pristine and lined with white marble, famous ancient buildings like the Guild Hall, Old Bailey and the inside-out Lloyds building. They circle back around through a labyrinth of tiny pretty winding streets to London Bridge.

"Can yer walk a little further?"

"Yes, of course Leo. Why?"

"Well those 'igh 'eels, they must be 'urtin'," he nods at her feet.

"A little, but that's not what I meant. I meant why do yer want to know if I can walk a little further?"

"I want to show yer somethin' in the lobby of that new buildin' over there." He points to an office block on the Southbank just east of the bridge.

"What? Another tree?" She loves the big trees she has seen growing inside some of the buildings Leo has shown her.

"A real Roman 'ouse!"

"Really! 'owever did they get it in there?"

"They dug it up. Now them 'istory people didn't want 'em to build and the people from the company wanted to pull it down, then somebody 'ad the bright idea of building the building around it, so everybody was 'appy."

"And that don't 'appen very often does it!" she chuckles. "Oh Leo look! They're opening the drawbridge, I ain't seen 'em do that since I was a little girl!"

112

And in her excitement she has taken his hand and just like a little girl, she balances up on her toes and points, Leo gently lets go of her hand and places his arm around her shoulders, drawing her close he kisses the top of her head. He feels her pull away. Oh no, now he has come on too heavy and blown it, after all he only met her a few hours ago.

"I'm sorry I ... " and reaching up she takes his bristly face between her hands, stands on tip-toe, and kisses him.

~

The party is in a large squat off Camberwell Green, formerly offices of the Department of Health and Social Security. The first challenge is to get into the building while the police are continuously circling. This is done by hiding in the shadows of a doorway then knocking just as they have driven passed. However one is not admitted immediately. Instead several representatives of the neighbourhood and the organizers barter a donation from you. These negotiations are taking on average two or three orbits, sometimes being obliged to move to a different door to create confusion for the police.

On gaining access, they go through a second pair of swing doors and find themselves in a room that takes up most of the ground floor. On the left are cubicles, an armoured glass screen cuts the counter tops in half. The near side stools are bolted to the ground and it is here a man sits conversing with his own reflection.

An acid-house party is in full swing and is illuminated by lights projected through hot-oil lamps producing a splendid psychedelic effect throughout the room. The multiracial dance floor is packed with teenagers who dress in baggy clothing and woolly hats or baseball caps, who in spite of their varied ethnic backgrounds, manage to look remarkably clone like. The main difference is the jewellery. The West-Indian adolescents favour gold, while their Caucasian counterparts go for beads strung on hemp, especially hematite.

"Upstairs." Nick shouts over the music into Kate's ear and he points to the door that leads to the looking glass side of the cubicles. A nondescript staircase leads up to the beginning of a long corridor, reminding Kate of the Hall in Wonderland with its many locked doors, only in this case the doors are all wide open.

From the two doorways at its far end comes the general humbug of animated voices and rock music. There are a lot of comings and goings between these two rooms and from what she can tell the lighter doorway on the right is the bar. She walks on, passing identical rooms on either side of her, each telling a different story.

The first room she comes to is on the right and lit with a black light bulb with a few rough, pseudo-pagan symbols inscribed on the walls in luminous paint on top of matt black; the chill-out room. On one wall posters have been glued and haphazardly scraped away and now a picture of Jim Morrison hangs there, the upper right hand corner curving downward. Several mattresses of sorts, a sofa and some arm chairs furnish the room. In one of the chairs a limp figure is sprawled, two of his friends stand over him, one administrating some small stinging slaps to his face.

"Come on Jim, come on man, stay awake, you can do. Wake up man, Jim, Jim! "

The other man has a bucket of cold water. He takes off his T-shirt which he soaks and then wrings out over the back of Jim's nodding head and he wipes it around his face and neck. The sickly heroin addict smiles and moans with pleasure. On the edge of a piece of foam a small young man lies on his side, out for the count. Half falling off the mattress, a trail of drool drips from the corner of his mouth onto the floor. Another man sits in a fetal position hugging a bucket like a buoy in a storm. Every couple of minutes he has been obliged to sit up and place the bucket between his legs, lean over it and vomit. At the back of the room two women talk gently, trying to calm down a fifteen year-old girl who thinks she has taken some bad ecstasy.

The next room she comes to is on her left and seems to be the territory of a white street gang. The men are yelling in some guttural caveman language and gesturing angrily with furious motions of the hands and index fingers. It is really quite alarming at first until one realizes this is their normal way of communicating. The men, who are in their twenties and early thirties, dress in donkey jackets which have been studded and chained to various degrees. They also wear black jeans and black leather shoes with stainless steel pointed toes. Each man jealously guards his own personal beer supply, cans of Carlsberg Special Brew for the most, which hang in threes from the fourth empty loop, which is threaded around their belts.

Their leader is easy to detect as he yells louder, gesticulates wilder and has the most studs and chains and beers. He is also the second largest member of the gang. His black hair is twisted and set in cones perpendicular to his skull and round his neck he wears a spiked leather collar. He holds a tiny golden Labrador pup with oversize paws snugly under his arm, warm and sleepy, already used to her strange new master.

Back on Kate's right the next doorway reeks of dope. The bass rhythm of some Reggie music can be heard under the din coming from some of the other rooms. A small group of Rastafarians sit on upturned milk crates and kitchen chairs in one comer, blood shot eyes under dark glasses, with a large spliff of pure ganja rolled to a filterless point. In the diagonally opposite corner two white, dread locked men with multiple piercing sit in their trench coats on a mattress with a female friend passing a joint and a large bottle of red wine. Another of their group lies on the bare boards. His hands are behind his head which he rests on his Rottweiler, breaking their stoned-stupid silences with idiotic remarks at which the other two men habitually laugh unenthusiastically and the woman looks bored to death. A few others sit propped against the walls, stoned redundant.

Next left is a room of working class men, mostly from Scotland or Northern England. They are enjoying a few beers and smoking fags or roll ups, while indulging in heated discussions about politics, trade unions and history. Some are split-up into smaller groups, allowing each other to express a little sentimentality, exchanging details about their families and memoirs of football and cars. This lot are not messing around, they are serious men with wives, children, even mortgages back home. They are looking for work in London and the prosperous South and finding it wanting. They are organized individuals, the foremost investment of their survival gear is a good quality, light weight thermally-insulated, waterproof jacket with a hood. They all have gloves, scarves, knit hats or balaclavas and thermos flasks. They carry small back packs with a change of clothes, wash stuff and sleeping bags.

Unmade bunk beds and single beds are pushed against the walls in the next room in which the adolescents and older children are having their own party. Some of them have babies and small children of their own, but other than a few tiny ones, who have sneaked in by their own devices, the age range is from about twelve to sixteen. The walls are adorned with pictures of popular singers and bands of their generation and those same performers boom from a boombox in the corner of the room. They dress like hippy versions of the teenagers downstairs, patched with brightly coloured and patterned fabrics and touched by punk rock-especially about the hair, make-up and jewellery. Some of them are children of the famous Stonehenge travelers, taking a break from the road, but there are a fair amount of runaways too. Some run from abuse, some have been encouraged by unemployed parents desperately trying to put food into the mouths of their younger siblings. A few seek adventure and some claim to seek adventure as they run from themselves, already under the grips of some addiction. A handful are already in trouble with the police.

An untidy middle-aged man with a long unkept beard and glasses comes out of the bar and walks down the corridor and into the room.

"David," he calls over one of the elder children, "David what did I say to you about showing respect to the younger kids and recognizing their need for more sleep and a regular pattern? I told you and I told you specifically out of respect to you as the eldest, that the younger kids had to be in bed by midnight."

"You have so many rules you're worse than bloody Thatcher!" And like a typical stroppy teenager David stomps off sweeping up a toddler in his arms as he does so.

"Come on everybody, we've got to put these kids to bed. Now Tracy, come on."

A line of grumpy adolescents cross over the corridor in front of her carrying various children into the next room to be tucked up for the night. The man continues:

"I also think it's time for anybody thirteen or under to go to bed." This remark is met with a lot of moaning and complaining. The man rolls his eyes at Kate.

"I'll be back later," he shouts and leaves, disappearing through the far right doorway at the end of the corridor. The others return and David shuts the door behind him.

Kate steps up and takes a peek into the children's room, where a blue light bulb casts a gentle light on the little sleepers.

The room has been painted ultramarine and scavenged wood furniture has been fixed up and painted a rainbow of bright glossy colours. Old blankets have been given a new lease on life, stitched on both sides with an array of colourful patches. Some sheets had been tie dyed and there is a fair collection of hand knitted and crocheted blankets. Numerous mobiles hang from the high ceiling, moving slowly as if half asleep themselves, some decorated with tinsel stars and glitter. A number of small beds, camp beds and cots fill the room. A couple of babies are wrapped up and cozy in some drawers and a new born sleeps blissfully in a cardboard box. In the middle of the room two women sit talking softly amongst the chaos of abandoned sticky toys. One breast feeds a large plump baby.

Next to the children's room is a cafe serving herb teas and vegan snacks. Long haired people sit at low tables having serious conversations. They wear long skirts or old jeans, clothes made of hemp with old T-shirts tie dyed and large loose sweaters which are knitted on large needles using thick yarn coloured with vegetable dyes.

The crash out room, as opposed to the chill out room, is set up for people who need to lie down to rest, or have overdone things a little, or just need a nap. Its lighting is warm, friendly and the room is full of old hospital beds. Surprisingly few people are making use of the facilities but those who are sleep peacefully under their coats. A couple, drowsy from barbiturates, are discretely having "why bother" sex under a blanket on the corner bed.

At the end of the corridor Kate and Nick take a right. A loud jolly scene meets their eyes, Vince's hyena laugh rises clearly above the rowdy voices. Nick points towards the centre of the floor and smiles at Vince and Barocco who are talking and joking with some acquaintances of theirs, but no Jake. Maybe he is listening to the band. The bar is on their right and across the room a pair of swing doors are propped open. This opening leads to a bathroom off the landing of the original back staircase of the house from which eighty percent of the building has been extended piece by piece, until it has become unrecognizable as the domestic dwelling it had once been. Sitting and standing around an old settee on the landing, a small group of deaf people dress in carnival costumes of bright green communicating with their theatrical gestures. They are very much involved with painting each other's faces and nails. A lone mime in black and white with a particularly steady hand paints the smaller details around the eyes with a liquid eye-liner.

"I'm sorry Kate," says Vince "I can't think what could have happened to him."

"Oh well, I'm sure we'll hear enough about it when he finally turns up, if he turns up!" Kate is getting bored of this crap and Vince did not blame her. Jake is a fool. He vows he is not going to lie to her any more tonight.

"When did you last see him?"

"Oh .., Tuesday, Tuesday morning." Oh what a tangled web we weave, when first we practice to deceive.

"I have some mescaline, would you like some?"

"Mescaline! Really?"

Kate finds the locket and hands her bag to Nick to hold for her while she carefully opens it and shows Vince the contents.

"Wow that's a great blue!"

"Cobalt blue, yes I love that blue." Kate smiles.

"Can I show Barocco?"

"Yes of course, I thought we could all do them."

"Barocco," calls out Vince, " come and take a look at this."

Barocco excuses himself from a conversation with two women.

"This better be good," he says aside into Vince's ear, "that little one's hot for me, maybe her friend too, you know what I mean!" Then turning his attention to Kate's locket he stares in awe for a few seconds.

"Is that what I think it is?"

"If you think it's mescaline," says Kate, "then yes, it is what you think it is."

"Wow! Where did you get mescaline from! Are we going to do this anytime in the near future?"

"Actually I was thinking that maybe now is as good a time as any, what do you think?"

"Always a man of action." Barocco has not given up getting into Kate's knickers, in spite of his continuous pursuit of anything with a vagina. Educated, rich and possessing a certain charm, he is also a difficult and ugly man who should be happy with what he gets instead of staying intent on what he lusts after.

"How much do you take?" asks Vince.

"I was going to take one now and then see what I think in about an hour or so. So I'll give you two each and you can take them whenever you like. But I'll warn you, this connection always sends something special."

Kate carefully places two apiece in the palms of their hands.

"Nick?"

"No thanks Kate."

"You sure?"

"Are you kidding?" says Vince." With all that organic food and clean living he'll still be tripped out in a week! "

"That's probably true." replies Nick.

Kate licks her finger and picks up one for herself. She shuts the locket and replaces it in her bag and then excuses herself.

Vince hands his mescaline to Barocco and opens up a new packet of cigarettes. He pulls out the top piece of foil packing from inside, taking back the two minute pills he wraps them up carefully and places them in the small pocket of his jeans. Barocco licks his palm and takes a swig of beer.

"What are you doing?" asks Vince. Barocco stares at him questioningly, with a stupid expression.

"Take one now and maybe one later. That's why I was wrapping those two up, weren't you listening?"

"Absolutely not, I was watching the way her mouth moves, she's got the perfect mouth. Did you notice when she put her finger in her mouth and sucked off the mescaline. Goodness Nick, I don't know how you run about with her so much, I'd be bending her over every chair, bed or what-have-you! I mean her breasts for a start ... "; and so on and so forth, oblivious of the increasing hostility radiating from Nick. Vince looks at Nick's face as he eye-balls Barocco. So that's it, him too, one would think that the woman is a bloody movie star.

"Have you ever heard Urban Crisis Nick?" Vince interrupts, bringing up the band in the next room.

In the bathroom Kate is unwrapping one of four packages she has purchased. This batch has a nice blue/pink tint, she likes that, she puts a little out with the corner of a credit card and snorts it. It is good, very good.

119

Vince fishes out the silver wrapping from his pocket and opens it up. He licks his finger and uses it to pick up one of the cylinders and places it on his tongue. He wraps up the other, replaces it in his pocket and takes a sip of his beer. He is the first to spot Kate coming back towards them, heads turn as she passes. He smiles to himself, he has to give it to her, she really should be a movie star. He hopes Jake has not blown it, they would make an interesting couple. Narcissus and Narcissess.

"I'm sorry Kate, where are my manners, can I get you a beer?"

"On me, on me. I'm buying! " And Barocco rushes off to the bar without even asking them what they want.

"Oh well, it's the thought that counts," and she takes one of her small but deadly joints out of her cigarette case and lights it.

After Barocco returns with beers for all; including the women he had been chatting up, of which the smaller of the two is sulking.

"Like to dance?" asks Barocco.

"Love to dance!" says Kate.

"Like to dance?" she asks Vince.

"Can manage a Polka and a little Watusi!" Kate smiles and contemplates Vince, surprised that she has not really noticed him much before today. He is good looking enough and seems to be a more intelligent, sensible version of Jake without the charisma, or rather a different kind of charisma, one that grows on you rather than blinds you.

"Come on Nick. Now I know you like to dance," she says.

Barocco hesitates as he watches the three of them funnel off into the next room, looking round at the pair of girls, back at his friends and at the girls again. Had they heard him ask Kate to dance? Without taking their eyes off him, the bigger one whispers something in the little one's ear and they give him a filthy look before turning their noses up into the air and walking across the room to strike up a conversation with two men standing near the swing doors. Barocco flips a hand in a dismissive motion and follows Kate.

The room is far bigger than any of the others on this floor, at least twice the size of the bar; not that any of this is going to matter to them in an hour or so. The atmosphere is intense and the heat is high. Large proportions of the audience are under the influence of some kind of hallucinogenic as they dance fanatically; mesmerized by the band.

The lead singer wears the highest platform shoes Kate has ever seen, more like stilts. They are black and shiny and buckled up like a sandal. On her legs she wears horizontally, wide-striped socks in white and navy which come above her knees like stockings. The shirt of her short blue pinafore dress sticks out almost as much as a tutu, under which she wears a plain white blouse with giant puff sleeves and a short red tie which sticks out over the bib top of her dress. She had parted her long blonde hair in the centre and plaited it with lengths of red ribbon which she uses to fasten the ends with big bows. She has also run wire down the centre of these plaits, bending them so they curl upwards and outwards, making the final touch to her schoolgirl caricature. Being unable to move her feet she dances from the ankles up, carefully avoiding over-balancing in any direction. Nick thinks this makes her look like a praying mantis, a thought he is soon to share with Barocco, much to his regret.

An exceptionally handsome young man stands behind an electric organ. He has beautiful long flaxen hair and beard which flows well passed his waist. He is dressed in an exquisitely tailored jacket in a gold embossed fabric cut in a regency style.

The bass player is a solid Northerner who looks like he could be Kevin the anarchist's brother. Not tall but strong with blonde going on ginger crew cut hair. No fancy clothes for him, he favors military camouflage trousers, a plain black T-shirt and a khaki U.S. navy jacket. He also sings backing vocals. Welding together the backbone of the band is an incredibly talented drummer, a tiny little guy whose feet barely reach the bass Pebbles. He is dressed in blue jeans, a blue pullover, thick tortoise shell glasses, has a wispy moustache and thin wavy mid-brown hair halfway down his back. He also possesses the supplest, strongest wrists in the Galaxy and that is how he plays, all wrists. He can keep it up for hours at a time, like tonight. He shimmers a little, sweat accumulates on his brow which runs down one temple as he modestly nods his thanks around the room during a roar of applause following his solo. On guitar and saxophone was a Jamaican father and son team. The guitarist, whose first love is the blues, is getting increasingly put out by his son's appearance. His son is only eighteen but already a prodigy and, until a few months ago, had dressed exceptionally, suit and tie, the works. However he has found Ras Tafari. Every so often the father looks at his son's feet in distress, sandals this time of year, covered in mud too, like the first eight inches of his trousers, which are too long. The young man knows what his father is thinking and is annoyed that he is right; his wet, cold, dirty feet have been bothering him all night. This fuels his performance further as he places all his anger, resentment, and discomfort into his music.

Kate looks around to see what that strange sound was behind her. She can see nothing to account for it when there is another strange sound to her right. This is it, she is starting to come up. Sounds always go first for her, bouncing and ricocheting all over the place. Nick and Vince have started to dance, Barocco is standing on the spot laughing like a madman.

Half an hour later the four of them are dancing like a bunch of maniacs. Everything seems to be getting faster and crazier as the music progresses. Vince is relieved he has only taken the one micro dot. They seem to be entering a high intensity zone and he knows there is still more to come, he feels incredible, weird but incredible. Kate feels good too. To her the walls of the room no longer exist and the ceiling has vanished. She feels as if she is at a fairground at night under a moonless sky, and time is both fast and crazy and slow and dreamy. The dancing is almost frenzied and the conversation inane and hysterical. Her ribs will ache the next day from laughing. However when Kate stops, and takes some time in the moment, the flowing undulations of the floor and any surfaces, upright or flat, makes her feel as if she is on the sea bed, with fauna moving around her. She even feels as if she is moving through water, floating and gliding a couple of inches above the silt. The smoke from cigarettes and marijuana has begun to glow and has taken on a slight magenta hue, she feels wonderful, almost spiritual. A short time later or maybe it is a thousand years, Kate suddenly snaps onto another level. Then the scene around her goes even deeper into slow motion and the sounds switch to lower octaves. Nick speaks to her. She does not catch the words he speaks, only the sounds he makes. He sounds so funny that she starts to laugh which sets them all off; except Barocco. Barocco stands as still as a rock, unable to move, totally freaked out and inarticulate. He feels like he has fallen and landed in Disney's Fantasia, and Mickey and cast have forced him to smoke crack with them. It is at this unfortunate moment that Nick chooses to share his observations about the singer.

Kate drifts away on a magenta cloud. The crash-out room is full with bodies, many sitting huddled up against the walls. Her attention is drawn to the plane of field created by the identical hospital beds so closely packed together. There is a flowing motion similar but different from the other room. The covers and protruding bodily extremities form a molten entity. Kate sees images of Pompeii and quickly reminds herself she is tripping and moves on quickly.

Someone has switched a brighter light on at the back of the cafe. Kate can see that it is deserted other than a plump women who is cleaning up the kitchenette. She dresses and looks the right age to have come out of Woodstock. Kate cannot make out whether or not the woman is making little squeaky rodent noises.

The doors to both the nursery and the older children's room are shut tight and not a whisper seems to be coming from behind either.

The main lights in the men's room are off and the majority of them sleep. Eight sit around a table in candlelight, seven talking in low voices and sipping tea or finishing up a final beer. The eighth slumps in his seat, arms dangling by his sides like a dead fish, his chin on his chest. With a tortoise like motion his head rises and he starts to sing. The other men hush him, his head drops again and he returns in a flash to Never-Neverland. An irritable voice grumbles from one of the sleeping bags.

She does not loiter by the gang's room but a quick glance into hell is enough to register drunken bodies snoring where they have fallen. Their Commander-in-Chief majestic, the upper half of his body raised with large cushions, his ankles crossed, beer clutched under one arm and puppy-dog snuggled up under the other.

The chill out room is even more distressing. Someone has turned on a lamp. Its shade is bent and ripped and the bare bulb blares. The light exposes all the room's cheap and gaudy effects, as well as the filthy carpet which seems to be composed of millions of ants. Only two bodies remain, both sunken into the pits of the grimy armchairs in which they are grounded. Luckily the sickly sweet aroma of vomit does not register; she just feels

123

overwhelming relief upon reaching the landing at the top of the stairs.

Now there is a new challenge. The moment she sets her foot on the first step the whole staircase starts to move like a rope bridge. She takes hold of the banister and concentrates on the task at hand, reminding herself to breathe deeply. She is tripping, that's all, just tripping, it is not really there. About halfway down a whole host of golden-silver butterflies fly in a great tide towards and around her and away, disappearing into the infinity of light below. She takes her foot off the step, a moment to smell the roses. This mescaline is something else!

"Aaarrrrrrr!" Barocco screams with horror, clutching the edge of the makeshift stage with one hand and pointing at the singer with the other. Vince and Nick know they should do something but it is just too funny.

"Come on mate, just a little girl in a costume that's all." A large good natured man, one of the travelers, tries to soothe him.

Barocco stands upright, still pointing a trembling finger while looking back and forth from the singer to the man, desperately trying to articulate. Finally he gets his lips around what he is trying to express.

"Aaaarrrr! Aaaarrrrrr!"

At the bottom of the stairs are doors leading to the outside world. The lighting is bright and a group of West Indian youths hang around, their incomprehensible conversation comes to an abrupt halt when anybody approaches and their eyes bore holes in the backs of those passing until they are out of earshot.

At least a couple of hundred revelers fill the dance floor in the next room. The lighting is much lower than earlier and so is the ceiling after spending so much time upstairs. Kate feels she is walking down a tunnel made of living murals, acid tones bouncing off the walls and the inside of her head. The man in the cubicle is still talking to himself, alone in his dreary interview, while everybody around him parties the night away.

She holds no desire to linger and heads or rather dances, as it seems the only way to cross the room, towards a doorway she had not noticed earlier. She finds herself facing a short corridor with a couple of smaller rooms off either side. Here is another bathroom and two small offices in which some middle aged Jamaican men in long leather coats, hats and heavy gold jewellery seem to be carrying out some business. At the end of the corridor she is left with the dilemma of identical swing doors on either side of her. She chooses the right and finds herself at the bottom of a staircase that looks more as if it belongs to a house than a government office. The stairs ascend in two flights and it is not until she reaches the top of the staircase that she realizes where she is. Behind her is a way into the old house, the door to her left is the bathroom, and the swing doors, which are now closed, lead into the bar. She is where the deaf people and the mime had been earlier. The space seems sad and empty without them. She picks something off the floor and examines it. It is a piece of ribbon that appears silver on one side and lime green on the other. It is just at that moment the doors bursts open and Jake draped over Little Wing, who is under the influence of half a blotter of acid he has spiked her drink with earlier, come staggering through. He takes two large gulps out of a vodka bottle and belches in Kate's face.

"Aaarrr ! Aaarrr !" Barocco is running around fanatically throwing himself at the walls like a moth at a window; he is causing quite a commotion. Urban Crisis's roadie is standing on the corner of the stage contemplating the situation. A strong-willed, bad tempered young man with little patience is reaching the end of his short tether. He stands still as stone until he decides on his course of action and wastes no more time once his mind is made up. Signaling to someone at the door to call security, namely the rather unfriendly young men at the bottom of the stairs, he jumps from the stage and advances.

"So what do you reckon?" says Vince. As tempting as it is to disown Barocco they know the time has come to rescue their friend.

"Aaaarrrrr!"

Security appears from nowhere, such is their rapid reaction to the call. They start to close in around Barocco who is trying to claw his way up the wall.

"Hey man, cool it. He's just got some bad acid that's all. He isn't anything to worry about. We're his friends, if you give us a minute we'll get him out of here." Vince throws himself at the mercy of the bouncers; luckily the roadie recognizes him from The Neanderthals.

"Well for fucks sake 'urry up Vince before he sets the 'ole room off on a bad trip, 'e sounds like a bloody were-wolf being done in."

Vince and Nick move forward cautiously.

"Hey Tarzan! Where are you going off to without your friends, ah?" Barocco stops clawing the wall and stands still but poised to resume his attempted ascent in a flash. He looks slyly over his shoulder.

"Do yet want to go climb some trees Barocco? Want to get outside?" asks Nick.

Barocco does not move but he begins to grin, somehow it is not reassuring. Then he slowly lowers his leg and arms and turns around. With the meekest face imaginable he looks from Vince to Nick and back again, stands up straight, looks very stem and rips open his shirt, (or maybe one should say Kate's shirt) exposing his chest.

"Me Tarzan, arrr ar-ar-ar ar-ar-ar, arrr ar-ar-ar ar-ar-ar! " and he leaps through a window to his left.

"Shit!" exclaims Vince. "Did that really happen?"

"Unless we're having simultaneous hallucinations, yes. Barocco just jumped through a closed window."

They run to the window, which the roadie and Nick have what remains of the frame open in a second. Their panic gives way to relief then confusion. Barocco, standing slightly to the side of the glass and carnage, tears off all of his clothes and runs off down the street like a hundred yard dash. There is a distant 'arrr ar-ar-ar ar-ar-ar, arrr ar-ar-ar ar-ar-ar' and that is the last they see or hear of him that night.

~

The cab speeds off furiously.

"Byeeee ...! " A staggering Jake waves into the dust and carbon monoxide before picking up Little Wing and throwing her over his shoulder. He attacks the stairs, it is a long hard halting haul up the single flight and at least twice Little Wing fails to stifle a scream as Jake falters dangerously backwards. A cat hisses ferociously before rushing past them preferring the street. Little Wing screams again.

"What the hell ...?"

"I'm sorry. Cats. I don't like cats."

He finds his keys, conquers the lock and lurching forwards into the front room, he trips, tossing Little Wing down onto her back on top of the mattress as he falls flat on his face at the foot of his bed. Crawling up next to her he starts tickling her, she giggles and rolls about quite helpless.

"So tell me Little Wing, why Little Wing? Tell me, tell me, tell me!"

"No!" she screams, Jake attacks more fiercely.

"No, no, no, no!" she squeals between shrieks of laughter.

"Tell me! Tell me!" Jake prods her with his finger while she curls up and flaps her hands in her defense, quite helpless and quite delightful.

"You don't want to know."

"Yes I do!"

"No you don't!"

"Yes I do!" Jake is suddenly serious, or at least he acts that way. He reaches out his hand and lightly smooths her left cheek with the back of his fingers.

"I want you too."

"Oh Jake I don't know, I ..."

"I want you Little Wing."

"Jake?"

"Little Wing?" He caresses her face and hair with fatherly tenderness.

"Why do you want me?"

"Why? Because you're beautiful Little Wing. I want to cherish you and know everything about you."

"Everything?"

"Yes everything. What you are, who you are, where you came from, your real name, why they call you Little Wing, why you're so beautiful, what you think, how you feel, how you got that scar, why ..."

She takes hold of his hand and holds a finger to his lips.

"I want to know Little Wing," says Jake in an insistent voice, stroking the small of her back.

"Have you ever been in love?"

"Oh yes! But that's.. it's all over now."

"A right bastard eh?"

"Oh no, not at all!"

"No?"

"Have you ever swum with dolphins?" she asks.

"No."

"Diomedes, Diomedes Eniopeus was his name. His grandfather had lived in America, New Orleans, for forty years and brought back all these records which, in the winter, we would play and sing along to for hours; he became my best, best friend in the whole wide world. My Auntie always said we were inseparable, like wings of the same bird, flying all over the island, never knowing where we were going to land next! So she named me 'Mikro Phtero' - Little Wing.

"In the long hot Greek summers we immersed ourselves in sunlight, swimming out to rocks off the shore, where dolphins gathered and the brisk blue sea sprayed our tanned bodies with its hissing foam. We slept under the stars, damp and naked between blankets, salt setting in our hair, fresh from the sea, where we swam intertwined under the full moon. Fluorescent currents embracing us with bright sparks, like fire flies that flew with the flow and shot from our fingertips and toes. We lay entranced for hours in these embraces, still as stone, breathing each other's life back and forth in an erotic trance of love and desire, with the call of the Scops owl and the sweeping tide for our lullabies.

"And then Diomedes had a motorbike accident......"

A tear runs down the side of her face and Jake, holding her chin ever so lightly, kisses the second away. There was silent for a while, then looking into her eyes he starts to sing:

"Well she's walking through the clouds,
With a circus mind that's running wild.
Butterflies and zebras and moonbeams and fairy tales,
Is all she ever thinks about.
Riding with the wind.
When I'm sad she comes to me,
With a thousand smiles, she gives to me free.
It's all right she says, it's all right,
Take anything you want from me,
Anything.
Fly on Little Wing."

128

"Did you just make that up?"

"Yes, just for you Little Wing, just for you! I love you Little Wing."

And he took her in his arms and into his bed, and she let herself be taken there.

SUNDAY

It is 5:00 am. As the dregs of Saturday night render to unconsciousness the Patels are rising. Or at least Mr. Patel is.

"I am not well, I am staying at home today," says Mrs. Patel.

Mr. Patel is aghast and genuinely confused. This has never happened before and he has no idea what to say to his wife as she lies there facing the wall.

"You are not well?"

"Yes, I do not feel well."

"And you are not coming to the shop today?"

"Yes, no work today."

He ponders momentarily.

"Mother will stay home too."

"No, I do not need your mother. I manage O.K."

"Yes, but she stays here anyway and looks after the children."

She decides not to make too much of a fuss, she doesn't want to raise his suspicions and he is right, it will be useful to have his mother to mind the children for a few hours.

~

Alec suddenly sits bolt upright. He has been fast asleep only seconds before dreaming of volcanoes exploding in a pitch black night. Screaming masses came pouring from the mountain tops followed by white hot lava, not that they ran from it, quite the contrary, they ran with it, the front line. It was like a giant Hieronymus Bosch painting come to life. 'Hieronymus Bosch, 'The Motion Picture'. He can definitely hear voices in the kitchen. It is not even light outside, he looks at the clock.

"Good God!" He flops back on the pillow.

He has tossed and turned for hours in search of sleep and finally found it about an hour ago, now this. He pulls the blankets over his head and prays for oblivion but finds only mounting rage. It is no good; he throws off the blankets and stomps into the kitchen. Just as he thought, the wife, bitch Monica, the idiot Alice, bucktoothed four-eyed Jenny, and fat bossy Wendy. Just what a

131

fella who knocked off the guru of the British Nazi party needs to wake up to.

It had taken over two hours the night before for the police even to start allowing people to leave the cornered off block on Hampton Road. His friends had tried to humour him but he was not having any of it.

"No, sorry," Gorky's mother went enthusiastically to hug him. He raised his hand. "No, I'm sorry your mother was in the Warsaw Ghetto Gorky, but I can't be her hero. No more heroes, remember?"

"Wait for me, I'll walk with you Alec," Kev was putting on his jacket.

"I'd much rather you didn't, I'm not in the mood for company."

With that he had left, only to fall into the ominous pit of insomnia.

"Oooh!" Ugly Jenny, noticing Alec naked in the doorway, jumps and drops a ceramic mug on the tile floor.

"Don't mind me, I only live here" he says. And goes into the bathroom and locks the door. Seconds later there is knocking on the door.

"Alec! Alec! Let me in." What a nasty voice Monica has.

"No."

"Stop messing around Alec! I need to speak to you."

"Sod off Monica."

Monica stands at the bathroom door, hand raised ready to knock again but amazingly she thinks better of it. Alec decides to take a shower, have breakfast and go back to bed. It seems like a good plan. Dripping wet with a towel wrapped around his waist he returns to the kitchen and makes coffee. There is an atmosphere of self-righteous hostility radiating from the four women.

"Are you just making coffee for yourself or for all of us?" says Wendy, taking charge.

"You drink decaf don't you?"

"Yes" the others nod. Monica has a very prominent back turned towards him.

"Decaf Monica?"

"Yes, if it wouldn't be too much trouble Alec."

"Well actually dear I haven't got any so it would be," he looks at Wendy, "sorry about that Fatty," and he wanders back into the bedroom and lies down. Monica comes running in after him.

"Whatever's got into you Alec? How could you talk to Wendy like that?"

"I can talk to Wendy like that because this is my home and she's a great fat interfering cow, who thinks she can just walk in here at some god damn unearthly hour in the morning, with my wife, who has failed to cohabit with me for months, and start telling me what to do. If I have any more crap out of her she will get a good punch in the mouth to send her on her way, and that goes for brain dead Alice and ugly Jenny too, and you know what you can do if you don't like it!"

"Oh that's right, threaten violence, isn't that just like a man. If I've 'failed to cohabit' as you put it, it's because I've been doing something to make this world a better place. Sleeping in a tent all winter while you lie around snug and warm in a comfortable bed."

"Is that what I've been doing Monica?" Monica feels uneasy; he is not exactly scaring her but his behaviour is unnerving all the same.

"So your mission has been successful?" She looks blank.

"Uncle Sam's taken down his nasty weapons and gone back home with a flea in his ear from Britannia's righteous sisters has he?"

"No, but that's not the point."

"So what's the point Monica?"

"The point is we're trying."

"No Monica, the point is to achieve. And you have achieved. You've achieved the last slot, the entertainment section, of the national news on a regular basis; you've created a soap opera!"

"You bastard!"

"Why thank you. Is that the kettle boiling? Oh yes, so it is. Goody!"

He goes back into the kitchen and starts to pour water into the filter for his coffee. The women are confiding quietly standing around an L shaped counter.

"Is this a private conversation or can anybody join in?" Alec says happily. He realizes he has not enjoyed himself so much for a long time. With a nod from Wendy, Alice, Jenny and herself step back from the counter and start retrieving their jackets and rucksacks.

"We'll wait for you outside Monica," Wendy says.

"Don't worry, I won't be long."

"Fancy a quick shag before you go Monica? No? How about an orgy. God, I could warm my ears between those mammoth mammaries of yours Wendy! Come on Jenny, don't be self-conscious, a man doesn't look at the mantel piece when he's stoking the fire. Alice, I understand you give the best blow jobs this side of The Elephant. Now don't be modest, I heard it from at least a dozen separate sources."

The door shuts behind Monica's friends, the corridor echoes her apologies. She storms into the kitchen, pale faced, eyes glaring. She stands in front of her husband for one second then slaps his face as hard as she can. Next thing she knows there is a loud pinging sound like a elastic band sounding in her skull and her own head jolts under the forceful swing and sting of Alec's open hand.

"So it's only men who resort to violence is it Monica? So much for saving the World, you can't even keep your own house in order. Get the hell out of here."

Much to his surprise she slides down the wall to the floor and starts howling. He takes her by the arm and none to gently pulls her to her feet. Picking up her rucksack and coat he starts to escort her to the door.

"Come along, your friends are waiting for you, you can tell them how you put me in my place."

"I don't want to go with them, I want to stay here with you." Monica manages to spit out between the sobs.

"Well you should have thought of that before you played the bitch, out you go," he is rattling with the latch on the front door.

"I'm sorry, I don't know what got into me, my hormones are all over the place at the moment, and I know it's no excuse, but the others are really getting on my nerves, especially Wendy. She decided we should all have breakfast together before going our separate ways, as if we haven't seen enough of each other, and somehow I got allocated. All I wanted to do was to get them fed so I could get them out of here. Please Alec don't do this, I know I've been a terrible wife but I do love you, and I'm so tired." She starts to sob again.

134

Alec stops fiddling with the lock and lets go of her arm. Fixing her with his eyes he speaks softly and very deliberately.

"Tell them to go away."

"O.K." she agrees meekly. Then a slight sly smile crosses her lips.

"Unless you'd prefer to do the honors." It seems like a long time since they had smiled together.

"I do believe I would! Run along and run yourself a nice hot bath, I'll be right back to cook us breakfast in bed, I dare say I may be able to muster up some decaf for you."

She gives him a big hug.

"Oh Alec! I don't give a damn if it's decaf or not, and I don't care what that bitch says, you're going to make a wonderful father," and she runs off down the corridor.

~

Maggie

I'd like to put a bullet through your head,
Just to give you a fright;
The very sound of your voice,
Makes me feel uptight.

I'd like to splatter your brain matter
Over every conceivable area of wall,
Because you infuriate me
With your constant talk of fuck all.

I'd like some cold, clammy hands
To come out of this decade of fog,
And throttle the life out of you
To end your patronizing monologue.

I'd like to be free from your reality,
Proletarian mass brain washing
And all this talk of money.
I'd like to put a bullet through your head,
But I'm fucked if I'll go to prison,
So I'll just sit here being bored,
Boring, apathetic, and unemployed instead.

Nick rips the sheet of paper out of his typewriter, crumbles it up, and throws it across the room into the wastepaper basket.

He is tying his laces, about to go for his daily run, when he hears a quiet knock on his front door. He is surprised to see young Mrs. Patel but immediately invites her in for a coffee. Seema approves of Nick, he is a good boy. He had helped them when they had first moved in and someone had sprayed graffiti on their front window, 'WOPS go home' and a swastika. He had gathered some of the other tenants and together they had helped them clean it off.

"No, no coffee, you go on with your running. I need to use your VCR for a private matter thank you."

Nick cannot see why not, though it does seem a bit strange as he knows the Patels have their own VCR. He takes her into the front room where he sets everything up for her and she then ushers him out.

"You go, run now," she says and shuts the door. Nick stands a few seconds, a little bemused at being turned out of his own front room. As he pulls the front door closed to he swears he hears a chorus of 'On the Street where You Live'.

~

Edith's step is light and buoyant; she wears a grin that could harpoon Moby Dick. It is a beautiful, cloudless, late winter's morning and outside the window, in front of the kitchen sink, a bird feeder hangs. The sparrows titter at the feeder while other birds are having operatic outbursts of early spring fever. Here Edith stands in a floodlight of golden sun-rays, washing-up a frying pan. The light pours through the upper right diagonal half of the window, highlighting the sparrows, the tops of the daffodils that sit in a white porcelain vase on the window sill, and Edith, who is humming happily occasionally breaking out into song herself. She looks positively youthful this morning, her fine full head of silver hair swept back into an Eva Poirt bun. She dresses very tastefully in a Marks and Sparks imitation silk kimono with an imitation hand-painted floral print in green and magenta on lilac, with matching slippers. Leonard stands in the doorway in her lavender house

136

coat observing her with a smile. She is still a damn fine figure of a woman and he is still not a bad lover!

"Good morning my dear, you are looking very radiant this morning if you don't mine me saying."

Edith looks over her right shoulder with a sly grin.

"And you were a very naughty man this mornin'!"

"And what about last night? Last night I'd like to think I was a very, very naughty man!"

"Come 'ere Mr. Three-times."

They exchange a little kiss and cuddle. He whispers in her ear and tickles her, Edith laughs and pushes him away as he gives her a resounding slap on the backside.

"Are yer by any chance unusually 'ungry this mornin'?" she asks, brandishing the frying pan in her hand.

"I could eat a horse."

"Me too."

~

Leo is in love. He looks down at her sleeping at his side, she is so pretty. He leans over to kiss her forehead and she turns on her back all warm and sleepy and sexy, and stretches out her arms. Opening her eyes she smiles at him, wraps her arms around his neck and pulls him to her.

~

Robert sits up in bed picking his nose and looking at a magazine. He farts loudly and starts groping himself under the covers. He flips over a page to a photograph of a woman and a donkey. Angela was surfacing, she is no stranger to waking up naked in strange places, and she takes acute hangovers in her near daily stride; however a rancid stench has somehow managed to penetrate her sleep. With an expression on her face as if none other than Satan's smelling salts have aroused her, she turns over slightly and looks over her shoulder, but whoever it is will not come into focus. A fuzzy hand looms out from the figure and smooths the back of her head momentary, then taking grip of her hair it starts pushing her head towards its crotch.

"Give us a blow-job Ang."

137

Giving a small scream, she pulls away trying to disengage Robert's hand from her hair. There is a small struggle before Robert releases her. He looks at her with narrow eyes for a few seconds.

"Get out of me bed yer useless, fuckin' slag."

Angela sits up frozen in disbelief. It is Robert, her ears have not deceived her, vile disgusting repulsive Robert. She would not be seen dead in bed with Robert, and here she is, in bed with Robert, wishing she was dead.

"I said fuck off yer old tart" and he raises his leg and with one kick pushes her out of bed and on top of the general refuse heap that surrounds his filthy old mattress.

~

There's mutants on the Walworth Road,
crooked shoulders, scooping, bald,
There's mutants on the Walworth Road.
Leering mouths and toothless grins,
a midget with a hunch-back kin,
Withered legs and hallow eyes, cauliflower
noses beetroot dyed.
There's mutants on the Walworth Road,
Like some unwritten biological code, the
DNA of inner-city ghouls,
Lead up their noses, ears deformed like
posies,
Stomach filled with grease and fat, now
they've got that Mc. D's crap.
Generations of eating poisons and breathing
pollution,
Now they're cutting down our rain
forests to promote this institution,
These mutants of the Walworth Road.

Nick munches on a packet of Baldwin's hiking mix, Baldwin's being an authentic herbalist in the Walworth Road established well over a century ago. The mix of dried diced apricot, currants, sunflower seeds, crushed raw cashews and peanuts was obtained from their adjacent health food store, recently opened for the nouveau healthy. It is market day and he leans against the railings with his back to the road contemplating the hordes flowing in and out of East Street. He remembers parts of a poem he had written some years before when he had been in a rather depressive state, and had started to empathize with the maniacs who let loose with semi-automatics in their local high street.

There seems to be so many deformed, aggressive and retarded people here. Here, in the centre of the London basin, pollution settles heavily. Six busy roads merged to form The Elephant and Castle. Nick blames the lead and what he believes to be deliberate poor education. A hushed up government white paper revealed the effects of generation upon generation of appalling diet. Apparently the average inner-city child ate more lard that fruit, it was a fucking disgrace.

Nick is about to make the final leg of his Sunday run which will bring him full circle back to the stairwell. First he has warmed up by jogging to the fish monger at the junction of Kennington Lane and Kennington Park Road. On Sundays they have a wider variety of fish, especially shell fish, than the rest of the week. He has treated himself to a large, live crab which he plans to dress before he takes his siesta. He carefully places the crab, submerged in a plastic bag of water, in his small rucksack and now is ready for the main part of his workout, an energetic run to the far end of East Street.

He runs up the rest of Kennington Park Road, veers right pass the Post Office and the Pizzeria, under the railway bridge, passes the 'Elephant Vindaloo' Indian take-away, and across the Walworth Rd, soon to take a left and zigzag through the back streets and eventually he comes up on the market from the rear.

About half way down, after a main cross street, the market changes from being busy to packed. Nick stops on the comer where the sarsaparilla man has his decades old pitch and has a pint of the traditional energizing drink. He listens to the calls of the stall owners, a language within itself, and as various as the trills of the dawn chorus.

Now he ventures into the bottom half of the market and starts shouldering his way through the throngs of people moving in patterns woven by the laws of chaos. Behind the stalls are boutiques and leather clothing stores for the most part. The stalls become less varied and more inclined toward fruit and veg, likewise the shops turn to those catering to gastronomic needs. First Nick works his way over to the left, towards a stall that specializes in more exotic fruit. Soft fruits: peaches, nectarines, plums, and tropical papaya, mango, and juicy red grapes. Also it has imported vegetables, plantains, okra and artichokes, amongst others. After this he has to fight his way over to the right to where the three other places he likes to shop lay one on top of the other.

He unzips his track suit top and pulls out a good sized canvas bag. The green grocer weighs out Nick's usual spuds, onions, carrots, parsnips and two or three green vegetables, plus some apples, tipping them all straight from his scales into Nick's shopping bag. He calculates the total in his head in a split second, unabashed but rapidly dealing with the extensive, endless lines forming at his stall. Nick places his carrier bag of fruit on top of the loose vegetables and fights his way a few yards back through the condensed narrow passage between the stalls and the shops to the centre of three adjacent butchers and examines the window display. Nick's diet includes meat though it did not feature it. He has given up trying to be a vegetarian after many failed attempts and excepts the true carnivore within, eating meat about two or three times a week and investing in quality. He is especially careful with beef, which he hardly touches and chicken which he loves. He does however have a weakness for breakfast meats, and eyeing the Cumberland sausage rolled into discs on their platters he decides to take a pound along with his usual half a pound of best back green bacon. To this he adds a couple of juicy fresh lamb chops and a thick slice of gammon.

He is almost done. Back down past the butchers is a marvelous cheese stall with an extensive selection. Here Nick can also buy free range eggs. Kate loves this stall, he cannot help thinking of her when he looks at the immense jar of olive oil which holds small goat cheeses marinated with rosemary and oregano. He nearly buys her one but catches himself. He has to stop doing this. She is his friend, not his girlfriend and never likely to be. He has to work on acceptance. He buys some hard Cornish nettle cheese and some Shropshire blue, and resumes the battle of the pavement, finally managing to burst out of the Walworth Road end of East Street.

After taking his little rest on the railings he picks up some flowers and heads homeward, first crossing over the road to where the stomach rumbling aroma of Arif's Bakery fills the air. He picks up a warm, crusty loaf of bread, a light sweet almond croissant, and a hot delicious Turkish boat pizza. Last night is catching up on him rapidly and he decides to eat now, sleep and prepare the crab later. His orbit finishes with a light jog, turning left passed the chemist towards home.

~

Jake is coming round, his head feels like a vise is just about to burst open his skull; his mouth and throat are as dry as a desert rock at noon and taste like shit. Lacking the strength to open his eyes, let alone go in search of relief, he drifts in and out of consciousness for what seems like hours. Eventually, unable to escape into sleep and tortured by his thirst and bladder, he opens his eyes. The light pierces his eyes, then his brain and refracts off the back of the skull and throughout the cranium in microscopic rays of pain and agony. Objects zoom in and out of focus, he is not alone, someone lies beside him. Slowly the room begins spinning, and slowly it gains momentum, faster and faster, he feels the need to vomit and defecate.

Half running, half stumbling, he almost nose-dives down the porcelain receptacle. Doubled up and simultaneously chucking up his guts he collapses to his knees. He heaves again; he is in agony, his sides feel both numb and sore as if his ribs are broken. Then in a movement unbelievably fast considering his condition, he spins up and around, landing heavily on the toilet. He has forgotten to pull the seat down and as he sinks, knees rising, he farts loudly, thickly pebble-dashing the inside of the chasm. The stench is foul and starts him gagging. He flushes quickly and once more drops to his knees, vomiting for the second time. Once empty his stomach convulses bile uncontrollably. When finally the cramping stops Jake is able to flush, open a window, and splash some cold water on his face. He shits again, cleans himself up a little, and heads out to the kitchen in search of great quantities of H20. Standing at the kitchen sink, still dizzy, he clings on to the edge, tilting his head back to drink. He feels a bit better in spite of his unquenchable thirst and the sound of his heart pounding his

141

ear drums. It is just then that a very young woman he has no recognition of whatsoever walks into the kitchen wearing his favorite T-shirt. Coming up behind him and putting her arms around his waist she gives his stomach a quick squeeze, nearly making him puke again.

Jake rapidly disengaging himself, makes another bolt for the bathroom and empties his bowels again. To add to his problems his splinter is beginning to burn like hell.

~

Kate is used to hangovers and can still pride herself on having never missed a day's work.
"That's my lass!" she can imagine her late father slapping her on the back as he hands her another Scotch.

But once, twice, maybe three times a year there are the killer hangovers. When her ears would ring so badly that if she picked up the phone she could not tell what was being said or even which language the caller was speaking, whether she knew them, or if this was a complete stranger. She would lie in bed motionless until she was nearly pissing herself because it hurt so much to move; those hangovers, and this one is one of them.

The first thing she notices is the excruciating pain in her head, it feels as if it has been cloven with a blunt ax. No start, no end, just pain throughout, as if the most painful part of a throb has been instilled permanently. The next thing she notices is the daylight, and then with the best imitation of a start her pathetic state can manage she realizes, with horror, that this is not her bed and she is naked. Though very weak she is suddenly very awake. She lies motionless with her back to the window and whoever. Whoever rolls onto his back and lets out a deep sigh, scratches, snorts and falls back into the deep, regular breaths of slumber.

The shock of her rude awakening has sharpened her instincts. He is a large man, she is sure, and she feels a sense of some kind of familiarity, which could be good or bad of course, but who? Who the hell...? She catches the reflection in the mirror hanging above the mantel piece. Oh no! Big Joe!

~

142

Jake finally emerges to the clash and clatter of saucepans, the noise reverberating through his brain sadistically. A greasy cabinet door obscures most of his view of his crouching guest. At a time less worse for wear he would have noticed her long chestnut hair, which flows down her back and hangs past lush taunt little creamy buttocks that protrude just below the hem of his T-shirt. A beautiful hand with long nails painted all the colours of the rainbow hold the door ajar, under which he would have noticed matching toenails as she balances on the balls of her feet. But now, right now, all he wants is for that noise to stop, to go back to bed and for her be silent or go home, preferably go home as he is not in the mood to face anyone. Just as he can bear it no longer, she stands up smiling radiantly, large frying-pan in hand.

"Are you hungry? I'm starving," she chirps merrily. " but I don't know about this milk, it smells off. What do you think?" She holds the carton out towards him.

"I think we should sit down and please, please, put that milk back in the fridge." He nearly pukes again.

"O.K!" She does so in a flash and seems to spring into a chair like a child at the fairground. Christ, how old is she anyway? She looks about fourteen. She places the frying pan down on the kitchen table with a penetrating clash. Jake takes a seat.

"Just a minute."

He gets up and goes to the bedroom, slips on a pair of jeans and returns with a pipe and a pill box.

"Look, last night. Last night was great."

Much to Jake's surprise she burst out laughing and then makes a visible effort to pull herself together.

"Well, it was kind of fun!" Laughing again she looks at him both with a little guilt and a lot of affection and adds:

"And special of course. Very special Jake, " reaching forward she squeezes his hand.

"Well anyway ..."   She starts laughing again, silently, holding her sides and rocking in her seat.

"Oh, I'm sorry, I was just thinking, it was so funny, so funny when you…, oh, excuse me."

She gets up and makes a dash for the toilet banging the door behind her and dropping the seat noisily. He can still hear her laughing. He opens the pill box and gets out a small dark brown lump of resin and heats it over a match and tries to piece together

143

some remembrance of the night before. But after Fen's Den he keeps drawing a blank. He burns his fingers, curses under his breath, sucks and shakes them. The resin has cooled and he has to heat it again and crumbles it with his index and thumb of his right, unscorched hand. The bathroom door opens, she stands there in all seriousness, looks at him for about two seconds, and doubles up again.

"I'm sorry, I'm so sorry." She takes her seat almost maintaining full composure.

"Well out with it."

"What?" she grins.

"What's so funny?"

He lights a match and puts the pipe to his lips. It will either make him pass out or feel a bit better, either will do. He is getting distinctly worried about the previous evening. Kate. He was supposed to meet Kate. His stomach is beginning to feel queasy again; he takes a deep drag on his pipe.

"Your agent's party."

Jake nearly chokes. She gets up and runs him a glass of water. Oh no, he must have taken her up to Knightsbridge and gate-crashed a private party his agent was throwing for a dozen or so of his most prominent clients.

"Thank you," he says meekly. "I'm sorry, what were you saying?"

His guest starts to reel off a substantial list of embarrassment and humiliation, each worse than the previous.

"... and then you placed the end of the water melon on your head, pronounced yourself 'King of the Fruits', turned round, dropped your jeans, oh and your under pants of course..."

"Of course."

"... mooned everybody and performed 'The Raspberry Fanfare to the Common Man'!"

Great. He has a horrible feeling he is going to have to find himself another agent.

~

Kate remembers leaving the party. She had turned heel, gone so suddenly it was as if she never was. She had run back down the staircase, dodging round groups of people, knocking into others, jumped the last six steps and burst through two sets of fire doors into the outside world about two seconds before a taxi pulled round the corner. She has been lucky lately, at least with taxis.

Jake had coaxed Little Wing galumphly in the direction of the toilet and slammed the door shut behind her.

"Come to me Aphrodite!" he had hollered, and run after Kate. Jumping several steps at a time, he had lost his footing and fallen, landing heavily on his knee. Cursing, he got up again limping, and fanatically he burst outside, every bit the monster in pursuit of his maker, only to see a magnificent seam-stockinged leg on a high heel, disappear into a taxi. The door had slammed, and gracefully and swiftly the taxi pulled away, turned the comer and had headed for the West-End.

~

"Don't forget you owe me half that cab fare Jake, I'll be broke otherwise. That driver was enormous-I thought he was going to kill you!"

"Thank you for bailing me out, excuse me."

"You're excused."

He has to go to the bathroom again and relieve himself once more. After which he does feel better, but finding himself nodding off as he sits there he realizes he really has to go back to bed. But first he also has to find out one more thing.

"What time was it when we finally got down to the other party? Can you remember?"

"God, it must have been about three o'clock!"

"Quite some party, what did you think?" he feels like a masochist, but he just has to know.

"It was such fun Jake, you're a great dancer! God, wasn't everybody out of it."

She yawns widely, showing off a set of perfect teeth and takes a little toke on the pipe before handing it back to him.

"Oh!" she giggles "Apparently you fell down the stairs. I could hear you shouting 'Come to me Aphro-die-tee!', and you fell and ..."

"Strained my ankle?"

"No, your knee. Don't you remember?"

"Of course I remember. Here."

He hands her the pipe, she raises her hand and shakes her head. Feeling his knee he winces.

"Look um, sweetheart, to tell the truth I'm really not up to breakfast. In fact I'm not up to much at all except getting some more sleep. Now I'm not saying you have to go but I'm being straight with you, I have to lie down and I have to lie down now. So you're welcome to join me or it may be a better idea for you to leave me your number and I'll catch up with you later."

"What's my name?"

"Oh sweetheart please ..."

"My name? What's my name?"

"Oh no, what's all this, I can't handle this shit, I've got the hangover from hell and ... " her look silences his self-pity.

"Oh god" he sits with his head in his hands," M something beginning with an M, don't tell me now, Mary, Maria, no? Margaret! No? I was sure it was an M, I'm terrible with names, but it will come to me, if not now later. Please, please sweetheart, I've.."

"My name is not sweetheart!" she yells, and storms to the bedroom. She dresses and leaves, her small feet and tears echoing and amplifying up the stairwell.

He shuts the door quietly behind her. Well that had gone well! Poor little thing, he could have shut up but oh no, he just had to go on, then trying to pull himself out just to sink further in adding insult to injury. He wishes he had the energy to go after her and buy her breakfast. Shit, he had even forgotten to give her the cab fare. He lies back down on the bed and tries to ignore the guilt and the shame. Guilt because, in spite of his conscience, he cannot help feeling relieved at getting rid of her, and shame because he just knows somewhere along the line he has acted shamefully. He would catch up with her later, when he had had a chance to catch up on some sleep. Then he was snoring, sleeping the sleep of the dead which will take him right through until much later that night, when Vince would wake him up and beat the crap out of him. So much for good intentions.

~

Kate recalls having the taxi drop her on the Southbank at Westminster Bridge, still heavily tripped out and feeling tormented

146

by anger, rejection and her damaged sense of dignity. Looking across a calm river on a flood-lit Houses of Parliament, backed by a sky resplendent with a billion stars she exhaled deeply, and allowed the city to work its enchantments upon her.

She had turned right, down some white granite steps and proceeded along the embankment on a wide stone path aglow with its own inner light. The River's ripples sparkled brilliantly and prisms alive with colour, radiated from the old gas lanterns and shone off any reflective surface. The path passed the old G.L.C.[10]offices of County Hall, the Jubilee Gardens and under a railway bridge that served Charring Cross Station, to The Royal Festival Hall. Here she abandoned the riverside and crossed The Thames at Waterloo Bridge, pausing, looking East and West to where the curvature of the river obscured her altered view. Once over the bridge she continued straight through the junction of The Strand and Aldwych, turning left into Tavistock Street. She had worked her way through the complexed maze of tiny streets, passed the Covent Garden Royal Opera House and the empty market plaza, until she hit St. Martin's Lane. She had turned right on St. Martin's towards Cambridge Circus and the lights of the theatre district, where animated characters were still emerging from different clubs and theatre stage-doors. This had absorbed her until well after she had peaked on the mescaline. Then with the streets emptying and small noisy groups of drunks coming out of the woodwork she had decided to avoid the end of Shaftesbury Avenue and Piccadilly Circus. Instead she had cut through Soho to a little back street cafe just off Regent Street.

Gary's Cafe's clientele were nightclub and restaurant workers for the most. That night four street walkers sat by the door in their flimsy clothing, shivering and warming their chilblained hands with their cups of tea. Their pimp stood at the window exchanging glares with Gary standing behind the counter at the back of the yellow and red cafe. Pimps were not welcome at Gary's but he had a kind heart when it came to the girls.

Other than greeting Gary, she had avoided eye contact and headed straight for the Ladies room. Retrieving the opened packet of cocaine and her compact from her bag she gently and carefully

---

[10]*Greater London Council*

tapped the white powder down the fold in the paper until a generous half gram lay out on the mirror. She folded up the packet and putting it away fished out her credit card and proceeded to chop and tidy the cocaine into one neat line which, with the help of a crisp rolled twenty pound note, she made short work of. After a quick cup of coffee she decided to go dancing at a sleazy basement nightclub she knew. That was when the real drinking had begun and then ... what?

Not thinking she rolls over abruptly onto her back, her sudden movement woke Big Joe; she could no longer shield sleep.

"Hey Princess! You O.K. Princess?"

"My head, my head is unbelievable, I'm afraid I don't remember much about last night, I mean, well, did we?" There is a short pained silence Kate is too desensitized to notice.

"No Princess, it's all right, we didn't."

"Oh," she sighs, with all too obvious relief. "Oh, I'm sorry Joe, I didn't mean it like that I just meant ..."

"It's O.K. Princess, it's O.K."

"I think I'd like to go home now whilst I still have the energy, if you don't mind."

"That's O.K., you go, your clothes are over there on the chair."

Kate gathers her things and heads for the bathroom. There are still so many questions unanswered. She had woken in his bed with him naked. She felt sure Joe was giving her a break and he is right, she would rather not know. She feels her crotch quickly, neither tender nor wet, nor can she detect an alien scent. Perhaps he is telling the truth, about that part anyway. At least she will not have to worry about being knocked up.

~

Jacket buttoned incorrectly and an earring light, she trips and nearly falls down the last flight of stairs, just catching herself as she turns her ankle. A pretty teenager with long chestnut hair nearly collides with her.

"Sorry" Angela hears her say through a flood of tears. Ascending footsteps get fainter and fainter until they reach the top of the stairs and a door slams.

Clutching her handbag in one hand and a nylon scarf in the other, she treads down tentatively. Her ankle gives way under her, a sharp pain shoots up her shin and she has to lean against the dirty, tiled entrance of the stairwell to stay balanced. A black cab speeds past.

"Taxi!" Angela hollers pitifully after it.

The cab keeps going. She starts coughing, a harsh, coarse, graphite cough, which chokes her and holds her bent. Suddenly she tastes vomit in the back of her throat and, as she stumbles out onto the pavement, a particularly violent cough projects an arch of brown tarred phlegm, bile, and bourbon into the gutter, where she promptly staggers and falls. And there she is, kneeling in the gutter in a pile of her own vomit, looking at the palms of her hands encrusted with gravel and filth through which beads of blood are now appearing.

~

" 'Ave yer 'ad ample Leonard?"

"Ample? Ample would be an understatement my dear! I am in a state of complete satisfaction."

Edith starts clearing the table but Leonard stands and takes the plates from her.

"You can't cook and do the washing-up too my dear, it's against the rules. You sit down and talk to me whilst I endeavor to accomplish the task."

So Edith sits at the kitchen table and drinks tea while Leonard delivers many amusing anecdotes. Eventually he finishes the job at hand, sits down and pours himself a cup of tea and continues to talk.

"Well, I suppose I better be getting back to that grandson of mine, see what trouble he managed to get himself into last night. And you my dear, what are you up to today? " he says, reaching for his third cup.

"Me daughter's picking me up soon to go to the zoo with me great grandchildren. Twin boys Jerry and Freddy six and the baby, Ruth, just gone nine months."

"Great-grandchildren, how wonderful! And such a youthful great-grandmother, and beautiful of course, and not to mention an effervescence of enthusiasm and passion!"

"What a load of bollocks," Edith thinks, "though 'e does it well."

Eventually he goes to the bedroom and returns dressed with his hat in his hand. He sits down and talks a little longer and finally after the customary exchange of phone numbers he leaves.

"Good God!" Edith shakes her head and mutters in disbelief, "I thought 'e was never goin' to shut up!"

~

A pair of running shoes and the elasticized ankles of a blue track suit appears between the two cars where she had fallen.

"Angela?"

Angela looks up at Nick, the epiphany of healthy living. She had not thought it possible to feel ever more of a worthless, useless piece of shit than she already felt; but she was wrong. It takes Nick all of about half a second to summarize the situation. She had been desperate to get home before resigning to the grief of her humiliation, but she cannot hold back her despair. She speaks to him as best she can though her uncontrollable sobs.

"I'm sorry ... with Robert .... so   disgusting   ...   can't remember ... I'm sorry ... me ankle ..., there's no point anymore ... wish I was dead......I'm sorry......"

" 'Ang on Ang, just a mo."

She gave way to her tears, not even trying to articulate any more. Nick puts his bag down on the steps and returns to help her to her feet. With him supporting her she tests her ankle again but it immediately buckles under the lightest pressure. Nick gets her over to the steps, sits her down and takes a look. It is so swollen it looks deformed.

"Come on Ang, let's get yer upstairs and cleaned up and phone an ambulance."

Angela starts to cry again, these were the gentlest words she has heard for a long time.

~

"BEV-ER-LY! YER FUCKIN' BITCH, I KNOW YER FUCKIN' IN THERE! BE-VER-LY!"

Leo feels her nails dig into his back as his dick goes flaccid. Someone's fist is smashing on Leo's door, it sounds just like Mean Mike.

150

"Oh my God! It's me 'usband!"

Leo has never known it was possible to dress so quickly. He pauses for one deep breath as he zips up Beverly's dress and lights a cigarette with a shaky hand.

"Why didn't yer tell me yer was married?" He is lacing up his boots at a rate that is making him dizzy. Beverly, white as a sheet, blabs over her tears:

"I meant to, 'onest Leo, but everythin' was so perfectly luvly, I didn't wanna spoil it, I didn't want it to end, I kept on saying to meself, after this I'll tell 'im I 'ave to go 'ome, but I just didn't want to, right up to falling asleep last night, I didn't mean to fall to sleep Leo, then I thought what 'arm would an 'ours nap do, it was so nice just layin' there in yer arms Leo. Please don't be angry with me, I know it was selfish but everything with Mike is so 'orrid, 'e's never nice to me Leo."

Oh God, tears. What to do about tears. He addresses her in a softer voice.

"Well, never mind all that now, let's find a way to get yer outta 'ere."

Leo stands and scratches his chin for a minute, Mean Mike pounds and yells at the door. Beverly walks around looking for suitable hiding places but nothing seems adequate. The phone rings. Leo dares the passage, passes the front door and gets to the sitting room.

" 'Ello."

"Leo, it's me, Barocco, thank God you're there! You've got to help me."

"Barocco I can't talk right now mate, yer gonna 'ave to call back."

"Then get me Vince man, this is an emergency! Come on Leo, please hurry up, you've got to get me out of here."

"Barocco, phone back in 'aft an 'our mate. Sorry, gotta go."

"Don't hang up Leo. Leo? You bastarrrr...! "

Leo places the receiver down and negotiates the corridor once more.

"Leo," she says "over 'ere," she beckons him to a window. Leo looks out onto the first floor balconies, which in their turn look out onto the workshops' yard.

"Leo, ain't that Ruby Rutt's balcony?"

151

They look down on a neat tidy balcony with everything in its place and put away for the winter. There are some large earthenware pots with evergreen miniature trees and shrubbery. Gnomes stand around here and there. There are some barren half barrels and window boxes painted a hi-gloss dark green to match the shutters on the windows and a long box that runs the whole length of the back end of Ruby's balcony. In the summer she grows honeysuckle out of this box, letting it flow into the yard below. On a hot day the lightest of breezes fills the entire yard and workshops with its subtle sweet seductive scent.

"Yea that's right. Do yer know 'er then?"

"She's me Nan's best-mate. Oh Leo we're saved. Yer 'ave got some rope or something ain't yer?" Leo thinks for three whole seconds.

"No."

"What yer mean no? Yer got to 'ave somethin', 'ow can yer be so sure?"

" 'Cause I lent it all to Sid and Vince for loadin' up the van for the gig last night, and they ain't given it back yet."

"Well take another look Leo, maybe yer missed somethin', I'll go and give Ruby a ring."

They look at each other. They both know what that means, she will have to pass the front door, where Mean Mike is alternatively kicking and bashing, yelling and trying to look through the letter box. She swallows hard, waits for him to start his hammering again and makes a run for it. It is with shaking hands she dials Ruby's number.

"I can't hear you dear, somebody's making the most tremendous racket upstairs, yelling and screaming and trying to smash the door down, you've never heard anything like it."

"Well actually I 'ave Ruby because I'm up there."

"You're where dear?"

"I'm upstairs in the flat above yer Ruby," she is scared of Mike hearing her if she speaks much louder, "and that's Mike yer can 'ear."

"You dear, what are you doing up there?"

"Well it's rather a long story Ruby, right now I need to get outta 'ere. 'Ave yer gotta ladder or some rope or something, so I can climb down to yer balcony?"

152

"Don't you worry dear, now just don't you worry. Auntie Ruby will take care of you," and she hangs up.

"What's takin' 'er so long?" says Leo. Beverly has made it back to the kitchen.
"It's 'er feet. Gout, bunions, yer know."
With that the door opens below and Ruby waddles out clutching a rickety old step ladder that. When she holds it up to the wall, even at a steep angle, barely covers half the distance. It was hopeless.
"Only one thing for it," says Leo. And with that he sweeps Beverly off her feet, as if she is no heavier than a feather, climbs onto the window sill and jumps.

~

She dresses and is out of the door quicker than she ever could have imagined possible even without her disgusting, still half inebriated state. Walking at a half trot, left eye closed and head turned away from heaven's fiery eye, she hopes and prays not to run into anyone she knows; laddered stockings and bruised, grazed knees.
It comes back to her in a flash. Dancing on a small round table, the table falls over, glasses, drinks, ice bucket and contents, all over the floor, being helped to her feet. She blushes even in recollection. God, she is lucky not to be cut to shreds. She remembers meeting some acquaintances at Gary's, a manager of a club and two bartenders from Stringfellows. They had gone to The Cinder Box, a sleazy grubby little joint in a basement off a low narrow alley. She had done a lot of drinking, she remembers at least three bottles of champagne being sent over before starting on the cognac. She also remembers several visits to the toilet to powder her nose. Then a sea of faces, noise and confusion, the incident with the table and then what? Nothing.
It has just gone noon. Around the next corner, first stairwell and she will be home and dry. Keys poised in a warm, sticky hand, she practically breaks into a run. Rounding the corner she collides with Fen. Fen is pacing the pavements at a fanatical rate cradling Scud in his arms; Nancy is running after him brandishing Tom's cut-throat razor. Knocked back and slightly winded, she coughs

153

roughly as Fen turns to meet Scud's assailant. He launches into one of his exhilarative monologues, accompanied by one gesturing arm, as his large spidery stature dominates the pavement. Just at that moment, a black taxi cab pulls up on the other side of the spectacle and an immaculate foot dressed in black Italian leather emerges. Mother!

Kate looks at her watch. Her mother is thirty-five minutes early. This is bad, very bad.

"I'm 'aving that dog's bollocks for me earrin's and I'll be drownin' 'is little bastards at birth!" bellows Nancy.

"Yer leave me Scud alone, 'e didn't do anythin' that didn't come natural!"

"Don't yer natural me, yer filthy men think anythin' and everythin's natural. It's that disgustin' creature of yours and me Pookie that ain't natural."

"Your Pookie's a slut!"

"Oh, ohh! " Nancy is actually speechless for some seconds.

"Why yer beastly, beastly man!"

Fen turns and runs around the corner with Nancy in hot pursuit. Seconds later a police car shoots by and can be heard screeching to a halt.

Doing her best to look as bright as possible Kate runs up to her mother, every stride jolting her sore shrunken brain against the rock hard interior of her skull.

"Mother!" Her Mother turns. A critical eye runs over Kate, noting every little detail in about two seconds. Kate shudders.

"So shall I ask the driver to keep the clock running dear?" asks her Mother, with a voice so sugary sweet.

"What do you think?" answers Kate. Kate's mother turns back to the window of the cab.

"Stop the clock driver." The sweetness in her voice has turned sharp and sour.

~

Not far away Big Joe lies curled up, weeping like a little boy.

~

Leonard stands on the street listening to the row coming from upstairs. Married women, what had he always told the lad about married women? Fun but trouble. And it would seem the lad had picked one with a psychotic husband.

"BEV-ER-LY!"

What to do?

By now a small crowd was gathering around the bottom of the stairwell. His roaming eyes settle on Mrs. Patel and instinctively he raises his hat. He is finding himself more and more taken by these graceful eastern beauties as he matured, but he is going off on a tangent here.

As it happens Leonard is one of the few people Mrs. Patel approves of. He has very good manners and his grandson works hard.

"Mrs. Patel, I was wondering if I may borrow your mother-in-law?"

Mrs. Patel could have smiled if it was more in her nature. He wants to take her mother-in-law up to where Mike the Mean is behaving like a murderous maniac.

"Why certainly Mr. Humbolt."

"Dear lady, I don't know how I am ever going to thank you, but thank you so much!"

What is it these English always say? Oh yes!

"The pleasure is all mine."

Leonard reaches Leo's flat with Mrs. Patel Senior on his arm. She has been briefed her part in the mission, translated to her by her daughter-in-law. Leonard is her husband and she is to hold onto his arm and agree to whatever he says.

"Excuse me young man can I help you?"

"What the fuck do yer want yer old git? BEV-ER-LY!"

SMASH, BANG, WALLOP.

"I don't know what you are expecting to find here but I think there must be some kind of mistake. My good lady and I abide here, there is no Beverly."

"Bollocks! This is that fuckin' Leo Humbolt's place, I 'ad three different fuckers' tell me."

"And they were right, I am Leonard Humbolt, would you like to see my library card?"

"What the fuck are yer on about?"

"Young man, you obviously have the wrong Humbolt."

"Ho, ho. Lost in valley of jolly green giant."

Leonard and Mean Mike forget their differences for a moment and stare at Mrs. Patel.

"What the fuck ... "

Leonard taps his temple as he rolls his eyes towards her and nods at Mike who continues.

"So yer live 'ere do yer?"

There is something familiar about the old cunt, but he can't place it. Maybe he has seen him around, these stairwells do look all the same after all

"And this is yer Mrs.?"

"Yes, yes." Leonard nods vigorously, looking pointedly at Mrs. Patel who does the same. Mean Mike starts to shift his weight around and pull at his cuffs. He looks up the stairs and down, and is just making up his mind to leave when heavy footsteps come from inside, bolts are drawn and Leo opens the door.

" 'Ello Mike, sorry to take so long I was 'aving a crap."

Wham! Leo receives a punch in the mouth that sends him flying down the corridor and onto the floor where he lies dazed. Stunned for a minute he becomes aware that Mean Mike is busy ransacking his flat, giving him a sharp kick in the ribs for good measure as he steps over him. Nothing! Mean Mike stands with his hands on his hips in the middle of the kitchen. Leo gets to his feet slowly using the walls to balance. Mike turns to leave but not before instilling a final threat. Pressing his face up about two inches from Leo's, he ogles.

"If I ever fuckin' find out that yer been near me fuckin' wife I'll kick yer fuckin' 'ead in! " and with that he head butts poor Leo, breaking his nose and departs, but not before spilling out a whole cesspool of abuse in Leonard's direction, until he looks up and sees Fat Sid coming down the stairs, where after he decides it best to leave, and quickly.

Leonard helps his grandson into a seat. Others arrives on the scene. Vince answers the phone while Fat Sid fetches ice for Leo's rapidly darkening eyes. His grandfather cleans the blood off his face and Nick checks his neck and ribs. And then the curious arrive such as Robert and young Mrs. Patel; even Dick the yuppie puts his head round the corner.

"Leo mate, if he had just been here a minute longer, I was preparing a little kick-boxing for him, la-ki!" Dick strikes a pose, impressing no one.

"I do hope it was worth it Sparky," says Leonard.

Vince returns to the room.

"That was Barocco, he's wants someone to pick him up from Maudsely Hospital. Apparently he woke up this morning in a padded cell wearing a strait jacket."

The older Mrs. Patel nods earnestly.

"There's a lot of ham in a can of Spam."

~

Kate's mother practically throws her hat and coat at Kate, Kate drops them. Her mother sits at the kitchen table, her aura pulsating with scorn and gleeful spite. She examines the various reading materials like a princess holding a navvy's prick and finally selects a 50's Vogue.

Kate sets to making coffee, a good idea she thinks. Grinding the beans nearly makes her head explode. When she opens up the filter compartment a soggy, cold filter with contents still occupies it. Halfway to the bin the filter gives out and the old coffee drops to the floor. After putting a new filter in place, she tips the freshly ground beans into the filter, mineral water into the percolator and switches the percolator on. Crawling around on her hands and knees in her pathetic state, it seems to be taking an eternity to clear up the mess. Suddenly she becomes aware of the smell of burning coffee. Kneeling up on her poor, sore knees she can see only about half an inch of fluid is actually in the pot and nothing seems to be dripping through. Raising herself with great difficulty on her ever stiffening joints, she opens the filter. Boiling water spills out all over the counter top and her left thumb. Stifling a scream she hastily turns on a tap and sticks her thumb under scolding water. Jerking her hand away her elbow hits the dish rack and two coffee mugs and a glass crash to earth. Her mother shrieks and places her hand to her chest.

"Goodness Katherine you don't seem to be able to do the simplest thing. Why don't you go and look after that hand of yours. And don't you worry about me I've quite gone off the idea of coffee now anyway! "

157

Kate's mother sits with the face of a martyr, not meaning a word of what she says.

"O.K." says Kate and walking past her mother to the bathroom she grabs the cord of the percolator and tugs it hard, but rather than pull the plug from the socket she merely loosens the wires inside, they touch causing the circuit to short and there is another big bang and a second shriek passes her mother's lips and all the lights go off.

She goes into the bathroom and shuts the door resisting the urge to slam it out of consideration to her cranium as much as anything. The shower is a mixed blessing, washing away the grime of the night before but increasing her consciousness of her circumstances. All she wants to do is sleep; drink great quantities of water to quench her unquenchable thirst and sleep. And that is just what she is not going to get. She steps out of the shower and is giving her face and teeth a good wash, when she becomes aware of pressure building up at the top of her neck under her skull. It runs up over her forehead, down her temples and to the back of her head again, in the form of a hot then cold sweat. She is going to faint, vomit then faint, and she can do neither, not with her mother and her bat ears in the next room. Quickly she drops to her knees, forgetting they are cut and bruised and turns on the cold faucet of the bath and sticks her head under the icy flow. Wetting a flannel, she sits leaning naked against the door, wiping it around her face and behind her ears and neck. Focusing on some deep breathing, she wills the nausea away. Just then there is a plaintive knock on the door.

"Kate darling, we have company. A gentleman caller."

~

So Nancy finds herself arrested for the second time in less than twenty-four hours. Taken away last night handcuffed to Dave, she now has to suffer Mean Mike. He has been thrown on top of her after a short scuffle at the bottom of Leo's stairwell. The police have been looking for Mean Mike all night, since witnesses had reported a fight involving him breaking out moments before the recently emptied cash box had been snatched up by a man later found to be his cousin.

"Three pounds and sixty pence. Where did yer think three pounds bloody sixty was goin' to get yer?"

The arresting officer, an Inspector Grey, seated in the front passenger seat, addresses Mean Mike. The driver sniggers.

"A one-way ticket to Brixton for six months, that's where it's goin', to get yer. Still on parole for that Woolworth's job aren't yer?"

Both men laugh. Even Nancy manages a little smile, she has never heard of a grown man getting caught stealing from Woolworths.

"Fuck off!"

"Now, now, Michael, lady present."

Mean Mike glances at Nancy out of the comer of his eyes; that snobby fucking bitch from The Rhinoceros.

"What the fuck are yer doing 'ere, robbed a church box?"

"Assaulting a police officer in the line of duty yesterday, and brandishing a lethal weapon the next. A bit out of yer league Michael, stuff which would make yer old man proud I dare say. I'd love to be a fly on the wall when 'e gets wind of yer latest contribution to the family legacy! "

"Fuck yer, yer cunt!"

"What was that Michael?" says the Inspector, in not too nice a tone of voice, his eyes become grim slits.

"Nuffink." replies Mike quietly, as he looks out of the window and sulks.

"Good."

~

She comes out of the bathroom towel clad. Professor Scribble sits in the corner, nose wrinkling, looking like an overweight rodent, two pinpoint eyes look down that nose through very thick glasses; he is holding a bunch of flowers. Kate's mother, on the edge of her chair affects one of her laughs, a laugh kept especially for men she is trying to impress. Looking over her shoulder at Kate she exclaims sweetly.

"Kate darling, you got the sack!"

She looks from her mother to Scribble and back again, Scribble wriggling his nose faster and faster. The glass and crockery still lie on the floor, the spilt coffee on the counter top.

"Excuse me," says Kate, and crosses the kitchen to get to her bedroom. Scribble holds out the flowers as she passes blocking her way.

"For you Kate."

"Why isn't that nice dear, such beautiful ..."

"Thank you, but excuse me," she brushes past into her room.

First things first. She sits down at her dressing table, opens a secret drawer and fishes out a tobacco tin which holds a small mirror, razor blade, half a straw and a packet made out of meticulously folded white paper. She opens the packet as carefully as she can with shaking hands and spills out the entire contents onto the mirror. Then she empties the contents of her evening bag out onto the dressing table. Shit, is that all she has left. She checks her compact and cigarette case to no avail, only one of the original four packages remain and that is more empty than full. She adds the contents of the second packet to the first and goes to work with the razor blade, chopping and smoothing the powder out into two little white lines. She leans over and snorts a line. There is a knock on the door and, not waiting for a reply, her mother bursts in. Kate lets the straw drop from her hand onto her dressing table and turning slightly towards the door she keeps her eyes on her mother as she opens the top draw and sweeps everything inside. Her mother fails to notice a thing, her usual vigilance being offset by her excitement. Shutting the door, with a stage whisper that Kate is quite sure Scribble can hear, her mother exclaims:

"A professor darling, Ph.D. from Balliol College Oxford! Like Uncle Jeremy dear and ..."

"Mother, could you give me just five minutes."

Kate's mother sniffs and stands stiffly, Kate has really done it now.

"Well I can see when I'm not wanted." She runs the same critical eye over the room as she had over Kate twenty minutes earlier.

"I will go and entertain YOUR guest for you."

"Mother you let him in, I've been trying to avoid the man for months. It's bad enough having to work with him all week without having him pestering me morning, noon and bloody night."

"You should consider yourself lucky to have someone decent and well educated interested in you my girl. You're not exactly a prize catch yourself. Living in a pokey little flat in South London and running around with God knows who, staying out all night and now you haven't even got a job and that was a good job too, more than you deserved and ..."

During her mother's bitchy outburst, Kate opens the door. Taking her gently but firmly by the shoulders she makes her take a step backwards into the hallway and quietly pulls the door shut.

"Perhaps this isn't a good time?" Kate hears Scribble ask.

"Nonsense Professor. You stay right where you are; Katherine said she'll be right out."

Kate was shaking inside, sometimes she felt as if she could kill her.

~

Edith opens the front door in her bath robe and a towel wrapped around her head. It quite throws Silvia, usually she opens the door with her coat over one arm, bag in the other, and keys in hand.

"Oh. Yer not ready" she says and checks her watch.

"That's right dearie. Why don't yer come in and sit yerself down, there's tea in the pot 'elp yerself."

"I've got Jerry and Freddy in the car."

"Oh yes, 'ow could I forget. I suppose it's just as well there's two of 'em then, they can talk and 'it each other for ten minutes can't they?"

Silva was just about to protest when she realizes her mother is right. They are tough little buggers who run around the streets half the time anyway, they can handle a back of a car for a little while. Besides she can keep an eye on them out of the window.

"I wonder 'ow Bev and Mikes' evenin' went. I 'ope 'e was able to pull off sometime 'alf decent for 'er. God knows she deserves it."

Silva sits at the kitchen table and flips through a magazine. Edith's voice comes from the bedroom.

"Did I 'ear yer say 'e'd invited that cousin of 'is up to stay the weekend?"

"Yes."

161

"What the 'ell's 'e thinkin, of! There's yer gone to all the trouble to look after those two little bastards of 'is, and then there's that friend of 'ers, nice girl, what's 'er name?"

"Linda."

"Yes that's right, Linda, who's taken the baby for 'er, and 'e goes and invites up that little shit."

"I know."

For a while silence prevails. All that can be heard is Silvia turning the pages of the magazine, Edith singing in the bedroom, the clock ticking, the birds a twittering, the constant dim rumbling and turbulence of city traffic, the pained moaning and groaning from trains, and the scream of the flight path over their heads.

Something is certainly amiss. Even Edith's attack on her grandson-in-law has only been half-hearted, lacking all its usually zeal of vindictiveness. And in spite of the fact she is running late she is very perky and relaxed, singing away like a jolly little cricket in the next room. Edith flounces into the kitchen in a flowery frilly dress smelling of lilies of the valley. She puts on her cardigan, and her shoes and coat, and picks up her handbag and keys from the mantelpiece. She looks slyly at her daughter with a crooked hat and a crooked grin and a daft expression.

"What's got into yer Ma?"

"What do yer mean?" Edith says grinning happily.

"You're actin' kinda odd."

"Can't a girl be late for once in 'er life?"

"It's more than just that, it's something about you, I can't put me finger on it."

"Well I'm afraid I can't 'elp yer there dearie. The only thin' I can think of that may 'ave the slightest bearin' on the matter is that I got me leg over last night, what do yer think?"

"Ma!"

"Hee hee hee, I thought that would get yer!"

"Who? Do I know 'im?"

"The gentleman in question goes by the name of Leonard Humbolt."

"That young man who lives over Ruby!"

"No, good God, now that would be somethin' at my age! At least if it wasn't for the, you know, 'is little visitors. No, 'is grandfather's visiting for the weekend, up from 'Astings. Mr. Three Times! Ha ha ha! "

162

"And 'ow do yer know 'e ain't got 'em, staying there and all that?"

"Oh, they got rid of the bed and everything ages ago! Besides we used johnies."

" 'E carries condoms around with 'im?"

"No, I supplied them, and guess what."

"I can't imagine and I don't know if I want to."

"We smoked some pow!"

"Pow?"

"You know, that calibus stuff that's good for yer arthritis and makes yer randy."

"Yer mean pot, Gordon Bennet Ma! Now don't tell me yer supplied that an' all. It's illegal, yer can be arrested for that yer know."

"I asked one of the youngsters and they gave me two 'joints', that's what yer call 'em, the cigarettes, joints. Anyway Leonard tried some too and 'e liked it and it made 'im randy ..."

"OK,OK, Ma. I get the picture."

"I've got some left would yer like to try it?"

Edith opens her hand bag and finds the half of the original joint she and Kate had shared. It is just then that the phone rings.

"I expect that's our Bev seein' what's 'appened to us, Miss Punctuality 'erself!" says Edith, and goes to the bedroom to answer the call.

"Silv it's our Bev, she wants to 'ave a word with yer. She's at Ruby's."

Silvia is just taking the receiver from Edith when something flashes past the window. Edith pushes up the window and looks down to meet the puce face of Constable Wright standing in a large puddle of water, his big blue-tit hat lays on the ground beside him.

~

Freshly made up and in a burgundy silk trouser suit, Kate re-enters the kitchen. Crockery, glass and coffee lie untouched and Scribble once more blocks her way with the bouquet. It is all she can manage not to snatch it out of his hand. However self-control rules and she takes them graciously, takes a pair of scissors out of the kitchen drawer, and removes all the ends with one clean cut. Ripping the cellophane off, she throws the flowers into a vase, and sticks the vase under the tap for a moment and very matter-of-factly places them on the table.

"Really Katherine, all those flower arranging classes gone to waste."

Kate's mother looks at Scribble and giggles, a coy girlish giggle. Scribble grins and wriggles his nose.

~

She is grateful for the warm, fleecy track suit Nick has given her but she is even more grateful for the little bit of dignity he has allowed her to restore by giving her the chance to clean herself up, even going as far as fresh towels and a toothbrush. He has handed her the track suit at the same time.

"Me Nan's Christmas present. The pink side of plum an' luckily at least four inches too short in the leg, so I don't even 'ave to wear 'em once for show, so yer most welcome to keep 'em! "

When she is ready, he calls the ambulance and finds her a pair of mega-thick hiking socks and a plimsoll for her good foot.

"Now these I do want back! " he refers to the socks, "I'm gonna 'ike the Appalachian Trail this summer, the longest continuous footpath in the World, takin' yer up the east coast of America via the Appalachian Mountains."

"How I envy yer bein' able to do somethin' like that. I'd love to see some of those places yer see on the telly. The pyramids, beaches with palm trees, Mount Everest."

"Mount Everest?"

"Oh yes, the biggest mountain in the whole World, imagine! When yer think of what these mountains are, so 'igh their 'eads are in the clouds, all covered with ice and snow, the biggest things on earth! Seeing Everest must be like meeting the King of the Giants."

"What would yet say if I told yer there's a way yer could go and see Everest?"

"Oh, I could never do somethin' like that luv."

"If you got some 'elp with yer drinkin' yer might, and I'll tell yer somethin' for nothin', yer'll be amazed at what a sober life will bring yer if yer let it. I thank God every day for the life I 'ave now. Well actually I thank God for 'avin' a life. The old Nick, drunk Nick, would never 'ad been flying off to go on a three thousand mile 'ike!

The old Nick would 'ave thought there was somethin' wrong with Nick. Five pubs within stumbling distance, an off-license and a nice comfortable bed to fall down unconscious on. What else could I 'ave wanted for?" Kate-beautiful adorable Kate; living just around the corner all this time. A weight in his heart and heaviness on his soul. He had loved her from a distance for so long, too long.

"I can't stop Nick," she starts shaking and crying, "and I 'ate meself. I 'ate meself for being so weak and pathetic. Every day for months now I've been saying today, today I won't drink and I get to about four o'clock and that's it, I cave. I feel so nervous, so shaky, sick."

"It's OK Ang, it's not you, it's the disease. We were all like that to begin with, this ain't somethin' yer goin' to be able to do on your own, yer 'ave to accept that and ask for 'elp." Nick gets up and comes back with a pamphlet and a handkerchief.

"When yer finish at the 'ospital yer could do a number of things. For instance yer could go 'ome, yer could go to the pub or yer could meet me 'ere."

There are footsteps and a knock on the door.

"Ambulance?" A man calls through the letter box.

Nick hands Angela the pamphlet, a line of which he has highlighted and goes to answer the door.

~

The mini-cab is also not a success, they sent a Renault 4 with a crossed-eyed driver. Kate's mother sits perched with her nose in the air.

"I can't believe you insistently invited him to Grandma's party in spite of the fact I asked you not to and he didn't want to come. You are such a control freak."

"And I can't believe that you would kick your mother so hard in the shin, that you bruised her leg and laddered her tights."

"And I've already apologized for that but you were told quite blatantly that the man irritated the fuck out of me."

"Katherine! Language. What do you think the driver will think!"

"London cab driver Mother? Been there, seen it, heard it. Do you think one little "fuck" is going to shock him?"

"Katherine!"

"Oh fuck-fuck-fuck-fuck-fuck!" and she finds herself reduced to the mentality of a five year old; her mother has triumphed once more.

The rest of the journey continues in silence, her mother trying not to smirk. Occasionally she raises her left leg to examine the nonexistent bruise, brushing off the nonexistent dust from the pair of very good tights Kate has given her.

She is actually grateful to Scribble for once. He had taken her on one side while her mother had been changing her tights.

"Kate sorry about my big mouth," he gestured towards the bathroom. "What I came to try to tell you is the job's yours if you want it. I have it on good authority that 'Mister' Pebble was not all together honest on his application."

Yes! She had known it, always trust gut instincts!

"Which means we're both in for a promotion soon, making me your immediate boss! Oh, don't worry. I know a beautiful young woman isn't going to be interested in a colossal bookworm such as myself, but I couldn't call myself a man if I didn't keep trying Kate. I have to say that over the past five years it's been a privilege to work beside such a talented and beautiful individual. Oh to hell with it; call me sexist; talented and gorgeous woman, and I think together we can make the department a happy working environment for everyone, as well as creating the best restoration workshop in Britain, maybe even Europe."

"Why thank you so much Christopher, that's a terrific leap of faith and I'm honoured, I won't let you down. I can't begin to tell you how relieved I am. It couldn't have been easy to get round Hawkings, you're a good friend."

"Well, he wants to see you half-an-hour early tomorrow morning. Don't worry, he knows you're valuable; he just wants you to eat a piece of humble pie. Apparently the derogatory remark about homosexuality wasn't apt, the museum being an equal opportunity employer etc." Kate giggles.

"I thought it was more of a derogatory remark against pineapples myself!"

They hear the door knob on the toilet door rattle and Professor Scribble rises and retrieves his hat from his chair.

"Ah, Prudence. I didn't finish my story. The gallery asked me to visit your daughter this weekend. They're anxious not to lose the good with the bad."

"Why that's so generous of them!"

"To the contrary, Kate's top of her trade Prudence, she could get a job anywhere and they know it."

Kate smiled for the first time that day, touched by his confidence in her, and grateful to see her mother looking most put out.

"So are you joining us Professor?" The woman was relentless.

"Thank you Prudence but no, I have some prior engagements."

"Anything you can get out of?" she giggled for no apparent reason.

"No." he answered bluntly.

"Oh." She was not used to not getting her way.

The mini-cab pulls up outside The Park Lane Hotel. Kate thrusts the fare plus a generous tip into the driver's hand and would have jumped out and run up the stairs if she could have managed it. However she raises herself cautiously. After holding open the door for her mother, she deliberately slams it a little too hard. Prudence jumps and Kate is reminded of her own delicate condition. A wave of dizziness spins through her, she hopes she is going to be able to make it through the occasion. If she passes out, or is sick or something, she will never hear the last of it. The lift from the cocaine is wearing off; she could have really done with that second line. She had sniffed around with the straw but had managed to scavenge more dust than powder. What she really needs is a-hair-of-the-dog and some not too rich food to soak up the acid in her stomach.

~

Carter Street police station, as all police stations, is a strange place. A seemingly inoffensive, almost pretty building on the outside, inside is a curious maze of pokey little rooms with incredibly high ceilings for their size. The reception area is no exception. A potbellied fat-legged station sergeant in too tight trousers sits on a high stool behind a counter not much bigger than a hat check. Beside him sits a fresh faced youth, his uniform still stiff with newness. The station sergeant told Alec to take a seat over an hour and a half ago. On one hand Alec is bored and pissed off at being kept waiting, on the other he is paranoid. He does not want to look at the camera because he does not want to behave suspiciously but at the same time he does not want to avoid looking and behaving suspiciously. It is quite a dilemma. Finally he takes a deep breath and decides to slowly check things out around the room, including the camera, an act done in the face of innocent curiosity.

"Hurray!" chorus the four plain clothes detectives and seven uniformed men. Detective Shaw stops the watch.

"One 'our, forty-two minutes and seven seconds."

"That's gotta be some kind of record!"

"It's up there," says Detective Healy, reaching in his back pocket for his wallet. He happily collects his winnings and the usual well-meant and not so well meant insults.

"Shall I brin' 'im down?" asks a pasty faced officer, none too pleased at losing a tenner. The detective says nothing for a while, as if he is bouncing the idea back and forth in his head, those who know him start to laugh at his sadistic dry humour.

"I suppose so…" he says in lazy resignation, his grin betraying his bored drawn out voice. Then quite straight faced he adds an afterthought.

"Inspector Grey go with 'im, I'd like yer both to escort Mr. Evans."

The phone rings at the front desk. Every one of the dozen or so of those waiting and their companions look up expectantly. The flabby policeman grunts into to the receiver three times over the next minute then places it down. Without looking up he picks up a newspaper, looks at it and puts it down again. He puts his hand in his breast pocket and fiddles with his pen while he talks inaudibly to the private at his side. Anxiety subsides to apathy. Shoulders droop and eyes are downcast again. About fifteen seconds later the gruff, bad tempered utterance of the crotch-pinched sergeant cuts into the atmosphere.

"Alec Evans?"

~

The Oak Room of the small hotel is just that. Its oak beamed ceiling is low but the banquet room suffers no loss of grandeur for it. The room is paneled in oak, stained Jacobean and enriched by centuries of elbow grease and polish. The floor's wide oak boards are exquisitely laid with bow-tie joinery.

To her left is a bar and lounge area, carpeted with a lush thick gold pile and decorated in emerald green and deep blood red. There are a number of beautiful sofas set between partitions of wooden lattice and cut glass. These booths hold hefty oak tables with three inch thick tops and low comfortable seating. To her right is the dining area with a traditional T-shaped table covered with embossed white cloths and with serviettes to match. Silver and crystal sparkle throughout and bouquets of spring flowers are placed periodically in cut glass vases engraved with the hotel's insignia. Oil paintings in gilt frames adorn the walls; portraits and typical English landscapes, the Fox and Hounds, and the like.

Across the room an impressive fire burns in a magnificent stone fire place. Here twisted and twitching in his wheelchair sits Cousin Georgie, Martini glass clutched in his poor deformed hand. His meditative stare flickers, continually roaming from the flames to the shapely behind of a very pretty young waiter. Kate walks across the room and plants a kiss on his cheek.

"You can have too much of a good thing you know!"

"Oh no you can't! Don't ever say that again! You look divine darling, if not somewhat shady around the eyes. Oh don't worry honey-pop, it quite suits you actually, adds to your feminine mystique. A real man would fine it sexy for sure."

"And there's not many of those around."

"Oh! You think you can complain! At least you can dream, I can only imagine. It's like dear Quinton said, 'the trouble with a real man is that a real man wants is a real woman'."

Here they both drift off for a second with thoughts of biceps, broad shoulders and the likes. Suddenly Kate notices the Vicar making a beeline in their direction.

"I better go and say hello to birthday girl, where is she?"

No sooner has Georgie pointed her towards the bar than he is confronted by the Vicar. With no visible means of escape he stares desperately after Kate who smiles and calls out:

"Enjoy!"

"Well hello Georgie, and how are you?" the Vicar asks him in a patronizing voice that holds a remarkable resemblance to Margaret Thatcher.

Georgie starts jerking and drooling.

"Bla, bla, bla, bla, bla!"

Kate finds her Grandmother holding court with a champagne glass in hand, surrounded by good-looking young men and fancy gift-wrapped parcels. The sortee is in honor of the old woman's eightieth birthday and as Martha has aged so has her contempt for social conventions and etiquette. She is skilled at saying exactly what she thinks when and as she thinks it, which makes her popular and unpopular, as well as something of a social liability as Prudence perceives it. Finding her mother-in-law's traits increasingly embarrassing and disturbing, Prudence has started trying to pass her off as a little touched, but she does not fool many people, so she has had to settle for fooling herself.

"Grandma!"

"Katie! Come and give your old grandmother a kiss. "

Kate gently shoves a couple of boxes out of the way with her feet.

"That's right, you just give those a darn good kick! Probably just full of toilettes anyway, why do people give old people so many toiletries? Do they think all we do is pee and crap in our pants all the time?"

A general titter sweep through her audience. Martha is never happier than when she is centre of attention. Kate carefully lowers herself onto one knee and they embrace.

"You just got here? Came with your mother ah?"

They give each other a knowing look.

"The bloody Vicar's here."

"Now Gran!"

"Whatever did she invite him for? She knows I can't stand the bloody man. All plaintive looks and solumn little pieces of advice about things he knows bugger all about. Idiot. You know he invited me to some pensioners coffee morning at the rectory? Coffee morning! I'd rather go to a Scotch morning. And what do I want to be surrounded by a lot of miserable grumbling old farts for? It's you youngens I like," she pinches Kate's cheek," it's you younguns that keep me going!"

"I hope so, look what I've got." Kate reaches in her jacket pocket and pulls out an envelope and hands it to Martha, who has it open in a second.

"Tickets for B.B.King at Ronnie Scott's; now that's my idea of a present."

"And afterward I thought we could go somewhere dark and sleazy if we feel like it."

"And do some dancing; that sounds like my kind of birthday. That's my girl! "

There is a brief silence whilst Martha holds both of Kate's hands and looks at her, a second of sadness passes over the old woman's face and then she laughs again.

"Now run along and get yourself some champers, we'll speak more later."

~

Selene can imagine how easy it must have been for an intelligent woman like Martha to get around the likes of Dick. Dick is an avid social climber and she expects that all Martha had to do is to drop a corporation here and a name there. She must have had him hanging onto her every word. She watches her husband smooth his hair in the mirror; he looks like he is going for a job interview. Idiot.

"Now let's take a look at you."

Selene is deliberately wearing an unremarkable blue dress from one of the acceptable yuppie labels. It comes down to her shins, buttons up the front to a little collar and has long sleeves gathered into buttoned cuffs. It is dull and boring, Dick likes it, he approves. She watches him strutting around the room like a rooster on speed. She had never known it was possible to hate someone as much as she hates her husband. In fact she even doubts she had known what hate was before Dick. She imagines a gun just lying on the coffee table near where she sits. Would she?

"O.K., I'm ready." Dick interrupts the flow of her thoughts. "Now don't forget, I expect you to circulate this afternoon not spend all your time drawing attention to yourself the way you do when you hang around with Kate and that cripple. I think you've

171

seen quite enough of them for one weekend. Martha tells me that your Godfather is the managing director of Exxon U.K.?"

"Did she?"

"Yes she did Selene. That along with a whole lot of other interesting tickle-tackle about her husband's side of the family. You've been holding out on me girl."

He pushes her shoulder playfully.

"I don't really take much notice of things like that."

"Meaning what?"

"Meaning I don't really take much notice of things like that." Oh no. Here we go.

"You know Selene, sometimes you can be a really stupid bitch. Get off your fat arse and get it in the car."

Robert watches them depart from his front window. Dick crosses over the road, opens his B.M.W. from the driver's side, gets in, buckles up and starts to drive off. Selene, holding a large gift wrapped package struggles with her seat belt, her door still half open. She manages to slam it as the car proceeds up the road and turns left onto the Walworth Road, before which Robert sees the passenger side door open briefly again as Selene frees the corner of her coat. He reckons on having at least three hours. Half an hour to drive there, if they are lucky, and half an hour back, and two hour minimum at the joint. Champagne reception served with hors d 'oeuvre, followed by a formal lunch; three hours easily. After overhearing about the party on Friday evening the details have been easy enough to obtain via the floorboards and the wonders of modern day audio.

He gives them twenty minutes to return for forgotten items over which time he lays out his tools in a way which would have made a surgeon proud. Then taking up a crow bar he starts to loosen several floor boards.

~

Kev is up at the squat having coffee with Vince and Little Wing, when Sid gets back with Barocco. He holds Jason and points out of the window at the bird feeder Little Wing has made.

"Birdies," he says, "birdies."

Jason laughs, waving his tiny arms around as he leans forward reaching for the sparrows. Suddenly a thrush comes to perch, scaring the timid sparrows away and breaks forth into song. Cautiously the sparrows return until within a short period of time, they are hopping around the thrush, happy once more.

Even with his back to the room Kev can tell something is wrong. Looking over his shoulder he speaks over Jason's coos and giggles.

"Sid?"

Sid is quite pale. He sits down heavily throwing down three different newspapers and spreading them out on the surface of the table. He lights a cigarette.

"Come an' take a look at this."

Of course, thinks Kev, the assassination, the riot. It already seemed like a dream. Twenty-four hours ago he would never have imagined all this, it is incredible the difference a day can make. He wonders how Alec is feeling. They all look over Sid's shoulder and yes, there it is, in two out of the three papers it shares the headlines. However the tabloid has been more exclusive and the headline reads:

ISLINGTON STRANGLER ARRESTED

Under which is a photo of Andy, their violinist. The article continues:

Police have now released the name of the man they have had in custody since last night and subsequently charged with the gruesome Islington Strangler Serial Killings, a chain of brutal murders which have claimed the lives of 12 women, 9 in Islington.

Andrew David Quinn 32, has apparently spent his 18 month reign of terror moving around cheap hotels, boarding houses and squats in and around the Islington area. His victims were all female poodle owners with exception of his first victim Susan Clarke 41, who owned a pug.

Quinn, described by squatter Timothy Vain 29, as a 'quietly spoken, intelligent, nonentity', garroted his victims with a violin string before tying and hanging them upside down by the ankles. He then disemboweled the women, also removing the heart, liver and kidneys, and fed them to the poodles before putting the unfortunate canines to the same fate.

"Good God." says Vince. The thrush sings on over the silence.

~

"It's quite simple Mr. Evans, when yer say an explosion do yer mean the shatterin' of a large, and therefore noisy window, or the petrol tank going up on a bloody car?"

Detective Healy sits with one cheek of his rump on the table and the opposing foot on the floor. He reaches inside his leather jacket for the cigarettes in his breast pocket. Taking out a cigarette, and stumping the end a couple of times on the table top, he puts it between his lips and lights it with his gold Du Pont lighter.

"Good idea," thinks Alec, reaching for his cigarettes, but he is wrong.

"What do yer think yer doin'?"

The room seems to have suddenly gone very quiet, even the traffic seems to have stopped. There is only an irritating buzz coming from a clock high up on the dirty, scuffed yellow-ochre wall.

"No smoking! No one smokes in 'ere, no one! Inspector who smokes in 'ere?"

"Never seen anyone Sir."

"Officer?"

"No one ever smokes in 'ere, Sir," says the pasty flat-faced cop.

"So let's take it from the top again Mr. Evans and again and again, until yer memory serves yer better."

"I had been at Mrs. Zaidorf's for about an hour ..."

"And 'ow do yer know 'er exactly?"

"As I said, I'm a friend of her son's."

"So yer a friend of the family so to speak?"

"Yes."

"I thought last night was the first time yer met 'er?"

"Yes."

"Seems yer 'ave a pretty strange idea of what a friend of the family is. Well go on."

"Oh, well um ..."

"Yer 'ad been there about an 'our Mr. Evans."

"Oh yes, yes. And we were about halfway through the first course and we heard an explosion. We looked out of the window and the back of a police car was burning and all the skinheads were running out into the street."

"Yer don't like skin'eads do yer Mr. Evans?"

"Oh well ... ," Alec is getting very flustered again, and suddenly has the mad urge just to scream: I did it! I killed Lord Mosley! He takes a deep breath and manages to pull himself together.

"Does anybody?" Does his voice really sound that high and squeaky?

Detective Healy looks down at him and says nothing. A knock comes at the door and the officer opens it and speaks in low tones to someone Alec cannot see or hear at all. The detective never takes his eyes off Alec all this time, not even when the officer comes to the table and, turning his back to Alec, whispers in Detective Healy's ear. The officer returns to his position near the door and Detective Healy allows the quiet to become uncomfortable before he blows smoke all over Alec and leaves the room.

"Inspector" he gestures towards Alec with a motion of the head.

Inspector Grey wastes no time. Even as the door is shutting Detective Healy hears him launching into a new attack. The detective smiles and shakes his head. That Dennis is an evil bastard, a thoroughly nasty piece of work, the sort that makes one feel grateful that he is on your side. It is too bad for Mr. Evans that Grey's brother had been one of the badly injured duo of the welcoming party last night.

"Anything for me Bob?"

Detective Healy addresses a short, bald, bearded, bi-focaled man. Bob is on top of his profession. Even though he is close to retirement he has kept up to date up with his career to even the smallest developments of forensics. He has become a sort of father figure to the boys in blue. His domain in the laboratories has almost a religious feel, a peace haven of intelligence and scientific investigation done in a true 'who done it' spirit which would have made Sherlock proud. With all his years and experience Bob has seen it all.

"Yes, but not enough to get you a search warrant yet. Yes they are Winstons, not exactly the most unusual brand in the World, and the only thing slightly detectable is half a very smudged right thumb print on the uncrushed one."

" 'Ow about the empty packet?"

"Better luck there surprisingly, left hand, fore, middle and thumb."

"Bob, do us a favour."

"What's that John?"

"Keep the lid on this one. I know everyone's thinking I'm barking up the wrong tree but I've 'ave a feeling about this one from the moment I first set me eyes on 'im. I can't explain why."

"What, this piece of chicken-shit John? Really? Well, my grandmother always said to trust gut instincts and she had her gas money stolen out of her sugar tin by a nice young man who said he was from the Mormons. But tell me, what first drew your attention to him? I mean he sounds like a neurotic little queer to me, I heard from the lads he took nearly two hours to look at the camera!"

"One 'our, forty-two minutes and seven seconds Bob." Both men laugh. "OK, OK, I get the point. But still that's strange in itself."

"That's big time chicken-shit John!"

"Fancy a friendly wager?"

"What would you suggest?"

"Fifty quid."

"Fifty! Come on John you can do a little better than that can't you?"

"OK, 'undred."

"A hundred? You really think you're right on this one don't you? All right, a hundred it is."

Dr. Bob looks at his watch.

"Got to run. Don't leave Dennis in there with him for too long John, you'll have him making a nasty mess in his underpants."

Detective Healy gives Inspector Grey a few more minutes while he finishes his cigarette and then goes back in. The Inspector is holding up Alec by the lapels of his jacket.

"Inspector Grey, what 'ave I told yer about upsettin' yerself like this! Now put Mr. Evans down an' take some nice deep breaths. I read in the paper only yesterday about stress on the job. It can ruin yer love life apparently. That's right, good deep breaths there. Stress ever given yer the droop Mr. Evans?"

"I think that's a rather personal question," snaps Alec. The men laugh.

"Gentlemen, if yer would please leave the room, I'd like to talk to Mr. Evans alone."

Detective Healy resumes his lopsided position on the table while the other policemen leave. Then he pulls a chair up and sits opposite Alec resting his elbows on the table.

"Yer can 'ave that fag now Mr. Evans, I don't think anyone is goin' to interrupt us. It's just that if they see me lettin' yer break the rules they'll let everyone do it."

Alec is not taken in by his fatherly tone but reaches for his cigarettes anyway. He needs one. He is searching his pockets for his lighter when Detective Healy produces his, and silently a flame flickers on before him. Alec is beginning to hate that bloody lighter, like a thorn in his side.

"Yer a family man Mr. Evans?"

"One on the way Detective." He cannot resist it, he is going to be a daddy!

"Why congratulations Mr. Evans. Yer said earlier that yer were an artist?"

"Yes that's right."

" 'Ad any shows recently?"

"No, nothing for a while."

"But I suppose yer 'ave somethin' comin' up, right?"

"Actually nothing planned at the moment."

"That would make yer unemployed then."

And he starts scratching out something in his note book and writing something else beside it. He is getting bored and he has nothing to hold him on, perhaps Bob is right, just so much chicken-shit.

"That will be all for now Mr. Evans but don't leave town will yer?"

"Does that make me a suspect?"

"Mr. Evans, everybody who enters these rooms are suspect. Now do yer think yer can find yer own way back to reception or would yer like Inspector Grey to escort yer?"

~

Georgie is beckoning to Kate.

"Come here!" he mouths silently. Kate crosses the room and bends down. He whispers in her ear,

"The message has been delivered via the cloakroom attendant, Seline knows what she has to do. Now wheel me round

177

the room towards the staff exit behind that wall. When I say 'go', head straight behind the wall and through the double doors. There will be somebody waiting for us."

"The champagne-blonde waiter with the great arse?"

"Exactly." Georgie grins; she is as sharp as ever. "He'll open the doors for us, then we're to follow him."

"O.K. Mr. double-O-seven and a half!"

Kate takes the handles of Georgie's wheelchair and they proceed as planned, stopping every so often in front of a painting. Just as they are loitering around the exit Martha starts a boisterous chorus of 'Patrick McGinty's Goat'. Prudence drops into an armchair, receiving sympathy from the Vicar.

"Go!" says Georgie.

Without hesitation or looking back Kate pushes him behind the wall. The doors block their way but as if by magic one swings open and Kate sees it is indeed the waiter in question. He raises his finger to his lips and beckons them to follow. Turning left, and through another set of doors, then right, and to the end of a corridor which finishes in a T. Straight ahead is a small service lift. The waiter signals to them to stop and he looks furtively around while opening the doors.

"Quick," he says.

As smooth as clockwork Kate whisks Georgie into the lift. The waiter presses a button and an accordion of lattice-work closes behind them, a brass latch snaps shut loudly, as a brass arm opens slowly, extending the two halves of the outer door until all that is left of their handsome young waiter is his face framed with security glass. Then elevator jolts into ascent.

Once Kate negotiates the latch, the accordion door flies open as easily as it had shut. She wheels Georgie out into the dazzling winter's light and the pleasantly crisp air to meet the spectacular panorama that circles around them.

Directly behind the hotel lies the exclusive labyrinth of Mayfair. Venerated on the Monopoly board as the last stop before Go, its exquisite Georgian and neoclassical streets opened up to the splendours of Berkeley, Roosevelt and Grosvenor squares, the latter home of the American embassy. Raising her eyes, Kate contemplates the considerable scope of the skyline. Her scrutiny wanders west to east, starting at the gloomy characterless Home Office, to Westminster Abbey and a tiny Big Ben. A small silver strip of the Thames sparkles in the distance and she continues to pick out various riverside landmarks well after the embankments become obscured by rooftops. She reaches as far as the distant Canary Wharf development before moving on to the less distant office blocks belonging to the financial district of The City Of London. A little further east and closer still, Centrepoint stands out prominently. Once the tower was a youth hostel for the recently relocated, as well as low-budget tourists. These days such a quantity of homeless adolescents appeared on a nightly basis that only the sick or injured had any chance of being accommodated. In-between Centrepoint and Mayfair lay the chaotic shopping district of the West End, its daytime traffic progressing at a speed slower than that of a horse and cart. Next her eyes pass over a large building in the Euston area, Senate House; the archives of all the students attending British colleges and Universities past and present are kept here. It has a claim to fame on the silver-screen, given to it by the man-eating plants of 'The Day of the Tripids'. Also standing out on its lonesome is the top-heavy Telecom Tower. Once holiday-camp entrepreneur Billy Buckling's rotating restaurant was its crowning glory, but now the restaurant is closed and not expected to be reopened due to its liability as a terrorist attraction. For a moment Kate rests her eyes on the American Embassy before stretching them further and further over the seemingly never ending mass of North London.

Kate wheels Georgie to the front of the building and the greenery of Hyde Park spreads out before them. Another river, the Serpentine, sparkles happily in the sunshine and immediately across the road they overlook a fountain where a couple of gilded, naked figures and four cherubs cavort gaily amongst the ducks and spray. Through the trees beyond they can make out the austere architecture of Knightsbridge, including the dark tower of the army barracks.

"What ails thee Aphrodite?"

"Funny, you're the second person to call me that in the last twelve hours."

"So what's up Doll?"

"Have you got any coke?"

"I may. What is the urgent need, may I ask?"

179

"I've got the hangover from hell." And with that Kate proceeds to relate the events of the weekend, plus a bit of background on Jake.

"Sounds like someone's slipping."

"Oh Georgie!"

"Come on Kate. The sack, waking up naked with a stranger, and a blackout."

"He wasn't a stranger. It was Big Joe, the manager of the Cinder Box."

"And is he someone you would have gone to bed with if you had been sober?"

"No."

"Did you use a condom?"

"He said we didn't do it."

"And you believe him?" Kate shrugs her shoulders.

"Well I got my job back! At least I got my job back!"

"Yes. This time Kate, this time. But you better make sure you make that eight-thirty appointment in the morning because you won't be able to afford cocaine on the dole."

"Really Georgie, you make me sound like a junkie!"

"When did you last go a whole day without a drink or a drug?"

"When did you?"

"I am a grotesque mutant homosexual, desperate for kicks. You, well I think these so called 'real men' should have a bit more fire in their blood, don't you? Why aren't they all bowing down to you! You're a Goddess! I'd bow down to you queer and all. Why look at you! You're gorgeous, intelligent, talented and young, the World's your oyster. Yours Kate, all yours! "

"And you're charming and brilliant only two years older than me and an unashamed flatterer! So don't let's pretend there's one rule for me and another for you. And you're not grotesque." Kate's eyes start to shimmer.

"Oh Katie, tears? You're not doing so well are you?"

"No I'm not! I know it's silly, but this Jake. It was the first time for a long time I felt an attraction to somebody. You know how I am Georgie, there has to be some sort of connection for me, and it's not just because I was raped, I've always been that way. I need some feeling of kindred spirit, more than just sexual. And well it's just that, that, it's just I suppose ... oh God-I'm so lonely Georgie!"

"My dearest Kate, didn't anybody ever tell you that the very beautiful are also freaks?"

~

"I suddenly came to and there I was, standing naked on a second floor window sill of a large Georgian house in Dulwich Village, screaming: Arrr! Arrr! Arrr! Arrr! and rattling the window like a madman. There was this little kid in bed and he was screaming, 'Mummy! Mummy! Mummy! Mummy!"

Poor strung-out Barocco sits and shivers. Wrapped in his hospital blanket and dressed in hospital pajamas and slippers. There is the sound of a key in the lock and the front door opens. It is Dolores yapping away as usual. She enters the kitchen, motor mouth going off at least 85 mph and continues at this pace for some time after she has taken Jason from Little Wing. Then looking from face to face she says:

"What's up with you lot, lost a fiver and found a quid?"

Vince steps back and motions to the newspapers which Dolores, after noticing Barocco, and looking him up and down a couple of times, duly inspects.

"Bloody hell! Shit! Serial Killer Andy's the Islington Strangler! I always knew there was something funny about him. Fuck! You see I knew I was right! What did I say? I always said he was creepy, didn't I Vince?"

"Yes Dolores. You did say he was creepy" says Vince, his voice full of wafer-thin tolerance, sarcasm and mounting anger.

"Errrr! Yuk! It says here he strung them up, gutted them and fed their liver and bits to ..."

"Please shut up Dolores." Vince uses a loud clear voice.

"What?"

"I said," Vince pauses and licks his lips; he speaks softly.

"I said," then he yells, "SHUT THE FUCK UP DOLORES! Please, just for once in your life, shut up! "

Jason starts to cry.

"Now look what you've gone and done, you've scared the living daylights out of him you stupid bastard!"

"Oh well; isn't that sweet! Well, let me tell you something about this stupid bastard. This stupid bastard, along with that fat bastard over there, for more than six months now have shopped and fed and looked after that poor little bastard, while his mother has been spending more and more time chasing the dragon, with that useless bastard over at Elston Street."

"It's none of your fucking business!"

"No? Well maybe I'm making it my fucking business."

"We'll see about that."

And grabbing a bottle from the fridge she kicks the door shut, kicks open the kitchen door and storms out of the flat without bothering to shut the front door behind her.

~

"And what's this? Sneaking off without me?"

"Selene!" cries Georgie, Kate smiles. They both look at her affectionately.

"Without the stiff!" He continues joyfully and tactlessly. Kate gives him a sharp look.

"So that's what you call him. Oh no, no, no, no, no, no, no, no, don't apologize, you're right; you can't begin to know half of it. How I hate him. Hate him with every fiber of my being."

With that she starts to unbutton and pull aside her clothing to reveal parts of her body, an arm, some of the back and front of her torso, lifting her skirt to show them her legs. They both gasped with horror at what they see.

"It all started as a bit of fun believe it or not."

"That's a bit of fun?" It takes a lot to shock Kate.

Georgie has turned himself around and is contemplating the horizon. He has put down his martini glass on a coaster built into the right arm of his chair and removes his glasses, which he holds in a crooked hand that shakes for other reasons than his spasticity. He dabs his eyes and returns the handkerchief to a pocket, puts on his glasses, takes up his martini and turns abruptly around.

"It all started with a little light bondage and then some spanking, in fact we took it in turns, it was fun once a week or so! You know me and sex!"

"Yes, all in the cause of true horniness" says Georgie.

"Exactly! Couldn't of put it better myself. Anyway, things progressed until it was about the only type of sex we were having, and he wanted to be the aggressor more and more of the time. Then he seemed to totally flip one day and emptied out the middle

182

room and he started to completely refurnish it. He brought a fitted rubber carpet, and mirrored most of the walls, sticking thick black plastic sheeting in the gaps and the ceiling he painted a kind of satin black; I think he was trying to make it look like plastic or leather or something. But then things started to get really crazy! He started to come home with these like kits he would assemble."

Here Selene shudders.

"Whether he was buying them or having them made especially, God only knows. Some of them attatch to the wall with some big bolts, but basically when assembled, through the nature of the apparatus and how it is structured, one can strap, tie, chain, or whatever, somebody into each one of them in various unusual and humiliating positions and have them at your mercy. He also modified various pieces of furniture, mostly leather pieces, oh, and one of those pole things they have in American titty bars. But the real feather in his cap is the bed. He sat up late and studied every night for two weeks before he launched on that particular project. History books as well as carpentry. In the end he built a four poster with grooves cut down the inside centre of each post to accommodate sliding panels that act as stocks. It's horrible. I mean I suppose it could have been fun on occasion, with a lot of role playing and trust but ... ,"

Selene's voice trails off and she starts to whimper.

"And it should have been for fun! Poor Selene" says Georgie.

"And then the whips and sick cruel things and you can't do anything about it, sometimes I couldn't even turn my head and..."

"Hush" Kate embraces her. She weeps on Kate's shoulder. After a while Kate asks her:

"So what are you going to do?"

Standing back upright one of Selene's quick mischievous smiles crosses her face. She reaches inside her hand bag and produces plane tickets, a passport and a wad of traveler's cheques.

"My suitcase is already in a locker at Victoria station. That took some doing. I had to take a few things at a time into work with me and save change, which I gave to a lovely lady in the office who brought a suitcase and took it to Victoria station for me. He kicks me out every morning at five-thirty to fetch the paper, one of the few times he ever lets me out of his sight. This Monday's going to

183

be different, this Monday I'm not coming back. By the time he realizes something's up, I'll be half way to Gatwick. "

She looks from one to the other of them.

"Well are you going to light up a joint or aren't you?"

"Well done! Now you're speaking! Let's lighten up a bit here and light up Kate." exclaims Georgie. Kate produces her silver cigarette case.

"Oh Selene, I'm so happy for you! Here you do the honors" she hands Selene the joint and lighter. Selene draws deeply and starts to cough.

"God it's been a long time," says Selene, handing the joint back to Kate while she regains control of herself.

"And this has been a long time;" says Georgie," the three of us together like this."

Kate is alternately placing the joint under the flame and blowing on it until it burns evenly. Finally she draws on it deeply a couple of times and hands it to Selene.

"Remember when we were children, all those long holidays by the sea? If only we had known then what we know now." Selene says sadly.

"Thank God we didn't!" retorts Kate.

"I'll second that!" puts in Georgie.

"Remember what we were going to do when we grew up?"

"Kate was going to be an artist, you were going to be a poet, and I was going to be a pilot and see the world. Are you all right Kate?"

"I hope that dope doesn't pass me out after last night." She is beginning to break out in a cold sweat.

"Never fear relief is here." Georgie says with tired, resilient acceptance, and he reaches inside his breast pocket and pulls out a neat little white packet between his fore and middle fingers.

"Oh thank you Georgie! Thank you, thank you. Hey! "

Selene snatches the package and holds it aloft; one of her Medusa arms wielding it in her fingertips. She also has a good four inches on Kate.

"Here doggie doggie, here doggie doggie!" Georgie is chuckling to himself.

"Not a junkie Kate?"

Kate sticks her tongue out at him. Selene gives her the packet.

"I want a line of that later."

"Good to have you back Selene!" says Georgie, as he toasts her with a hip flask of cognac.

~

"They had me down there for two hours Kev, it was that bloody explosion thing, I couldn't remember what we had agreed on."

"You should have asked for your phone call, then kept your mouth shut, you prick."

Gorky was right; Pookie!

"Well I wasn't under arrest! I couldn't be too uncooperative, they would have got suspicious! As it was they left some psycho in the room with me."

"Inspector Grey?"

"You've heard of him?"

"Yes but never mind, go on."

Suddenly Kev is all ears. What are they doing moving a ball buster like Grey in on little Alec? Surely they couldn't have anything on him.

"Well it was like I said. Detective Healy just kept going over the same questions, over and over again. There was a short intermission with Inspector Grey, and then Healy comes back and orders the others out of the room. Then he sits down opposite and tells me I can have a fag. Oh, there was this whole cigarette thing earlier." Alec relates the cigarette story blow for blow,

"And he has this really weird thing with this gold lighter, gives me the creeps, yuck!"

"Come on Alec, get a grip, a fucking lighter!"

"Oh, it's all right for you! You weren't there. All by myself with a Detective, two uniformed guards and a fucking psycho Inspector! "

"How can you be by yourself with a Detective, two uniformed guards and a fucking psycho Inspector?"

"Oh that's right, you take the piss."

Alec stands and grabs his jacket. He puts a cigarette in his mouth and struggles with his jacket, getting it all twisted up in his haste.

"I know I'm just a joke, something for Gorky and you to tease and pick on. But think. If they are on to me then they'll soon be on to you and Gorky, and that crackpot of a mother of his. Think about that! Now where the fuck is my bloody lighter? I only just bought one on the way over here, someone keeps stealing them!"

"Come on Alec, now you're getting paranoid man."

"Sure. Now I'm paranoid. Whatever the fuck could I have to be paranoid about?"

"Alec ..!" Alec is at the front door.

"Fuck you Kevin and tell Gorky to go fuck himself too!"

And he leaves, making his exit felt with such a leviathan slam that Kevin is surprised the door surround does not come away from the wall.

~

"Never underestimate freedom." Georgie says, looking pointedly at Kate.

"From what I can see from my viewpoint is that these 'relationships' aren't all that they are made out to be. They shatter dreams, they crush individuality, they stifle passion and personality, they get into people's very souls turning them neurotic from the inside out. The romance always goes out of it they say; as they fart and pluck their nasal hairs in front of the television. No wonder! They are festering; and worst of all the boredom! In the days of Constantinople before the church came under Roman rule, there used to be an eighth deadly sin; Acedia. Meaning to allow one's self to become insistently and unceasingly bored. In my mind this should be the one and only deadly, unforgivable sin!"

"Here, here!" shouts Selene, toasting no one in particular with the cognac. She is getting sloshed rather quickly.

"And you dearest woman; by the way are you going to grow your hair again?"

"Yes!"

"Good. Anyway, as I was saying, Selene you've got to focus. You've still got to make it through the next twelve hours or so and old Mr. Head may not be too bright but he's cunning, and he'll smell a rat if you aren't careful. If I was you I'd give that ticket and stuff to Kate and ... are you listening?"

Selene is singing 'If You Want to be a Bird' from Easy Rider and dancing, or rather prancing around, arms askew and flapping.

"Kate, she's going to blow it!"

186

"No she will not. I'll not let her. First I'll get half of this up her nose," she waves the little white packet in the air, "that will sober her up and yes, that's a good idea of yours, I can have a mini-cab waiting too."

It is at that moment the service lift reappears.

"Mr. Lanseer, Mr. Lanseer Sir," the waiter calls out.

"And away we go! Back to sing-a-long with Marvelous Martha!"

Kate wheels him back into the lift and then with some difficulty recovers Selene. Who stands cross-legged, leaning into the corner of the elevator and hiccups.

"You've got a great arse," she says to the waiter.

"Hands off, I saw him first!" Georgie rolls his eyes, the waiter blushes. Kate tries to give the young man a reassuring smile which only makes him colour up more. Georgie passes around some mints.

"Now let's not get sloppy!"

The lift descends and Georgie slips the waiter a hundred pound note as they reach their destination. Hushing them, the waiter gestures to them to stay put while he takes a look around, Selene gets the giggles. Then, after a speedy ride through the corridors, they casually as possible enter the banquet hall.

They do not see Dick hiding around the corner. He walks up behind them, grabs Selene violently by the arm, digging his thumb into a nerve and hanging on hard.

"Where the hell have you been?"

Dick's eyes narrow, and his mouth takes on a particularly harsh sneer. It is a nasty moment; Dick finally revealing his true character, with all its vile jealously, cruelty and contempt.

"For goodness sake Dick," says Kate, "she's only been with us."

"Oh yes Kate, and that's supposed to make me feel better is it?"

"And what exactly do you mean by that?"

"I mean you're not exactly the kind of company I want my wife keeping. I mean how was Jake on Friday night, a good fuck was he? Obviously not by the state I saw you in this morning on your way home, groupie for the whole fucking band are we now? I'm surprised you're not shagging that waiter over the toilet bowl as we speak."

"Goodness, you too?" interrupts Georgie. "Just give me half a chance!"

"You keep out of this, you turd-burgling spastic!"

"Charming!"

"You stay away from her Kate. I know you artsy types. She's a respectable married woman now, with a respectable sensible job ..."

"Yes, with an oil company responsible for at least half the erosion in Africa."

"You're a fucking little shit-stirring slut. Socialist bitch! You fucking fag-hag ..."

Wham! Martha stands waving her cane, its bone handle having successfully brought Dick down. Dick lies with his head in his hands rolling on the floor moaning. Selene starts laughing hysterically and Prudence shrieks.

"Martha! Your blood pressure."

Kate is getting high from the adrenaline rush; she cannot believe what she is seeing.

"You bastard! You leave my lovely girls alone, you little shit!"

Now it is the Vicar's turn to step in with a little sermon:

"Now, now Martha, violence on the Sabbath and profanity, even on your birthday ..."

"Oh shut up you silly old sod."

"You old cow, you fucking cracked my skull."

"Obviously not enough," says Martha, raising her cane. Georgie is in heaven, Martha strikes again.

"Get the old bat off me! She's crazy! Get her off!"

Dick's voice is getting shrill. He rolls around on the floor, covering his head and testicles as best he can as he dodges the blows. Both guests and staff run to intervene.

Kate turns and runs, hand over mouth, it is mind over matter which allows her to make it as far as the Ladies room. Not even taking the time to close the cubical door behind her, she throws up the entire contents of her stomach with one big heave. As she coughs and spits the awful acidic juices from the back of her throat Selene, all knees and hands flapping, runs in.

"Are you O.K. Kate?"

Kate puts down the lid of the toilet seat and sits down limply. She tears off some toilet paper and wipes her mouth and blows her nose. Then, reaching inside her pocket she tosses the cocaine package down on top of the system, opens it and turns the entire contents out. As quick as a flash she takes a credit card out of her wallet, chops and divides the silvery-pink white powder into four lines, rolls a crisp ten pound note, gives her nose another good blow and snorts two lines.

"Here," she hands the rolled note to Selene who makes short work of the remaining lines. Suddenly there is some commotion outside as two particularly large members of the hotel's staff restrain Dick from entering the Ladies room.

"SELENE!" he starts shouting at the top of his lungs, "SELENE!" Selene goes pale.

"I better get on out there before he suspects something. Are you going to be all right Kate?"

"You don't have to go back out there to him" protests Kate.

"It's all right Kate, remember?" she lowers her voice into a whisper, "Just one more night. The next time you and Georgie hear from me I'll be as free as a bird! I'll be looking out for you both this summer on the beach." She hugs Kate and kisses her on the cheek and then she is gone.

After a few minutes Kate starts to gather her things and her wits about her. She carefully touches up her make-up and reapplies lipstick. She is starting to feel a lot better. Then she realizes she has forgotten to get Selene's travel documents from her.

~

"I tell you he was shitting himself man! It took a whole hour just to get rid of that squeaky voice thing he gets when he's worked up."

Gorky is genuinely concerned. Bullying someone for a couple of hours is neither here nor there. It is what the police do best after all, especially when they have nothing better to do. Even setting that Inspector on him could simply be a matter of entertainment; they are sick bastards after all. He thinks briefly of the recent events that have forced him to flee his native Poland, but he cannot afford to get side-tracked. Gorky had really believed that the assassination would be the making of Alec. He had expected to find a tough little bugger underneath that wimpy exterior once he had been, admittedly, somewhat shoved off the wall. Secretly

189

he agrees with a lot of what Alec believes in. He has a good mind; it is that pathetic whinging, Pookie-faced stuff that let him down, and he was always on the defense. His mother sits in the corner knitting and listening to her polkas on the radio. After Kevin leaves she places down her knitting and turns the radio off. She sits with her hands in her lap looking with stern seriousness at Gorky.

"This Alec could be the ruin of us all, you know that don't you?"

"Yes mother, I do."

"What were you thinking?"

Gorky held up his hands, palms upwards, shrugging his shoulders and shaking his head side to side at the same time, his mouth was open for words but somehow none would come.

"You cannot afford romantic notions anymore. If that young man can go to pieces in a routine interrogation what use can he be to us? He's a liability not a recruit! You can't change people Peter, how many times have I told you that in your life time. They have to want to change. Now he could have been a use to us in the future, on our propaganda, and he wouldn't have even needed to know of a military attachment. But an assassin? For any recruit on a first mission!"

"I'm sorry mother. I think it was a male thing. Having to listen to him argue, good arguments, but all the same, argue and complain night after night but never doing anything about it. It was so irritating and so, well, so British and down-trodden. Moaning and pickling their sorrows on corporation beer every evening in full acceptance that they cannot do a thing about their lot."

"That is what we are here to change. Meanwhile we have to protect the cell, which is you and I and it would seem young Kevin. Now I like that boy. I can see that one taking a good beating and not saying a word. I dare say he would fight back. But note the first advice he gave Alec, about demanding his phone call. An amusing touch of irony, an anarchist demanding their 'rights' under the law of the society they seek to overthrow!

"Now, as for the cell. He wasn't wearing gloves when he came in the flat that evening?"

Gorky wore a worried expression as he searched his memories.

"You recruited an assassin who didn't even have the sense to wear gloves?"

"So it would seem." Gorky hung his head. His mother was right; he really had not thought the whole mission through seriously enough.

"Can you retrieve the pieces of plumbing?"

"Yes."

"Leave the barrel somewhere where it will be found."

"Mother! I can't do that! Besides won't that give us all away?"

"No, because when we are questioned we will put up an initial resistance, then break down and tell the truth, that Alec was late and arrived just after the attack. He asked us to say he was with us at the time because he said it would avoid a lot of unnecessary fuss, but the lie lays too heavily on our conscience and we have broken down and told the truth, so help us God.

"He's going down, believe me, they have something on him. Can you imagine how many people they must have asked or brought in today to question about this? Yet the detective in charge of the case and the station henchman spent two hours with him. Believe me, just because he's destined to fall, we don't have to fall with him. And Peter,"

"Yes mother?"

"I never want to hear you dispute a direct order from a commanding officer ever again."

~

He was surprised and put out by his wife's sudden appearance at the shop. His brother from Tottenham, apparently in the area by chance, has popped in to say hello. After the two men return from the stockroom Seema picks out a magazine and heads towards the toilet. This means she will be a while. He cannot believe his luck.

When she finally returns to the store front her brother-in-law bids her adieu.

About an hour later the phone rings. Seema answers and speaks politely, if not a bit abruptly, in Hindu to the caller and hands the receiver to her husband.

"The Sound of bloody Music over and over again, and something called Winnie Phoo and one Dirty Dancing." His brother projects an urgent whisper down the line.

He hangs up; Mr. Patel stands mystified. He had suggested his brother check his minivan for another Tesco's bag, otherwise Mr. Smith must have made a mistake, which seems so unlikely. It is just then that his wife interrupts his train of thought.

"What's the matter Krishna? Doesn't Ram like Julie Andrews?"

~

The atmosphere at the squat can at best be described as abysmal. Various people drop by but none of them stay long. The pathetic Barocco is whisked away in a taxicab, much to everyone's relief. Vince takes the flickering portable black and white television into the front room and the three of them sit down to stare at it together. Vince and Sid are silently getting very stoned and rather sloshed, and Little Wing is feeling the emotional toll of the last forty-eight hours, not to mention the last six months, in which everything in her life has so radically changed.

She looks from Vince to Sid. That is enough to make her want to put her head in the oven. Vince has slid down low in his seat at the other end of the settee and has his feet on the coffee table. He rests his jaw in his left hand. The picture on the telly starts turning and Sid heaves himself out of the armchair, waddles up and starts twiddling various knobs on the back and hitting the upper left hand corner every so often. Vince stares straight ahead as he has been doing for at least the last hour. She cannot stand it a moment longer. She fetches her jacket, tripping over a pile of rope and bungee cords left besides the door.

"I'm going for a walk," she announces, and without giving either of them a chance to reply she steps out of the front door and closes it behind her.

She has no idea where she is going. She ascends the stairwell onto the roof; all she knows is that it feels good to feel the sharp cutting breeze, a sea breeze. She looks up at the sky. It has clouded over thick and fast, the clouds are coming carried by the wind. She realizes she has forgotten to change her sandals for boots. Heavy black clouds are appearing on the horizon. She gives it two hours, five minutes behind the last of the seagulls.

Descending to the pavement she walks around the corner and finds herself confronted by a white, giant lop-eared rabbit. The rabbit hops up and starts to nibble her toes.

"Hey stop that you!" Crouching down she strokes him.

"Now where did you come from big-foot?"

There seems to be only two choices, the entrance to some workshops, a few yards ahead on her right, or else he has just come hopping down the street. She carefully picks him up. It seems he is used to being handled, so she proceeds through the gates and into the yard, looking left to right at the workshops as she passes. They are all empty, some because of the inevitable decline of conditions under ill or nil maintenance of the landlord, Southwark council, and as for the others, it is a cold miserable Sunday afternoon and nobody feels like working. No one except two large gentlemen, who look as if they could be friends of Mean Mike's family. They are shifting several rails of designer label clothes out of the back of a van and into a workshop with blacked out windows.

She starts to hear music and finally reaches the end of the yard where a tall stick figure has kept running in and out of view. The music is coming from the first floor of a workshop that stands by itself, with its own little yard looking back up the cobblestones to the main entrance. Immediately to the left is the smaller side entrance to the main yard, which she decides must have been where the stick man has vanished. Turning around she swears she catches a glimpse of him passing right to left across the main entrance were she has just come from. Then he runs passed left to right. Just as she is wondering what she should do he appears again, stands still for a few seconds, and then starts running down the yard towards her. His animated figure becoming more real with every stride until it pulls up opposite her larger than life itself. He throws open his arms.

"Zeus!" he cries out, "Oh Zeusie, Zeusie."

Little Wing suddenly realizes he was addressing the rabbit and goes to hand him over. Big hands take hold of Zeus as if he were a new born baby, and as Fen holds him one great big tear rolls down his bristling grubby face.

"Bad Zeus! Bad Zeus scared Master! "

Little Wing turns to go.

"Yer 'ave to 'ave a reward! Oh yes a reward, follow me, shut the gate behind yer."

Fen runs on ahead leaving Little Wing standing where he has met her. The first floor window opens and is wedged with a piece of wood. Fen's head appears.

"Come on!" he says. Then the wedge disappears, the window shuts and she hears Fen drop the piece of wood on the floor and start to sing along with some dreadful piece of music.

"Oh, oh, oh, it's magic, you know-oow, never believe it's not so!"

Her curiosity gets the better of her and she goes in, pushing the creaking gate. She finds herself in the small yard, half of which is undercover and serving as a stable for Queenie, the rest houses a small cart, various flower pots and garden tools. She follows the trail of the scavenger up steep creaking steps which threaten to collapse at any given minute under the weight of his collections.

Upstairs she finds Fen busily decorating the milk crate next to the dirty old wine-colour armchair, which he then ushers her into and serves some surprisingly good tea. Scud sleeps in front of the stove, Zeus hops up to him and nudges his nose and scurries away to hide. Scud looks up heavy eyed, looks lazily around and drops his head. Zeus repeats the performance. Scud's head shoots up this time but he looks in the wrong direction and misses him. He lowers his head, more wary, his eyes look from side to side, alternate eyebrows rising. Scud's eyes slowly close again and just as he is drifting off again Zeus hops up and gives him one all mighty whack. Scud sees him this time and chases him around the back of the stove and reappears around the front again. They keep this up until Zeus changes the direction, and then changes it again, and so after a while it becomes impossible to tell who is chasing who.

Meanwhile Fen is mumbling rapidly under his breath as he works his way around the room, opening and shutting every door on every piece of furniture he can find. Then he stands and scratches his chin for about two seconds before throwing himself with equal enthusiasm onto the doors of the cookers and microwave ovens. Nothing. Well, of course every square inch of every cupboard is loaded, and every shelf in every oven is stacked, but not with whatever it is he is looking for. Then he thrusts his fist into the air. Triumphant, he spins one-eighty and pushes a mattress to one side revealing several refrigerators. The second largest in size is an antiquated round cornered model from the fifties. Fen pulls it open by the large handle which had once operated the broken latch. Inside are hinged metal boxes, most of which are rusted and dented: tool boxes, fishermen's tack boxes, children's lunch-boxes, small tins which have once held tea or tobacco, money boxes plus the usual you name it array one associates with Fen. He takes down a badly dented box of which the right back corner must have been exposed to moisture once, for the rust is all the way through at this point and badly flaking. If one wished, one could take a thumb and collapse the whole corner quite easily. This area of rust has also included one of the hinges which someone had forced open and subsequently broken. Pulling up a foot stool, Fen sits at Little Wing's feet and starts a glissando with his fingertips. From what she can see, the contents of the box consists of dirty cheap costume jewellery, and not very interesting at that, even in kitsch terms. Fen removes the tray from the top of the box and stares into it as if it holds great visions, then he plunges in his hand and pulls out a ring.

"Yes!" he says, more to himself than to Little Wing as he pauses to look at a ring. Then he hands it to her.

She likes the ring. It has three oblong flat clear stones cut very tastefully around the edges with a small number of facets. The larger central stone is set long and on either side of it, mounted into wide settings, are the smaller stones. Either side of these small round stones, in diminishing size, are set directly into the band. She presumes the stones are crystal; she notices the hallmarks on the gold and thinks she has gotten lucky. She wears the ring to her dying day, after which it is valued at seventeen thousand pounds.

The gate creaks twice.

"Hello there!"

Fen slams closed the box, shoves it back into the refrigerator, closes the door and pulls the mattress back into its original position. He seems to leap to the top of the stairs. Another record drops on the turntable and Abba starts coming out of the portable mono record player.

"Gorky!" Fen starts skipping from side to side.

"Thank you Fen my friend. But I see you have company, a lovely young lady; I hope I'm not intruding?" Gorky smiles at Little

Wing in a way that tells her he is not talking over her, he just enjoys teasing Fen.

"No no no no." Fen scuffles around moving some glass photographic plates off an upright chair and then beckons Gorky to sit. He seems to have gone a little shy all of the sudden.

"Gorky at your service," he holds out his hand towards her, "I didn't catch your name."

"Little Wing," she says accepting his hand shake. "My name's Little Wing." She feels the need to identify with herself, as much as to instill her name in Gorky's brain. Both men stop still for a moment and brake forth into chorus.

> " 'She's walking through the clouds,
> With a circus mind that's running wild.
> Butterflies and zebras and moonbeams and fairy tales,
> Is all she ever thinks about,
> Riding with the wind.' "

"Arr! Mr. Hendrix," Gorky sighs, "the world's most underestimated poet! Yes, fly on Little Wing."

"He wrote that?"

"Yes. I presumed that was where you got the name."

"No. I've never heard of a poet named Hendrix."

"Jimi Hendrix was a black, American rock guitarist, and singer/songwriter of the late sixties until his death in nineteen-seventy from an accidental drug overdose."

Fen serves tea to Gorky. Gorky looks at the sugar display and gets the giggles. Zeus appears from somewhere behind Little Wing and hops around the milk crate and bites Gorky's toes, which luckily for him are enclosed in heavy boots.

"There he goes, sticking up for his master! Sometimes I'm sure he understands every word we say."

Fen, whose back is turned on his company whilest he fiddles about in a drawer making an awful racket, spins round and stands upright, arms by his side.

" 'E does! " he looks deadly serious, " Margaret says 'e's Einstein!"

Fen folds over at the waist with one of his manic shrieks of laughter. Gorky laughs until he cries. He is dabbing his eyes when he addresses Little Wing.

"Excuse us Little Wing, you don't know Margaret. I apologize. Margaret thinks everybody she meets is a reincarnation of someone of great historic fame."

"Like always Cleopatra but never her lavatory cleaner?"

"Exactly."

"Who does she think she is?"

The men started laughing again then Gorky points to Fen.

"Queen Elizabeth the first."

The men continue to laugh and she even manages a little smile.

"How long have you known Fen?" asks Gorky. Fen starts feeding his animals.

"Just met him outside this building about twenty minutes ago, I found Zeus hopping down the street."

"So you haven't seen the best of Fen's Den yet! Fen. Hey Fen. Are you checking on Athens soon?"

Fen looks unsure and shifts from foot to foot, his eyes moving in the opposite directions to his feet.

"Oh come on, you can introduce him to Little Wing, she won't disturb him, he'll like her, I know he will."

Fen stands up straight, looks at them and smiles. He has made up his mind and nods his consent. He finishes feeding Scud, Zeus, and four cats. Little Wing is grateful that he puts the cats' bowls at the other end of the room. She does not want to be near them. Maybe it was the cats that set her off.

Fen is on the go again, not that he ever seems to stop. This time he is looking for a long shinny cardboard box, which he finally finds in a drawer of a Welsh dresser. Inside are some leather archery arm guards. He helps pick out and buckle up one for each of his guests.

"We have to tread softy now." Gorky whispers in her ear from behind, he places a hand on her shoulder as he does so.

She is getting an anxiety attack. What is she doing creeping sideways down this corridor, barely twelve inches wide, being jam-packed with junk like the rest of the place, with two men she has only just met, one behind, and the one in front definitely deranged? They are going into a back room where it is doubtful, even if it was not a Sunday, anyone would be able to hear her scream. She shuts her eyes for a second and tries to breathe deeply but her breath keeps on catching short. Fen opens the door into the back room. This is it. The moment she is inside Gorky will shut the door and they will rape her, maybe kill her. A sharp gust of wind cuts her face and she feels less light headed for it and opens her eyes. Ahead of her she can see Fen already standing in the centre of the room. In front of him an owl sits enthroned upon a perch. She exhales slowly noticing the cooing of the doves.

This room is the most amazing contrast to the rest of Fen's Den. There are thick heavy curtains on the two windows, one of which is cranked open, just as the curtains are slightly open, to allow Athens to come and go as he pleases. At one time Fen had collected leaves to carpet the floor but had found they disturbed Athens when they dried up and crunched under foot. So he has replaced them with maple leaves, which he gathered at the peak of their autumn glory, and pressed them to preserve the colour. He keeps the orange and red leaves swept around the edges of the room and the effect is striking against the gray dusty boards of the workshop. In the far left corner is another staircase, even steeper and more precarious than the other. The landing at the top of these stairs is wired off to make an aviary. There is a small window within the compounds of the aviary which Fen will open in the spring. Meanwhile an infrared bulb gives off the necessary heat to keep the doves happy. Fen says the doves help Athens sleep. And then there is Athens himself. Beautiful, proud Athens has already stepped off his perch on to Fen's arm and the two of them are taking a good look at each other. Gorky encourages her forwards.

"See if he'll come to you."

Athens swivels his head clockwise and she finds herself eye to eye with the nocturnal predator. He elongates his body, the long tufts on his ears stand to attention and he takes a long hard look at her. Athens is a young owl with a fine plumage of ashen gray, vibrant rust and black. His pale breast is marked with Maltese crosses. He clicks his beak twice stating his approval and steps from Fen's arm to hers.

"Why it's a Scops owl!" she exclaims.

"How do you know that?" Gorky is genuinely intrigued.

She suddenly feels a sharp scratch and sharp little teeth attack her left foot. The door has been left slightly ajar and some kittens have snuck in. She looks up at Gorky, she has trouble making out his features with the dim light source of the room behind him, and then she could have sworn the stairs creaked.

~

"Yer should 'ave seen 'im after the ladder collapsed, danglin' there on the window sill by the tips of 'is fingers! I don't know 'ow 'e made it back up there."

Bev stops laughing and looks affectionately at Leo, Leo with his broken nose, two black swollen eyes and fat lip.

Ruby looks around the room. She is getting bored of all the repetition and is eager to move onto the Scotch decanter. Edith dabs her eyes, Leonard smiles. Ladies, how he loves the ladies. And the grandaughter, what a pretty little thing; a shame about the husband. She reminds him of a blonde Bernadette, the one who got away. It was not until years later that he realized what a fool he had been to let her slip through his fingers. He had been so young then but old enough to have known better. Silvia comes back into the room and all eyes turn.

"I spoke with the station sergeant, and 'e says what with 'im bein' on parole and all, only the Magistrate can post 'im bail, and that won't be 'til the mornin' of course, which apparently is most unlikely given 'is past record, which 'e says is as extensive as it is feeble."

"So what's it like being married to a celebrity dear?" giggles Edith.

"Oh come on Ma. Stop being such a bitch. She was fifteen years-old and made a mistake."

"Don't yer mean two mistakes?"

"Where are Freddy and Jerry?" asks Beverly, suddenly serious. She looks from her mother to her grandmother; both seem to be avoiding direct eye contact.

"Mum? Nan?"

"Well yer could say that they're visiting their daddy, the little darlings!" says Edith.

"They dropped a condom full of water off the roof and 'it a policeman."

"Knocked 'is 'at off!"

"Oh God!"

"Oh don't worry luv," her mother reassures her, " we all agreed a couple of 'ours cleanin' the lavs down the police station would do 'em the world of good! So they're safe and sound being aptly punished and that's the last we'll 'ear of it. Look at it as a couple of timely 'ours of free baby sittin'. Now let's get down to important matters..."

"Oh yes dear, what a good idea," says Ruby. "The Scotch is where it always is, over there on the sideboard and there's plenty of ice and mineral water in the fridge, glasses in the usual place too."

"Allow me to do the honours dear lady," says Leonard. "Now where did you say the glasses are?"

Ruby busies herself bossing Leonard about, who takes it all in his usual good natured swing of things, while Leo fetches the ice and water.

Grandmother, mother and daughter look at each other; Bev knows it is up to her to start off the discussion.

"I've gotta get away from 'im" she begins.

"Oh at last, at last!" says Edith.

"I thought I was never goin' to 'ear yer say that luv. Thank God yer come to yer senses!"

"About time!"

Silva shoots her mother a dirty look, she would kick her if she could reach.

"I mean a good time, a good time for new beginnings. Spring around the corner and all that," Edith relents.

They all know Bev is not the brightest, but she is a sweet girl never-the-less and deserves a lot better than Mean Mike. How he had laid the charm on for her, twelve years her senior too. Then the moment he had got the ring on her finger, after dually knocking her up, he had dropped all pretenses and reverted to the truly nasty bastard everyone had tried telling her he really was. But she had not wanted to listen; he was her nasty bastard and he loved her. The fact that he treated the rest of the world and its inhabitant's as his personal latrine just went to show how much he loved her, she was his princess. And that was how she found herself, not long passed her sixteenth birthday, down on her knees, eight months gone, scrubbing someone else's toilet to make ends meet. Everyone thought he had done it on purpose for the quick council flat and the guaranteed dole and they were right. It did not do him any harm to have someone to clean up after him and his friends either.

"I can't stay around 'ere, it would be too easy for 'im to find me and yer know 'e'll go ballistic when 'e finds out I've left 'im. 'E probably won't get out tomorra but I don't want to bank on it. With a bitta luck they'll keep 'im down Brixton 'til the Magistrates 'earin' and with a bit more luck they'll send 'im straight down from there. Otherwise they'll probably let 'im out on bail 'til Crown Court and yer know 'ow long that can take."

"So basically my dear you need somewhere to hide out until you can find out what happens tomorrow, and possibly something more permanent after which or farther down the line."

The women look at Leonard.

"Please don't think me rude ladies, I dare say it isn't any of my business but I couldn't help over hearing and I think I may be able to help."

Leonard looks from face to face to make sure he is not offending, you have to be so very careful with the ladies; but the only looks he registers are those of enquiry. So he continues:

"Why doesn't dear Beverly take a little holiday at the seaside? I live all by myself in a three story house with attic and a two bedroom basement flat I rent out in the summer. It's totally empty the rest of the time. Turn right out of the front door, a couple of hundred yards to the end of the street and there's the sea! Bring the kiddies, I have plenty of guest rooms and tomorrow you can take a look at the flat, examine the option, you don't have to cross that bridge until you get to it! "

"What's 'e talking about?" Bev bends forwards and speaks into Edith's ear as she pretends to have an itch in her ankle.

" 'E's saying if yer don't like it yer can tell 'im to stick it."

"Exactly," agrees Leonard.

Ruby is unable to restrain herself a moment longer.

"Are you going to wait until every ice cube in that Scotch has melted before you hand it to me or will just one or two do?"

~

Dick starts on her the moment the front door slams. The noise alerts Robert who is busily and happily working away. All has been going smoothly, without a hitch. He has tested everything, everything works, it is just a matter of neatening up the hole in their ceiling, mounting the transmitter on a beam, soldering the

201

wires and replacing the floorboards in which notches had already been made to take the wiring. Robert looks at his watch, not even two hours; shit!

Dick drags her indoors by a twisted ear, slams the door and without any warning whatsoever punches her full force in the face. Selene lies where she has fallen everything spinning around her, her head throbs and everything suddenly sounds under water, or rather that she is listening from under the surface of the sea, her vision is out of focus too.

Between the threats, Dick is shouting every conceivable piece of filth that a man of his unexceptional vocabulary can find to fling at a woman. Something is tickling her under her nose, she reaches up with a shaking hand and touches the spot, focus zooming in and out as she examines her fingertips. Blood. Dick has never been happier. It felt so good smacking the rich spoilt bitch right in the face. He has hit her in the eye and already it has ballooned out to the size of a large orange. It is then he notices the contents of her handbag spewed out around his feet.

"What's this?"

He is screaming spittle and waving her travel documents in her face.

"You think you're fucking cleverer than me do you? Is that it? You think you've got half a brain in that thick skull of yours? Off to Barcelona in the morning without me were you? You bitch, you fucking bitch!"

Selene has managed to push herself up onto her elbows when he kicks her in the head. All goes black for a moment then out of the darkness comes the sound of pitiful crying. She is being dragged down the corridor by her hair which periodically slips from his grasp, each time her head hits the floorboards he takes hold of it again. The crying she hears is her own. She starts kicking and rolling from side to side, trying to release herself from his grasp, trying to no avail to remove his hand from her hair.

He should have thought of this hair thing before. He would have her grow her hair, not like that wavy hippy crap he had made her cut off, but straightened and bleached platinum blonde with a fringe. He waits by the door of the sex room until she is trying her upmost to free her hair, then he lets go. Her head falls hitting the floor with an almighty crack. He chuckles to himself and draws back the heavy bolts. He kicks the door open and taking hold of an arm he pulls her limp body into the room. He drags her across the floor, stripping and ripping her clothes off before lifting her like a piece of dead meat up onto the bed. She starts to moan as he lowers the stocks around her neck and wrists. Then he ties her legs tightly to the bed posts with leather straps. Lighting a cigarette he examines his handy work.

He is at eye level with Selene's navel, around which an incredibly colourful, detailed butterfly had been tattooed some years before when she and Kate had done some low budget traveling in America. They found themselves in a tattoo parlor in downtown Oakland, California, under the careful eye of Madame Lorraine, tattooist extraordinaire. They had both ended up having the butterflies around their navels. Kate had chosen the Peacock, so in character, and Selene had gone for the native Monarch.

Robert has not dared to look through the hole in the ceiling. Scared of disturbing the plaster and attracting attention, he lies on his mattress and listens, penis in hand. This is great! It is different from anything he has heard before. Then there is bloodcurdling scream.

"From now on, one for every time you disobey me!" Dick hisses. And the door slams and bolts are drawn.

~

Little Wing does not pause until she reaches the bottom of the stairwell. Then she leans against the wall and pants. Her eyes are shut and she tries to calm herself down. She is beginning to hyperventilate, and out of that other dark loft, the loft she thought she had all but forgotten, had come a horrific dream from long ago.

She could have sworn the stairs had creaked, that someone had been climbing, no, creeping up them.

"I have to go!" She suddenly blurts out into the silence, and manages to keep it together long enough to hand Athens over to Gorky. Then she bolts. She takes a cat by surprise as it is waking and arching its back. It jumps and hisses, she screams, concerned voices come from the back room.

"It's all right, I'm O.K." and she scrambles down the stairs, slipping on the first step and nearly falling head first down onto the concrete below.

She then exhales and takes the steep steps as slowly as she can manage, until she reaches a spot where she is low enough to turn round and use her hands also. It is at this point her head begins spinning and she finds herself hanging on for dear life, willing a fainting spell away. Then she realizes she is holding her breath. It takes thirty seconds or so before she opens her eyes and the first thing she sees is Fen's battered boots. Then a cat sticks its face in hers. She screams and nearly falls again.

"What's the matter Little Wing?" Gorky's voice echoes Fen's.

She opens her mouth to reply but words are not forth coming. She is having a flash-back.

She is falling forwards, her face flat into the nest of kittens, a strong male arm around her neck. They spit and scratch, as two of them manage to scatter, their minute, razor sharp claws rip the child's skin. One kitten is partially trapped under her right neck and shoulder, it frantically meows as it tries in vain to pull itself free. Then the full force of the assailant's weight knocks the wind out of her. Another kitten, caught by a single claw embedded in her left check, springs free, taking a chunk of flesh with it. There is a crunch as the trapped kitten is crushed under her, its blood and innards squelch out, their warmth and wetness spreading under the right side of her face. Then sweet oblivion for a just a few moments, followed by the most excruciating awakening. She hears a loud piercing scream, not realizing from whose lips and throat it comes. The arm tightens around her neck, while a hand stuffs old, dusty, smelly straw in her mouth; it tastes bitter like moldy bread. And then the terrible, repetitive pounding into her. Her teeth biting down so hard that her face, so lined with fear and pain, looks eighty not eight. Dark blood, blood to match the bruising, spills sticky moisture on the dry dirty floorboards, blood from a womb which would now never procreate,. And all along, through all the vile and painful acts he commits on her, all she can hear is her name uttered by his lips, over and over and over, until she can bare the sound of it no longer...........

"What's the matter Little Wing?" Gorky's voice echoes Fen's.

"Look, I hate cats. O.K.? I just hate cats!"

And with that she had jumped the remaining steps and bolted.

Little Wing opens her eyes and looks up sadly at a circling seagull.

~

Angela does not want to show the pamphlet to the driver but her voice is shaking, her head is aching, she feels exhausted, and her eyes are having trouble focusing. The cabby smiles and hands it back to her and pulls away. She wonders why he has not switched the clock on. He parks the cab and switches the engine off.

"What do I owe yer?"

"Nothing, we 'ave the same destination so yer got a free ride. I'm a friend of Bill's too."

"Well actually a friend of mine, Nick, gave me the leaflet."

"First meeting?"

"Yes."

"Thought so. I'm Joe."

"Angela."

"Welcome Angela. Keep coming back. Let's get yer inside, these clouds are ready to burst. Cor blimey! Famous last words!"

An indignant cry of a lone seagull calls out to the rapid dusk.

"Are there any newcomers who would like to introduce themselves? We ask you this so we can welcome you." Nick smiles encouragingly. She raises a timid hand.

"Me name's Angela and I'm an alcoholic. This is me first meetin'."

There is applause and a lovely elderly lady with a big smile hugs her and gives her a coin. She turns it in her hand trying to look at it though her tears. She manages to control them just long enough to make out the words:

'To thy own self be true.'

~

Gorky sits on the arm of the sofa, his legs crossed and his jacket folded neatly over his knees. He observes Kev as he paces around the room, stopping once to perch on the edge of the sofa.

All knees and elbows, he picks up Gorky's cigarettes and lighter from the coffee table, lights up and stands up again.

"Shit!" he said and threw the cigarettes down angrily and put the lighter in his pocket. Interesting, thought Gorky.

Kev resumes his pacing then stops at the window. A seagull flies over the small patch of sky and cries out to the approaching darkness, a wave of immense sadness sweeps over him for a moment or two and then he is back, sharp and to the point. That is what Gorky loves most about Kevin. He shifts his weight onto one leg, smooths the back of his hair and swings around.

"I don't like it Gorky."

"I'm sorry my friend, this must be very painful for you. I know this must go against the fiber of your Anglo-Saxon sense of loyalty and male bonding ..."

"Fuck male bonding and loyalty Gorky, and fuck all the rest of your crap. It's Alec we're talking about here, our friend Alec. Whatever we tell him or not, whatever we scheme or plan or say, right now we're talking about our friend Alec, 'Poor Little Alec' as you've so often referred to him as, maybe going down for life, and I don't think I need any other reason to explain why I am upset."

"Sorry Kevin, you're right. I apologize." It crosses Gorky's mind that if he was interrogating Kevin this would be the perfect time to ask about the lighter. All was quiet for a while, peaceful even. Kev continues to look out of the window and smooth the back of his head. Gorky examines his hands and fingernails pushing back the odd cuticle.

"I say we tell him." Kev turns round and is looking intently at Gorky.

"And what would be gained by that?"

"I think he'd understand." Gorky is silent. "I think he'd understand, I think it would help him feel some sense of purpose because he went down to save the cell, and I also think the least we can do is give him the option of making a run for it, or having some nights to remember before they send him down. If they send him down."

Gorky has to admit it, Kev has a solid argument. Solid, fair, even noble, but completely emotionally impractical. There is no way to wager how anyone would react to the news that they are about to go to prison for the rest of their natural life, let alone someone so apt to panic as Alec. He could turn bitter and take them down with him, just because he could, or he could find God and confess all. He had seen that happen once. Truth was certainly stranger than fiction. He relates these thoughts to Kev. Kev is not stupid, he does not want to be incarcerated for life any more than Gorky wishes to be deported back to Poland. Therefore he will not tell, presumes Gorky, and he is right-but not for the reasons he has presented but for those to arise. Kev is right also, Alec did understand.

"Do us one favour Gorky."

"And what would that be Kevin?"

"Let's not decide right now, let's decide tomorrow."

"He doesn't understand yet, it hasn't sunk in," thinks Gorky, "he's burnt his bridges. When he stepped foot on that roof last night and helped Alec and then took aim and twisted the switch himself his, mine, and Alec's lives were changed irretrievably. He doesn't realize he's in a militia now and I'm his commanding officer, leader of the cell as far as he's concerned. We'll have to work on that next, but not now."

"Let's surprise him with a Chinese take-away and I've got some of that beer he really likes, and I'll go and see if Vince will sell us a sixteenth or lend us a couple of joints worth."

Kev made a quick calculation on his fingers of how much money he had, divided by the number of days to his next Giro.

"All right my friend, if that would make you happy it makes me happy. Also, I believe Casablanca is on B.B.C. 2 later and Alec, if my memory serves me, has a splendid television set."

"How come foreigners speak better English than the English Gorky?"

"I don't know Alec."

"You mean Kevin."

"Yes, of course, forgive me Kevin."

"I'm not offended Gorky."

~

Little Wing quietly shuts the front door and listens. There is shouting coming from the kitchen.

"Are yer crazy? Who's goin' to look after Jason when yer smacked out of yer brain?" Sid's voice is indignant.

207

"And since when did you start telling me what to do! Who do you think you are, my bloody father?"

Vince scrutinizes Danny Day who hovers around the doorway aware of his unpopularity.

"What the fuck are you doing here?" he says.

"He's come to help me get my things."

"Your things?" asks Little Wing as she steps silently into the room.

"Yes that's right, I'm moving to Elston Street."

"Elston Street?"

"Bloody hell, it's not Timbuktu, it's around the bloody corner. You can come and see me whenever you want!"

"But Dolores, I don't want to visit you there, it's horrible! And what about Jason?"

"Jason is my baby not yours, I'll do what I think is best for him, not you. I think you're all being very selfish, especially you Trudy, Little Wing, Scar Face, or whatever the fuck you call yourself these days. You turn up out of the blue, follow me up here, I find you a home and this is how you repay me. Well don't come and visit me then. Fuck you!"

Little Wing starts to cry and Danny slides out into the hallway.

Silence prevails in the kitchen as Dolores's angry nonstop voice could still be made out through the thick brick wall in the next room. Little Wing sits down at the table and weeps silently; Vince crouches down and gives her a hug. Sid at the cooker snuffles and sniffs as he fixes Jason's afternoon feed. Dolores, returning in her usual hurricane style, empties all the cabinets of baby food and collects Jason's bottles.

" 'Ere." Sid hands her the warmed bottle.

"Thank-you," she pronounces curtly and then she is gone.

Little Wing runs into the next room and slams the door. Vince wanders around the kitchen aimlessly and then crouches down to retrieve something caught between the wall and the table leg. He stands and stares at what he holds in his hands. It is the small teddy bear Jake had been clowning with only yesterday. How one day can make such a difference he thinks. Fat Sid sits glumly and looks from the teddy-bear to the newspapers, to the teddy bear again, and bursts into tears.

Meanwhile Little Wing swallows hard. Through her tears she focuses in on the loose piece of shirting. It comes away easily in her hand, Dolores has not even bothered to replace the knot. Behind it is nothing but plaster dust and a few old mouse droppings.

~

"Are yer sure yer don't mind luv?" Mother and daughter are wishing final farewells on Ruby's threshold.

"No Ma. I told yer. Yer stay 'ere and keep warm. There may be a film on the telly later. It ain't 'alf turned nasty out 'ere, yer'll freeze. I've got Leonard and Leo to 'elp me, I'll be fine."

"Well as long as yet sure luv."

"I'm sure Ma, oh I nearly forgot." Bev starts rummaging around in her handbag and pulls out a key.

"Could yer give this to the 'Odgins and tell 'em I'm sorry I couldn't give 'em notice?"

"I'll tell 'em they owe yer a good spankin'!"

The two women stand and look at each other for a second before they embrace, Silvia has the urge to cry but controls herself. Leo is talking to the mini-cab driver and Leonard is ... she hears her mother ululate a shrill shriek and giggle. Behind her in the passageway Leonard and Edith are fooling around like a couple of teenagers.

"Mini-cabs waiting, Leonard," says Silvia. Bev giggles and runs off down the steps.

"Bye bye Ma, I luv yer."

"I luv yer too Bev, safe journey."

More giggling comes from behind her, Edith seems to be beating Leonard while he holds up his hand in mock distress.

"Oh for goodness sake Mother put 'im down!" They stop and smile at Silva.

"All ready and waiting?" Leonard asked her.

"Yes Leonard."

"Well in that case Ladies, au revoir!"

He gives Edith a great big smacking kiss on the lips and waves a final salute to Ruby in her arm chair. Stepping outside on the landing he takes Silvia's hand between his and speaks softly.

"Don't worry Mum, I'll look after her."

Silvia looks at him gratefully, her eyes start to mist over.

"Now, now, we'll be having none of that. The Humbolt men specialize in smiles not tears." He pulls out a silk handkerchief and dabs the corners of her eyes.

"Thank you Leonard, I don't know what came over me. It was like all the time she was with that bastard I couldn't cry, I couldn't afford to break down, I never knew when she would need me. 'E used to beat 'er yet know, the last time quite bad, 'e put 'er in the 'ospital. 'Is old man and some uncles and that took 'im on one side, I don't know what they said to 'im but 'e never lay an 'and on 'er since. But I was always scared 'e might do it again, perhaps even worse. And then there was just the everyday things, never knowin' when 'e was goin' to be arrested again, never 'avin' any money for nothin' but 'is beer. And now that she's left 'im, it's like there's 'ope, 'ope that me little girl may find 'appiness after all. Trouble is she ain't that bright."

"The boy neither," Leonard sympathizes, "but he's a good worker, same job since sixteen, trade, a carpenter, union job, makes good money with bonuses."

"Oh," says Silvia happily surprised, "and 'ow about 'is little friends?"

"Long gone, bed and all."

"Good." They smile together, the two conspirators.

Leo has put Leonard's carpet bag, Beverly's suitcase and the twins' small back-packs into the boot, and is holding Baby Ruth while Beverly and the boys climb into the back seat. Leonard arrives with a smile and Leo hands Ruth back to her mother. Leonard sits next to the driver and Leo walks around, gets in and slams the door.

"Waterloo East please." says Leonard, and they pull out into a gust of wind and the rain.

The phone rings and Silvia answers. She places the receiver down at the end of the conversation and joins the old ladies back in the sitting room. She is trying to keep a straight face but the comers of her mouth kept twitching and give her away.

"Well out with it!" demands Ruby.

"That was Constable Wright. Apparently somebody put cling-film over all the toilet bowls and urinals!"

~

Mean Mike sits on a narrow backless bench and leans against the wall, numb-arsed and his arms crossed over his chest. Everybody else has been bailed out or taken away on remand. Even Dave, it seemed, had a warrant out for his arrest for non-payment of fine, and has gone off with a group of lads to Brixton, where they have an uncle doing seven years for fencing gem stones. Dave will be well in there, probably having a joint right now. All Mike knows is that fucking bitch has not even brought him down any baccy.

There is a jangling of keys. Someone is coming. He can hear several sets of footsteps and the door being locked again. Inspector Grey passes with long strides clenching a truncheon followed by Rick who was moaning and barely conscience. His arms are wrapped around the necks of two uniformed cops who drag him down the corridor towards another cell.

Mean Mike leaps to his feet and runs up to the bars. Grabbing them he starts to shout.

"GREY! YER FUCKING BASTARD! GREY!"

There are sounds of metal against metal as hinges swing a door open and shut. They drop Rick onto the concrete and then there are two pitiful screams of terror and of agony followed by hallowing bestial utterances of torture and despair. Mike can hear the soft dull thud of weapon, fist and foot against what sounded like a bag of flour.

"RICK! RICK! LEAVE 'IM ALONE YER CUNTS. YER FUCKIN' KILLIN' 'IM! "

Mike hears the door of the cell swing open and footsteps. Inspector Grey is at the bars with an enquiring look. The weapon in his hand has blood on it.

"Something bothering yer Michael?"

"Leaving 'im alone yer fuckin' bastard!"

"I don't know about that Michael, yer saw the way 'e was when we brought 'im in 'ere. Kickin' and punchin', screamin', causin' 'avoc! These niggers are all alike when it comes to resistin' arrest Michael."

"Leave 'im the fuck alone Dennis."

"There yet go again Michael. The F word. You ain't 'alf got a dirty, dirty mouth there Michael. Pity yer mother didn't 'ave more time between prison visits to give it a good scrub with soap and water because now I'm going to 'ave to teach yer some manners. 'Ere's an idea for yer. 'Ow about every time yer use a naughty word yer nigger friend gets a slap. 'Ow does that sound to yer? Officer Jones?" The Inspector calls back down the corridor to the other policemen.

"Sounds good to me, Sir."

"Officer Murray?"

"Most apt Sir, never could stand vulgarity."

"Yer ..."

"Officer!" calls out the Inspector. There is another thud followed by a weak moan.

"I didn't say anythin'!"

"Tell me Michael, what's a nice white boy like you doing running around with a nigger?"

" 'Is old man saved my old man's life, yer cunt! Oww! "

"Did yer 'ear that Officer? " Another thud.

"Yer just can't help yerself can yer Michael. Open yer mouth and out it comes, like so much diarrhea."

"Inspector!"

"Yes officer?"

Inspector Grey looks back along the corridor, his brow becomes knitted and his forehead ceases. He suddenly losses all interest in Mike and struts off back to the other cell. Mike hears a heated frantic exchange. Then Inspector Grey gets on the radio and Officer Murray passes by fast and shifty.

"What the fucks 'appenin'? RICK! RICK! "

A short time passes after which Officer Murray returns with Dr. Bob. They ignore Mean Mike and head straight to the other cell. For a few minutes there is an eerie silence that is followed by a hushed panic.

~

Bang, bang, bang, bang, bang!

"What the hell?" Kate's fuzzy head rises off the pillow. It is dark outside and the old window rattles in its frame. Rain beats on the glass, rivers of water streaking the panes like tiger-maple.

Bang, bang, bang. She pulls the bed clothes over her head.

"For God's sake, go away" she groans. Then a sobering thought hits her, maybe it is Selene. Oh dear, that's who it must be, why else would anybody be knocking on her door like that.

Bang, bang, bang. She throws her quilt aside and is putting on her dressing gown as she strides down the corridor to the front door.

Bang, bang, bang.

"I'm coming" she shouts.

Kate opens the door but instead of the desperate figure of Selene clutching toilet paper to a bloody nose she is greeted by the glare of a stout, middle-aged Jamaican woman. She stands like a rock, feet planted firmly apart and her fists on her hips. She is armoured in a transparent sky blue plastic mac and a clear plastic folding hat with polka dots. A puddle is forming around her as she stands with water running off her onto the concrete.

"Kate Lanseer I presume?" Kate gets an urge to laugh which she quells immediately.

"Yes?"

"My name is Maria Howard, I'm Joseph Howard's sister, mean anything to you?"

Kate searches the recesses of her cranium her brow creases. Joseph Howard? Joseph Howard?

"Oh, you mean Big Joe."

"That's right, good of you to remember, after all you only spent last night with him!" Maria's sarcasm was not lost on Kate.

"Look Maria, I don't quite understand what you're so upset about but if you'd like to come in…"

"Have you any idea how long my brother's been holding a torch for you?"

"Me? Maria I …"

"I'm not here to socialize and what I have to say won't take long. Stop messing him about. If you're interested do something about it, if you're not leave him alone and let his broken heart heal."

"Maria I had no idea that was the situation …"

"Well you do now." Maria is starting to shout.

"And if I had I would have dealt with Joe differently. But we are both grown-ups and I consider him a friend …"

"Then leave him alone you white bitch, I told you once, leave him alone."

Maria's teeth are clenched, her voice lowers. She bends her knees slightly and pushes her upper body forwards as if preparing for attack. It is not like Kate to back away from confrontation but she considers Maria's solidly contained bulk and stance, and realized as far as the other woman is concerned there is no argument.

"I'm sorry Maria, you're right of course but I ..."

"There are no buts."

"I really didn't know that was how he felt. Could you tell him I'm sorry?"

The initial flare of Maria's fury seems to have become more subdued. She relaxes her muscles and shifts her weight; she turns to go but stops as if to take a final look at Kate.

"Any other messages?"

"And that I'll miss his friendship."

Maria snorts and raises her eyes to heaven and starts down the stairs. Kate quietly shuts the door behind her and leans forwards resting her left arm and forehead on the door. Someone taps lightly. Kate wonders if Maria has changed her mind and has come back to give her a good sock in the mouth after all. To her relief it is only Nick, Nick with a bunch of flowers that looked like they have seen better days.

"East Street, two pounds a bunch or three for a fiver," he steps in and hands them to Kate. "They're 'aving a bad 'air day!"

"So am I!" Nick could always make her laugh and she feels like a bit of companionship. She could not have hoped for anyone easier, he is never any trouble.

"As I couldn't 'elp over 'earing, that was one scary lady."

"Oh, that's not half of it."

"I'm all ears, if you want 'em." The phone rings.

"I'll wait in the sitting room, no hurry I want to look at that Ensor book of yours anyway. Can I make a pot of tea?"

"You must be a mind reader," she answers. She goes to her bedroom and answers the phone.

"Kate, it's me Big Joe."

"Hello Joe." What now.

"Look my sister ..."

"Been and just gone Joe."

"Oh, sorry Princess. I couldn't stop her."

"She's quite something!" She could hear Joe laughing.

"That's for sure Princess, that's for sure." There is an awkward silence.

"Princess ..."

"Joe, I ..." they both start talking at the same time.

"You first." says Joe.

"I'm so sorry Joe, I had no idea you felt that way about me."

"It's all right Princess, how were you supposed to? I played my cards tight to my chest, but they were close to my heart."

"What were you going to say Joe?"

"I was going to say, I don't suppose I am the man of your dreams am I?"

"Oh Joe ..."

"That's all right Princess, just seemed silly not to check while I have you here. I think I'm going to go now if that's all right with you. Could you do me one small favour?"

"Sure, what's that Joe?"

"Say, sweet dreams Joseph."

"Sweet dreams Joseph," and then a small click on the line and they are disconnected.

Kate sits looking at the receiver in her hand for a long while before placing it on the handset.

~

It has taken only a short time for the skies to open up, and after two days of premature spring the weather was back to usual for this time of year, atrocious. The Hastings train pulled up alongside platform 2.

"Fast to Sevenoaks then Hildenborough, Tonbridge, Tunbridge Wells, St.Leonards, St.Leonards Warrior Square, and Hastings," the recorded announcement announces.

Leo looks down at Bev, she is yawning, little Ruth cradled in her arms. He starts to smile before a sudden pain reminds him of his broken nose. Leonard has opened the carriage door and is getting the boys, who are cooperating splendidly, if not a bit loudly, onto the train.

"Well I guess this is it," says Bev.

"Yes." Leo picks up her suitcase, neither of them move.

"Yer know, I don't 'alf luv yer Bev."

"Oh! I luv yer too Leo."

215

The guard is shouting at Leonard who is holding the door open. Leo quickly puts the suitcase in the carriage, Bev hands Ruth to Leonard and after one passionate embrace she jumps onto the train and Leo slams the door after her. The guard blows his whistle and the train immediately starts to pull away, Bev opens the window and waves.

"I'll phone." Leo shouts, but his words blow away with the wind.

~

One bleak, chill Sunday night, and the east wind blows. It blows strong and constant. Its damp, icy fingers penetrate your skin, flesh and joints, to the very marrow of your bones. Rain crashes to earth directed by a relentless gale, pounding the tarmac, pummeling the tinny swarms of traffic. A saturated canvas, loose on a trailer, flaps sadly as a torn sail on a ship destined without hope. Wheels endlessly orbit wheels, these two great adjacent circles, this giant junction of South London. The Elephant and Castle; like some dark, primitive, Boschian machine, its two main cogs turning eternally in this tempest straight from the shores of hell. It spits as it spews: cars, buses, taxis, motorbikes, lorries and cyclists, dark waif-like figures surface from its flooding, subterranean, piss-stinking subways. A thousand puddles reflect a thousand lights. Long splinters of water form on the road's tired surface sparkling the red neon words 'take-away'. Opposite, from the foot of the railway bridge the steamy windows of 'Elephant Vindaloo Indian take-away food' looks homey and inviting. Tires splash, people pass, their bodies bent. With one white knuckled hand they clutch their jackets, wrapping them close. The other numbed fist holds the lapel, pulling it up and over their heads in vain attempts to keep dry. Three survivors of a crazy, lost weekend, on a miserable Sunday night in the grim 1980's of Thatcher's sad and confused Britain, wait for Indian food and sleep.

"A thumb?"
"By all means Leo me good fella, a thumb. Floatin' in mid-air as if still attached to its original owner."
"Meanin' it 'ad more than one owner?"

"Meanin' that the original owner was once flesh and blood like us, and is now merely the invisible spirit of 'The Rat-Man'."

"And 'e's carryin' around 'is thumb. Gotta be pretty pongy by now, gotta stink!"

"No, the thumb does the 'auntin' it's only the thumb yer see. That's why they call it 'The Ghost of The Rat Man's Thumb', not 'The Flying, Green Turd, Fish-Thing' "

"So where's the Rat-Man?"

"Dead of course! Bleedin' Nora, 'ow can there be a ghost if 'e ain't dead, Christ almighty Leo!"

"Me Nan believed in ghosts of the livin'. She said she saw me once quite clearly standin' at the end of 'er bed. It was 'er birthday and I said, ' I'd like to wish yer a very 'appy birthday Nan'. "

Nick looks sideways at Leo with the tolerance of a Saint. He manages a slow, firm, quiet utterance:

"Do yer want to 'ear the story or not?"

"Yer, go on."

"Once upon a time in Southwark ..., " Nick begins again but is soon interrupted.

"So there was only one thumb and one Rat-Man?"

"Yes" confirms Nick

"And only one ghost thumb?"

"Yes"

"So the ghost thumb wasn't attached to its original owner!"

"No, 'e's DEAD!"

"But yer said it floated around attached to the original owner."

"As if attached, Leo, as if."

"Ohh!"

"So ..."

"Which one?"

"What!?"

"Left or right?"

"I don't kn -, the right, definitely the right."

"How do they know?"

"I don't know Leo, they just do."

"Ain't much of a story so far." Leo mutters. Exasperated Nick looks round to check on Kate.

"All right Kate?"

The establishment, a tiny triangular room has one seat, makeshift and fitted to the obtuse corner next to a fish tank placed on top of a miniature counter. Here Kate sits, heavy head propped up by a weak arm, chin cupped in a cold clammy palm. Sleepy eyes follow the golden-silver waves of light that gently ripple down the amber fish. A turbaned man, chin also cupped, sits behind the counter. Dreamy, unfocused eyes with a Cheshire Cat grin, he stares at her.

"Yeah," she manages a half smile, her head nods slowly twice.

A fish turns revealing a large oval of ragged, pink, bloody meat, surrounded by a beautiful ring of rich golden scales. The occupants of the aquarium, about a dozen gold fish, are behaving like dope smoking cannibals. Serenely and gracefully they swim the length of the tank, turn and glide back. Every so often, with a movement more like a snake than a fish, they take a mouthful out of a companion. They all have puce, minced open wounds.

"Your fish need feeding."

Turbaned man smiles on!

"You've forgotten to feed your fish." repeats Kate.

"Yes, oooh, yes." He nods his head slowly, up and down, up and down.

"No! The fish. You have to feed the fish! "

She gestures with both index fingers at the aquatic horror show to her left.

"Yes, yes pretty lady. Yes." He grins on. Lazy smile, sleepy smile, happy smile.

"Stop looking at me, look at the tank, the fish tank, just take a look at your bloody fish tank!" she gestures, then gestures fanatically.

"They're eating each other, the fish, the fish, look at the fish!"

Turbaned man sits up straight, his grin has taken on a sour look and he looks nervously from side to side. He is beginning to wonder if Kate is a nut.

"This guy, the Ratman right, lived about a 'undred years ago on Iliffe Street. The Ratman was the local vermin exterminator, that's 'ow 'e got 'is name, Ratman. Anyway, 'e was scared shitless of fire, terrified of it. So 'e lined 'is place with lead, completely fire proofs it, right? Then one night 'e falls asleep with 'is candle still alight, and it catches the bed clothes and well, you can imagine, his worst nightmare came true. And after the fire 'ad completely gutted the place all that was left of the Ratman was a pile of ashes and 'is thumb, 'is right thumb. And to this day they say, if you burn a candle in that flat you may see the Ghost of the Ratman's Thumb, floating 'as if' still attached to its original owner! So what do you think of that little ditty me old friend?"

Leo's brow is creased by a frown, as if contemplating some profound concept.

Somewhere from within Kate's exhausted brain and body a last drop of adrenaline is stirred, causing her hands to shake, a cold sweat, lightness of the head and a strange nervous sensation in her stomach. Whether from lack of sleep, or the remnants of high living in her system, currents of crystalline light seem to flow from the fish, the golden scales shine as bright as the Phoenix's egg. As for the wounds, they have taken on the appearance of badly poxed faces, corrupted flesh, misshapen dung heaps of matter. Mouths distort into horrific grimaces, eyes swollen almost closed into dark crimson slits, bloody eyeballs assimilating bottomless pits of disease and despair. Collapsed, rotting noses oozed slime and maggots, seemingly desperate to escape the grotesque death masks but imprisoned by red hot rings of armor. Finally Leo speaks:

"I still don't get the 'original' bit, if there was only one Ratman."

"The fish are eating each other! The fish are eating each other!"

Kate is on her feet, her voice shakes and shrieks as she points at the fish tank with one hand and tears at her hair just above the temple with the other.

"Feed the fish, the fish, the goddam fucking fish!" and then she does something that in all the years Nick has known her, he has never seen her do before. Holding her head between her hands she burst into deep guttural sobs. Nick takes her hands gently away from her face and places them together, holding onto to them he frees his right hand and smooths her ruffled hair.

"Yer gotta to calm down, 'e doesn't understand yer Kate. O.K.?"

She almost whispers:

"Nick, the person who feeds the fish has forgotten, they're eating each other."

"It's O.K. It's O.K." Stroking her hair, he glances at the tank, he looks back at her momentarily, jumps and sticks his face right up to the glass. Just at that moment the small square kitchen hatch opens and a small brown paper bag appears. The turbaned man picks it up and calls out Nick's name in broken English.

"Yer need to feed yer fish mate," says Nick taking the bag. The turbaned man stares at him blankly.

"Come on, let's get out of 'ere Kate."

Stepping outside, the lashful force of the wind and rain slashes and pelts their faces. Nick pulls one lapel up and over his head. Kate plunges her hands deep into her pockets, wrapping her coat closely around herself, and runs.

~

"No sweet and sour pork Kevin?" Gorky is amused and somewhat surprised. Kevin usually insists on his sweet and sour pork with considerable obstinacy.

"No! Not tonight. Tonight we're ordering all Alec's favourites."

Which means the meal would taste insipid thinks Gorky. He wonders how many vegetarians would know a good meal if it came up and bit them in the backside, let alone know how to cook one. He will be glad when this Alec business is over, and he has been arrested and sentenced. He could see more and more clearly what a fool he has been. Mother was right to be furious. He had endangered the cell and the distraction was almost as dangerous, especially now when he needs to be more alert that ever. Also, there is Kevin's autocratic tone he has taken to addressing him with. He decides to deal with that tonight after they have been to Alec's. Any prolonged insubordination would have dramatic repercussions. Then there is Kevin as an entity, so long dreaming of the frontline and now after getting a taste of it is reverting back into a child before Gorky's very eyes, and in less than twenty-four hours. A child, who after hurting his friend's feelings for the first time realizes that he loves him. Maybe Kevin is also in mourning for the child within, the child he had killed the moment he decided to help his friend kill. Gorky planned to exhume those remains and bury them tonight also.

The weather is filthy, typical, but filthy. They stand on Alec's doorstep dripping and waiting. Kevin pounds on the door loudly for the second time. The fact that he could be out without them is not something they have considered. Kevin feels like an arrogant prick and Gorky wonders if he has already been arrested or maybe committed suicide. He is the dramatic type after all and it would be so very convenient but that is wishful thinking. There are footsteps in the corridor behind the door and ... and giggles!? Alec opens the door. He is wearing his dressing gown and is all smiles.

"Oh!" The smile drops from his face like a ton of bricks.

There are footsteps in the corridor behind him and a little face pops up under his arm and smiles at Kevin and Gorky. The smile has dimples and is on a pretty face with a short honey-blonde bob. She is tiny but full breasted and a little plump. Gorky finds her very attractive. He is sick of looking at pale anorexic women, dressed in black with crisp black, chemically treated hair.

"Hi, you must be Gorky and Kevin. I recognize you from Alec's descriptions of you, I'm Monica," she looks from one to the other, "his wife?"

"Of course!" said Gorky, "I must apologize, I had completely forgotten you were going to be here."

"That's all right! Alec didn't know either, did you Alec? I surprised him. Alec? Alec, aren't you going to invite your friends in?"

"Oh no! We wouldn't dream of intruding."

"Nonsense!" says Monica. "You've gone to all the trouble of going out for a take-away in this disgusting weather and I'm hungry even if Alec isn't. Casablanca is on BBC 2 soon, so why don't you take off your shoes and hang up your coats, and take the food and drink into the front room. We can pig it in front of the telly. Besides Alec and I are celebrating."

~

Little Wing had cried herself to sleep and woken to the darkness of the night. The rattling of the window in its frame and the gravel sound of rain blown on the powerful wind brings her back into consciousness. She puts on the light and looks at herself in the mirror. Her head aches and the reflection seems fuzzy around the edges but although her eyes are a little out of focus her image is clear enough. She looks awful. Her eyelids are so inflamed that they look like blisters and her eyes are bloodshot, beneath them is dark and swollen. She is very pale other than the red roughness under and around her nostrils, sore from where she has successively blown her nose. Her lips look white and her lush crowning glory hangs tangled and as bedraggled as seaweed.

Silently Little Wing creeps out into the corridor and places her ear up against the door of Vince's and Sid's room.

"Of all the bars in all the world she...."

They seem to be watching a film, though they themselves are very quiet. She wonders if they are asleep, she has no idea what the time is. Her hands shake and she is sure that if she starts to talk her voice will shake too. She is getting sick. Sick like she had been when she first arrived in Greece, before she could talk or smell or taste or see colour. It takes her so long thinking about whether to go in or not, that by the time she has decided to knock she has built up such a wall of paranoia that she cannot broach it anyway.

Turning around she once again stumbles upon Leo's bungee cords and rope. Picking up a coil she holds it in her hands and stares.

~

Mr. Patel is sulking; he had wanted to watch Rocky but is not going to get his way now or for a very long time, if ever. Though his mother's anger would distill in the passage of time, he could foresee no way out of the disgrace his wife would make him suffer, who by a little pout of the lips, a slightly raised eyebrow or even the supplest of eye movements, would instill shame on a daily basis for years. The fight is over, it had only been a question of time. He has always known Seema would swat him like a dung fly, eventually. The rain washes away Ingrid's tears while her saintly husband holds open the plane door.

"Ha, ha, Lady love Milk Tray." The older Mrs. P, cross-legged in front of the television, looks over her shoulder at her daughter-in-law and gestures at the white plane in the rain shuddering down the runway, desperate to be airborne.

Seema watches the back of the old woman's head. She is somewhat horrified. It is the third time this week her mother-in-law has cracked a joke. Somehow she seems to be developing an

222

awful British sense of humour. That is all she needs on top of everything else, a comedian.

~

'.... each night seems like a thousand years old, I can't lose these young boy blues .... '

The old blues master soulfully wails. Little Wing's eyes cloud and she finally gives way to tears; remembering a night that seems so long ago, another life, yes. Wet and naked, snuggled up under a blanket, laughing at the stars, picking some out for their particular characteristics and admiring others for their beauty. He had made her laugh a lot, maybe it was not what he said but simply him. They had ravished each other for the first time that night and afterwards when he had tried to relieve her of his weight she had wrapped her legs tightly around him.

"Please don't move" she begged him. They had held each other like thus until he woke to find the horizon aglow with the peach light of dawn, her arms and legs pulling him into her and her hot, intense breath by his ear, on his neck and rasping, uncontrollable animal gasps.

'.... every time I kiss your lips so fine, makes me feel so blue .... '

She had cut out a cartoon and stuck it on the wall. The cartoon depicted a man standing in front of a chair. A noose hung loose around his neck and he wore a surprised expression. Looking in, the occupants on the top deck of a double-decker bus laugh hysterically. The caption read:

"Look at that silly bugger, he got the rope too long!"

She has not smoked for over a year but tonight, her last night, she has purchased a packet of ten. Two remain and she takes up one and lights it.

'.... every time I find someone new, I make believe that it's you tonight .... '

They had said it would be impossible to estimate the brain damage while he lay comatose, in fact it was a miracle he was alive at all. She kept a vigil by his bedside as he slept the months away until he finally came to. Of course it had to be the weekend she had gone to the island for her guardian's saint's day.

"We didn't want to get your hopes up," the ward Sister had told her "but you just go and take a look for yourself. He gets drowsy spells of course, and is suffering short periods of disorientation, but otherwise he seems perfectly aware of his surroundings and circumstances."

His name had spilled from her lips, the very sound of which she caressed. She slid the tip of her tongue down her sensitive pallet and exhaling in a slow, low gasp, her mouth opened slightly, pushing her full lips forward to blow his name; a lush kiss from a lush flower. All her love, passion and desire translated into the utterance of that singular beloved word. He grabbed her wrist and looked her straight in the eye, then rudely pushed her hand away.

"Who the hell are you?" he said.

And then her beloved guardian had died and she had been sent home to her parents.

~

Leo lays embryonic, like a sack of potatoes that has slightly melted, snoring. Sylvester Stallone cries.

"A-DREE-AN, A-DREE-AN" and slobbers over the ropes with a face like a monkey's arse.

The remains of the eastern feast with all its encrustations and congelations lay in disarray around him. As he rolls on his back his elbow sinks into a crumpled aluminum platter of takka dill, spreading the hot lentils like diarrhea. Rolling back onto his side he scratches his elbow and wipes his hand through his hair.

~

Tom cuts no slack with either last call or time. Dead on ten forty-one, his customers find themselves out on the street with the doors being bolted behind them.

224

Leaving his brother to clear up and ring up the tills he goes upstairs to Nancy. He finds her in their frilly pink bedroom, in a frilly pink dressing gown, with a box of tissues. She is sitting up in bed in front of the television, blowing her nose noisily and dabbing her eyes. Little, freshly shampooed, impregnated Pookie sleeps soundly at her feet.

The filthy weather outside complements the film excellently as Ingrid and Humphrey act out their famed climactic scene of lost love. After the film's conclusion, Tom picks up the controls and mutes the volume.

"How's me girl?"

Nancy carries on blowing and dabbing and shrugs her shoulders. Eventually she gets an 'Alright' out.

"Now come on luv, things ain't that bad. I spoke with the station sergeant and 'e say's Constable Wright was startin' to see the funny side of it, and it looks like the charges will be dropped. And as for the other matter, 'e said what with yer clear record, two or three good character references, and Fen being agreeable, yer both should be bound over to keep the peace for a year and then everythin' can be forgotten."

"But the disgrace Thomas! I just don't know 'ow I'm going to face anybody. I don't know what got into me, but it seems every time I try to do something nice, someone 'as to come along and spoil it, someone even pulled up one of me geraniums." Here she resumes her weeping.

"And poor Pookie! I 'ad this lovely little dog Trickster all lined up for 'er through The British Poodle Association, but I thought she should wait a little and now that filthy creature got 'old of 'er. Goodness this must be just 'ow poor Silvia felt when that dreadful Mike Jarvis got 'er Beverly into trouble."

Tom shakes his head and raises his eyes. It is around this time he usually losses patience with his wife, but she is not acting up this time, this time it is genuine.

"Now, now. Come to Tommy." He rocks her gently in his arms like a sick child.

"It was goin' to be me next, wasn't it? Me and our poor little Pookie."

"Sssh!" That bloody violinist. Christ Almighty that has shaken her up, it has shaken him up too.

"I've been thinkin' about that bed an' breakfast idea of yers and I've decided that it seems silly to wait 'til our retirement before gettin' goin' on it. After all it's gonna take time to find the right place, we 'aven't even decided on the town yet. And then I 'ave to fix it up, yer 'ave to make the curtains and stuff. So why don't yet 'ave yourself some time with yer sister this week, and take a trip down to the seaside, and do a bit of 'ouse 'unting while yer at it."

"Oh Thomas, do yer mean it?"

"Will it make yer 'appy?"

"Yes."

"Then I mean it."

"Perhaps we should take a look at 'Astings first, we could go and 'ave tea with that nice Mr.'Umbolt."

"I'd like to be a fly on the wall when that old bugger gooses Penelope!" Tom laughs.

"Oh really Tom, 'e's such a sweet old man with such lovely manners too, I can't imagine him be'avin' so uncouth."

"Well send 'im my regards."

"I will."

~

Lushness withers,
Loves lost luster tightens,
A web around my bleeding heart.
Fine lines, cold as steel,
Cut down to icy chambers
Where passion's radiant joy once fired.
And only the long, lost soul,
Of whom once I was,
Can cry for you,
My Lost Love.

Little Wing had reached the end of words. She folds the sheet once, slips it into an envelope and places it on the desk with a letter to the parents she neither knew nor liked, though for some reason she could not help but love, even her mother whom now she hates. She throws the packet with its singular cigarette down on top.

She has run Leo's rope over a giant hook that went through the ceiling into the rafter. Dolores had bossed someone into putting it there for her hanging wicker chair, the irony was not lost on Little Wing.

"Fuck you."

The words are still ringing in her ears. Well fuck you too Dolores. That is the last of her family ties severed, and good riddance. She is sorry about Baby Jason but he was not enough.

"And what could I do for him anyway, even if I did stay?" she thinks," Good luck little man."

She has used all the correct knots, as one brought up around seafaring folk would, and remembers the theorem behind the snap-not-swing equation used for Ruth Ellis, she places a pile of phone directories on the chair to increase the drop.

Everything is ready now. She puts the noose around her neck and tightens it. Looking down everything starts to ripple like water; she is not afraid to jump but something stops her. The floor has turned turquoise and sparkles, and below its surface two dolphins swim. Their movements are full of joy and a light shines through the water shimmering from their streamlined bodies. She smiles, feeling a tremendous relief, shutting her eyes she takes her last breaths deeply. With her arms stretched out like a bird waiting for some strong, brisk wind to carry it away she goes to take the fatal step. All of the sudden she hears Diomedes's voice as he releases a cry saturated with horror.

"NO!"

Suddenly she is very awake, awakened to the harsh, brutal reality of her situation. She is alone now and it is just another normal, boring, wet Sunday night all over London town, and nobody gave a shit anyway.

The room looks different than it had a few moments earlier. It feels different too. No one will be breaking the door down, no one will have to cut down her swinging body. The police will not be called, her corpse will not be carried out in a body bag while unknown neighbours and passersby crane their necks, speak in hushed, serious voices, voices which would have exploded into the ghastly whine of innuendos and fresh gossip the moment the ambulance rounded the corner. The letters will never be read and she will continue as destined, whatever that is.

She goes to remove the noose. As she leans her head to the right the emotions surrounding her whole scenario swell to the surface, and she starts to weep angrily. Roughly wiping the tears from her face with the back of her hand, she tears at the rope. Snot runs down her face and she stops to wipe that also, and pulls on the rope again and tries to pull it over her head. Trying to loosen it further she tightens it by mistake, her tears and mounting fury flow faster. Taking death's umbilical cord strongly in both hands, she focuses her attention on the job and starts to smoothly slide open the noose. Just then there is a tremendous crash, she is startled, nearly losing her balance. She lets go of the rope and just as it would seem she had regained her footing the glossy cover of one of the telephone directories slides on its newsprint causing the book to fan out, sending the whole pile to the floor.

Outside a seagull with a broken wing and neck crashes to the rooftop and tumbles down the first flight of stairs, coming to rest outside the squat.

~

The skies have darkened until the small coal fire in the grate and the T.V. are the only flickering sources of light. Crystal tumblers and decanters, ice cubes, the gem stones of the ladies rings and Ruby's and Silvia's spectacles sparkle on and off, and the dark polished wood of the antique furniture captures a deep rich fluctuating glow.

"Can't see what she sees in 'im anyway, he's a drunken, chain smoking, bar owner that's all, he's not even better looking than the other one."

"Sssh!"

"Maybe he's got a big one. Are yer crying Ruby?" Ruby raises her glasses and wipes her eyes then blows her nose.

"No."

The phone rings.

"I'll get it!" Edith pushes herself up from her oversized armchair and shoots from the room. She is gone for a good while giving Silvia and Ruby ample opportunity to dab their eyes and expel their snot in peace. They can hear Edith in the other room every so often, speaking coyly and giggling.

The desperate flight finally gets airborne and Sam is at last free from ever 'playing it again'. Edith comes back to the room and Ruby switches a lamp on.

"They've all arrived safe and sound. Leonard sends 'is regards. Says 'e's got all the rooms aired and warm, and that she was in the bathroom with the children getting ready for bed."

"Bless 'im, I'll sleep all the better for knowing that."

"Yes," says Ruby raising her glass, "here's to quiet times ahead."

"Quiet times," echo Silvia and Edith.

And then the most almighty crash comes from next-door, nearly giving Ruby a heart attack and shaking the floor so violently that the decanters on the sideboard sing like tuning forks.

~

"Bravo!" exclaims Gorky.

"I think I could watch that film a hundred times and not get bored of it." Monica says as she stretches.

She could be very feline Gorky observes with pleasure, and mixed with the glow of pregnancy she is delightfully, perfectly ripe. She springs up and starts clearing the coffee table of the leftover Chinese food.

"No you don't." Alec takes the crumpled foil containers out of his wife's hands.

"You sit down and talk to Kevin, Gorky and I can do that, I'll put the kettle on while I'm out there."

Gorky picks up a pile of empty pallets and some empty beer bottles, and follows Alec out to the kitchen. Alec places his load down on the counter and turns to him.

"Gorky, quickly, while I've got a chance. I've been thinking. I really screwed up last night and nearly blew everything and I want to take full responsibility. It could have been the death of you and Kevin, so I just want to say there's no need for us all to go down because of me. If it turns out they do have something on me then say whatever you have to say. Say I didn't arrive until after the explosions if you have too."

"Alec I ..."

229

"And look after Monica, you and Kevin. Make sure she and the baby are OK at least until someone decent comes along."

"Yes Alec, I promise you that with all my heart."

And then the whole ceiling shook as if it had been hit with a thunder bolt.

~

Kate lays on the settee fighting the delicious feeling of oblivion as sleep tries to overtake her again and again. Nick stretches out on the floor, hands behind head, head on cushion. Humphrey Bogart speaks.

"Maybe not today, maybe not tomorrow, but soon and for the rest of your life," and Ingrid Bergman sheds a tear.

Ingrid's plane accelerates down the runway and Rick and Louie start their beautiful relationship. Kate takes her cue.

"Nick, I've got to call it a day."

"Give us a minute, I need to take a slash."

"A minute for what?"

"I'm walkin' yer 'ome."

"Don't be silly, it's only round the corner and you'll get soaked."

"I don't mind."

"I do! You've already been soaked to the skin once tonight, you'll catch pneumonia."

"What about yer?"

"I'll going to take a hot shower when I get back."

"I can take a 'ot shower when I get back."

"But you don't have to get soaked, I do."

"Kate, what's the big deal?"

"Nothing. I'm sure the fresh air will do you the world of good."

"Unless yer rather I didn't walk yer 'ome for some reason?"

"Oh God, here we go!"

"I'm just asking, for all I know yer could.., why are we arguing?"

Nick has suddenly realized he is beginning to shout.

"Why don't you tell me?"

Nick pauses to moisten his lips. Suddenly and unexpectedly Kate has thrown all the cards on the table, if he backs down this time he feels sure he will never get another chance.

230

"Maybe I want to make sure yet get 'ome safely because..."
and then there is an explosive crash which shakes the stairwell
and drowns out the words:
"I love you."

There are screams and hurried footsteps on the stairs, the
sound of a hasty key turning and worried voices. Leo wakes up
momentarily, rolls over into the tandoori chicken and goes back to
sleep.
"There's a thumb in me mulligatawny," he utters.

Nick and Kate run outside. They descend just in time to see
the door to Selene and Dicks' flat burst open and the neighbours
stampeding in, pushing Silva to one side and almost trampling
Ruby. Edith wins and throws open the door to the middle room.
Up tail-end Ruby scuffles in complaining loudly and takes a
position next to her best friend. They all stare at a room filled with
floating specs of white dust settling on a white carpet of plaster, it
looks like a snowscape made of thick soft flakes.
It seems a long time before anything happens.
Robert has Dick pinned down so to speak. A horrific scream
both loud and shrill had shaken Dick's larynx as Robert's impact
winded him. Then the groans and stifled little screams of pain
came from the general mound upon a bigger mound which was
once a bed. It starts to move like an animal in a bag coming alive.
The two old ladies step slowly into the room arm in arm
moving as cautiously as a two-headed asp as the serpentine of
spectators coil in behind them. Solemn as a crowd at a funeral,
they form a crescent around the door. There is a great gaping hole
in the ceiling that had allowed Robert and other refuse through;
mugs with their gut wrenching festering milky tea, magazines,
disgusting underwear and socks. The white shroud was a blessing
to the eyes but in did not help the stench. A page from a magazine
graciously spirals its way on to Ruby's head where she promptly
pulls it off and inspects the sticky paper. After a few seconds she
screams and faints into Fat Sid's arms.
The top of the mound flips over, like a playing card, and the
disgusting Robert reveals himself, a screwdriver still clutched in
his hand. Ruby opens her eyes, lets forth another cry of distress
and faints again. The five Patel children are having the time of

their lives, chasing each other around the mound, squealing with delight in the mock snow, and jumping up and down shrieking with high-pitched laughter. They point from Robert's dick to Dick's arse, which is now the summit of the dilemma, stripped of its snow cap and standing out boldly.

Seema eyes the gamut of whips and swishes.

Dick manages to disengage himself and stagger a couple of steps clutching his arse.

"Christ almighty." Vince has caught a glimpse of Selene before Kate tears off her coat and throws it over her. He did not mean to stare, but amongst the horrific bruising and cuts of the many months of abuse is the most incredible butterfly. But something is wrong. It takes him a second to realize what it is. The butterfly is in fact the most incredible tattoo, a tattoo with the stub of a cigarette ground out on it. He pulls out a pen knife from the back pocket of his jeans and cuts her legs free and goes to assist Kate who is trying to open the stocks.

"It's padlocked," she says.

Sid has now come over, leaving Ruby with his pullover under her head and Silvia and Edith fanning her. He takes one look at the lock, one look at Selene's face, and one look at Dick hovering around in the far corner holding his arse and howling like a baby and nods at Vince and Nick. Nick gets Dick locked in a hold and Sid does a swift and to the point interrogation.

"Where's the key yer fuckin' cunt."

"It's somewhere over there on one of my belts."

"Aaaarrrrr! Aaaarrrr! Get offa me ! Get the fuck off! " Seema is lashing Robert with a cat-of-nine-tails. The more he screams and retreats into the corner the more vicious she becomes.

Nick and Fat Sid have dragged Dick over to the belts where Sid holds him by the hair, yelling in his face while he fumbles and boohoos his way through them.

"They're not there!" Dick blabs pathetically. Sid has had enough of this shit and delivers a punch to the belly.

"What the 'ells going on 'ere!"

"Bleedin' Nora!"

Detective Healy and Detective Shaw stand in the doorway of the sex room.

" 'Elp me! 'Elp me! " Robert desperately screams, now covered with welts.

Vince crosses the room with a key ring that looks like it belonged to a dungeon and manages to open the padlock on his third attempt. He and Kate gently slide Selene down the mattress cradling her neck and supporting her head. Monica and Kev go to fetch water and first aid stuff, as they pass the Detectives, Monica notices their badges.

"Could you radio in for a female officer please?"

Detective Healy walks across the room to where Selene lays, takes one quick look at her face and nods to Detective Shaw who immediately gets on the radio. Monica sits down on the other side of Selene from Kate, and Kev places the bowl of warm water on the floor. He has carried it in from the kitchen, but not before bumping into and spilling some on Detective Healy.

"Sorry Sarg," he says, smirking. The detective returns a long cold stare.

Kate rinses out a flannel and starts to tentively clean Selene's face, while Monica holds her head still. Nick has found a bag of frozen peas which he places on her eye, which by now has swollen closed.

Dick lays on the floor crying. He is getting on Sid's nerves and Sid decides a dozen or so good kicks may act as a fine remedy. The Patel children tear around the room in delight and Mr. Patel turns traitor on his fellow conspirator and ignores his pleas for help. Instead he takes to trying to control his mother, who having taken a look at Selene's unrecognizable face, is cheering on Sid in his endeavors.

"Kills all germs!" she shouts, giving Dick a quick kick herself.

" 'Elp, 'elp!"

"Madame my name is Detective 'Ealy and if yet don't stop whipping this gentlemen I will be forced to intervene."

"This man is not a gentleman, he's not even a man, he is a filthy pig."

Seema drops the cat-of-nine-tails and takes a riding crop from a hook on the collapsed bed and points it at Robert as he cowers.

"He spies on us all and puts us in his dirty videos!"

The detectives look at each other with raised eye brows. Nuts.

"Now, now, Madame. I'd like yer to give me the riding crop, that's right, the riding crop. Carefully does it, just 'and it over nice and gentle."

233

Seema stands with her hands on her hips, riding crop held firmly in her hand.

"You don't believe me! You think I'm a crazy woman! "

"No! Whatever makes yer think that. But the gent... 'e's 'ad enough, you've made yer point. Now 'ow about that ridin' crop! "

"I tell you he spies on us all and puts us in his dirty videos, all except the Humbolt boy with the crabs."

"Not the geezer who 'ad that party last summer? " exclaims Detective Shaw, shocked.

"Yes!" choruses the room in unison. The detectives look at each other with expressions of curdled milk. Seema continues:

"Fat boy likes to get spanky, spanky."

"Ar fuckin' great!" moans Sid.

Nick sniggers and Seema turns her attention to him.

"Mr. Nick dresses up with high shoes and ladies underwear with long red wigs, and the blonde boy has threesomes with Rita from Ali's and her friend Rachel."

She points at Vince with the crop. Vince colours up. He is glad Little Wing is not there. Next is poor Ruby, who has only just begun to come round again.

"You kiss a picture of a young woman and put it under your pillow at night." Ruby screams and swoons once more.

"And Mr. Gorky and Mr. Evans get drunk, and have prostitutes. Mr. Gorky likes it with men and women."

"That's not true! Is it Alec! Alec?" Monica is indignant.

Kev is astonished. He stops playing with the recently acquired lighter in his pocket and thinks about it. And the more he thinks about it, the more it makes sense. The bitchiness recently between them, and it was truly amazing that Gorky had managed to get Alec to carry out that assassination. In fact it is unbelievable.

"Does yer 'usband know about that fuckin' great vibrator in yer top drawer? The one yer like stickin' up yer arse, yer fuckin' bitch! "

Robert has scurried around to hide behind the detectives. Seema glares-if looks could kill! Mr. Patel is ecstatic. For the first time ever in their marriage he has some ammunition and he is just about to shoot off to claim the evidence when something extraordinary happens, even by that day's standards.

"Alestiere Evans. Yer under arrest for the murder of Lord Oswald Mosley. Yer 'ave the right to remain silent. Anythin' yer say will be taken down and may be used in evidence against yer. Yer 'ave the right to legal representation ..."

"Alec, what's happening?" Monica is beginning to cry, it suddenly seems very quiet. Even the children are silent and allowing themselves to be led away without making a fuss. Piercing the stillness, Leo's terrified cries bounce off the walls of the stairwell.

"The Ratman's thumb! The Ratman's thumb!"

~

Far away, a young man has been sleeping. He dreamt that he was sleeping under an olive tree not far from the sea. A bright uneven line of silver from a setting sun separated the sea from the sky and reflected off the waves and the inky tide that swept the beach. The sky was black and starless, no moon shone there and the sea was dark and ominous. A foreboding hung over the atmosphere as if awaiting a terrible storm, but the sleeper slept on peacefully-unaware.

She swam up and leaving the water, she came to him and took him by the hand. Still deep in slumber, his spirit rose and she lead him back to the sea. Like dolphins they swam in the fathoms of clear blue sparkling water. But then his head rose above the waves, breaking her spell and he found the sea turbulent and dark once more. She stood naked upon a great rock that protruded from the depths, her arms wide open, embracing the wind that blew through her hair and fingers. Her hair had grown very long and heavy with the spray of the waves that exploded on impact with the worn granite and as it lashed around her, slapping her face and body, it wrapped around her neck and flew upwards catching an overhang of rock above her head. He climbed up beside her and she looked into his eyes taking his hand once more and placed it in a large wound that had opened between her breasts. His fingers touched a heart so icy cold that it burnt him, and so brittle that it shattered leaving its precious pieces embedded deep in his skin, and still she held it there.

"Feel my heart?" she whispered, "It's broken." And then she jumped.

"NO!" His own scream awakens him. A seagull falls from the sky, landing beside him with a broken neck and wing. The glass he is holding shatters in his hand which bleeds profusely and then he remembers; he remembers everything.

His Little Wing, his dearest, his love. He will find her-he must find her! Yes; then everything will be alright.

~

Jake's trembling bloody hand raises a cigarette to his distorted split lips. He has never taken such a thrashing in all his life, nothing close, and from Vince, Vince of all people. What the hell would have made him do a thing like this, bad acid, angel dust? He lays flat on his back on the bed; he has taken such a vicious kicking he can hardly move. He smokes and shivers and shivers and shakes. He is going into shock.

Why? He did not even tell him why. He had just kept screaming 'I told you not little wing, not little wing.' fucking maniac. He starts weeping again, he cannot control his emotions. One keeps surfacing after the other. And then he is numb for a while, detached, but soon he starts to shake again and his senses seem heightened. The phone rings, music comes on and a happy Jake greets the caller.

"Hello you've reached Jake Lawrence, unfortunately I'm not here to speak to you personally but leave your name and number and we can make up for it later. Beep."

"Jake! You rascal! Its Albert, are you there? No? Well I guess not. So who's a naughty boy? Gate crashing my party! Well everyone found you and your darling little sister delightful! Iris wants to speak to you next week, Shakespeare, Jake! May not pay well to start, but the work it will bring you; producers love to see Shakespeare. And that's not all! I want you to phone me the moment you get this. Stewart from Calvin Klein phoned me this morning and he's anxious to set up a date for a photo session this week in lieu of, wait for it, the possibility of you being their next billboard boy! Imagine Jake Lawrence a hundred feet high-New York, Tokyo, Rome! Well that's all for now. Oh, Desmond says he's so sorry about that scar on Little Wing's face. Apparently she was exactly what he's been looking for for Nivea. But he's interested in

236

speaking to her anyway, wants to hear her sing. Well that's it for now, au revoir 'King of the Fruits'. Ha, ha, ha ..."

~

Two sets of automatic doors buzz and slide slickly apart. Two sets of eyes lock. Georgie looks hassled; his usual impeccable grooming habits obviously unobserved under the dire circumstances. She would have found it quite endearing normally. She stands and moves hastily to meet him.

"She's going to be alright, the doctor spoke with me a few minutes ago. They're just making her comfortable."

Georgie's face and hands are a sickly ashen gray.

"The bastard! If only I could get out of this darn contraption. I'd throttle him with my bare hands, if it wasn't too good for him. I'm going to kill the bastard, I swear it!" And here he starts struggling, trying in vain to raise himself from his wheelchair, as if willing his disablement away by brute force.

"Hush," says Kate placing her hand upon his shoulder, "hush," and she kneels to hold him as he weeps. He sits back, blows his nose and returns his handkerchief to his breast pocket.

"You'll have to brace yourself when you see her," Kate warns him, "she's a mess. The swelling does make it look even worse of course, but the doctor said that should go down considerably within the week. Her nose is smashed to pieces. They're going to operate on that tomorrow given that the CAT Scan results are favourable. Her lip is slit twice but miraculously she escaped with an intact jaw, though she's missing four teeth. The main thing they were worried about was her neck, skull and possible brain damage. However the X-rays came back fine, thank God, so it's as I said, we're waiting on the CAT Scan."

"Lucky to have an intact jaw, lucky she hasn't got a cracked skull, just waiting on the bloody CAT Scan! I can't believe what my ears are telling me! Oh my God! I felt something awful was going to happen. I knew. What did I say at Martha's? I begged her you know, while you were in the loo throwing-up, before he had his psycho act. I had such a horrid feeling, I begged her. I said please, please dearest, come back with me. But she wouldn't have any of it."

237

He retrieves his handkerchief again and blows his nose, it sounds like a fog horn.

"What's happening with him?" asks Georgie.

"They're throwing the book at him, with a lot of help from material supplied to them by Robert Smith, in return for a hefty plea bargain in his case. They want to charge him with attempted murder, amongst other things, but they don't know if they will be able to make that stick."

"Yes, what on earth was all that Robert Smith stuff about? I couldn't make head or tail of what you were saying, dearest. It was as if you were trying to tell me a buggering peeping-tom crashed through the ceiling with all the neighbours watching! "

"It's a whole other story."

A nurse comes though the swing doors. They both look up anxiously, Kate stands. The nurse walks over to a grey-haired couple and starts talking to them in low earnest sentences. The elderly couple listens attentively, nodding simultaneously and hanging on to her every word. Georgie's and Kate's shoulders slump. Kate sits down and stares at her feet.

"Miss Lanseer?"

"Yes?" Another nurse has approached them from along a long corridor.

"You can see her now, for a while, if you'd like to follow me."

Mercifully the main lighting is off and only a dim reading light shines on Selene. In spite of Kate's words Georgie is horrified. He cannot relate the creature in the bed to his lifelong friend. The Selene-thing rotates the single slit-eye of its bulbous head slowly in their direction. The effect shocks him in the pit of his stomach, nearly causing him to retch. Even from the doorway her face is obviously vastly disproportionate and asymmetrical; a potato face.

"Hi." Georgie jumps. It seems unbelievable that Selene's voice, however weak and distorted, could emerge from this hideously bruised mask of inflammation and deformity. He approaches the bed powerfully, shadowed by cowardice and the urge to turn tail and run. The few yards stretch before him like an ever elongating path.

"Hello my dearest," he speaks softly, taking hold of her hand that rests limp and useless on the covers. A hiss of pain escapes Selene's lips.

"I'm sorry. It's the torn ligaments and things, I can't move my arms." And she starts to cry. "Please don't be angry."

"Why on earth should I be angry?"

"You told me not to go back with him, you said ..."

"Selene my love, this isn't your fault. O.K.? You've suffered enough without laying out self-flagellation! And you were taking steps, great steps. You were off in the morning. You were doing the right thing. You were leaving him."

"Kate could you wipe my face?"

Kate leans over from the other side of the bed and with tender loving care begins to dab away the tears that run down her friend's face.

"Thank-you," says Selene softly and smiles. One of the slits in her upper lip reopens. A heavy vermilion line abruptly appears and runs down her chin, pouring onto the neck-brace below and she starts to cry again.

"Oh my God! Hang on darling, hang on."

Georgie grabs a handful of tissues from the box on the bedside table and hands them to Kate.

"We better call the nurse."

Kate nods and holds the wad up to Selene's mouth.

"I think you better say good-night," the nurse says kindly, "I'll be back in a minute to give her something to help her sleep."

They watch the nurse leave then return their attention to their friend.

"Well I guess that's it for now my lovely. Sweet dreams." Georgie kisses his finger tips and blows.

"Good night Selene." Kate kisses her gently on the forehead.

"We'll be back tomorrow. We love you."

"There's just one thing."

"What's that Giraffe-neck?"

"Ow! Don't make me laugh!"

"Wow she really does look like a giraffe now you mention it Georgie!"

"Always did!"

"You two are so mean!"

"What is it Selene? What is it you want to know?" Georgie smiles affectionately and for a brief second he looks beautiful.

"What's all this about that Leo guy upstairs and pubic crabs? I mean he's not the first person in the world to have crabs is he?"

Georgie and Kate look at each other and grin.

"You tell her Kate."

So Kate began:

"The reason that his infamous party of last summer will not, and probably never will be, forgotten is because he, or maybe one should say his bed, infested well over forty of his guests with crabs, who in their turn put them around their nearest and dearest, and what have you, and what resulted was an epidemic. The bedroom, being as is usually the case, the smoke room, saw a lot of traffic over the course of the night, a lot of whom sat on the legendary bed. They had to set up a special mobile unit at Guy's hospital. Apparently the crabs were of a particularly resilient strain. It made the evening news on ITV; he actually seemed quite proud of the accomplishment at the time I seem to recall!"

The nurse returned and gave Selene an injection. She went out like a candle.

"Come on dearest," sighs Georgie, "back to the asylum!"

~

Kevin stuffed one pair of jeans, a pair of shorts, three T-shirts, three changes of socks and underpants, sandals, and his toothbrush into his duffel bag. He and Gorky had been taken in for questioning and eventually released after duly breaking down and telling the 'truth'. They were under strict orders not to leave town. What with that, followed by Gorky's megalomaniacal verbal assault on him, he was getting the fuck out of the Elephant and Castle, and fast.

He examines the contents of his refrigerator, takes out a bag of fruit and hurriedly makes up a whole pile of sandwiches. He has very little money. Gorky, as usual, has forgotten to pay his half of the Chinese food and he has been forced to trust in an acquaintance, who has forwarded him his social security money in exchange for the key and rent book of his flat. All in all he has less than eighty pounds.

Kev opens the long thin cupboard in the corner of his front room and switches on the light he has installed especially for the purpose of illuminating his collection of stolen lighters. There are five shelves and on the cupboard floor is an immense heap of Bics and other disposables, in every colour of the rainbow and shade and tint thereof. But he had become bored with Bics, too easy, and so has become more specialized over the course of time.

He had given Alec a shelf all to himself, this shelf also held an impressive collection of disposables. His friend has also unwittingly contributed three Zippos, some interesting old flint and petrol lighters, and some device he had picked up in Amsterdam which operated a red hot coil.

Gorky, being of sly character, had proven much more challenging, especially as he had a habit of pocketing his cigarettes and lighter immediately after he had finished with them. Luckily Kev could be sly too and he has managed to obtain seven Bics, a Zippo, a small silver Ronson, and an interesting old Polish model of which Gorky had mourned the loss. Gorky shared a shelf with twenty-two of the giant Bics Tom likes to keep behind the bar at The Rhinoceros.

The top shelf's specialty is table lighters. He has his Nan's three Wedgewood lighters that he had obtained from his mean-tempered uncle's bequest. As far as he knows his family is still bitterly divided over their disappearance. There is a stainless steel egg that opens cleverly along an invisible seam. This he had taken as emotional compensation from his ex-girlfriend when she had given him his marching orders. One lighter is made from a large piece of dyed rock, exorbitantly over-priced, which he had immensely enjoyed stealing from a yuppie shop in Covent Garden. There are also three silver pieces, of which two are very attractive antiques, and a pewter piece shaped like a beer tankard with a lid that opens, igniting the flint.

The two shelves below held all kinds of lighters, most of them quite fascinating, as well as pieces made specifically for advertising; 'Drink Star Lager' says one, 'Guinness is Good for you' another. However, the crème de la crème was on the centre shelf; the best examples of his antiques and some designer names. There are two simple but striking enameled art-deco pieces: one in gold and black and the other silver and blue; also an Austrian piece decorated in a tiny, detailed patterning like lace. There are the best of his Ronsons, Du Ponts and Colibris, some set with motifs in gem stones, and a ridiculously expensive, fashion-of-the-moment lighter of Dick's he has almost regretted stealing. Dick had moaned about nothing else for months after and still brings it up from time to time. And in the centre of it all, monumental to all his efforts, stands Detective Healy's solid gold Du Pont.

He leaves the cupboard door open with the light on and the rest of his flat in darkness. The weather is nasty, very nasty, with an east wind that seems to cut through flesh and muscle to the quick of his bones. He plans to venture through the back streets until he hits the Old Kent Road, where at a particular petrol station he hopes to catch a lift with one of the lorry drivers, who habitually fill-up there for their journey to Dover and Europe. He places his wallet and passport safely in the inside pocket of his coat, lifts his duffel bag over one shoulder and his old tent and sleeping bag over the other.

Stepping outside, the curious angle of the front door makes it possible for him to look back and see his front room with the glow that radiates from its corner.

"Sod it," he mutters. Striding back into the room he snatches up his trophy and drops it in his pocket. Without looking back he slams the door and walks out into the night.

Jefferson. Richard Daniel, suddenly last Sunday, aged 29. He is survived by his Father David, his mother Josephine (nee Cooper) brothers David, Joshua, Zackary & sisters Rachel and Elizabeth. Funeral pending investigation.

Saunders. Trudy Katherine, suddenly last Sunday, aged 16. She is survived by her father Derrick, mother Audrey (nee Viner), sister Dolores and nephew Jason. Arrangements by R.G. Flint & Sons (0732) 657101.

FINI